THE
OCEAN

100TH ANNIVERSARY COLLECTION

Off-Trail Publications

Elkhorn, California

Acknowledgements
With gratitude to Gene Christie for helping get this project underway; and to Frank Robinson, for additional assistance.

THE OCEAN
100TH ANNIVERSARY COLLECTION
Copyright © 2008, Off-Trail Publications
ISBN-10: 1-935031-03-1
ISBN-13: 978-1-935031-03-1

OFF-TRAIL PUBLICATIONS
2036 Elkhorn Road
Castroville, CA 95012
offtrail@redshift.com

Printed in the United States of America
First printing: October 2008

CONTENTS

— — § — —

Stories from THE OCEAN

— — § — —

Lost at Sea
The Story of THE OCEAN

John Locke

FRANK ANDREW MUNSEY IS THE GEORGE WASHINGTON OF THE PULPS, the Founding Father. On the 25th anniversary of *The Argosy*, the magazine he founded and eventually turned into the first pulp, Munsey wrote of how it came about. An ambitious young man, he'd grown bored managing a Western Union telegraph office in Augusta, Maine. He became interested in publishing and dreamed of starting his own publication. The title came first: *The Golden Argosy*. Munsey moved to New York, ready to pour his accumulated earnings into the venture. Financial difficulties prevented him from bringing out the paper himself; however, an existing publisher agreed to go forward with the plan, retaining Munsey as manager and editor. The paper, an 8-page illustrated weekly for boys and girls, featuring stories by Horatio Alger, Jr. and other popular authors, debuted in December 1882. After five months, the publisher failed; *The Golden Argosy* went into receivership. Munsey struggled, but obtained a precarious control. He had little money and paid subscriptions to fill. He minimized costs by writing most of the magazine himself. "It was a question of swim out or sink," he wrote. The swim turned out to be years of difficulty—a marathon. Munsey gradually discovered the drawbacks of his readership: juveniles continually outgrow the publication and have to be replaced by new readers; and they have no money to appeal to advertisers.

By 1887, the magazine was making money. Advertisements and circulation were up. Page counts and cover price had been increased. "Golden" was dropped from the title. In 1889, still haunted by the decision to publish for juveniles, Munsey hedged his bets by launching a ten-cent adult magazine, *Munsey's Weekly*. After two years, Munsey zeroed in on the real problem: weekly publication, which put him in competition with the big Sunday newspapers. In 1891, *Munsey's Magazine* debuted as a twenty-five-cent monthly. Two years later, still unsatisfied, Munsey conceived a bold plan, to reduce the cover price of *Munsey's* from a quarter to a dime, a decision destined to resonate through magazine history. Munsey felt that consumers recognized only five price increments below fifty cents: one, two, five, ten, and twenty-five; thus the initial price and the big drop to a dime. His monolithic distributor, The American News Company, balked at the low margins from a ten-cent monthly but finally agreed to go forward when Munsey's attempt to self-distribute raised public interest. The magazine was a great success, soon rising in circulation to 700,000, and, as an added benefit, saved *The Argosy*

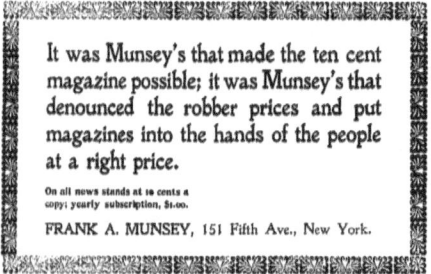

It was Munsey's that made the ten cent magazine possible; it was Munsey's that denounced the robber prices and put magazines into the hands of the people at a right price.

On all news stands at 10 cents a copy; yearly subscription, $1.00.

FRANK A. MUNSEY, 151 Fifth Ave., New York.

Newspaper ad, January 21, 1893

from demise, at least temporarily. To make the rescue permanent, Munsey reworked *The Argosy* as an imitation of *Munsey's*, a ten-cent monthly, no longer strictly youth-oriented. Circulation for *Argosy's* last weekly issue had sunk to 9000; as a monthly, it debuted at 40,000. But, as the neglected stepbrother of *Munsey's*, *Argosy* did no better than that—until its last great change. To differentiate it from *Munsey's*, Munsey made his next bold move, changing *Argosy* to all-fiction with the October 1896 issue, printing it on cheap paper. Circulation quickly doubled, and the pulps were born. After a few flat years, circulation began to rise again. By its 25th anniversary, it stood at a half-million.

Despite Munsey's role as the founder of the pulps, that was to be the lesser part of his destiny. In 1891, he bought a daily newspaper. It lasted less than a year, but revealed Munsey's ulterior motives. Ten years later, he bought the New York *Daily News*, *The Washington Times*, and, in 1902, *The Boston Journal*. After that, Munsey's ardor for the newspaper acquisition apparently cooled for some time. Then, in 1908, he acquired *The Philadelphia Times* and *The Baltimore News*. Starting in 1912, he launched a series of acquisitions and consolidations of New York papers. At one time, he controlled seventeen separate newspapers.

During the 1902-08 interim, Munsey devoted his energies to other businesses, including the magazines. He must have noticed other publishers entering the field he established with, for instance, *Young's Magazine* (first issue, April 1903); the not-to-be-ignored Street & Smith with *The Popular Magazine* (September 1903); and *The Monthly Story Magazine* (May 1905, later retitled *Blue Book*). With the issue of January 1905, Munsey responded with his second pulp. This time, the name made the contents clear: *The All-Story Magazine*. In March 1906, he started another general purpose magazine, *The Scrap Book*. Its circulation quickly matched *Argosy's*.

The next new title, *The Railroad Man's Magazine* (October 1906), marked another milestone. It was the first specialized pulp, though not all-fiction. It mixed in a great quantity of articles and features with its short stories and serials. Railroad fiction, itself, wasn't revolutionary—*Argosy* had already demonstrated success with it.

In an introductory essay in the inaugural issue, Munsey described the vast impact of the railroads, and laid out his rationale for the magazine:

To-day with its various ramifications and allied interests, the railroad business is the biggest industry in America with the one exception of agriculture. And yet there is no magazine of general interest, so far as I know, which contains special features of direct interest to the railroad workers and their families.

It is singular that this is the fact when there are perhaps as many as five hundred publications of one grade and another that are published for the farmer and his family—publications that contain a considerable percentage of reading of a technical farming nature, together with fiction, general information, biography, poetry, and such other items and articles as make good, wholesome, and interesting reading for the home and fireside. The fact that there is a demand on the part of farmers for all these agricultural journals makes me marvel that no publisher hitherto has thought to issue a publication for the railroad man, who represents the second largest industry in our Western World.

He also explained the combination of fiction and fact features:

My experience in the publishing business justifies me in saying that, if all fiction were to be eliminated from the magazines of America, their combined circulation would speedily dwindle to not over twenty per cent of the present total. If this deduction is correct, and it is not a careless bit of analysis, it is clear that the story with love and adventure—the good old-fashioned kind that never grows old and never will lose its charm so long as human nature remains human—cuts a very big figure in the periodical publishing world and fills a very big place in our lives as a people—including all the people who can read at all.

It is this fact that leads me to issue a magazine for the railroad world which shall be something more than a mere technical thing—a magazine that shall be filled with human interest stories in fact and human interest stories in fiction. And fortunately for this publication, the railroad in its very nature is so dramatic that it furnishes thousands of themes in real life which are as thrilling and daring and brave as the fancy of the most active story-writer can invent and vitalize into probability.

Munsey's approach opposed the idea of popular fiction as escapist entertainment. He created *Railroad Man's* to fill what he saw as an unmet market niche: people in the railroad industry will want to read about themselves. Looking back on how the pulps actually developed, we can safely say that adventure stories were not written specifically for explorers, nor detective stories for law enforcement officers, nor aviation stories for pilots, and so forth, but for ordinary readers wishing to travel to places attainable only in the imagination. Munsey, while probably wrong in theory, succeeded with *Railroad Man's* for other reasons. The railroads did, at that time, represent to the wider public a technological frontier, an exciting symbol of the modern world and its possibilities, similar to what aviation would soon come to represent. The magazine thrived into the teen-years before eventually merging with *Argosy* in 1919. In 1929, after railroad enthusiast William Edward Hayes announced his own railroad pulp, The Munsey Company revived *Railroad Man's*, co-opting Hayes as editor. It was retitled *Railroad Stories* in 1932, then *Railroad Magazine* in 1937, under which it ran for several more decades, proving the long-term commercial viability of railroad-oriented fiction and fact.

Munsey also discussed sea stories in the introductory essay to *Railroad Man's*:

> Before the days of the railroad and ocean-going steamers, writers found that the ocean furnished the most dramatic possibilities. But with the disappearance of the sailing ship and with the subjugation of cannibals and savages, the ocean no longer compares with the railroad in the variety and multiplicity of dramatic and thrilling possibilities.
>
> The weather bureau, the lighthouse, the life-saving station, the telegraph and telephone, the wireless telegram, a better knowledge of the ocean and its habits and a more complete record of its most dangerous places—all these, together with the big stanch ships of to-day, have robbed the sea of much of its dangers. It is still far from a placid thing, and it can be very ugly, very treacherous, very wicked, but to a large extent man is getting the mastery of it. Our big modern steamers can run away from a storm, fight a storm, defy a storm. All this about the sea to show that its old-time dangers and terrors are disappearing, while railroading has come into the foreground and is the most thrilling and dramatic phase of human endeavor. Every minute that a great train is thundering along at sixty or eighty or a hundred miles an hour it is not only subject to many perils, but is actually skirting the very edge of disaster. And because of this danger—this tensity of life on the rail, there is an excitement and fascination to it that cannot be found and does not exist in the more placid and more secure occupations.

Munsey seems to have been spellbound by the fascination of speed to see the rails as inherently more dangerous than the oceans. Perhaps that was a general perception in 1906. He probably wouldn't have written that passage after, say, 1912, when the *Titanic* went down, killing fifteen-hundred people in a matter of hours.

Curiously, though, within a few months Munsey defied his instincts by introducing THE OCEAN, a magazine of sea stories and lore structured like *Railroad Man's Magazine*, a thick, 192-page pulp with a balanced combination of serials, short stories, and fact features—all for that magical ten-cent cover price. The first issue debuted with a date of March 1907. Munsey didn't supply introductory remarks, perhaps not caring to contradict himself in print so soon after his remarks in *Railroad Man's*. However, when THE OCEAN folded—after a mere eleven issues—Munsey reflected briefly on its origins in "To the Readers of THE OCEAN," included in the final issue (January 1908) (and reprinted in full in this volume):

I wasn't very keen for "The Ocean" as a title in the outset. I should have preferred "The Earth," but I found that that name was already being used. There was, however, the bare chance that tales of the sea might interest a wide circle of readers. The only way to know was to find out—to put the theory to the test. The experiment has been interesting and profitable—profitable both in actual money and in the development of an established magazine.

The Ocean, as the title of a magazine, gives no latitude for wanderings on shore, and there are many scenes along the Rialto and in other choice places of earth that furnish themes for good journalism. It is an inelastic, unyielding term . . .

He made clear that the magazine had not failed:

The Ocean is doing fairly well, and has done fairly well from the start. That is to say, it is paying a net profit, and has paid a net profit on every issue. But it isn't doing well enough to be tremendously exciting. I fancy there is too much water in the title, and water isn't especially popular just now.

The remarks led up to an explanation as to why The Ocean was being retitled *The Live Wire*, a general purpose pulp with a similar mix of fiction and fact. Assuming Munsey is giving us the complete—or complete enough—story, The Ocean obviously could have continued. In his history of *The Argosy*, the theme that comes through loudest is Munsey's sheer perseverance, his willingness to go to the bitter end to turn a magazine into a winner. But that was a younger Frank Munsey, a man with far fewer attractive options. Munsey is showing a different side here. He's no longer so steeped in the business that he's writing fiction for his own product. The sink-or-swim cycle had been shortened to a sprint, not a marathon. The issue was opportunity cost: why continue one magazine at a certain profit when another in its place could do better? We can assume *The Live Wire* didn't make a better success, however, lasting only eight issues (February-September, 1908). But it also had the added burden of proving a new color-printing process, as Munsey describes in "To the Readers of The Ocean," and his introductory remarks for the first issue of *The Live Wire* (also reprinted here).

History aside, let's look at the content of The Ocean.

At first thought, the sea-story genre does sound somewhat restrictive, falling short in "the variety and multiplicity of dramatic and thrilling possibilities," as Munsey put it. This doesn't really bear out. The sea story can travel far and wide, backwards and forwards in time, with a historical sweep from *The Odyssey* and Noah's Ark to *The Perfect Storm*, with a literary sweep from *Moby Dick* to *Waterworld*. Settings can range from the Great Lakes to the Seven Seas, from tropical seas to the Polar regions. Vessels can range from ocean liners and battleships to submarines to sailing ships of all sizes to rowboats and canoes, even to rafts supporting shipwreck survivors. The vessel's purpose can range from sport to commercial to naval to scientific exploration. Characters range from captain to deckhand, from passenger to stowaway, from prince to pirate. Sea stories can be contemporary or historical, encompassing all of maritime history; they can involve naval battles, sadism and mutinies, survival ordeals, treacherous water and weather, fishing experiences, adventures in seamanship and engineering, and, because it's not exclusively a male-oriented genre, romance at sea. Endless possibilities, all of which can be multiplied many times over by the variety of human complications the characters provide.

Though his name does not appear in the magazine, Robert "Bob" H. Davis was managing editor of THE OCEAN, as he was for *All-Story*, *Scrap Book*, and *Railroad Man's* (Matthew White, Jr. edited *Argosy*). His challenge was in finding the authors to present the variety inherent in the genre.

This collection attempts a representative sampling of THE OCEAN's wares, with a few disclaimers:

1) Every issue of THE OCEAN, with the exception of the first, had four serials running. For reasons of length, only one serial, a two-parter, is included here. The magazine had as few as six short stories an issue, and as many as ten; the average was eight. The majority ran about 2-5000 words in length.

2) Fiction in THE OCEAN is predominately male-oriented, by about a 2-to-1 margin. A number of stories featured female characters either in central or subordinate roles. Several female writers appeared, including Izola Forrester, whose short from the first issue is reprinted here. However, due to your editor's preferences, this collection is probably a little more male-oriented, action-oriented, than the totality of the magazine itself.

3) Some stories were heavily weighted with the inarticulate, ethnic speech of working-class seamen, and it's not always clear whether this was done with affection or derision, for realism or for humor. At any rate, it results in an overdose of apostrophes, and often requires deciphering the dialogue. Your editor was willing to risk accusations of snobbery in limiting the inclusion of such stories here.

4) Though, in general, the magazine featured well-written material, as this collection endeavors to establish, a number of poorly-constructed stories turned up, and were of course excluded. The existence of these stories speaks more to Davis' challenges as editor than his competence. A general-fiction writer, a landlubber by nature, can, no doubt, generate a reasonable sea story from time to time. But, ultimately, the quality of THE OCEAN rested on the ability of writers with authentic and original takes on the genre, the kind of knowledge that grows from genuine experience. Thus, on one hand, THE OCEAN featured stories with intriguing human and technical situations,

which failed owing to the author's inability to create a completely coherent narrative; and, on the other, it featured solid storytelling from generalists which lacked firsthand insight into the intricacies of the sea-going life. The preferential group, that small subset of knowledgeable quality writers, did find their way into the magazine; several, T. Jenkins Hains and L. Frank Tooker, for instance, are included here. But you don't really need to know who they are ahead of time. In the authentic story, you can practically feel the breeze and taste the saltwater; in the generalist's work, the boat is merely a stage for actors to play upon, or a means of transporting characters to and fro, and themes become obvious and predictable, i.e. the story of the man who fears himself a coward, but comes through a hero in perilous circumstances.

With the first issue, the format was all but set. Three serials were initiated. Six short stories were included. One "complete novel" (actually a novelette), "Bullseye Higginson" by Philip Robert Dillon, was included. This was the only non-serialized long story in the run. There were four poems. Poetry appeared in every issue. Often, they were classics by Longfellow, Byron, or such, but originals appeared, as well. There were six "special articles." Some of these were series, such as "Rough Riders of the Sea" by Captain Jack Brand, which provided historical profiles, and "Unsolved Mysteries of the Sea" by different contributors. Additionally, there were a dozen or two brief articles on nautical subjects, filler material.

A number of regularly appearing authors were names familiar in other Munsey pulps of the time: for instance, Burke Jenkins (*Argosy, Railroad Man's*), John Barton Oxford (*Railroad Man's*), or Charles Francis Bourke (*All-Story*). Old standby, William Wallace Cook, contributed a five-part serial, "A Deep-Sea Game" (July-November). Some young authors—Clarence Budington Kelland, for instance—were relative unknowns in THE OCEAN, but went on to become bigger names. (Profiles of the authors included in this collection appear in "Authors and Others.")

Sam Moskowitz, in his book *Under the Moons of Mars*, gave the impression that THE OCEAN contained a lot of science fiction. The most notable fantastic work is Epes Winthrop Sargent's two-part serial, "In the Land of To-Morrow" (reprinted here), a scientific romance in the mold of stories that would be better executed a few years hence by writers like Edgar Rice Burroughs and George Allan England, though Sargent's story is entertaining enough. Another story Moskowitz cites (which we also reprint) is Edwin C. Dickinson's "The Passing of the Waters," a brief account of a fictional battle over the newly-completed Panama Canal. This could only be considered science fiction under the broadest and least demanding definition of the term. It would be fair to say that modern readers looking to THE OCEAN for more examples of early fantastic fiction would be disappointed. It really is a sea-story magazine. But the sea story blends well with the ghost story, and we include one such from THE OCEAN, Izola Forrester's "Devereux's Last Smoke."

Toward the end of the run, the sea became a less important element of the stories. "In the Land of To-Morrow," which ran in the last two issues, is only marginally a sea story. It features a secret island city, approachable only by submarine. But that's a question of transportation; the story is concerned with other matters. Other stories are completely land-bound. "By Right of Justice," in the last issue, is a western short; a sea story only under the terms of this line from the Koran quoted in *Lawrence of Arabia*: "the desert is an ocean in which no oar is dipped." It seems that the transition to *The Live Wire* was underway before the actual change of title. Sea stories were gradually phased out in *The Live Wire*; perhaps a matter of using up purchased inventory. At the time of THE OCEAN's demise, three serials remained to be completed. They carried through into *The Live Wire*, and were joined, in the first issue, by a Mary Roberts Rinehart mystery serial.

One doesn't leap to consider the legacy of a magazine that only ran eleven issues. Perhaps Munsey, with more patience, could have turned THE OCEAN into a long-term winner. It seems, in the end, to have been doomed by the prejudice he brought to the project. Since it didn't take off as quickly as he had hoped, he must have assumed he'd been right in the first place. Still, it was the second specialized pulp and, owing to its brief run, a rare magazine today.

THE OCEAN may have had its greatest impact in lessons learned. First, the even mixture of fact and fiction may have revealed that two separate readerships existed, one for mostly fact, another for mostly fiction, and perhaps neither camp would have been satisfied with a half-appealing magazine. The readers that liked the composite format may have been a minority. As the pulps developed, fact features became commonplace, but they were seldom more than a few pages. On the other side, many predominately nonfiction magazines included a small amount of fiction.

For Munsey, the brief life of THE OCEAN may have inhibited the introduction of other specialized pulps. Had he been a little looser in his thinking, he might have been first to exploit the possibilities of the detective- and western-story pulp, which at their roots also address occupational categories, though we don't normally think of them that way. We have no way now of knowing whether THE OCEAN negatively affected other publisher's plans, but it's something to consider. Other specialized pulps entered the market haltingly. *Top-Notch Magazine*, a youth-oriented outgrowth of a dime novel, came out as a pulp in March 1910. *Adventure*—as broad a genre as you could define—had a first issue date of November 1910. *Women's Stories* came out in 1913.

Detective Story Magazine (1915) and *Western Story Magazine* (1919), also evolved from Street & Smith dime novels. It wasn't until the '20's that the idea of pulps as ephemeral publications evolved, when publishers no longer expected their creations to outlive them. Titles, and even genres, were rapidly introduced and killed as a way of keeping up-to-date with changing reader tastes.

We should note that while THE OCEAN died a quick death, the sea story never went away. They became a staple of *Adventure, Short Stories*, and other adventure pulps. Perhaps the lesson is that readers enjoy sea stories, but only mixed in with other predilections: jungle stories, westerns, foreign legion tales, etc. Street & Smith introduced *Sea Stories Magazine* in 1922; it lasted, mostly as a monthly, into 1930, a moderate success for a pulp. But by then, readers could vary their pleasures simply by buying multiple titles off the newsstand. Other than *Sea Stories*, the genre never took hold as an independent niche in the pulps. There were other attempts, for instance Gernsback's *Pirate Stories* and *High-Sea Adventures* in the mid-'30s, but they failed to last. It may simply be, as Munsey had felt in 1906, that the ocean was passé in the modern world. The wide, and sometimes inexplicable, success of the aviation pulps stands in contrast.

After Munsey died on December 22, 1925, from appendicitis and peritonitis, his life was compared to the fictional self-made successes celebrated by Horatio Alger, Jr. But Munsey's role in creating the greatest medium for popular fiction to date, the pulp magazine, was barely a footnote. It created the capital by which Munsey built a newspaper empire, the thing that *was* celebrated. Munsey's funeral was attended by the cream of New York society, the Astors, the Vanderbilts, the Rockefellers. His passing was memorialized by the President of the United States, the Governor of New York, the Chief Justice of the Supreme Court, Senators, publishers, and bank presidents.

When *Argosy All-Story Weekly* ran a six-part article in remembrance of its founder, "The Story of Frank A. Munsey" (February 20 - March 27, 1926), neither *Railroad Man's Magazine* nor THE OCEAN received mention. Both were magazines of yesteryear, footnotes to a footnote.

Bibliography

" 'Bob' Davis Honored By Fellow-Authors." *New York Times*, June 17, 1931.

Britt, George. *Forty Years—Forty Millions: The Career of Frank A. Munsey*. Farrar & Rinehart, 1935.

"Editorial Comment on the Death of Mr. Munsey." *NYT*, December 23, 1925.

"Leaders of Nation at Munsey Funeral." *NYT*, December 25, 1925.

Moskowitz, Sam. *Under the Moons of Mars: A History and Anthology of "The Scientific Romance" in the Munsey Magazines, 1912-1920*. Holt Rinehart and Winston, 1970.

"Munsey Began Life on a Farm in Maine." *NYT*, December 23, 1925.

Munsey, Frank A. "Just a Word About This New Magazine." *The Railroad Man's Magazine*, October 1906.

———. "A Great Event for *The Argosy*." *The Argosy*, December 1907.

———. "To the Readers of THE OCEAN." THE OCEAN, January 1908.

———. "Just a Word or Two by Mr. Munsey About This New Magazine." *The Live Wire*, February 1908.

"Noted Men Laud Dead Publisher." *NYT*, December 23, 1925.

"The Story of Frank A. Munsey." *Argosy All-Story Weekly*, February 20 to March 27, 1926. Six-part serialized article which quotes heavily from "A Great Event for *The Argosy*."

Authors and Others

MOST OF THE STORIES IN THIS COLLECTION were chosen on the basis of suitable content; so the following biographies provide a near-random look at the kind of authors to be found in THE OCEAN, or, for that matter, any Munsey pulp of the period. The authors range from the prestigious to the up-and-coming to the journeymen to the anonymous, as history finds them. The list also hints at the number of writers who were eventually lured into the film business.

The bulk of the information comes from newspaper reports, obituaries and book reviews. The online FictionMags Index provides much of the publication records; information is sketchy from the early 20th Century, particularly for prestige magazines, but many of the Munsey pulps have been indexed. Additional information came from *Fred Cook's The Argosy Index 1896-1943*, by Denise Cook Uhler (Adventure Fiction Press, 2001); and the *Science Fiction, Fantasy, & Weird Fiction Magazine Index: 1890-1998*, by Stephen T. Miller & William G. Contento (Locus Press, 1999).

Bourke, Charles Francis (~1865-1914) ["The Lone Mutineer"]: Born in Detroit, the son of Irish immigrants. In 1898, he sent a short story from Detroit to the artist Albert Beck Wenzell who sold it to P.F. Collier. Collier subsequently brought Bourke to New York to edit *Collier's Weekly*, a job he held for seven years. Following that tenure, about late 1905, his freelance writing career appears to start in earnest. He placed stories in *Harper's Weekly*, *Leslie's Weekly*, *Munsey's Magazine*, and others. He's a regular presence in Munsey pulps—particularly, *The All-Story* and *The Cavalier*—from 1906-14. Many of his stories shared the byline with his wife, S. Ten Eyck Bourke, daughter of a wealthy Albany and Brooklyn family; they married around 1904. C.F. Bourke died August 4, 1914 at home in NYC after an acute attack of gastritis, age 49. Two weeks later, Mrs. Bourke survived an apparent drug overdose. She continued to publish under her solo name for a few years.

Davis, Robert "Bob" H(obart) (1869-1942) [editor of THE OCEAN]: Born in Brownville, Nebraska, March 23, 1869, son of an Episcopal clergyman. Both parents had come from New England to perform missionary work among the Indians. Later in 1869, the family moved west. When Bob was four, the family was living in Marysville, California; later they moved to Carson City, Nevada. "One of the first jobs I ever had was the position of advertising agent for a prepared food company." He eventually worked for the Carson *Daily Appeal*, published by his much older brother, Samuel P. Davis. Bob delivered papers, collected subscriptions, and set type. Sam died March 17, 1918, age 68, with a reputation as a humorist, poet, brilliant editor, and significant figure in the history of Nevada journalism. A greater influence on Bob, however, was his other brother, Willis (Will or Bill) (d. 1943), two years his senior. Bob wrote of his boyhood in *Tree Toad, The Autobiography of a Small Boy* (1935). "Tree toad" was Bill's nickname for Bob after he'd talked Bob into painting himself green and "camouflaging" himself in a tree. Bill became a newspaperman for the *Appeal*, the *Stockton Independent* and the *Los Angeles Express*. A fourth sibling remains unidentified.

Following his apprenticeship with the *Appeal*, Bob Davis moved to San Francisco, about 1894, to set type at the San Francisco *Examiner*. Once, while setting the type for an account of a baseball game, the copy blew out the window. Davis, who had seen the game, wrote up his own version, which so pleased the editor, he was promoted to reporter. He reported for other San Francisco newspapers, the *Call Bulletin* and *The Chronicle*, and founded a short-lived newspaper named *Chic*. In 1896, grubstaked by "two Irish gentlemen," he relocated to New York with his friend, the artist Harrison Fisher. He married the former Madge Lee Hutchinson of New York in 1899.

While writing for *The New York Journal* and *The American*, he became a well-known reporter. In early 1903, he joined Joseph Pulitzer's *New York World*, editing fiction for the Sunday edition, whereby he pursued and hired the young writer O. Henry, thus beginning a celebrated friendship.

Later, Munsey hired Davis to edit the *New York Sunday News* at double his salary at the *World*. After Munsey killed the *Sunday News* in 1904, Davis was shifted to fiction editor for *Munsey's Magazine*, and Munsey's expanding line of fiction magazines (excluding *The Argosy*). He became managing editor of *The All-Story* (1905), *The Scrap Book* (1906), *Railroad Man's Magazine* (1906), *Woman* (1906), THE OCEAN (1907), *The Live Wire* (1908), and *The Cavalier* (1908). At the peak, Davis was managing the 40,000 manuscript submissions Munsey received annually. He wrote one author: "I read as many thousands of words as any man in the country." He considered himself a conduit through which most of the fiction written in the United States passed. "Nothing good gets by." He built a reputation for discovering authors and publishing "first" stories. He's credited with the discovery or development of such well-known authors as Rex Beach, Max Brand, Edgar Rice Burroughs, James Oliver Curwood, George Allan England, Fannie Hurst, Zane Grey, Frank Packard, Mary Roberts Rinehart, and dozens of others. Encomiums for Davis from veteran writers are easy to find in the writers' mags. For example, Harold Hersey wrote in *Author & Journalist*, July 1927:

> He has been called "Cent-a-Word" Davis. To some this nickname may be anathema. To me it proves the man's sterling qualities. Nicknames are given

only to those we love. This man would take hold of the young writer, labor over him, and out of the rough clay molded many a name seen nowadays emblazoned across the covers of the big periodicals. It may be true that he paid only a cent a word, or some similar sum, but the work he purchased was capitalistically worth more.

He was especially known for his helpful correspondence, even with rejected manuscripts. Thomas Thursday wrote in *Writer's Digest*, July 1940:

> His letters were classics. He could say more in one sentence than the average editor could say in sixteen pages. And when a cuss word was in order, you would get that and like it. You would like it because you would know that Bob Davis wanted to be your friend and aid you. There was nothing snooty about the fellow. He was down to earth and he would see that the writer stayed down there with him.

Another author received this response to a submission: "Some mystery, kid. It certainly had me fooled. I thought it was never going to end—and it did."

A detailed history of Davis' editorship of the Munsey pulps can be found in Sam Moskowitz's *Under the Moons of Mars: A History and Anthology of "The Scientific Romance" in the Munsey Magazines, 1912-1920.*

In addition to his duties with Munsey, Davis found time to write three plays, one in collaboration with former *Scrap Book* editor and popular Munsey contributor, Perley Poore Sheehan. Davis and Sheehan also wrote a novel together, *"We Are French!"* The story resulted in a 1916 film, *The Bugler of Algiers*, and a 1924 remake, *Love and Glory*. Davis' stories resulted in five other films, including the Eddie Cantor hit *Whoopee!* (1930).

In 1897, Davis, having never seen a prizefight, was sent by the Hearst papers to cover the Bob Fitzsimmons-James J. Corbett heavyweight championship, since it took place in his former home of Carson City. In 1913, Davis wrote a two-reel screenplay with a boxing plot for Fitzsimmons that was to be produced by Mutual Film. We have no record that the film was actually made. In 1926, Davis published a well-received biography of Fitzsimmons.

Davis' introduction to the film world came in the late 1890's. He and several partners set up the Miragraph Corporation to film boxing matches. ("Miragraph," Davis explained, is Latin for "wonderful pictures.") Their first match resulted in a knockout after twenty-eight seconds, rendering the film unmarketable, the investment of thousands lost. "Come easy, go easy," Davis concluded.

In late 1920, Davis mostly retired from editing to start a Munsey-sponsored literary agency, Service for Authors. Moskowitz wrote: "Other people involved with the Munsey magazines say that Davis resigned as a result of deep disagreements with other members of the Munsey editorial staff, chief among them R.H. Titherington, veteran of *Munsey's Magazine*." We say mostly retired, because Davis remained involved with *Munsey's Magazine*. We should also note that *Railroad Man's Magazine* merged into *Argosy* in 1919, then *All-Story* merged with *Argosy* in July 1920. Davis may have sensed his world contracting. Financial matters may have become an unendurable annoyance. In a July 1929 interview in *Writer's Digest*, he made these revealing remarks:

> Money is the trouble with writers today. They have become so tied up with the demands for luxuries that they sell their artistic souls for dollars. They write for money, and not because they want to get something out of their mind and soul. They do some creditable work, and the moment editors become interested in them they tie themselves up in such a maze that they have to go on writing, writing whether they have anything to write about or not.

The comment reflects upon the nature of the art of fiction which, aided greatly by the pulps, had transitioned into a mass-production medium of absurd dimensions.

In a brief 1924 profile, author Frank Condon wrote:

> The full name is Robert Hobart Davis and what you see upon entering his office at 280 Broadway, New York, is a thick-shouldered individual, with a bent-over manner about him, which probably comes from leaning over manuscripts, which he has been doing, as an editor, for roughly twenty years. Roughly is correct. Bob Davis is the only editor in the world who barks at authors and continues friendly and the statistics on file now show that he has more writing friends than any other man alive.
>
> Mr. Davis (quiet laughter at the thought of calling him Mr. Davis) is a person of widely diversified interests and not only edits magazines, encourages budding authors, consoles poets and warns them against starvation, but he is likewise an authority on fish, knows fish thoroughly, writes about them in out-door publications, plays golf, talks about golf, writes poetry and as a matter of historical fact is the father of the "I Am" school of poetry. He wrote the first "I Am" poem about a printing press, which declared that "I am the mighty voice of the people," and since its appearance everything from washing machines to blackhead eradicators. [Davis' "I Am the Printing-Press" appeared in an ad in the July 1911 *Munsey's*, and was reprinted widely.]

Davis continued to write in the side, producing literary biographies of his friend, Irvin S. Cobb (1924), and Mary Roberts Rinehart (1925).

Frank Munsey died on December 22, 1925. He bequeathed Davis $10,000. On Munsey's instructions, William T. Dewart, company general manager, vice-president and treasurer, was promoted to president. Dewart soon offered Davis what was widely considered a reporter's dream job, a thrice-weekly column in *The New York Sun* which Davis wrote for the rest of his life. Dewart's mandate was "that you see everything and write about it in your own vein. To you in the future, the whole earth is a local story." Davis wrote about experiences he'd had in the business, people he'd known. In time, he took extended trips, both in the U.S. and abroad, accompanied by his wife, and recorded his observations. The column was called *Bob Davis Reveals*, and it earned him a reputation as one of the great reporters of his time.

The title of the column reflects the name under which he became extremely well-known to the public. He'd started life as Robert Hobart Davis, but shortened it for everyday usage to R.H. Davis; but this led to him being occasionally confused with his contemporary, the novelist Richard Harding Davis. The final ascendance of "Bob Davis" seems to have occurred in the '20s, due to the insistence of "a unified public." It was how he was known for the rest of his life, often preceded by "the legendary."

As a sign of his fame, in November 1930, Davis was featured in a Lucky Strike ad that ran in many newspapers, an honor usually reserved for movie stars, not editors and columnists.

Collections of the columns were frequently issued as books with titles like *Bob Davis Recalls*, *Bob Davis Again*, *Bob Davis Abroad*, etc. Fannie Hurst's preface to *Bob Davis Again* (1928) describes him thusly:

> At fifty-eight, he is a notorious fisherman; a poet who likes red meat; a chronic enthusiast; a world traveler who explores the Bronx with the same zest that he treks a jungle; a king-pin editor; an incorrigible amateur photographer; one of the few post-prohibition after-dinner speakers worth his filet-of-soul; a champion of champions; man of parts; hobnobber with poets and cauliflower ears; an inspired and inspiring friend.

In his reporting, Davis meticulously noted the names, addresses, and other pertinent details about everyone he encountered; his notebooks eventually counted some 32,000 names. A *Time* story on Davis (June 16, 1930) stated, "it is scant exaggeration to say he has 'been everywhere, knows everybody.'"

In 1926, Davis obtained an interview with Premier Benito Mussolini for The Associated Press, for which they made him an honorary life member. In 1931, he produced a noteworthy biography of another friend, O. Henry, *The Caliph of Bagdad* (with Arthur B. Maurice). On the occasion of this book, and to recognize his long record of achievement, Davis was honored at an all-star luncheon in New York, attended by Irvin Cobb, Achmed Abdullah, Ellis Parker Butler, Lowell Thomas, Theodore Dreiser, Rube Goldberg, and many others. Sinclair Lewis sent a telegram. One speaker described Davis as "the most lovable figure in American literature today."

A number of the guests had been subjects of Davis' portrait photography. Davis jokingly called himself the "foremost amateur portrait photographer in the world." He eventually made over 3000 portraits of prominent people, which he called "psycho-graphs." Many were taken in his office, with no artificial lighting or special treatment. He turned down a $50,000 offer to sell the collection. A selection was published in the 1932 book, *Man Makes His Own Mask*. A *New York Times* review of a gallery exhibition (February 16, 1930) called Davis "a true and sincere artist," and called the portraits "extraordinarily fine photographs . . . Mr. Davis discovers in our faces what we are trying to hide."

Davis' later column collections reveal travels far and wide, e.g. *Let's Go with Bob Davis to India, Ceylon, Venezuela, the Caribbean, Puerto Rico, Alaska and the Yukon, Gaspe, Chesapeake Bay* (1940). On October 11, 1942, he died of a heart ailment in Royal Victoria Hospital, Montreal, age 73. Canada was one of his favorite destinations, and the subject of numerous columns and his 1937 book, *Canada Cavalcade*. His funeral, at St. Bartholomew's Protestant Episcopal Church in New York was attended by 500 people.

Legendary, indeed. More than sixty authors, many of them well-known, dedicated their books to Bob Davis; yet he, modest to the last, could quip as he did in a 1928 piece, "What little success I have achieved as an editor is due entirely to the fact that I have never at any time considered myself a better writer than my contributors. Nor have they."

Dickinson, Edwin C. (1880-1956) ["The Passing of the Waters"]: Born in Cromwell, Connecticut, March 11, 1880. Graduated from Hartford Public High School in 1898, Yale Law in 1902. He apparently had considerable success writing short stories early in his career, as late as 1916. He was a member of the Connecticut Cavalry from 1911-17 and did service on the Mexican border. After private law practice, he began a judicial career in 1917, eventually rising to associate justice of Connecticut's Supreme Court. He loved sailing, usually accompanied by his wife and colleagues.

Doran, Charles ["The End of the Iron Monarch"]: No information. Only known publication.

Durham, W. Hanson [" 'Don't Give Up the Ship' "]: Current records indicate a dozen published short stories from 1906-14, including four in *Argosy* and three in *The Black Cat*. From 1912-14, Durham wrote stories and scenarios for the Vitagraph Company in Santa Monica, California. For several weeks in 1913, he wrote from a hospital bed, keeping three directors busy, while he recovered from a broken knee.

Forrester, Izola (1878-1944) ["Devereux's Last Smoke"]: Born Izola Louise Wallingford, November 15, 1878, in Pascoag, Rhode Island, to unmarried parents. Her mother, a stage actress, believed herself to be the daughter of John Wilkes Booth. Izola frequently acted with her mother on the stage. After her mother's death in 1892, Izola was adopted by family friends Harriet and George Forrester. George was editor of the *Chicago Tribune*.

At age 14, Izola began selling stories to magazines like *Woman's Home Companion*. By 17, she was virtually self-supporting as a writer. One of her editors doubted her authorship, suspecting she might be fronting for her adoptive father. He subjected her to a writing test in his office. She proved her ability and sold the editor the resulting piece. She was published in several Chicago newspapers until 1901.

In 1899, Izola married Reuben Merrifield, a painter for the Ringling Brothers Circus; they had five children. After a brief period in Chicago, they moved to New York. Izola started publishing books for young girls, e.g. *The Girls of Bonnie Castle* (1900). She became a feature writer for the *New York World* from 1901-14. She published many short stories in the pulps, the bulk of them from 1907-14, including a number of appearances in THE OCEAN and *The Live Wire*, and quite a few in *The All-Story*.

In 1913, Izola left Merrifield to marry playwright, Mann Page. According to a family story, they succumbed to love at first sight at their boardinghouse on Washington Square in New York. They had three children together. Izola continued to produce girl's books, including the *Polly Page* and *Greenacre Girls* series. Together, they collaborated on 35 stories for film (the Internet Movie Database shows 24 completed films from 1914-34, including one based on Izola's 1920 novel, *The Dangerous Inheritance* [*How Women Love*, 1922]). In the sound era, the family moved to Hollywood.

Izola's later magazine work appeared in higher-grade magazines like *The Saturday Evening Post, Ainslee's, The Ladies Home Journal* and *Woman's Home Companion*.

In 1937, she published her most noteworthy book, *This One Mad Act: The Unknown Story of John Wilkes Booth and His Family*. Her research skirts the border between history and conspiracy theory. There have been numerous theories that the man killed near Port Royal, Virginia on April 26, 1865, twelve days after the Lincoln assassination, was not in fact John Wilkes Booth. Izola argued that he lived on, and had a secret marriage which led to the birth of Izola's mother, who went under the name Ogarita Booth, in 1866.

In 1940, the family moved to Keene, New Hampshire. Izola Forrester Page died on March 6, 1944, age 64.

(Numerous biographical details were obtained from the web pages of Harvard University's Schlesinger Library, which holds the Izola Forrester papers, and the Spring 2006 issue of *News from the Schlesinger Library*.)

Greener, William ["The Terror of the Doomed"]: No information. Possibly William Greener, a journalist who published an eyewitness account of the Russo-Japanese War, *A Secret Agent in Port Arthur* (Archibald, Constable; London, 1905).

Hains, T(hornton) Jenkins (1866-1953) ["When All Were Equal"]: Jenkins was born in Washington, D.C., in the home of his maternal grandfather, Rear Admiral Thornton Jenkins, from whom he took his name. Hains' father was General Peter Conover Hains, a distinguished engineering officer who helped drain the Washington Tidal Basin (Hains Point in D.C. is named after him), and build the Panama Canal. T.J. Hains was educated in public and private schools and also did one year at Columbian University, Washington. At 12, he went to sea on the schooner *Pharos*, an apprenticeship that lasted four years. In time, he was licensed as a navigator for large ocean steamers. He was the only male in his immediate family, including two brothers, who didn't pursue a military career.

He began writing in 1889, but an early event threatened to derail his career. On June 12, 1891, off Hampton Roads, Virginia, Hains went sailing in a canoe with a friend since boyhood, Ned Hannegan. When a squall headed their way from the James River, Hannegan, according to Hains' trial testimony, insisted on returning to shore. Hains, a skilled sailor, refused. Hains claimed his friend lifted an oar to strike him. Hains shot him twice, once in the heart. He stood trial for murder three months later. As both killer and victim were sons of Washington privilege, the case received a great deal of attention.

Prior to the trial, Hannegan's father claimed that Hains had caused his own father a great deal of trouble. Hains was described as a small man, but powerful. He was generally agreed to have a "surly disposition," and was "a careless, dare-devil sort of a fellow, and a ready shot with a revolver, which he was never without." He was reported to have drawn his revolver on people several times in the previous season without serious provocation. There were hints that a disagreement over a woman was the real cause of the tragedy. It was a friendship of opposites. Hannegan, four years younger, was considered as gentlemanly as Hains was rough.

Hains' defense team was described as a "brilliant array of legal talent." Witnesses disagreed on whether an oar had been raised. The only witness to bolster Hains' account was one Lincoln Smith, a "nomadic negro." Hains proved to be an effective witness in his own behalf, pleading self-defense. He received a powerful summation from his lead attorney. The jury, largely farmers, acquitted Hains after four hours of deliberation, this sparing him a hanging. The community was shocked and outraged. Over a thousand people gathered at the courthouse to denounce the verdict. Even the judge admitted that the jury had brought in the wrong verdict.

It was Hains' first famous murder trial.

In 1894, he published his first book, a short story collection, *Tales of the South Seas*. He eventually published twelve books, all dealing with the sea. Many stories were based on journals he kept during his own voyages. A 1901 novel, *Cruise of the Petrel*, dealt with events in the War of 1812, based on his grandfather's logbook. A 1903 collection, *Strife of the Sea*, spelled out the harshness of the sea, from the points of view of different animals, the whale, the turtle, the pelican, the shark, etc. All along, he had been appearing in magazines; nearly every English-language magazine, he claimed. He developed a significant reputation.

General Hains was a high-ranking member of the Nicaragua Canal Commission (1897-99); for some of that period, Thornton was in charge of the New York office and compiled statistics on dredging costs.

He married, in 1896, Mary Jones of Bensonhurst. A daughter was born in 1900. It's clear that life for Mrs. Hains presented challenges. In December 1903, accompanied by Mary and crew, Hains sailed his 30-foot sloop, the *Edna*, for Florida and the West Indies. They were struck by a hurricane and blown several hundred miles off course. After losing the rigging and rudder, the *Edna* became unseaworthy. The party was rescued by a passing ship. The rescuers found Mrs. Hains lashed to the mast. The *Edna*, valued at $6000, was abandoned. The *New York Times* commented that the experience would improve the authenticity of Hains' already commendable books. In 1906, Mary died after childbirth on a yachting trip in Florida. The following year, Hains had a child with his French maid, with whom he was living.

On August 15, 1908, Hains and his younger brother, Peter Conover Hains, Jr., a promising young Army officer, went to the Bayside Yacht Club, Long Island, on the afternoon of the ladies' day regatta. Peter Hains confronted his close friend, William E. Annis, advertising manager of *The Burr McIntosh Monthly* magazine, who had just won a race. He pulled out a pistol and emptied the magazine—eight shots—into Annis' body, in front of hundreds of society witnesses, who stood by without intervening. Annis' wife and two sons witnessed the murder. During the crime, Thornton pulled his own pistol and stood guard. Afterwards, the brothers waited to be arrested. Thornton calmly smoked a pipe and told a bystander, "No one could be more sorry for this than I am. I have tried my best to keep him from doing it for weeks."

It was actually Thornton who had started the ball rolling the year before. He wrote letters to Peter, stationed in the Philippines, keeping him up-to-date on incidents of an affair between Peter's beautiful young wife, Claudia, and Annis. Upon Peter's return to the U.S. in May 1908, he allegedly extracted a confession from Claudia. "He was vulgar and depraved, but I loved him," he reported she said of Annis. The Captain doubted the legitimacy of their youngest child. The couple separated; divorce proceedings were initiated. Finally, the Captain could contain his anger no longer. . . .

The two brothers cooled their heels in jail while the legal machinery ground, and the case became a front-page sensation across the country. In preliminary proceedings, the brothers' attorney attacked Annis as a womanizer and absinthe drinker. Thornton passed time in his cell by writing of his experiences. The state moved forward with separate trials. Thornton's began first, on December 14. He took the stand on his own behalf, January 4. His testimony took the better part of four days. He hadn't understood Peter's motives in attending the regatta, he claimed. He had counseled Peter repeatedly not to seek revenge. He testified that he always carried a gun, from his habit of visiting dangerous places on his sea voyages. Witnesses disagreed on whether he appeared to know of the murder in advance.

His attorney then tried to establish that Peter had acted out under "the unwritten law," that essentially gave cuckolded husbands a claim of insanity in acts of revenge; and that Thornton had also been temporarily afflicted under a theory of contagious insanity. It took fifteen ballots to achieve unanimity, but the jury of twelve bought the defense's case. Announcement of the "not guilty" verdict caused an unruly eruption of joy in the courtroom. A *Times* editorial called the verdict a "shocking failure of justice." Finally free, Thornton planned to write a long novel, around the idea of "the unwritten law." He promised it would be his masterpiece.

Captain Hains went on trial in April 1909. His attorney surprised the court—and the public—by declaring that "the unwritten law" would not be invoked, that it would be a straightforward insanity defense. In the courtroom, the Captain did his best to present an appearance which lived up to the claim, seeming to be oblivious, occasionally babbling "meaningless, purposeless words" to his father. To a great extent, the trial was a family affair. General and Mrs. Hains both took the stand, testifying, in essence, that Peter had been the runt of the litter, a weak, nervous, and excitable child, plagued by sleeplessness and nightmares. Mrs. Hains testified to her own history of hysteria, which was backed up by her behavior in the witness box. The third brother, Army Major John Power Hains, testified. Thornton testified on his brother's behalf, telling his story to a jury for the second time. The judge rebuked him for his "theatrical manner." The case boiled down to this: Captain Hains had a fragile temperament and his wife's confession of adultery pushed him over the edge. The defense's alienist called it "impulsive insanity"; the prosecution's alienists disagreed. Ultimately, this jury wasn't as compliant as Thornton's. The Captain was convicted of manslaughter in the first degree, and received an 8-16 year sentence in Sing Sing, prisoner No. 2,002. General Hains, who essentially spent his retirement savings defending his sons, worked tirelessly for a pardon from New York's governor, and finally received one. Peter Hains, Jr. was released in October 1911.

Thornton's masterpiece never came to pass. He continued to write, however. His name must have been poison to publishers, because his post-trial stories appeared under the suggestive pseudonym, Mayn Clew Garnett, a tip-off of his identity to loyal readers—Garnett was a favored character who appeared in a number of Hains' stories. Garnett's stories appear primarily from 1910-14, in *The Popular Magazine*, *Top-Notch*, *The Cavalier*, and other pulps, as if the higher-class magazines would no longer take him. He achieved pseudonymous fame with the publication of a short story, "The White Ghost of Disaster," in the May 1, 1912 issue of *The Popular*. It described an ocean liner colliding with an iceberg in the Atlantic, the sinking of the vessel, and the fate of the passengers and crew. The issue had come off the presses as the *Titanic* prepared her maiden voyage. When the *Titanic* sunk, Garnett's story became a sensation. There were rumors that he had foreseen the real disaster in a dream while sailing on the *Olympic*, and written his story as a result. But the public, while fascinated, had no idea who Garnett was, as, for example, this editorial in the *Reno Evening Gazette* (April 23 ,1912) reveals:

> Prescience is not a recognized science. It ranks with telepathy and other alleged cults, but it is without doubt that this man Garnett, if he be a man, and not an intuitive woman, possesses a power that is uncanny. He looked into the future and told what he saw.

The story led to Hains' first book since 1908, and the last book of his career, the collection *The Chief Mate's Yarns* (1912), by Captain Mayn Clew Garnett, with "The White Ghost of Disaster" as lead story.

We have no record of publication—under either name—between 1914 and 1922. Then Hains resurfaced in the pulps, primarily under his own name but with a few as Garnett. He has a deep list of appearances in *Sea Stories*, and a scattering in *Complete Story*, *The Danger Trail*, *Adventure*, etc. Many of them may be reprints. In 1922, for example, under Hains' name, *Sea Stories* ran two adventures of a character named Bahama Bill. Both are from Hains' last collection before the Annis affair, *Bahama Bill, Mate of the Wrecking Sloop Sea-horse* (1908), although *Sea Stories* doesn't identify them as reprints. (Unacknowledged reprints were common in the magazine.) Curiously, in 1924, they ran two more Bahama Bill stories under Garnett's name; these were not from *Bahama Bill*, and may be originals. The last known publication of Hains is "Death in the Moonlight," in the November 1930 *Excitement*, the short-lived retitling of *Sea Stories*.

Hains' remaining years are a mystery. He would have been about 65 in 1930, so retirement is a likelihood. He died August 19, 1953 and was buried in Portsmouth City, Virginia. No obituary could be found. For a figure with a solid literary reputation *and* the tremendous notoriety of the 1908-09 murder trial, he passed from this world with barely a murmur.

Hall, Gifford (1882-1948) ["The Backslider"]: Published several short stories from 1903-08. No other information. Birth and death dates unconfirmed.

Hall, T(homas) Victor (1879-19??) [artist, "In the Land of To-Morrow"]: Illustrator and landscape painter. Born in Rising Sun, Indiana; studied at the Cincinnati Art Academy and worked in New York. Magazine work includes covers for *The Argosy* and *The Scrap Book*; interiors for *Adventure* and *Triple-X*. Book illustrations include *At the Earth's Core*, by Edgar Rice Burroughs. Last known credit is the book *Red Morton, Waterboy*, by Alan Drady (1932).

Hamblen, Herbert E(lliott) (1849-1908) ["A Crusoe of the Antarctic"]: Different accounts have him born in either Lovell, Maine or Ossippee, New Hampshire, two towns about 30 miles apart; December 24, 1849. He came to New York City and attended public schools. At the age of fifteen he went to sea as a cabin boy, and spent fifteen years as a sailor (1864-78), leaving as a chief mate. He worked as a railroad engineer from 1880-94.

An omnivorous reader, Hamblen struck up a friendship with a New York City librarian, William Stone Booth, who was enthralled by accounts of his life and considered him a born storyteller. Booth encouraged him to commit his sea experiences to paper. Hamblen's poor education barely qualified him to understand grammar, much less write, but he persevered and delivered to Booth a hard-to-read, pencil-written manuscript. Booth helped Hamblen shape it into a book, while retaining its rough appeal. Macmillan published it in 1897 as *On Many Seas; the Life and Exploits of a Yankee Sailor*, under the penname Frederick Benton Williams. It told many stories of hardship and brutality on the high seas, course language intact. Hamblen stirred up a certain amount of controversy with his depiction of the ill-treatment of sailors at sea.

Hamblen's natural follow-up was an equally harrowing account of life in the railroads, published under his real name. It was serialized in *McClure's Magazine* before reaching hard covers as *The General Manager's Story; Old-Time Reminiscences of Railroading in the United States* (Macmillan, 1898). A series of books about either the sea or the railroads soon followed.

His articles and stories appeared in *Munsey's Magazine* and *The Saturday Evening Post*. He seemed to be perfectly situated when Munsey expanded his pulp line to include both *Railroad Man's Magazine*, and THE OCEAN, which published four of Hamblen's stories. One senses from his record, though, that he ran short of material, as his list is somewhat thin after 1902.

Hamblen was employed by the City of New York, Aqueduct Department, when *On Many Seas* was published, as "the engineer of a stationary engine" at a Manhattan pumping station. He apparently never gave up the job to become a full-time writer. He died in Woodhaven, Long Island, April 6, 1908.

Jenkins, Burke (1879-1948) ["Under the Black Flag"]: Born in North Carolina. He published a book, *Waggishness, the Philosophy of Arch Fools*, in 1904. The record shows a solid block of primarily short stories appearing in the pulps from 1904-13. The majority were in *Argosy*. A 1923 film item referred to him as "former editor of *Argosy*," although, if true, it certainly would have been in a subordinate position. He was known as a writer of sea stories and westerns. A February 12, 1908 syndicated item in the *Washington Post* discussed Burke's lifestyle:

> Mr. Jenkins' yacht is a thirty-six-foot auxiliary sloop. During the summer he cruises about the Sound, and occasionally goes South by the inside route. Mrs. Jenkins is his midshipmite [sic] and crew of the captain's gig. He writes his stories of raging storms and red-handed pirates while the yacht is becalmed in peaceful waters.

The point of the article was Burke's unique living quarters during the cold weather:

> Every man in the big apartment house at Manhattan avenue and 110th street, excepting the landlord, is hitching his trousers nautically, doing hornpipe steps and humming, "Yo-ho, lads, yo-ho!"
> For Burke Jenkins, amateur sailor and writer of magazine stories of the briny, has cruised among them and shown them a new and delightful fashion of housekeeping. To save the bother of buying and subsequently storing land-lubberish furniture, Mr. Jenkins has simply moved the fittings of his yacht into the flat. And with folding cots, folding chairs, folding tables, and collapsible cooking and table utensils, he is enjoying a salty winter close by the raging Cathedral Parkway.

Jenkins has a record of writing for smaller film companies from 1920-27. He died October 19, 1948, in Ventura, California.

Kelland, Clarence Budington (1881-1964) ["When His Chance Came"]: Born in Portland, Michigan, July 11, 1881. "I came from poor but Republican parents." Of his boyhood reading, he remarked:

> I used to read "Frank Merriwell" in nickel form behind the barn, because the dime novel was looked upon by my parents as little better than petty larceny; however, "Frank" was issued in a book with cloth covers, and my

uncle gave it to me, and my father and mother smiled with satisfaction when
I stayed at home of nights to read it.

The family moved to Detroit when Kelland was ten. His father operated a
grocery store. Kelland attended public school in Detroit, but dropped out in
the tenth grade to work in a factory. After he read Paul Leicester Ford's novel
The Honorable Peter Stirling and What People Thought of Him (1894), he
decided to become a lawyer. After three years of night school, he graduated
from the Detroit College of Law in 1902. Instead of pursuing a career in the
law, his old interest in writing asserted itself:

> All my life I had been writing things for fun. I even wrote epic poems,
> and so, when it became necessary to eat, I turned naturally to the newspaper
> business—and my real education started. I believe three or four years in a
> good newspaper shop to be the most profound and practical education a man
> can have.

The "shop" was *The Detroit News*. He stayed there from 1903-07, starting
as a reporter, covering sports as one of his beats, later becoming a political
editor. His working hours were three p.m. to three a.m. He continued writing
fiction on the side, working on Sundays and early afternoons. It took seven
years before he made his first freelance sale, a short story for *Young's
Magazine*, for which he received $3.

In 1907, Kelland married Betty Caroline Smith of Ludington, Michigan;
they eventually had two sons. Soon after the marriage, the couple moved to
Vermont. He explained: "My wife's father was dubious about sons-in-law
who thought literature was a profession, so he induced me to give up editing
to go to Vermont and help run a clothespin mill." This was in conjunction
with his brother, with whom he shared ownership of the mill. Kelland
also lived in Maine, owning a lumber camp. These were either short-term
experiences, or his involvement was tangential, for in 1907 he was back in
Detroit, working for *The American Boy*. He was hired as a proof-reader and
quickly promoted to editor. When he started, the circulation was 90,000;
when he left in 1915, he had built it up to 360,000.

He continued to write, primarily fiction for boys. In *The American Boy*,
characters he would make famous first saw print: the corpulent boy sage,
Mark Tidd; and the kindly old philosopher, Scattergood Baines. His first
novel, *Mark Tidd*, was published in 1913. From 1913-15, he lectured at the
University of Michigan on writing and juvenile literature.

After he left *The American Boy*, he became a full-time freelancer. He
started pitching his stories to a general audience. He landed in *The Saturday
Evening Post* with another popular series character, Efficiency Edgar. His
1917 novel, *Sudden Jim*, brought him into prominence. He was well on

his way to becoming one of the most popular and well-paid authors in the country for nearly a half-century to follow. His chief markets were *The American Magazine* and the *Post*. He sold 55 serials alone to the *Post*, his total sales exceeding a million dollars. Many of the serials were turned into books; he published over 60 novels, and hundreds of short stories. In 1938, he estimated his annual output at half a million words, and his annual income at over $200,000.

Everything seemed to work for him. His two boys had an Airedale, so he turned it into a book, *Into His Own; The Story of an Airedale* (1915). *Scattergood Baines* (1921) collected the popular short stories into hard covers; Kelland bought a boat, named it *The Scattergood*. The family moved to New York and lived in a nice house in Port Washington, Long Island.

Kelland was a speedy and fluid writer. He wrote for four hours every morning and took the rest of the day off. He never reread or revised. He claimed that the one time he worked and polished a story, the effort took three months and he couldn't sell it. He billed himself as "the best second-rate writer in America"; thought Booth Tarkington was the country's best fiction writer.

His stories were about common-sense, everyday Americans. His genre was described as "old-fashioned Yankee wisdom, canniness and simple honesty triumphing over the entanglements and sham of a world continually growing more complicated." He always seemed to be looking back:

> Those years from the beginning of the eighties to the middle of the nineties, before speed came into the world, as the serpent came into Eden, and destroyed tranquility forever, appear to me to have been mankind's happiest time on this earth.

Critics charged that his characters were essentially the same; that he made small-town people sound like yokels. He considered himself an entertainer, not an artist. He didn't think plots were paramount: "when you have a character people like, your main job is simply to keep him in character."

Where entertainment leads, the movies follow. Starting in 1917, Kelland's stories were turned into films, about 30 to date. His best period was probably the '30s, when his stories produced such worthy comedies as *Thirty Day Princess* (1934, starring Cary Grant, from a *Ladies Home Journal* serial), *The Cat's-Paw* (1934, starring Harold Lloyd, from a *Post* serial), and his most famous story, *Mr. Deeds Goes to Town* (1936, starring Cary Cooper and Jean Arthur, directed by Frank Capra, from *The American Magazine* serial, *Opera Hat*; remade as *Mr. Deeds*, 2002, starring Adam Sandler).

In the 1936 film, inside jokes gave Kelland a bit of comic celebrity. Gary Cooper plays Longfellow Deeds, a modest small-towner who unexpectedly receives a multi-million dollar bequest. The New York law firm handling the matter is named Cedar, Cedar, Cedar, and Budington. Much sport is made of the Budington name. Deeds writes homespun verse for postcards, and a running gag is his inability to find a rhyme for Budington. When we finally meet Budington, he turns out to be a milquetoast. In the climactic scene of the film, Budington is rudely shoved in the face by his partner John Cedar, the thwarted villain.

Kelland was on the radio, too, of course. *Scattergood Baines* was a 15-minute weekday serial that ran on CBS from 1937-42. It inspired a series of Scattergood movies, distributed by RKO for the Pyramid Pictures Corporation, starring Guy Kibbee in perhaps his signature role: *Scattergood Baines* (1941), *Scattergood Pulls the Strings* (1941), *Scattergood Meets Broadway* (1941), *Scattergood Rides High* (1942), *Scattergood Survives a Murder* (1942). The good-hearted cornpone found rapidly-decreasing favor with the audience, leading RKO to change the title of the sixth and final entry from *Scattergood Swings It* to *Cinderella Swings It* (1943). Scattergood returned to the airwaves in 1949, as a 30-minute comedy-drama on Mutual.

Television wasn't immune to Kelland's charms, either. *Mr. Deeds Goes to Town* ran for 17 episodes during the 1969-70 season.

Kelland maintained an active life outside of his fiction career. In 1918, he wore a uniform as publicity director for the YMCA in Paris. He wrote behind-the-scenes articles about his observations and experiences that were widely reprinted stateside, articles like "Americans Lay Down 720 Ton News Barrage From Trenches" and "War's Scars Show Stuff That's in Our Boys."

In the mid-'20s, Kelland became president of New York's Dutch Treat Club, a toastmasters organization whose membership consisted of writers, actors, artists, and editors. The weekly lunches often featured famous guest speakers whom president Kelland—"Bud" to his friends—introduced in a humorous damned-with-faint-praise style. His association with the club lasted for decades.

Kelland was a director of The Bank of North Hempstead in Port Washington. It failed in 1932, tying up most of his securities. Also in '32, he refused to pay a $3,313 bill that his wife had run up in a Manhattan gown shop. Kelland argued that the shop had no right to extend so much credit. The shop sued Kelland, and won; the tiff was front-page news in many papers. In March 1933, no doubt the fallout from the bank failure, Kelland declared bankruptcy, with liabilities of $188,492 and assets of $260,000, mostly in illiquid real estate. He was able to pay off his debts by August, when the bankruptcy was dismissed, "largely through my literary efforts since March, 1933."

In 1937, Kelland bought a house in Phoenix, Arizona to spend the Autumn and Winter. This seems to coincide with his emergence as a voice in national politics. He was as conservative in political view as he was in literary bent, and the New Deal had provoked his wrath. He attacked it as "insane." He became known for his colorful invective. In early '40, he characterized the coming national election as a "holy war" in defense of the Constitution. He provoked particular outrage when he said, "the fifth column [i.e. the New Deal] in this country is headed by that fellow in the White House." In May, he was named Arizona's Republican National Committeeman, a position he held off and on into 1956. In the keynote speech at the 1940 State Republican Convention, he said:

> We are fighting a tapeworm known as the New Deal. This unsavory, parasitic growth . . . consists of yards of useless hungry body and one-half inch of head. The only effective treatment is to destroy the head and then the loops of brainless body disappear quietly.

A month after Pearl Harbor, Kelland, now 61, said, "Greater love hath no man than this—that he shall lay down the life of his son for his country." Pearl Harbor, as *Time* pointed out, had changed him from a "tub-thumping isolationist." *Time's* editors seemed to enjoy characterizing Kelland as "pint-sized, vitriolic," "caustic," and "pugnacious."

In 1942, Kelland was named publicity director of the Republican National Committee. His effectiveness had diminished by '44, however, as his fellow Arizonans refused to reappoint him state committeeman. It didn't muzzle him, though. Later in the year, he made headlines by blaming FDR for Pearl Harbor. He could always be relied on for a sharp comment, increasingly against his fellow Republicans. After Truman won the presidency in '48, he criticized the Republican candidate: "Dewey's campaign was smug, arrogant, stupid, and supercilious." In '54, he criticized Eisenhower's men as "the dolts who have usurped control of the party." In '58, he denounced Eisenhower's appointment of Earl Warren to the Supreme Court as "incredibly stupid"; Warren "did not know the difference between a law book and a farmers' almanac"; Eisenhower was "a façade with no solid structure behind it."

Kelland considered Senator Barry Goldwater a political protégé, but that may have been a bit of hubris. After his flirtation with actual politics in the '40s, Kelland had probably metamorphosed into a quotable gadfly. He remained a highly-productive writer throughout. He became a vice president and director of Phoenix Newspapers, Inc., which published *The Arizona Republic* and *The Phoenix Gazette*. He was often away from home, trailing major sporting events. He'd been an avid golfer for many years. He'd published a high-profile interview with Jack Dempsey in 1927.

In a 1941 interview with the *New York Times*, Kelland lamented the state of fiction:

> The old-timers who knew how to tell a story have dropped away. Some are dead, others have quit writing. Where's Peter B. Kyne? Why doesn't Ben Ames Williams write more? Why no stories from Irv Cobb? Of all that old *Saturday Evening Post* gang, do you realize that only Tark and myself and, now and then—too seldom—Mary Roberts Rinehart, are left?

He may as well have lamented his own fading relevance with such sentiments. In the interview, he devalued socially realistic fiction. He referred to Steinbeck, not by name, but as "this fellow who wrote about the Okies." In a 1954 review of his latest novel, *Time* characterized Kelland as "a prominent U.S. author to whom U.S. literary and critical magazines pay no attention whatever." In his books, "The good always wins, the boy always gets the girl, and they are married in a nice church ceremony—just after getting the deed to a nice piece of real estate—while a kindly old homespun philosopher stands snapping his galluses in the background."

Kelland's last published novel was *The Monitor Affair* (1960), from a *Post* serial. The final chapter of his last *Post* serial, *The Big Swindle*, ran in the June 17, 1961 issue. But the *Post* had been suffering declining circulation, and, in a major format overhaul, severely cut back the amount of fiction—it wasn't only the pulps that had been hurt by television. Walter Winchell reported in his column that Kelland's $150,000 annual guarantee didn't figure in the new plans.

There were more words to come from Kelland's typewriter, but he had entered *his* last chapter. In a somber story in the *Times* (August 25, 1963), Kelland admitted that his writing days were through. He was confined to bed, his energy exhausted, his eyesight dimming. "Writing fiction has become too hard work." He died six months later at his suburban Scottsdale home, on February 18, age 82.

Meyer, George Homer (18??-1926) ["When Famine Drives"]: A native of Sonoma County, Californian. Sparse information puts him in Oakland in 1891; serving as a local staffer of the San Francisco *Daily Morning Examiner*; and starting a new magazine, the *Bear Flag Monthly*, devoted to California content. His three known books are *Lamara, and Other Poems* (1878), *Almiranté: A Romance of Old-Time California* (1890), and *Nine Swords of Morales: The Story of an Old-Time California Feud* (1905). He has three known short stories in magazines, all from 1907, two in THE OCEAN.

Osborne, Maitland LeRoy (1846-1918) ["The Guardian of the Gold"]: Born in Maine. Osborne wrote for Boston's *National Magazine*. The bulk of his listings in the FictionMags Index reflect a solid block of bylines in the *National* from 1899-1901, mostly articles and poems, and several short story listings from 1911-14. In between are a few pulp appearances in *Blue Book* and *The All-Story*. *National Magazine* published two of his books: *Old Whaling Days in America* (1899) and *Recollections of P.T. Barnum* (1900). A 1908 book, *Pipe Dreams*, was published under the pseudonym, A. Vagrant.

Oxford, John Barton (1876-1944) ["A Son of Trouble"]: Born in Malden, Massachusetts, May 14, 1876. His first job was with a wholesale drug firm in Boston, 1892. He worked on the staff of the Boston Public Library for eight years, beginning 1895, during which time he began writing fiction, finding his best success with humorous works. He published under his real name, Richard Barker Shelton, and the Oxford pseudonym, which predominated after 1905. In 1903 he began work in the advertising business; married in 1904. Starting in 1906, he was a reporter for the *Boston Herald*. He resigned in 1911 and moved to Hampton, New Hampshire to become a full-time freelancer, basing a number of his stories on the rural New Englanders he encountered.

He was a steady presence in the pulps into the late teen-years. He hit all the Munsey titles, and was a consistent seller to *Blue Book*, *Red Book* and *Green Book*. From 1919-24, he placed a number of stories in *The Saturday Evening Post*, *The American*, *People's*, and other higher-grade magazines, under the name Barker Shelton. He primarily wrote short stories, although several serials turn up in the record.

Three of his stories were filmed as shorts in 1914-15. One, *Virtue Is Its Own Reward* (1914), included Lon Chaney in the cast; another, *The Availing Prayer* (1914), was directed by Donald Crisp, and featured Raoul Walsh and Dorothy Gish in the cast. A circus story, *The Man Tamer* (1921), was filmed as a feature by Universal.

In 1928, he was elected managing secretary of the Portsmouth, New Hampshire, Chamber of Commerce. In 1935, he left that job and became publicity director for a power company. He died at home in Cambridge, Massachusetts, of a heart attack, May 23, 1944, age 68; and was buried in a family plot in Hampton.

Pennell, Herbert ["Nemesis on the High Seas"]: No information. Only known publication.

Sargent, Epes Winthrop (1872-1938) ["In the Land of To-Morrow"]: He was born in Nassau, the Bahamas, where his father, Epes Sargent, was a correspondent for the *New York Times*. The family returned to the U.S. in 1878, and was in New York from 1891 forward. Sargent's first job was as an usher in Washington, D.C.'s Bijou Theatre. After that, he was employed for a series of periodicals: reviewed concerts for the *Musical Courier*;

conducted a vaudeville department in the *Dramatic News*; critic with the *Daily Mercury* and its subsidiary the *Metropolitan Magazine*; joined the staff of *The Sunday Mercury* where he wrote under the name Chicot, after the fool in the Dumas novel, *Chicot the Jester*; carried the name to *The New York Morning Telegraph*. In 1905, Sime Silverman hired Sargent (and Al Greason) to help him establish the Broadway trade paper, *Variety*. At *Variety*, Sargent shortened his nom de plume to Chic; Chicot and Chic were names that became very well-known in the theater world. As a critic, he was known to be vitriolic when he didn't like something; his commentary was described as "severe and frank"; and no amount of advertising in the paper would cause him to temper his remarks.

Pulp writing was a minor chapter in his career. He was a presence in the Munsey pulps from 1907-12 with shorts and the occasional longer work.

At some point, an argument at *Variety* caused him to leave and start his own paper, *Chicot's Weekly*. He also became a press agent and scenario writer. He's credited with 122 films from 1912-18, the majority for the Lubin Manufacturing Company. In the mid-teen years, he wrote a department for *Moving Picture World*. He published several leading books on the film business, e.g. *Technique of the Photoplay* (1912), *Picture Theatre Advertising* (1915).

He was rehired by *Variety* in 1928, where he remained for the rest of his life. He died December 6, 1938, age 66, of a stomach ailment, at home in Brooklyn.

Spears, Raymond S(miley) (1876-1950) ["Teche's Canoe"]: Born in Bellevue, Ohio. He published his first story at age 12. His father was John R. Spears (~1851-1936), a much-traveled reporter for *The New York Sun* from 1883-98 who was known for his coverage of international yacht races; he began writing books in 1898, including many works of naval history. Raymond S. Spears followed in his father's footsteps. He reported for the *Sun* from 1896-1900, before becoming a freelance writer. Spears was a prolific author of western and outdoor stories, which reflected his own love of the outdoors. He also wrote many articles on hiking, camping, and other outdoors subjects.

Many of his stories appeared in leading pulps, *All-Story, Argosy, Western Story, Short Stories, West*, and numerous others. He also wrote a number of detective stories, the majority of which appeared in the early years of *Detective Story*, 1917-21. In addition to his own name, he wrote under a number of pseudonyms, principally Jim Smiley. While not technically a sea-story writer, Spears could be called a river-story writer, as he set many stories on America's rivers. He also wrote many stories about animal trappers, and was himself Conservation Director for the American Trappers' Association in the '30s. In a 1942 address to The Manuscripters of Los Angeles, he told this story:

> I wrote 40,000 words about a wolf trapper. Bob Davis of the Munsey periodicals bought it. He wrote me that he was breaking all records.
> "This story has no plot, only one character, and it is nothing but fresh air and varmints." . . .
> In that story I told how French Louey saved all the money he received from wolf bounties and wolf hides. He changed it into gold. He kept the gold in a poke, or rawhide bag. I thought this was good imagination. I told how he shook the bag in the air and the gold jingled as he bragged his prowess, killing wolves. That I thought ought to be true, though it was just a figment of fancy, based on wolvers and their habits of thought. A few weeks after the story was published in *Munsey's* magazine, an officer in the Great Lakes Naval Reserve wrote me a letter that he had seen that old trapper waving his wolf gold in a rawhide bag.

The anecdote highlighted the fact that Spears wrote convincing fiction built on a strong foundation of research. He was against any sort of fakery or invented data in fiction. In the same address, he said:

> In order to write fiction we must know as many facts as though we were writing history, or news, or science. Knowing this, I have spent my time gathering information and writing it into fiction or into articles. If I write a story about stealing lands from the state or from individuals by lawing them to death, you can depend on my knowing that subject. To cover a certain phase of politics, doing a newspaperman's citizenship duty of gratitude, I went through the titles of about 4,000,000 acres of lands in the Adirondack Mountains in New York. I read scores of public documents, collected thousands of clippings, studied uncounted books of history.

Spears married C. Eleanor Shepard in 1904; they had two children. As early as 1925, he was living in Inglewood, California. A couple of his stories were filmed. His 1920 pulp serial, "Janie of the Waning Glories" (*All-Story*) was turned into the 10-chapter Pathé serial, *The Bar-C Mystery* (1926). He occasionally wrote magazine columns, e.g. *Reel, Trap, and Trigger* for *Western Story* (1921); *Outdoor Trails* for *North-West Stories* (1926). His publishing record reveals a three-year gap during WWII, suggesting service of some sort. He published a number of books, both fiction and nonfiction. He died at home in Inglewood, January 25, 1950, age 74.

Stephens, Charles ["Till Russia Shall Be Free"]: One other published story known, in the February 1912 *All-Story*. No other information.

Suverkrop, E(dward) A(lbert) (1864-1921) ["A Treasure in Turtle"]: Born

Washington, D.C., May 6, 1864; educated in Scotland and Germany. He served an apprenticeship in the Canal Basin Foundry, Glasgow from 1882-87. Following this, he traveled the world for five years as a marine engineer. From 1892-94, he worked at the Cramps Shipyard, Philadelphia; Gloucester Manufacturing, Gloucester, New Jersey; and Geometric Lathe, Philadelphia. He opened a machine shop in Camden, N.J., in 1894; then opened a larger shop in Philadelphia in 1897. In 1904, he joined the staff of *American Machinist*, writing technical articles under his own name and the pseudonym, E.A. Dixie. He belonged to the American Society of Mechanical Engineers.

He was known for his wide interests. In 1901, he published an article in *Scientific American* on ants; and also discovered a new orchid on one of his multiple trips to South America, as part of continuing contributions to the Herbarium in London. Two stories in THE OCEAN represent his only known published fiction.

(An Edward A. Suverkrop received a degree from the School of Mines, Columbia University in 1913; was a member of the American Institute of Mining, Metallurgical, and Petroleum Engineers; and was living in Dayton, Ohio in 1916. Our Suverkrop would have been about 50 in 1913, making it more likely this was a son.)

Suverkrop resigned from *American Machinist* in July 1919 to develop a manufacturing process. He died July 29, 1921, of blood poisoning, as the process was coming to market.

Tooker, L(ewis) Frank (1855-1925) ["At the Spur of Danger"]: Born in Port Jefferson, Long Island. Tooker came from a seafaring family, and spent much of his spare time as a youth around shipyards and on ships. He graduated from Yale in 1877. In 1885, he joined the editorial staff of *The Century* magazine, where he remained for the rest of his life. He recounted his experiences in the 1924 memoir, *The Joys and Tribulations of an Editor*, published by The Century Company. One of his key anecdotes concerned a manuscript he received from an unknown writer. He highly recommended it for publication in the magazine, but was overruled by the president of the company, who asserted that Tooker was too prejudiced in favor of sea stories. Thus did the magazine pass on Joseph Conrad's *Typhoon* (1902); Tooker considered himself the first admirer of Conrad in the U.S.

Tooker wrote many stories and poems, himself, often dealing with the sea. His first book was *Call of the Sea, and Other Poems* (1902). His first novel, *Under Rocking Skies* (1905), a romance set aboard a ship, was serialized in *The Century* before being published as a book. The *New York Times* review concluded, "The best thing in *Under Rocking Skies* is the author's unfailing power to paint the sea in many moods, and always so vividly as to impart a wonderful sense of reality." Other books include *John Paul Jones* (1916), and a second novel, *The Middle Passage* (1920). The story included in this collection is his only known appearance in the pulps.

Tooker died September 17, 1925, age 71, in Greenwich, Connecticut, from an illness following a stroke.

When His Chance Came
Clarence Budington Kelland

Wherein a Mate Learns that Fog Is Not Always a Foe

THE BARGE AMOS MCGARRY WAS STEAMING NORTHWARD through the waters of White Fish Bay with a cargo of anthracite for the coal-docks at West Superior. Under her rounded bow the water boiled and eddied, piling up in a foam-topped wave that pressed and surged against her as if trying to halt her in her passage. All about her the blue and white of the sky was reflected by the thousand mirrors caused by the almost imperceptible ripple of the bay.

Far to the westward was the hazy outline of the Michigan shore, and to the eastward the pines of Parisian Island reared themselves in the clear air like monuments erected to some ancient chief. Through this scene of tranquil beauty the McGarry plowed, a blot of heavy black smoke trailing behind her.

Far above, Captain Henley was pacing backward and forward upon the bridge, suffering and anxiety in his face. The captain was ill. It had taken all the force of his strong will to keep upon his feet to this point, and now an additional and unexpected weight of responsibility had been placed upon him. He nervously fingered a yellow telegraph form, which he now and again uncrumpled and read; and at each reading the lines of worry about his mouth deepened.

The first mate stepped from the pilot-house and was descending to the deck, when the captain perceived him, and raising his voice, called, "Mr. Cooke!" The mate turned and remounted to the bridge to ask, "What is it, sir?"

"This telegram," said the captain, "was handed me at the Soo. It is from the owners, saying that we must be unloaded and at the Duluth ore-docks by Thursday or we will forfeit our present carrying contract. Do you think it can be done?"

Jimmy Cooke turned and looked at a line of black smoke far astern and said:

"We can make it, all right, sir, if we can beat the Meadows, yonder, to the coal-dock at West Superior. If she gets there first, we will have to wait a day, and perhaps two, for her to unload, and then we could not make Duluth before Saturday at the earliest."

"We've got to beat her," said the captain. "Tell the engineer to crowd on every ounce of steam. We've got to push the old McGarry as she was never pushed before! I'm sick; if I become too bad to take my watch, I depend upon you to do all that I could. I'm going to lie down for a while. My head feels as if it were going to split."

Jimmy walked aft and gave the captain's orders to the engineer. Then he returned to the bow and stood leaning against the rail watching the cloud of smoke from the Meadows' stack. His thoughts soon took wings and flew miles away, and Jimmy was walking through the mazes of a day-dream, now and again raising his eyes, half unconsciously, to gaze at the distant vessel which it was so important to keep astern.

"Good morning, Mr. Cooke," said a voice behind him. "Are you looking for a mermaid?"

The mate turned as if a current of electricity had touched him, his face turned rosy red, embarrassment depicted in every feature. "I—Miss Ransom—good morning!" he ejaculated.

To an observing eye it would have been evident that the presence of this young lady was very disconcerting to Jimmy. Indeed, she was a young lady who might have disturbed the peace of any one. She was a tiny thing; a trifle over five feet tall, slight and willowy, with unruly brown hair blowing about her cheeks. The daughter of Marvin Ransom, managing owner of the fleet, she had come aboard from the marine reporters' boat at Detroit.

The first day out, Jimmy Cooke fell in love with her, and was, consequently, a most miserable young man; more miserable through the recognition of their relative positions, for he fully realized the chasm between the daughter of a wealthy boat-owner and a common mate, however capable. And then, too, Jimmy was diffident. Every time that he came into her presence he felt as if something had come loose and were flapping about within him like a rope's end in a hurricane.

"I hope you are well this morning," he stammered.

She paused for a moment. "Upon reflection," she said soberly, "it seems to me almost certain that I have heard a remark like that before." And she looked at Jimmy without the sign of a smile. He felt like a man overboard in a heavy sea. He struggled hopelessly for something to say, and was unexpectedly saved by the cloud of black smoke astern.

"I was watching the Meadows, yonder," he said.

"Oh!" exclaimed Miss Ransom; "will she pass near to us?"

"I hope she won't pass us at all," responded Jimmy. "We're doing our best to show her our stern all the way across Superior." Then he explained the circumstances to her, and before he realized it he was talking pleasantly with her without a thought of his previous embarrassment.

After a time Jimmy went down to the captain's cabin to report and to receive orders. The captain was lying upon his berth, tossing feverishly and muttering to himself. As Jimmy approached the captain began to sing a foolish little song, and appeared not to notice the mate at all.

It was evident at a glance that the captain was ill—very ill—and Jimmy felt his heart sink, for it placed the whole weight of responsibility upon his shoulders—the responsibility of taking the boat across Lake Superior with a strange crew, of making an unusually rapid and important passage, and of taking care of his superior officer. And all this he must do in addition to standing both the captain's watch and his own. As this passed through the mate's mind his blue eyes grew firm with determination.

"My chance has come at last," he said. "I'll get the old McGarry through in time if I have to stoke her myself."

He did what he could for the sick man, then he called one of the hands to send the steward forward. In a moment the man entered the cabin, and Jimmy ordered him to prepare some home-made remedy which, in his experience, had served to allay fever. The steward looked indifferently at the captain; then striding over, peered into his face. With an oath he turned and dashed out of the room. Jimmy followed him in angry astonishment.

"What's the matter with you, anyway?" he demanded.

"Smallpox!" exclaimed the steward.

Jimmy paled. "The crew!" was his first thought. "How will they take it? Can I manage them? Miss Ransom!"

The two wheelsmen were Irish, and pals. Jimmy immediately turned his attention to them, for he must be sure of his helmsmen. With trouble in the pilot-house he would be powerless. "I expect Matt and you to stick by me," he said to Dan, the man whose trick it was. "The men may make trouble. Are you with me?"

"Wid ye!" exclaimed Dan. "We'll be wid ye t' th' finish an' afther." And Jimmy looked into the man's face and knew that it would be so.

"This is mostly a new crew," he said, "and I'm not fond of the looks of a lot of them. It wouldn't surprise me if they cut up rough."

"Faith, sor, d'ye think so?" said Dan hopefully, the lust of battle in his eyes.

Jimmy smiled. "I believe you'd be sorry if we didn't have a row," he said.

"What row?" asked Margaret Ransom, from the door of the pilot-house.

"Shure, ma'am, 'tis no row at all, worse luck! Mr. Cooke an' me was jist jokin' wan another."

Margaret cast a glance at the anxious face of the mate and knew that it was not true. "What is wrong?" she asked.

"It's best you should know, I guess," said Jimmy, and he told her, warning her to give the captain a wide berth. Then he walked aft to the stairs from the forward to the main deck to see how the crew was taking the news. A knot of men were gathered forward of the bunkers, talking and gesticulating excitedly. As soon as they saw him they came forward in a body, headed by the second mate.

"Mr. Cooke," said that individual, "we have just heard that the captain has smallpox. Is that so?"

Jimmy stood at the head of the stairs, leaning upon the hand-rail, his six feet of height and broad shoulders, outlined against the blue of the sky, appearing even larger than they really were. He removed his hat hesitatingly and ran his hand slowly through his blond hair, but in his eyes and about the squareness of his jaw there were no signs of weakness or indecision.

"The captain is ill, Mr. Roberts," said he—"very ill. He has a high fever and is delirious. Whether he has smallpox or not, I don't know."

"The steward, here, has seen him and says that he has," said Roberts, with a touch of insolence in his tone.

"Well?" replied Jimmy.

The men moved restlessly and muttered among themselves. It was evident that they were in a nasty humor. "The crew has talked it over," said Roberts, "and are afraid of catching the disease."

"There is little danger of that," said Jimmy. "The captain is forward and alone; no one runs the slightest danger of infection."

"We think differently," said Roberts shortly.

Jimmy's face flushed at the tone, but he said evenly, "Well?"

There was a growl from the men, and Roberts retorted sharply:

"We demand that you put about and run for the nearest port. We refuse to stay on this vessel with a case of smallpox."

"It is impossible. We have our orders to be at Duluth on Thursday," said Jimmy.

"Orders or no orders, this old tub is going to turn and run for port," shouted one of the men.

Jimmy looked at the man and smiled.

"You're mistaken, my friend," he said. "We're going straight on to Superior. And"—he put a note of authority into his voice—"you men get back to your work and drop this foolishness."

Without the slightest warning, without even a yell of anger, there was a rush for the stairway, a gigantic stoker in the lead. Jimmy faced the stairs, and as the man came within reach dealt him a crushing blow with his fist. The stoker stumbled, tripped, threw up his hands to save himself, and plunged backward upon his friends, blocking the stairs. Jimmy took a step to follow, but as he did so he felt a touch upon his shoulder.

"Take this," said a feminine voice, and he felt the cold steel of a gun-barrel shoved into his hand. He looked down at the rifle that always hung in the captain's room. "How did you get this? Is it loaded?" he cried.

"I got it out of the captain's room, and it's loaded," said Margaret. "The captain loaded it last night and was going to shoot at some gulls, but I wouldn't let him."

Jimmy turned his attention to the men once more and covered them with the rifle.

"Stand out there, you fellows," he said, and his voice was cold and hard and full of determination. "Stand out there in line!" The men, cowed by the weapon, obeyed. "Now, then," ordered Jimmy, "all on watch go aft about your duties. The rest come up here."

Sullenly, six of the men went aft and the remaining five mounted the stairs.

"For the rest of the trip," said Jimmy, "all men off duty will bunk here on the deck under my eye, and"—he raised his voice so that all might hear—"at the least sign of trouble, if the engines are interfered with, or if any attempt is made to turn this steamer back, I will shoot these men like dogs. I shall watch from here to port, and I can shoot straight!"

He paused a moment, and raising his voice again, he said: "The owners of this craft were depending upon the captain to get this boat into Duluth by Thursday. Now that responsibility has fallen upon me, and I'll do it if I have to kill every one of you with my bare hands and work her in alone!"

He sat down in a chair, the gun across his knees. As he watched, the air grew cooler, a dampness weighted the atmosphere, and the sun appeared to shine less brightly. He looked ahead over the bows, and the distance had taken on a grayish tinge. Near the surface of the water long, wisp-like ribbons of fog swayed and unfolded themselves, now melting into a single mass and fleeing before the breeze, now breaking up into little scudding cloudlets. To the right and left were grayish bellowing clouds that moved upon the breeze, breaking and sending forth before them long tendons, seeming to grasp at and cling to the surface of the water.

Slowly the vessel was enveloped and the sun was obscured. Jimmy looked aft; the mainmast and smoke-stack were no longer visible. Thicker and thicker came the mist, until at length objects ten feet away could not be distinguished. From the direction of the engine-room Jimmy heard a cry, and moving closer to the mutineers upon the deck before him, shouted:

"If you men aft value the lives of your friends, here, you will obey my orders. At a sign of trouble I will shoot, and shoot to kill!"

For an hour he sat thus. Margaret came and spoke to him, but he motioned her away. "I dare take no chances," he said, so she sat down silently by his side. Another hour passed, and still the vessel remained buried in the ghastly opaqueness.

Warned by some instinct of approaching danger, Margaret looked behind them. Jimmy heard her shriek, and jumped to his feet not a moment too soon to avoid a belaying-pin which crashed through the back of the chair upon which he had been sitting. Then the place where he stood became a mass of cursing, struggling men. Jimmy struck out to left and right, and laughed as his fists landed upon his assailants. In the dimness and confusion it was hard to distinguish friend from foe, and this worked to his advantage.

Suddenly he was grasped about the knees. He staggered, tried to free his legs, and plunged headlong to the deck. Then they were upon him, kicking, pounding, trying to batter out his life. He fought on as best he could, but his strength grew less and less. He suffered intolerable pain in the chest, where one of the heavy boots of the men had found a mark; his head was swimming; and he scarcely realized what was going on except that he must fight, fight, fight.

Then, indistinctly, as if in a dream, he heard a crash and the tearing and crushing and grinding of splintering timbers. The air was filled with cries of fear, and his head sank to the deck and he knew no more.

When he returned to consciousness again he became aware of a peculiar humming, droning sound. Where had he heard it before? What did it mean? He listened a moment, and it brought to his mind the sinking of the Meteor, upon which he had been wheelsman. Then he knew that it was the sound of a vessel filling with water. Again he listened, and now he knew that the engines had stopped and that the vessel listed far to starboard. He tried to raise his head, and felt a soft hand placed against his brow.

"What is it?" he asked. "What has happened?"

"Lie still a moment," he heard Margaret's voice say. "Drink this; it will give you strength, and you will need all you have."

He drank the liquor and rose painfully to his feet. "What is it?" he asked again.

"There has been a collision," she said, with a quiver of fear in her voice, "and"—she tried hard to conceal a sob—"I'm afraid the boat is sinking."

"But the men!" he cried. "The men! Where are they?"

"They have gone," she said faintly.

"Gone! Gone! I've got to get this vessel into Duluth Thursday," he said, wildly. "The men gone—I can't get her in alone. I sha'n't get there in time." He buried his face in his arms and sobbed. "I've failed," he muttered. "What will the owners think of me?" He looked around at Margaret, and realized for the first time what her presence meant.

"The curs!" he shouted. "The brutes! And they left you on a sinking ship to perish!"

"They would have taken me," she said. "They forced Dan and Matt to go, but I hid, and they went without me. I couldn't bear to go and leave you alone and unconscious. I wanted to go," she said piteously. "I wanted to go. I was afraid to stay, but I couldn't bear to leave you to drown alone!"

Jimmy's heart swelled within him, and something twisted and hurt in his throat. "You did this for me—for me!" he said. He threw back his shoulders and stood erect. "We have no time to waste," he said. "There is still hope."

He began prying at the planking of the cabin for material for a raft. But at the exertion he turned faint and giddy and sank, groaning, to the deck. The punishment he had received had done its work. He struggled to rise, but in vain. His muscles would not obey his will, and he sank back, sobbing at his impotence.

"It's not for myself," he muttered brokenly, "not for myself! Give me strength to save her. Just that little strength. Nothing for me, but grant me her life."

Margaret crept close to him and thrust her hand within his. He looked up into her face. "I love you," he whispered, and once more he sank into unconsciousness.

Slowly, slowly, the vessel settled. Little by little the list to starboard increased and the end drew near. Margaret felt a breath of air upon her cheek. She raised her eyes, and saw the fog moving, shifting, breaking. All was silent save the vessel moaning in her death-agony and an occasional groan from the captain, lying deserted upon his berth.

Suddenly, far away, she heard a shout. She sprang to her feet and called in answer, straining her eyes to pierce the swirling, thinning mist. Now came the sound of dipping oars, and she saw the dim outlines of a boat.

"Help! Help!" she cried. "This way! This way! Quick!"

They heard her, and pulled rapidly toward the McGarry. She rushed to Jimmy's side as he opened his eyes. "Jimmy! Jimmy!" she cried. "Get up! You must get up!"

It seemed as if she raised him to his feet by the simple strength of her will. He saw their rescuers, and staggered to his feet and caught her in his arms.

"You are mine," he whispered—"mine! The fog is lifting—the sun shines through. You have brought my heart out of its fog, to be forever in the sunshine." And he bent over and kissed her softly as the rescuers from their late rival, the Meadows, carried the captain over the side and stood up in the boat waiting to receive them.

Devereux's Last Smoke
Izola Forrester

The Sea Claims Its Own and Despatches a
Collector Who Will Not Be Denied or Put
Off

"DID YOU EVER HAPPEN TO NOTICE," asked Barnaby irrelevantly, "how a man looks smoking a cigar in a fog? You can see the light of the cigar as he draws on it, but not the man behind. Sort of headlight effect, you know. Once, when I was crossing on this same boat four years ago, I saw the light from a cigar, but there wasn't any man behind it."

"It was a ghost cigar."

Reardon laughed from his end of the settee.

"Barnaby, boy, you're liable to see anything, afloat or ashore, given favorable conditions. What had you been smoking yourself?"

Barnaby lighted a cigarette and ignored the speaker. The rest of us in that corner of the smoking-room listened.

It was the fourth day out from Sandy Hook.

The Königen Teresa was plowing an unsteady course through a dense fog, gray-white, like the edge of an August thunder-cloud. It had kept up for a day and a half, so far. On deck it was raw and damp, as only mid-Atlantic can be in March. The waves lurched choppily against the boat. You could hear the steady, monotonous breaking of them, but not an inch of sea was visible in the grayness.

Barnaby had just come in off deck. He was aggressively cheerful and buoyant, under the circumstances. The weather had reduced every one else to a state of limp endurance. The fog had settled on everything, including brains, and when Barnaby came jauntily in we were ready to welcome anything as a diversion, even Barnaby.

Every other minute the fog-horn mourned dismally.

"Wish that thing would hush itself," said Barnaby. "It always makes me think of a cow crying after the calf the butcher has taken away, and I'm awfully sympathetic by nature. And it makes me think, too, of that particular cigar I was speaking of. I don't believe in ghosts. I want to say that, first of all, before I swear I saw one. Any one present remember the late Charlie Devereux?"

"Wasn't that the fellow who married Irene Irving?" Reardon asked lazily.

Reardon's partner at whist looked up at Barnaby for the first time since his entrance from deck and waited for Reardon to play, but the dramatic critic laid down his hand and turned his chair toward Barnaby.

"That's the one," said Barnaby. "Used to be all-around good boy from Union Square up to Times. Not a coupon-cutter, you know, nor a coin-flasher. He had to work once in a while, like the rest of us, but he had a nice little anti-worry sinking-fund planted somewhere, so that when the rainy day happened along he never went out minus an umbrella. And the umbrella was silk at that. Any one else here knew Charlie Devereux?"

Nearly all of us remembered him, although four years is a large cairn to raise over a person's memory along Broadway; but Devereux was different, and the crowd at the card-tables in that end of the smoking-room followed Reardon's suit and laid down their hands. It sounded better than fog-bound whist.

"If there was a man behind that cigar, or, rather, the ghost of a man, that ghost was Charlie Devereux," Barnaby went on. "Who's to the listen?"

"Fire ahead," said Reardon. "But stick to facts, Barnaby. Cold, foggy facts, you know. Never mind local color in chunks."

"The story tells itself," retorted Barnaby with dignity. "I merely happened to be the phonographic record. I don't believe in it myself, even though I know I saw the whole thing. But for Charlie's sake it should be told, because it shows a degree of sagacity and general long-headed cleverness that no ghost ever let on to before.

"I met Charlie for the first time about a year before he married Miss Irving. One night I found myself cornered up around Forty-Second and Sixth with a crowd of good fellows and only ten dollars left in my own private bank. Charlie Devereux staked me. It was particularly decent because he had only known me about fifteen minutes and the stake was yellow paper. He told me to take it, and said that a man who wasn't good for twenty dollars wasn't good for anything, and it was worth losing twenty dollars to find him out."

"That's like Devereux."

"Why, sure it was. He was simply great in that line. I guess he'd loaned twenty-dollar bills to nearly every new youngster who fell broke along that way for ten years."

"More than that," said Reardon. "And some of the old ones, too."

"But he didn't lose much on the game," Barnaby replied. "The youngsters generally paid up, because it was like lending money to yourself. You could always go after it the next time. Anyway, one day we heard he'd married Irene Irving and they had sailed for Europe in a hurry on the Königen Teresa. It was glad news to the little isle that loved him. We wished him well, especially as he had picked out the loveliest girl of that season's Broadway stage."

Barnaby paused to light a fresh cigarette, and Reardon's partner leaned across the table and offered his match-box.

It was a small ivory death's-head with jeweled eyes. Barnaby looked at it with quick interest, and for an instant met the glance of its owner, then went on:

"Nobody along Broadway seemed to know anything special about Irene Irving. She just happened. It was her second season, so she said, and she had a glorious voice, and a face that didn't need any make-up. She got her chance without the asking.

"When they put on 'Fleurette' at the Casino Dunbar he saw a chance, and gave her a song to sing about breaking hearts and sighing waves, and that sort of stuff, with a mermaid mixed up in it, and at the end of the second act Irving sang it dressed in a five-thousand-dollar fish-net hung with real pearls. It was a joyous stunt, and the first-nighters hunted up her name on the program when the curtain fell."

"Devereux found it quick," said Reardon slowly. "They were engaged the next week."

"And married the fifth." Barnaby looked up quizzically at Reardon's partner. "They sailed for Europe on their honeymoon on this very boat, and we all lost track of Charlie except the rumors that floated over of a touring-car and general joy-bell state of affairs. Charlie had to be back in August, and he booked their passage on the same steamer. Point of sentiment, I suppose.

"The rest is left to hearsay and the press-agent, so to speak. Nobody knows how it happened. He was seen walking on deck that evening with Irene, and they seemed to be having trouble, but she left him and went to her stateroom, so that let her out, you understand. But somewhere in the deep sea at that particular point the mermaids are feeding pearls sautés to one good fellow—Charlie Devereux."

"And she wore violet mourning."

"That's correct," said Barnaby. "Lord, I can see her now swinging up Riverside with the neatest team on the path. Didn't seem to take to the gasoline after Charlie's death. Went in for the swell seclusion, and all that. Dressed in violet from head to foot. Violet crape widow's veil, even, and her hair was baby golden. Remember her, Reardon, old chap?

"French crêpon violet gown, elbow gloves in violet suède, and shoes to match. It didn't do a thing to little Manhattan. Broadway in September is like an impressionable kid at twenty-one. It is ready to worship anything just as long as it is something. And the violet widow of Charlie Devereux dawned on it with the tender pathetic glory of a purple-and-pearl twilight—and took.

"But she declined to mingle with the happy, care-free throng of climbers. Charlie had left her a bully little fortune and not a single restriction to the will except that she wear the violet for at least a year. And just exactly six months and four days after he had been transformed into submarine sauté, aforesaid, I met the widow as a fellow passenger on this boat and she was on her way to marry Jack Beaufort Crane."

"Don't know him," interposed Reardon.

"Hardly any one did, but he was all right. The *Review* had him out in the Orient for about ten years as special correspondent. He missed home comforts, but had the luck to get shut up in Port Arthur at the siege, and the better luck to get out. Charlie helped him, and when the honeymoon was shining brightly on the other side he thought he'd look up Jack."

Reardon's partner tapped softly with the little death's-head match-box on the felt-covered table as Barnaby paused, and again his eyes met those of Barnaby, but he said nothing.

"Crane was connected with the American embassy in Paris, so Mrs. Devereux told me," continued Barnaby deliberately. "I happened to be the only one on board whom she knew, and that means a good deal with a six-day sea trip ahead of one. Before we had passed through the Narrows she had told me how dear and sweet and lovely Charlie had been to her, but that she was going now to the only man she had ever loved.

"Well, anyway, along about the third day we struck this sort of weather and Irene grew reminiscent. Took to walking deck and not eating regularly. I didn't mind it so much, because she usually let me trot along for cheerful company, as it were. Sort of fog antidote, don't you see?

"And she had dropped the violet on New Year's as a good resolution. Used to pace deck in a long dark-blue cloak lined with Stuart plaid, and a cap to match on her blond curls. I rather preferred it to the violet myself. She seemed to dread being alone, and I didn't blame her, as we drew near the probable spot where Charlie had dropped, overboard.

"I was sitting in here smoking, the fourth afternoon, sitting right over where Dillingham is now, when she sent for me to come at once.

"It was so thick on deck you couldn't see your own hand an arm's length from your face. I groped about until I found her standing over the port rail up forward, and the instant she caught sight of me she gave a frightened little cry and caught hold of my arm.

" 'Barney,' she exclaimed—'Barney, for the love of Heaven, tell me I am not going out of my mind. Tell me you see something there—there, right in front of us. Oh, Barney, can't you see it?' "

"Stick to facts, Barnaby, boy—cold facts," warned Reardon.

Barnaby did not notice him. He was keeping one eye on the face of Reardon's partner, but this time there was no answering glance. Barnaby threw away a dead cigarette-stub and leaned forward in his chair, his elbows on his knees, his jolly, boyish face a bit moody in its expression.

"I said I didn't believe in ghosts, didn't I? Well, don't forget that as one of the facts in the case. But what I saw was this, and it was daylight, too—about three in the afternoon, I should say.

"Right there in front of us, not four feet away, was the light of a cigar, and

I'll swear there was no living man behind it. You could see it as plainly as I can see the light on your cigar-tips now, except for the fog-haze, of course. It glowed steadily there in front of us, every now and then brightening and darkening again, as a lighted cigar does when you draw on it."

"Was there any smoke?" asked Reardon, leaning forward also.

"I couldn't tell, on account of the fog. And while we looked Mrs. Devereux suddenly slipped beside me in a dead faint and the light died away. Not all at once, mind, but as I held her up from the deck in my arms I saw it move slowly in mid-air out beyond the rail and so fade away.

"When she was able, she talked with me down in the cabin.

"She had seen it every time she went on deck, she said, since the boat had reached the open sea. Whether she walked on deck in daylight or at night, it had appeared beside her, and followed her as she walked, as though some one kept her company and smoked as they walked.

" 'Just as Charlie always did,' she added to me. 'Sometimes I fancy I can even catch a whiff of the particular tobacco he liked. When you have been with me, though, it has never appeared until now.

" 'It is Charlie—I know it is. Why, it follows me from one side of the boat to the other. I have tried walking on both sides, just to test it. I did not dare tell any one but you, for fear they would think I was going out of my mind. If you had not seen it also today I should have believed so myself, but you did see it, didn't you, Barney? Tell me you saw it, too, and that it is the light of a cigar.' "

"Maybe you were both crazy," suggested Dillingham pleasantly, as the silence grew oppressive. "Don't lay it on too thick, Barney. The fog may lift."

"It did lift the next morning," said Barnaby. "It was clear and sunny, and we never saw a sign of the ghost cigar all day. Mrs. Devereux did not show up, though, until afternoon, and then she looked mighty bad. I tried to jolly her out of it, and even said I wasn't sure myself that I had seen the light, but it was no good, she only continued to stare out at the water, and would not talk to me.

" 'What's the use?' she said. 'It's Charlie. I don't blame him for troubling me if he is able to. I would if I were in his place. We had quarreled that last night over Jack. He asked me if I wanted to be free, and I said I did, of course, but I didn't mean the freedom he gave me. I didn't want him to die; I only wanted to be free, so that I could marry Jack.'

" 'But if he wanted to make you free and happy, and would go so far as to kill himself, why on earth should you suppose he would come back to smoke ghost cigars around you now and set you nearly mad?' I asked her.

" 'Oh, but he doesn't mean any harm,' she said. 'I know him so well. He doesn't do it to—to haunt me—that's what they call it, isn't it? If he loved me well enough to die for me, surely he would not harm me now that I am going to Jack.'

" 'But the year limit,' I suggested, rather cautiously.

" 'I didn't think it mattered, and Jack wanted to be married at Easter. Easter is so pretty in Paris, and we were going to have a violet wedding.' "

"Half-mourning bridal in memory of the late lamented Charlie," suggested Reardon. "I never did care very much for widows."

"But the ghost cigar had settled the violet wedding," Barnaby continued. "She just wouldn't see it any other way but that Charlie wanted her. The fifth day, that was. I tried to cheer her up by saying we would hit Cherbourg the next day, but she couldn't get the old point of view back again. She had lost her grip. After dinner I found her at the same place on deck, leaning over the rail.

" 'I want you to do something for me,' she said. 'When you reach Paris I want you to send or give this package to Jack for me. It belonged to Charlie, but it's a gift that Jack sent to him himself from Japan, and I want him to have it back. He will understand how I feel about it.'

"I tried to argue with her, but she persisted, and was so nervous and unstrung that I took the thing to humor her, and promised that Crane should get it on my arrival in Paris. Then, when it grew dark, I coaxed her inside to try and get her mind off the thing, for she was watching all the time for that fool cigar-light to show up any old place at all, and I didn't like the look in her eyes.

"They were having a concert in the saloon, and I found her a good corner, and some jolly talkers to brace her up. It must have been after ten when we missed her.

"Kalman was playing—Kalman Vorga, the Tzigane violinist. You know the sort of stuff he runs to, Reardon. It makes you feel as if you were either crazy or wanted to be—one of the two. I left the crowd and hurried out on deck with that music chasing me. And when I saw Mrs. Devereux I knew it had driven her out, too, to the darkness and the waves, and Devereux's ghost of a smoke."

"And you found her?"

It was the first time that Reardon's partner had opened his lips since the entrance of Barnaby, and everybody turned to look at him. He was bending toward Barnaby, his face white and tense with emotion, his lips set and stern. Even Barnaby was impressed, and the rest of his story was told directly to the man with the match-box, and not to the rest of us.

"Yes, I did find her, but it was too late to do anything. It was late, you see, and everybody was inside listening to the concert. There wasn't a soul at the point where she stood. The light shone near her this time, not an arm's length away. From where I stood you would have sworn a man was beside her, smoking.

"But all at once the light flickered and moved away. She did not stir, but watched it, as though hypnotized, her beautiful eyes wide and staring. There was no fear in her face—nothing but a strange sort of wonder. The light moved, as I say, away from her, and suddenly she followed it, as though obeying an unheard command. Straight ahead it went, steadily, deliberately, like a cigar-light would move smoked by a man walking leisurely.

"But when it reached the rail it did not stop."

Reardon's partner rose abruptly and leaned across the table toward Barnaby. Between them lay the little ivory death's-head.

"And she followed it?" he demanded.

"She followed it," repeated Barnaby. "With her arms outstretched, as though she obeyed a call I could not hear. She was over the rail before I could reach her. I saw her slip down into the darkness, and the light glowed for an instant, then vanished, too, not quickly, but steadily, slowly, just as the last tip of a cigar goes out. I believe that it was Charlie Devereux's last smoke."

No one spoke.

Reardon's partner stood for a minute staring ahead of him with wide, thoughtful eyes; then he suddenly turned on his heel and went out into the fog.

Barnaby bent forward after he had gone and took the little Japanese match-box in his hand to look at it.

"They make those things awfully well, don't they?" asked Reardon, to relieve the strain.

"Yes," answered Barnaby, "indeed they do. I haven't seen this one for four years. Not since I mailed it in Paris back to Jack Crane. They make them extremely well. Won't some one please go and bring him back? We're just about nearing the place where the aforesaid pearls sautés was possibly served, and the fog gets on one's brain. I happen to know."

"You said you didn't believe the story yourself," said Dillingham nervously, as he started to light his cigar and then let the match burn out, staring at the tip of the cigar.

"I don't." Barnaby stood up and slipped into his cravenette. "I don't believe a word of it—that is, on general principles and a certain prejudice I have against ghosts. I don't mind ghosts as long as they mind their own business and keep to the graveyards, but when they come around Atlantic liners and walk deck and smoke ghost cigars, then I am willing to hand them out the benefit of the doubt. I'm going out after Crane."

"Just a minute," called Reardon. "Was there any smoke to that ghost cigar?"

But Barnaby had swung out on deck after Jack Crane.

The rest of us sat about the table with unlighted cigars, staring at the little ivory death-head's match-box before us and thinking of Charlie Devereux's last smoke.

Teche's Canoe
Raymond S. Spears

Of Its Long and Stormy Voyage and the
Cargo That It Brought Into Port at Last

THE THIN CLOUDS OVER CHESAPEAKE BAY spread out in a broad white fan. The weather-wise oyster-tongers gazed at them askant and then looked away to northward, where the sky was turning lead-color and the waters of the bay were losing themselves in an opaque mist that shut out the view of the dredgers maneuvering over the "rock" off James Point. The tongers were praying for bad weather, which would drive the dredgers off the bay and shoot the price of oysters skyward, to the benefit of the canoemen.

It seemed as if the prayers of the uncharitable tongers were about to be answered for once, for the whiff of the changing wind had the tang of a norther in it, and toward noon of the December day the dredges were obliged to take in sail.

The unfortunates at the windlasses groaned as they lugged, for it seemed as if the palms of their calloused hands would freeze fast to the iron. From the culling-boards came the curses of the oyster-sorters, whose hands were numb, and cut by the lips of the shells.

Among the men in the canoes in Little Choptank was Byron Teche, a black-whiskered, raw-boned man who handled thirty-five-foot tongs with a grace and skill that was the admiration of all the bay. More than one man, in the intervals when rheumatic pains and sheer fatigue compelled him to rest, watched the tireless Teche jumping the oysters from the bed at the rate of a canoe-load a day.

And all the men knew that Teche was more than equal to his task, for they had seen him driving out into the bay at night to do illicit hand-dredging at the very spot and time when the police, armed with 45-70 rifles, watched in their boats for just such pirates as he. They listened in envy to his far-heard whistling, asking themselves how flesh and blood could stand the task, and how did it happen that Satan found it in his evil heart to favor a son for so long.

Teche, as much as any one, rejoiced in the wild weather he saw coming. The thicker it was, and the wilder it blew, the better chance he had to ply his craft in the forbidden waters. Finding, toward night, that the storm was really at hand, he knocked off tonging, hauled in his anchor, and raised his sail, unreefed.

The heavy four-log canoe raced down the wind for Taylor's Island, while Teche scanned the fast-fading sky for the signs by which to foretell the night winds. He was first to the Bridge, and first to land his catch.

By the time his fellows were eating supper he was overhauling his hand-dredges, and by the time most men were abed was beating out of the creek against the storm. Whatever it might be to most men, the night-work was full of joy to Teche. It did his soul good to "beat the police," and to rob the State of its toll. This was the kind of night to do it, and Teche laughed with the wind.

But it happened that Captain Dad Flowers was in Little Choptank that night. Captain Flowers was the police-boat captain whom it did Teche's soul the most good to beat. It was Teche's boast that he had dredged all around the bug-eye Eugie Willis off Cambridge harbor one night, and the boat had worried Captain Flowers "plumb sore."

He had now come down to Teche's own ground, unheralded, and was standing down the six-fathom channel when Teche threw his dredge on the nine-foot spit. Not a thousand yards was between them, but in that murk one could not see a cable's length. Captain Dad's hope was to catch his man unawares in the thick weather and run him down before the dredge could be hauled in or buoyed.

The burr of the wind in the rigging and the whine of the sleety snow on the sail made music for the storm-lovers. Only such would be out on a night like that. Captain Dad crept down the channel to the twelve-foot rock, crossed to the eight-foot bar, and then beat upwind toward the nine-foot spit. As he worked into the wind Captain Dad heard a sharp slapping sound ahead. Instantly he called his mate, who was below, and together the two looked for the sail, the cause of the sound.

A minute later the pointed shadow of a canoe-sail loomed through the snowy "dust," and Captain Dad drew down his rifle and fired across the oyster pirate's bow.

As always before, "the devil was with Teche." He had just hauled in the hand-dredge when the shot flashed in the night. He had only to leave it on the splash-board and stand by the rudder-lever watching his chance to dodge the bug-eye. It was not in Teche's heart to surrender. Stooping low, and beating toward the open Chesapeake, he pretended to be waiting for the police-boat to come up, when he was, as a matter of fact, shaking out the reefs in his sail and watching his chance to make a dash.

The police-boat drew nearer, and Captain Dad waited to see what would happen next. The canoe had not changed its course a point, neither had it come to, but this was proper, considering how bad the night and considering that the bug-eye was gaining all the while.

Suddenly, the canoe came about. The next moment, with the sail full, Teche drove headlong before the wind within twenty yards of the bug-eye, and Captain Dad, bringing his own heavier boat about, emptied the ten shots of his rifle at the mast of the canoe, hoping to cut it in two.

"I didn't want to kill the man," the captain said.

But even then Teche wasn't safe. The Eugie Willis was a noted speeder, and she came into the wake of Teche's canoe so handily that the pirate was not lost in the gloom. He was forced to head toward the island strait, crowded closer and closer to the shore all the while.

Now and then Captain Dad took a shot, but in the night he could not see to shoot the rigging. His mark was the great shadowy triangle waving in the thickness of the night.

"If he takes to the strait I'll chase him through," Captain Dad told his mate. "Keep after him till he has to cut up to pass the East Prong, then keep off a bit. If he runs into the bay, we've got his canoe. He won't dare to take to the big bay with the water roughing like it is to-night. Ugh!"

But Captain Dad didn't know the deviltry of Byron Teche.

He had vowed never to be caught or cornered unless he drove the mast out of his canoe. Working across the wind, he headed for the West Prong, watching his chance to lose his pursuer in the little bay. But the Eugie Willis was too near. In five minutes the canoe was in the calm rippling waters of the strait, while behind soared the huge police-boat.

"That man's Cap'n Dad!" Teche said to himself. "What's he doin' yere-away—um—m. Hits me he's atter. Lawd! but that bay's a growling!"

Before him was the great Chesapeake, frothing and roaring. It wasn't the kind of night even Teche would have chosen for a pleasure-ride in a thirty-four-foot canoe, but there was nothing to do but risk it or surrender to the police-boat.

The latter was not an alternative to Teche. Hugging the lee shore till he felt the drag of the bottom, Teche headed for the broad water. Astern came the Eugie Willis, keeping to the narrow deep water.

"Lawd alive!" Teche exclaimed to himself as he felt the bound of the reflected waves, "this yere's ol' Teche's night o' glory!"

The canoe turned down-wind and caught the waves aslant. The bug-eye had to run across the canoe's stern, hunting deeper water, and as they passed, once more not a hundred feet apart, the rifle was emptied, apparently without avail.

Out of the north came a smother of snow. In half a minute the canoe was out of sight and the Eugie Willis coasted down Taylor's Island hunting it in vain.

Teche had escaped the police-boat, but he was in the grasp of a norther, battling for life in the tumult of snow, waves, and wind.

Many times he had heard the shot "ping" overhead, but that did not worry him. Twice, however, he had heard the "spat" of a bullet hitting something—whether mast or frozen sail he could not tell in the gloom. He hoped it was the sail.

As soon as he was clear of the strait he headed for Cedar Point, across and down the bay, instead of running down the shore of Taylor's Island, which Captain Dad felt sure even so reckless a man as Teche must do. Thus, the boats separated in the night.

Teche held his course for a time, and then, finding his pursuer shaken off, took notice of the scrape the night had led him into. Holding the tiller, he had to bail with the leather scoop, for the water splashed over the wash-board, filling the open boat. Bailing kept him warm for a time.

Undaunted, he broke the icicles from his black beard with a shake of his head and started the blood circulating through his hands by beating them on the splashboard. For comfort, he scanned the jumping waves and gray crests pouring by in the gloom.

"I should come into the lee of Cedar P'int d'rectly," he said to himself. "I should pick up the light d'rectly. Huh!"

The roll of the waves told him when he was out in five-fathom water, and when he reached the sixteen-fathom channel he could "smell" it. He reckoned he must be somewhere off Cove Point by that time, but he couldn't be sure. After a time, when the raw chills pimpled his skin and stiffened his muscles, he began to scan the gloom ahead for sight of the Cedar Point below the mouth of the Patuxent.

"Hit's shore almighty oncomfy, this is," he admitted to himself, "but hits better'n payin' a hundred dollars an' bein' laughed at by ole Cap'n Dad an' them others. I should say so!"

The storm had shut down around him so thickly and so heavily that he began to doubt his senses. He began to question his ideas as to the water-depths, his only means of knowing where he was. When the time came for him to see Cedar Point light the gloom was thicker than ever, and the raw chill was frightful to bear.

Old bayman that he was, the like of that night had never come to his experience before. He wondered if he was really getting old, as his years seemed to indicate. He banished the thought.

"Hue!" he said to himself. "I'm jes' a thumpin' an' a humpin'. Hue! This yere's—ah-h-h-h!"

Suddenly in the dense gloom ahead appeared a vast cloud of yellow light. In another moment the vast hulk of a bay steamer loomed through the murk, pounding her way toward Baltimore in the frothing bay.

"Lawd alive!" exclaimed Teche. "She looks plumb comfy!"

He heard a short whistling, but a minute later he was far down the lee, while the pilot wondered what on earth a bay canoe could be doing off the Potomac on a night like that.

Teche had overrun Cedar Point by twelve miles, and had only just begun to look for it. Worst of all for him, the wind was hauling around to the west, point by point. He was steering by the wind, and he was headed straight down the bay toward the whistle-buoy off Smith's Point.

" 'Peahs like my Salymander ain't a travelin' like she mostly does," Teche said to himself. " 'Peahs like I'd orter see Cedar P'int light now er hear the breakers—um-m."

Crouching low, hanging to the tiller itself, he cowered under the blast.

It was a blizzard now, raw with stinging snow and bitter wind. Because the time dragged so slowly he thought his craft must be "mos' anchored," and that the Cedar Point light must be somewhere not far ahead. He gazed anxiously, lest he run into the breakers, losing his canoe, perhaps his life. This last seemed most unlikely to him. His kind could never believe death was near, not even when it stared them in the face.

The first inkling that something was wrong came to him when he heard a moaning shriek in the night.

"Lan' alive!" he exclaimed, straightening up, "where's that whustle?"

A faint haze appeared ahead of him—the yellow of a light of some kind.

"Fog-horn!" Teche exclaimed aloud. "Hard down!"

Thinking it was Cedar Point, Teche ran to eastward of the light off Smith's Point. Then, having passed it, he turned in to find the lee of Cedar Point. He held his course for a long time, and still the fury of the waves did not abate, nor did he come to land.

"Where in the world am I?" he said to himself. "This yere ain't Cedar P'int—hit's—hit's—mebbe hit's P'int No P'int. Breakers! Spit breakers! Lawd of love!"

There was nothing for it but to claw off toward the deep water again, and Teche found himself in the midst of the storm, headed for no harbor that he knew, lost in a Chesapeake Bay norther. Then his spirit rose, his black eyes flashing through the iced lashes.

"By the law, I'll drive clean to Lynn Haven!" he shouted.

Pride in his craft, pride in his baymanship, and his fierce heart rose to the occasion. Whatever the storm might be, and wheresoever it might take him, did not matter now. He divined that he was far down the bay somewhere, it didn't matter where. He could only hold his course and hope that he could make the Lynn Haven Road by daylight.

His feet were like lumps, and his hands were without feeling. The cold was doing its deadly work. Teche did not think of that. He was looking to pick up his bearings by some red segment or some white light. He could tell if he could time one. The truth dawned upon him.

"Hit war Smith P'int light. That was the whustlin'-buoy! Mother of me! but my ole Salymander is a goin'—a goin'!"

How long he sailed thus, bearing first to the east and then to the west, feeling the wind and rubbing the water, Teche could not tell. Now and then he dipped his hands over the side to judge by the pressure how fast the canoe was going. The tang of the bitter cold was like hot iron, but he rejoiced nevertheless.

The canoe was all that he had ever claimed for it, and more, too.

"How she does ride!" He laughed to himself exultantly.

The laugh was choked in his throat.

A harder blast than ever came down from the sky, and above the roar he heard a sharp crack.

"That damned man hit the mast!" Teche shrieked. "The bestes' stick a man ever stuck into a canoe!"

Thereafter Teche heard the mast splintered fiber by fiber.

There was no help for it. He could only swear at Captain Dad and the policeman's luck shooting in the night. He worked to westward as fast as he dared, hoping that he would accidentally find a lee point or one of the salt rivers. But luck was against him. There was a smash and crash up at the bow. The canoe heeled far over, and Teche sprang for his life to clear away the wreckage.

It was a wild scramble. The waves half filled the canoe as she lunged and rolled in the water, but somehow they seemed to have become gentler all of a sudden, although the wind was unabated. Teche scarcely noticed them in his effort to get rid of the broken mast and mass of canvas. He lifted the butt out of its place and threw it overboard bodily. Then, still dragging it by the sheets and other ropes, he fumbled with the oar till he had the craft bow to the wind, with the wreckage serving as a sea-anchor.

It was the work of but a minute or two, and when it was done he began to bail.

He threw the water overboard till his joint creaked. Somehow he worked his fingers limber again, but from his knees down there was no sensation— just heaviness and dullness.

"Lord alive," Teche thought to himself, "this yere driftin' is death on a man!"

He knew there was nothing to do but keep bailing, and so he fought the wish to lie down in the lee of the bow, bailing the drops from the bottom as they fell in, scraping the snow and sleety spray from the splash-board and bottom.

But the time came at last when, as a faint gray light appeared in the thickest of the storm, spread over the face of the ghastly water, and flickered in the driven smother, Teche paused in his task, turned his broad back to the gale, and sat down to rest "for jes' a minute."

The minute lasted a long time. The man dozed, and suddenly fell asleep, with his head bowed forward and his hands under his arms.

Two or there times he started up, shook his head till the icicles on his beard rattled and cracked, but it was too much for him. The spray swept over him, and some drops rattled down the yellow slickers in pellets of ice, while large drops froze fast and hung down over the motionless figure, till it was cased in corrugated ice.

Snow drifted into the boat, and water splashed over the sides, casing the whole craft in a pale mass that rolled and plunged heavier and harder as the waves below New Point Comfort became freer in sweep.

Two days after Teche sat down to rest the canoe floated into Lynn Haven harbor, rocking gently in the brilliant sunlight.

Some oyster-tongers caught sight of the strangely shaped ice-mass and came down to see what it was.

They saw the man-shape in the glistening block.

"Lan' alive!" one of the tongers exclaimed. "Hit's a man got ketched in the norther! Huh! An' theh's a han'-dredge, too! I bet that man's ben night-dredging up in Maryland. But ain't that a dandy cunner. Huh! Hit ain't filled quarter full! Rid the water like a duck, hit did! I wonder will that man's widder sell hit? I bet she will, les' him's got some boy—hope she ain't. Then I kin git that cunner! Huh!"

To this day the story of the endurance of Teche's canoe is the joy of the bay canoe-builder's heart.

The canoe, one hears, is down at Lynn Haven—some "tonger" down "that-away" bought it off the widow Teche.

The Terror of the Doomed
William Greener

The Story of Three Men Without Hope
and the Great Fear That Fell Upon a
Whole Ship's Company

"EVERY MAN EITHER HAS BEEN AFRAID OF THE SEA or has got to be," and Nicholson, with commendable precision, lighted a fresh Maltese cigarette from the shortest stump it was possible to finger.

"It's no discredit to a man to feel fear," said the second mate, "though ordinarily it's disgraceful to show it."

"I'm thinking maybe ye've been skeered yersel' some time, noo, Mr. Broon?" chuckled the engineer's assistant.

"Aye—one of a whole ship's crew in a dead funk."

"An' nae doot ye contracted the sickness from the chief engineer, or maybe from a Maltee fireman? Whaat?"

"No. It was on a wind-jammer."

"Then ye had the feeling from some puir Lascar, or a Seedee boy, or some black trash?"

"The crew were British—every man Jack of them."

"Ye dinna say sae! Then the ship was bad-like?"

"The Palatine? No better ship ever sailed from London or rolled over in the 'roaring forties.'"

"Th' elements would be against ye?"

"Oh, aye, there was a storm—but I've lived through worse."

"Man, there's a vast o' mystery anent this skeer o' your'n. It's an extraordinary instance o' the spontaneous generation o' fright in the bosom of a brave sailor-man."

"Well, judge for yourself," replied the second mate, "only I would ask you to remember that I was just a boy at the time. It was only my second voyage.

"I have said that the ship was good, and that we had a picked crew. The Palatine was an old East Indiaman, built on the lines of a frigate; she was high, very roomy, with a poop-deck and quarter-gallery. She was sound, and had the qualities and disadvantages of her type, being a bit slow and rather slack. But she was commodious, and a favorite vessel with emigrants to Australia and New Zealand.

"Captain Symes, a man of good family, was well liked by the men, by his officers, and by passengers. He had never lost a ship, nor the life of a passenger, and by reason of being lucky and oversuccessful, was a trifle negligent, perhaps.

"The first mate, Thompson, was a first-class sailor and a fine man. He was more attentive than the captain, saw farther ahead, and made up for the other's lack of intelligent anticipation by being overprudent.

"The weakest link in the chain—always excepting the apprentices—was the second mate, Jack Darvel. He was physically unfit; that was all that was the matter with him. He had consumption, which developed rapidly after we crossed the line; but he held on bravely, making light of his illness, and intending to leave the ship at Sydney and go up into the Blue Mountain country to be cured.

"Really, I think he doubted if he would live so long, and, anyway, if he were laid up, the senior apprentice was competent to assume his duties.

"We had fair weather out, and made a good voyage round the Cape. The crew knew their work, and did it without a grumble; the passengers were a pleasant company, in high spirits, and everything went well. We shipped our ill luck at Port Natal, with two passengers who came aboard from Durban.

"The first was an old pioneer, down with jungle fever, who was carried on to the ship by four bearers. He had been told that a voyage might do him good, but he was too far gone for anything, and he knew it.

"He was as yellow as the quarantine flag, thin as a lath, had eyes so far back in their sockets you could not see them, and his voice was a whisper none could understand at first. He had been up-country among the Massi-Kessi, the tsetse flies, and swamp-rats; had had beriberi, black-water fever, and Heaven knows how many other complaints, until he was quite played out.

"We did not know his name, but called him 'Davy,' meaning Davy Jones, for he looked like a death's-head, and we only hoped that he would live long enough to be carried off the ship at the next port.

"The other passenger came aboard in chains, between two of the Victoria police. He was Joseph Willets, the Geelong murderer, who was wanted in Melbourne for killing the mate of the Frankley. A well-built, determined-looking young chap, lithe as a cat, civil-spoken, and uncowed. He had fair hair, very light-gray eyes, a bronzed skin, and good manners—just such a man as any skipper would delight to ship.

"But he was doomed. The public and the papers had condemned him already, and he would swing for certain within a month of the day we put him ashore at Port Melbourne. He knew it, too, and didn't seem to care.

"I do not know why—unless it was natural—we boys were in mortal fear of these three doomed men. After one peep to satisfy our curiosity, not one of us would approach the little calaboose in front of the cattle-pens, and we hid away anywhere when the prisoner walked back and forth between two warders along the deck early in the morning watch.

"Nor would any of us remain on the poop an instant longer than necessary when the deck-chair under the awning was occupied by the ague-shaken pioneer. His quiet way of dying seemed most awful of all. I remember having to go by his chair once when I thought he was in it and, finding it empty, imagined that he had simply evaporated.

"We were just as chary of being alone with poor Jack Darvel, especially when he had a sharp fit of coughing or a bad attack of hemorrhage. The doctor and the head stewardess—who had been a hospital nurse—were his companions.

"Our fears were shared by the fo'castle hands. The superstitious believed that ill must befall a ship with such freight, and even in fair weather they cursed each of the three stricken men as a Jonah. Lord, what a monstrous wicked thing is ignorance!

"There was one exception—our leading A.B., Dick Starkey, captain of the fo'castle and of the foretop. He was a great big, heavy-limbed, muscular giant, of a jovial temper, and always merry. I have thought since that perhaps he had no real courage—that his pluck was only the outcome of pride in his immense bodily strength, and incidental to his health.

"Anyway, he was as good as three men when a pull was wanted on the main-brace, the right man for the weather-earing when double-reefing in a stiff breeze, and he took the bunt when furling topsails, which needed a man, for our yards were over seventy feet long.

"We youngsters just loved Big Dick—it was quite impossible to feel afraid of anything with him near by to protect you. He pooh-poohed the fears of the fo'castle, and went where duty called him. All the same, he did not seek the company of the doomed men. Not he!

"I don't know whether those three ever felt their isolation, but I hope not. What I noticed was that the men whose next voyage was to be to another world had no dread of one another; perhaps that very fact made them intimate. Anyway, Jack Darvel would often place a stool near the invalid's chair and hold long confabulations with the dying man.

"And at times, for he picked up a little after a few days at sea, 'Davy' would totter along the deck to the penthouse and converse with the prisoner. The old pioneer was a good sort, too, for he induced the warders to take off the man's chains, and he was handcuffed only when taking exercise on deck. I dare say the three found enough to talk about—I doubt if it would have been interesting to us.

"Trouble came when we were thirteen days out from Port Natal. Thompson expected dirty weather. He was generally right in his expectations, but he expected such a long way ahead we did not take any more notice of him than we were obliged to. The day before he had had us bend two new topsails of double storm canvas, and when we had reckoned up the day's work he got fidgety, though there was no change of weather indicated by anything we could see.

"That afternoon it was his watch on deck, and he got in the stunsails, took the awnings off aft, and left standing only the one over the cattle-pens. He actually commenced furling the light sails before the breeze freshened.

"The storm did not come upon us. It seemed to grow out of us, as though the ship were the beginning of it. To windward the water was almost without a ripple, but the breeze was whistling through our rigging, and to leeward the sea was working itself into a fury.

"Gradually, almost imperceptibly, the ship heeled over with the force of the wind, and the list increased as we shortened sail, for by the time we had dropped the topsail-yards to the masthead we were in a raging gale. By working like demons we got the courses furled, and still she careened more and more.

"I was on the poop, when I felt a trembling. Looking round to find what it was that was loose, I saw the 'old man' hanging on to the rail and just shaking with fright. Then for the first time it occurred to me that the ship was in danger. We were right where a storm was making itself, and no one seemed to know what would happen next.

"The old Palatine settled it by righting herself for an instant, giving a tremendous shiver like the death-shake of a whale in its agony, and then careening over until tons of water poured over the taffrail.

"The next thing I knew was that a great spare spar we carried on deck had broken loose from its lashings and was part rolling, part floating, about the ship's waist. Next minute it caught Mr. Thompson on the shins and broke both his legs just above the ankles.

"Big Dick ran to his rescue, picked him up as though he had been a child, and carried him aft into the saloon. The captain followed. Above the roar of the storm, the clatter of smashing crocks, and the screams of the passengers I heard the whisper of 'Davy' to the second mate.

" 'Captain's funked.'

"Then Jack Darvel climbed up the companion and came to me on the poop. The men at the wheel called out that they could not hold the ship to her course; she yawed like a barge.

" 'Take in the spanker!' Darvel spoke to me in a whisper, but there was no shake in his voice, and I was reassured.

"While I, with a couple of our watch, was getting the sail stowed, Dick Starkey, directed by Darvel, was securing the loose spar, but they did not succeed until it had half wrecked the cattle-pens and damaged the bulwarks.

" 'Haul down the staysails!'

"It had grown dark suddenly, and the fury of the storm was increasing.

"The lamp-trimmer came out with the starboard light, but dared not venture along the deck, still less get into the rigging. Big Dick, with a laugh, took the lantern from him, gave the lashing a turn round his wrist, and staggered aft.

"We shipped a heavy sea which swept Dick along the deck aft of the main-rigging and carried him overboard. But the lamp caught under the taffrail, and ten seconds later Big Dick's face was visible, and it wore a grin as he drew himself up. He recognized me.

" 'Almost had me that time!' he said, and laughed as he cocked one leg over the rail. Then another big sea rolled aft. It lifted him and the lantern as high as the poop, and carried him, with that smile on his face, right away into the evermore.

"That was the first time I had seen death close to. It frightened me.

" 'Come below.'

"I followed Darvel behind the weather-boards protecting the wheel. On the other side of the passage, holding himself up by a guard-rail, was 'Davy.'

" 'Tor-na-do,' he whispered; 'beam-ends unless—'

"Darvel turned to me. 'Square the yards; put the helm up,' he said in a voice that was scarcely audible. I hurried forward.

" 'Man the lee braces! Ease away gently! All hands!'

"Only about half a dozen followed me aft, but the bo's'n led a dozen to the mainmast. The helm went up; the ship wore round, and, running straight before the wind, went easier for a time.

" 'Where's Big Dick?' somebody asked.

" 'Overboard!' I answered unthinkingly.

"Then terror seized on the whole crew; some ran forward shrieking; others fell on their knees and prayed.

"I went behind the weather-board and watched. The big ship plunged through the water; harder and harder blew the wind, faster and faster went the old Palatine; the waves got bigger and bigger, and instead of stopping to climb them, she began to drive through them.

"Once the port leech slackened and the maintopsail flapped ominously. We were all but taken aback, and the helmsman was so frightened that he fell at the wheel in a swoon. I dragged him toward me; his face was white; I thought him dead, and was dumb and useless with horror and fright.

" 'Take the wheel,' whispered Darvel.

"I couldn't. I couldn't even answer. He himself put a guiding hand on one of the spokes, and with the other held on to the weather-board.

" 'She yaws so!' I heard the other helmsman whine. I knew he was crying like a kid. I was just tearless and dumb.

"The Palatine would have ridden out that storm quite comfortably had she been under bare poles, but with so much canvas spread she would not rise to the seas, and the storm made a plaything of her. As the force of the wind increased something was certain to happen.

"It was so dark one could scarcely see the leeches of the mainsail; one felt the ship gripe and yaw, and Darvel must have steered by feeling or have possessed second sight. Otherwise he could not have kept both sails full. If we were taken aback the ship would be on her beam-ends in a trice and held down flat until she foundered. That seemed the probable end.

"There was nothing likely to carry away and so save us. The ship was too good. Thompson, careful and prudent, had not left any weak spot aloft, and the old ship was so well balanced that, like the elder's 'one-hoss shay,' when she went she would go to pieces everywhere at once.

"I have no doubt Jack Darvel and 'Davy' knew the danger and were praying for something to blow away—a sail, a yard, a spar, a mast—any of the top-hamper that would ease her.

"I could not do a thing. I was passive, paralyzed. I could see, hear, feel, but I could not even imagine or dread a thing, only know what was happening. That is the way fear serves you.

"The sea and wind combined in order to wreck us, water and sky met half-way to do us mischief; and what I thought was cloud tumbled on our deck as black salt water.

"I felt that we were going under forever that time, but the black water broke into dark-green waves and brown foam. In it floated the carcasses of rams from the cattle-pens, balks of timber, planks, spars, and tangled coils of rope, and above the noise of the storm, of churning water and debris, came the wild shriek of a horse.

"But even as that died away I heard the wheel turning and the drag of the steering-chains. All was not over yet.

"Then there came a vivid flash of lightning which revealed the wreckage about the deck. It was accompanied by a burst of thunder right down on the mizzen-truck. In the darkness and comparative quiet that followed I heard howls and screams from below; some came aft, as from the fo'castle, others were shot at me from behind, and by me was still the certain slow, quivering rattle of the wheel-chains in motion.

"Would nothing ever give way?

"There came another long flash of lightning. That revealed a fresh object. On the deck, near the foremast, stood the murderer. I never saw such a beautiful figure of a man. He might have been on solid earth, his poise was so grand, and he did not even put his hand to the fife-rail or take a rope to steady himself.

"He was erect, solitary, and perfectly at ease. He looked like a storm-king, and he might have been either a god or a devil, so absolute was his unconcern. The storm, the ship, our stress—he was beyond all.

"Yes, all that and more than I can explain was revealed to me in the space of a single flash. Time is annihilated on occasions. I seemed to understand a great deal while the thunder was booming overhead, but I lost comprehension of all but what was happening in the darkness and roar of the storm.

"I waited anxiously for the next flash, my gaze fixed upon the spot at the foot of the foremast. And what a time it seemed before the darkness was broken again! The flash came—I saw the wreckage, the open space near the mast—but the figure had gone.

"The grating cackle of the wheel-chains remained; the ship was as it had been.

"Suddenly from out the blackness came the face of the murderer, peering at us around the weather-board.

" 'You called, sir?' he asked.

" 'Cut away—top-hamper—thing!' I caught of Darvel's husky whisper through the storm.

"The man came abaft the wheel, brushed against me, stooped down over the still prostrate steersman, turned him over with his foot, unbuckled his belt, and strapped it round his own waist. Pulling the knife from its sheath, for an instant he looked at its edge in the light of the binnacle, then stuck it behind him, and groped round the weather-board into the darkness beyond.

"The storm raged as badly as ever, the seas poured over our deck, the flashes of lightning showed nothing but the stout masts and spars and the bellied sails above, and an incomprehensible tangle of boats, pens, spars, ropes, and water on the deck. Near us was the ever-oscillating wheel, the grinding clank-clank of its restless chain.

"Then I saw something—the murderer clambering up the mainmast by the falls. The darkness hid him; the frequent flashes revealed his slow progress. Next I saw him crawling along the topsail-yard. Now he was holding on to the jack-stay with one hand and jabbing at the sail with his knife in the other.

"Then came a great sea, a roar of surging water, a crashing of timber, a ripping and tearing and rending, the noises of an explosion, of a collision, and of a ship running ashore. The sail, the mast, the man—everything must have gone, I thought.

"The next flash showed him still flat on the yard, jabbing and cutting with his knife, but our decks were clear of everything except water, and the starboard bulwark had gone clean.

"We waited a long time. When next I saw the man he was standing on the lower yard, leaning forward against the life-line and holding to the leech of the topsail itself. It was quite dark when the sail went. It gave way with a gentle hiss—blew out of the bolt-ropes and caught against a forestay, hung there some minutes, and at last tumbled over the starboard rail into the sea.

"The man came aft and took the wheel as though it were his of right. The ship went easier, the great danger was removed, and although the storm increased in force, it was powerless now to injure us more seriously. The tension was released, and we breathed again. I remember, too, that Darvel had one of his terrible fits of coughing.

"After, I know not how long, rain fell in torrents, the lightning was less frequent, the wind gradually dropped. Then I left the group, went aft to the steward's pantry, groped my way to the saloon galley—for all was in complete darkness—and there made coffee. I took this to the men. Darvel and 'Davy' thanked me by accepting it eagerly; the prisoner would have none, for the ship was in his hands, and in his alone, for hours.

"Day broke at last. The storm had passed, the rain had put down the sea, the ship was rolling and pitching, but, it seemed to me, simply because of what she had gone through, for there was nothing to cause it now. Darvel sent me to call the watch and get the wheel relieved, and soon the day's work began as usual.

"Darvel sent the man into his own cabin and ordered me to take him some coffee—the Palatine was a teetotal ship—while he and 'Davy' talked about what was to be done with him. 'Davy' determined that he should be properly defended at the trial; he would start a subscription list; all the passengers would contribute when they knew it was for the man who had saved the ship and their lives. They couldn't do less.

"We started to right things. We put life-lines where the bulwark had stood, and set some of the fore-and-aft canvas. Then one of the hands aloft sighted a sail.

"As it grew light we saw she was flying the 'N.C.,' and we bore down upon her, for the Palatine never disregarded a signal of distress. She proved to be a French barkentine, which had lost her foretopmast in the storm and was short-handed.

"What could we do? Not much, but an idea came to 'Davy.' He disappeared for an instant, and when he returned he remarked to Darvel:

" 'He can swim.'

"That was all, but I guessed what was passing in their minds. I did not know all, though.

"We signaled the barkentine and ran straight for her. Darvel went forward and got poor Dick Starkey's discharge papers from his chest. 'Davy' wrapped them up, with five sovereigns, in a bit of oiled silk, and when all was ready and we were within a couple of hundred feet of the dismasted ship Willets, stripped to his pants, left the cabin and slipped overboard.

"That was the last of 'Jonah' Willets; by that dip he was christened Starkey.

"There was a rope waiting for him, too. We saw him pulled on board; then we hoisted 'Good Luck,' and so bade farewell to the bravest man I ever met.

"Captain Symes? Oh, he minded his own business; he was an excellent head carpenter, and no mean shipwright. There was enough for him to do on the Palatine for the rest of that voyage.

"Yes, we put both 'Davy' and Darvel into the water long before we sighted Cape Otway.

"No, I have never met Starkey since, but I've heard of him several times. He was sailing in an American five-masted schooner called the Fame last time. I dare say he is master of her by this."

When All Were Equal

T. Jenkins Hains

Wherein the Hero Tells How the First
Mate Gave to Every One a Fair Chance
and What It Cost Him

SEVERAL DAYS OVERDUE, the San Blas came in from Gibraltar through the teeth of a wild nor'wester. She was iced as high as her funnel-tops, and the rays of the rising sun made the liner look like a huge crystal ship. Long festoons of icicles hung from bows and rails forward, and at first glance her missing small boats were not remarked in her mantle of shimmering frost. But they were gone, for all that, and a closer inspection showed that the whole of her deck-house was smashed and torn, bent and twisted, as though she had received the broadsides of a battle-ship.

She was not a pleasant sight for a ship-owner to contemplate, and we knew that Skidmore, her master, was not the man to make a show of himself and his vessel if he could help it.

She docked without delay, and we had the pleasure of seeing a delegation of passengers, headed by a United States Senator, thank Captain Skidmore for his heroism in saving them from a watery grave. For the San Blas had been near the Port of Missing Ships, and she had returned.

The papers gave the incident first place. The head-lines were five inches deep in some of them, and the hero of the whole affair was my friend and former shipmate, Josiah Skidmore, master of the fifteen-thousand-ton liner. I had sailed with Skidmore. I had been mate over him and had been mate under him. We were "lime-juicers" together in the earlier days, and had spent six months at a time, once, in a ship's forecastle from New York to Seattle in an old wind-jammer.

I had known Skidmore, and I still knew him, to be as able a seaman as ever trod a deck. But hero? Well, did any one ever know a hero intimately? The word always had a doubtful sound to us of the old sailing days. It savored of "pull" in the office ashore, and there were many men who had "done things" at sea.

And so I waited until the three hundred passengers had handed in their resolutions, accompanied with a gold watch, and until Skidmore had slept twenty-four hours and loafed twenty-four more, before I slid back his door. He was sitting comfortably back in his chair, smoking a cigar.

"Congratulations be hung," he growled as I held out my hand. "Don't be a fool. Sit down and smoke. These are rather good—the banker sent ten boxes with that watch."

Silence fell upon the room, broken only by the sound of the donkey-engines handling cargo.

"I go out of her to-morrow," he began finally in a low voice, as though speaking to himself, "and you'll be in temporary command. I go ashore for good. I'm well fixed for the rest of my time, and I'm glad of it. I'm tired."

"But you are a hero now," I said, without sarcasm. "Better stay a little longer and see what's in it."

He glared at me steadfastly for half a minute, and there was that in his eye that meant trouble for the man who would give intentional offense. He saw I meant what I said.

"Hero!" he roared finally. "Did you ever know a hero? Then why do you come here with your talk? Don't you know me? You know I've always tried to do my duty when its passengers and the company are acting decent—same as you yourself. As for Martha, she knows how the world wags well enough by this time. We're both old—nine children—and I'm through with the sea."

"It brought you your wife," I suggested, thinking of the old story.

"So it did. I was lucky—that was all. They made the same outfly about that, too, at the time, but it was simply hysteria—same as this. Case of lucky dog—as it always is.

"Hebron was engaged to Martha, as you remember. He was mate of the four-master John G. Grimes, of Bath, Maine, and I was second mate under him. That was in the eighties, and it was my first voyage on the coast in a schooner. We poked our noses into just such a thing as I've come in from, and it seems like yesterday. Same falling glass and cold weather, with a brassy sunrise.

"Yes, it was the same time of year, just the last end of the hurricane season, and we were bound south, light, to load lumber for New York.

" 'Lookin' sort o' bad,' said Hebron as I relieved him that morning.

" 'We've ten men, all fishermen and smacksmen used to fishing off the Banks,' said I, 'and they claim down East that half the fishermen are fit to navigate a ship. We ought to keep her going.'

" 'Ten fools,' said he. 'Do you learn sailoring in a fifty-ton-smack two days' run off shore? Fit to navigate? Navigate a sand-barge in a canal. Better get your men below and get what rest you can, for they'll need some strength when the time comes, for there's trouble coming, sure.'

"He was right about that. The air grew warmer, and the water lost its smoke. We were on the edge of the Gulf Stream, about twenty miles south of the light-ship—the Diamond Shoal—and about thirty offshore. Then came that big southeast sea, lifting, rolling, and finally rising to a live hill that burst and rolled with a dull snore. There was no wind to speak of. There never is, as you know. It was just that huge sea and the falling glass, with the haze thickening up, that told as plain as mud what was coming along up the Gulf.

"Those fellows had never been in real trouble before. You don't often get a 'snorter' on the Banks. The real thing in circular storms always shies off along the Stream, and is pretty well offshore long before it gets as high as forty north. The winter gales of the eastern coast are bad enough, but they are nothing but the ragged edge of the hurricane that starts in the West Indies and comes sailing up the coast as far as Hatteras, which pokes its nose out into the Stream and gets it blown off as they come past.

"We had her down to the lower canvas before there was a good sneeze, and those guys laughed at Hebron. They would have carried topsails on her. But Hebron knew his business, and when I came on again I took in the mainsail, close-reefed the foresail, rolled up the mizzen, and set the spanker double-reefed with the forestaysail and a bonnet in the jib. We lay dead on the big rolling sea, with just enough way to keep her pointing northeast. And then it grew dark suddenly.

" 'All hands!' I bawled, and old Captain Brown, who had not taken the trouble to come on deck since morning, limped up the companionway. He had broken his leg, and it was now all wrapped in splints and bandages.

"By the time the watch got clear of the forecastle it struck us. It came with the usual rush, and it laid that sea out as flat as a board. The Grimes laid her lee rail under and slid away to leeward like a crab, going sideways over a sea as white as milk with the foam and spume.

"It blew ninety-six miles an hour for two mortal hours at the Hatteras station that day, and the glass there was four-tenths of an inch higher than where we were, so it must have blown some in the Stream. We had landed mighty near the center of the fracas.

"Well, it peeled off our staysail in about ten minutes. The foresail, brand-new double-O canvas, as stiff as iron and close-reefed, sailed away half an hour afterward. Then a puff like the blast from a cannon, warm and wicked, ripped the jib and spanker out of her and bore her over until the hatch-coamings were level with the smother to leeward. It was blowing some, and Hebron was hanging on, watching the compass.

"His face showed plainly how he felt as the shift began. More and more to the northward worked those squalls, until they were clear up to northeast by north. Then we knew there was something doing.

"Before midnight two lights showed plainly to the southward of us. It was the light-ship, plain enough. We were slipping on to the Diamond Shoals.

"If we had only had half a cargo in her we might have been able to hold her a few hours longer—long enough for the shift which was bound to come from the northwest. But she was light, clean light, and when we clapped the canvas on her for the fight, giving her a little gradually, she wouldn't hold on worth a cent.

" 'Wear her an' let her run for it—maybe she'll go past,' said Brown. But she was going too fast. When we wore her, which we did in half an' hour, the light-ship was bearing south by east, and there wasn't room to go past with her sliding sideways, as she was.

"Those fishermen worked all right. They certainly didn't need hustling handling the canvas. They were all right when it came to the strenuous work, and they did their share.

" 'It'll be northwest in half an hour, an' we'd go clear,' said Hebron, 'but we haven't got the half hour. It's a damn shame.'

"We were jammed fair enough. The shoals were dead under our lee, and not far off. It was a case of calculation, and we had done all we could. We let go both anchors three miles inside the light-ship, and then cut away everything above the deck, but we couldn't stop her. It would have been better if we had run her head inshore at first.

"When she headed up to both anchors with a hundred and fifty fathoms' scope she rode those seas with a dry deck, only ramming her nose into them and lifting her fore foot clear out. But it was no use. It was blowing too hard to hold on even with nothing but her bare hull to get the weight of it. She began going back, and in the gray light of the morning she struck in four fathoms, where it was breaking white and rolling in.

"The wind was still holding, but had swung up to the north'ard, the squalls coming in fierce puffs. We were in the breakers of the Diamond Shoals. No vessels leave that place.

"Of course, you know how it is. After she once hit the bottom nothing made of wood or iron would stand for long. First one and then the other cable parted, and she swung off broadside into the surf, fetching the ground hard about three miles offshore. In the growing light we could make out the form of the Hatteras tower showing like a ghost through the swirl. We knew we had a good ship under us, and calculated how long she would hold together, and how long we could hang to her with the seas making a clean sweep over her decks and smashing the timbers out of her with each thundering crash.

"It was the old, old story. The deckhouses went first, and hung alongside, fetching up into our lee with each swing of the sea. Then the main-hatch, with four men clinging to the top, passed into the hereafter. The only place where any one could lash himself was in the lee of the poop, where the stump of the mast gave a sort of poor shelter and broke the tremendous smash of the water as it fell over her.

"Hebron and I made the skipper fast here. Four fishermen and the cook were left, and we hung in a bunch and struggled with the inevitable, watching the schooner break up. A heavier comber than usual smashed me so hard to the deck that my arm was broken above the elbow. The line around my waist was the only thing that kept me aboard.

"But it couldn't last. No one could live there long, and I could see by the mate's face that he was figuring how to make a get-away. He had a sweetheart to live for, and I can see him now, with his teeth shut and his streaming face lined and drawn with the struggle, a powerful and fine-looking fellow. Of course, there was little love between us, although we got along all right and never had a row.

"It was a time when every man was looking out for himself, and no one there was thinking of dying for the other fellow's sake. It was just struggle, breathe, and struggle, with the wind, now as cold as ice, howling over us and the frost of the winter in the air.

"Hebron and a big Down-East Yankee got together and started to do something with a piece of the wreck which floated close in our lee. I don't know how they did it, but they managed somehow to get a line to it between the seas. They were both very able men.

" 'It won't hold us all, but we'll all have a fair chance,' yelled the mate when they finished.

"Captain Brown couldn't go. He was too badly used up, with his broken leg. I was given a fair enough show by Hebron. He was straight. I was an officer and had my chance, but my arm was useless and—well, I didn't care to be under the especial care of the big mate. I shook my head.

"The cook, poor fellow, tried to make it, but failed. He was drowned alongside. The three fishermen who were left managed to get aboard all right. One was washed off before they got twenty fathoms away, but the rest made themselves fast and held on. We watched them between breaths as they went to leeward, and they were soon out of sight.

"But they were in hard luck. The wind, which had been swinging more and more to the northward, now began to shift to the westward of north. The fellows on the raft would have to make the beach quickly or be blown offshore again, unless the surf was strong enough to carry them in. I doubted it, for we were well out in deep water and the wind was going fast to the westward as the storm-center passed up the Stream.

"As the wind went round the storm lifted and the live-saving crews saw the wreck. She had gradually bumped and pounded to within a quarter of a mile of the beach, and what was left of her, the high poop we were clinging to, was rising higher and higher as the wind beat down the sea and the tide fell.

"They got a line over us finally, and I managed to get old Brown into the breeches-buoy. It was desperate work with only one arm, and the old fellow appreciated it. His leg was swollen as large as his waist by this time, and he was helpless. But I managed to make the tail-block fast to the stump of the mizzen, hauling in the line with one hand at intervals and taking up the slack by bearing the weight of my body upon it. He got ashore all right, and was thankful. I came in afterward, as became my position as second officer.

"As for the mate and the rest, they all went but one. A little, thin, wiry fellow who weighed less than a hundred pounds came ashore, soaking wet, the next day four miles below. The tide had carried the raft well down the beach, and the wind had kept them from making the land until they were all done up except this little fisherman and Hebron. Being almost continually under water, they had drowned one by one until these two were the only ones alive on the raft.

"The little sailor was carried ashore by the life-guard, and as he was unconscious for several days, I never heard the details of the ending until a year afterward, for as soon as he could walk he went to Norfolk, shipped in a vessel for China, and disappeared. It seems that Hebron and he being left, and the raft getting into the surf on the shore, the thing broke up, splitting into two pieces. There was one big piece and one little piece, hardly enough to float a large man.

" 'We're all equal here,' said Hebron, 'and we'll all have a fair chance.'

"He let the little fisherman take the piece he was fast to—the big piece of the wreck—and he, the mate, who had authority to take what he wanted, took the small float. It was not enough to keep him out of the foam, and he drowned in the roll on the beach within a few feet of the guard. He was exhausted, and the sea had been a little too heavy for him, and so he died.

"I was the hero—the real hero of the fracas. Brown told it himself—how I stood by the ship when Hebron had deserted with the rest of the cowardly crew, leaving us to shift for ourselves. When and how my arm was broken, and what part it had played in the affair, was left out.

"I hadn't gone on the raft. If I had—and I certainly would have gone if I could and taken the old man with us to take his chances with the rest—I would not have done the heroic thing of saving the captain's life at the risk of my own, and all that sort of foolishness the papers published, the same as they published how I remained on the bridge of this ship during the hurricane last week. I had done the only thing I could do with reason, and I was the lucky dog, as it happened.

"As for the missus, well, of course she read about it. Hebron was dead. We were married, and it was years afterward she learned how he really died. By the sailor's own showing, he could have saved himself, but he gave all a fair show and went."

"He was a good one, all right," I said as Skidmore finished. "He had something of the hero about him."

"Yes—yes, I reckon he had," said Skidmore, "but so has every man who does the best he can."

A Son of Trouble
John Barton Oxford

***Wherein One Member of a Distinguished
Family Finds that His Great Name Is a
Grievous Burden***

A CERTAIN MR. MORAN—KNOWN TO HIS ASSOCIATES, by reason of professional deftness, as Oily—sat on an inverted trawl-tub near the end of a pier, idly watching the flash and sparkle of the sunlight on the water with languid eyes. To all outward appearances Mr. Moran's soul was steeped in gloom; yet so closely allied sometimes are the visual evidences of joy and sorrow in this vale of tears, that nothing could be further from the truth.

Mr. Moran was at peace with all the world.

What with the warm spring sunshine, the sparkle of the water before him, and the inner satisfaction of the newly fed, his heart overflowed with pleasurable emotions. Moreover, in his pocket was the gratifying certainty of the twenty odd dollars he had lifted from a gentleman the evening before.

The fact that for several days he would be beyond the pale of pecuniary worry, that he need toil not neither need he spin, still further enhanced his tranquility.

And because of all these things Mr. Moran sang. Anon he lifted his voice in nasal strains of joyous exuberance and caroled in a voice which had the carrying power of a foghorn. His repertoire was limited, his entire energy being expended in the monotonous repetition of a ditty in which he wailed:

> *Oh, Annabel, my Annabel,*
> > *How could you treat me so?*
> *Oh, Annabel, my Annabel,*
> > *You've filled my heart with wo.*

There were few craft tied up at the pier, but two fishing vessels lay at their respective berths—a seiner, her hold recently iced, now merely waiting for the favorable tide of late afternoon before she slipped her moorings, and a trawler lying in readiness to discharge her cargo of ground fish. On the deck of the seiner not a soul was visible; on the trawler a solitary Herculean figure in a dingy red sweater and heavy sea-boots moved ponderously about.

As Mr. Moran's somewhat raucous warblings rudely disturbed the morning's quiet, the man on the trawler's deck came to the port rail, and, since the tide was low and the schooner's deck was considerably below the level of the wharf, stood there for a moment in stolid disapproval, looking up at Mr. Moran on his perch.

"Say you," he bawled at the singer, "stow that!"

Mr. Moran gave no evidence of having heard the injunction. His supplications to Annabel still went on stridently. The man on the trawler sucked in a deep breath of morning air. When it came forth it took the shape of a hoarse bellow.

"Hi, there, Bill, choke that off!" he roared.

But this brought no better results. Oily Moran's unbroken lamentations ascended heavenward. By the schooner's rail stood a crate of fish. The figure in the sea-boots stooped quickly, and deftly drew forth a fifteen-pound cod.

Gripping the tail firmly, he swung it several times around his head, and then loosed his hold. Straight as an arrow sped the missile. It caught Moran squarely on the right ear.

The song ceased abruptly. There was a clatter, a smash. Mr. Moran toppled from the trawl-tub and struck the wharf with violence, while from the deck of the trawler came great guffaws of laughter.

Moran scrambled to his feet and blinked uncertainly for a moment. His gaze rested with some enlightenment on the prone codfish, and then with more enlightenment on the bulky figure by the schooner's rail. He caught up the fish by the gills, and, dragging it beside him, advanced belligerently to that point of the string-piece which was just above the schooner's quarter.

"Who done it?" he demanded thickly. "Who t'rew the fish at me?"

The man below him gave vent to another spasm of merriment. His sides shook and his laughter boomed out along the wharf.

"Was it you, you fat lobster?" said Oily, shaking in his wrath.

"Now keep your shirt on, lad," the other advised. " 'Twas no fault of mine it hit you. Sure, 'twas a flyin'-fish that we forgot to clip the wings of, that flew out of the hold an' collided with you."

The eyes of Oily Moran narrowed angrily. He dropped the trailing fish, and, clenching his fist, shook it vindictively at the man below.

"Come up here," he invited in a voice hoarse with wrath.

"Come down *here*," the other returned imperturbably.

Moran took a step forward. And here let it be known, that it was with no intention of accepting the big man's challenge, but merely that he might the better voice the scathing anathema which was seething on his tongue's end. Alas for the better part of valor, to which it was his full intention rigorously to adhere!

As he took that one uncertain forward step, his foot slipped on the string-piece; for a moment he poised uncertainly in mid air, trying vainly to recover his balance; then he shot downward and landed sprawling on the schooner's deck.

Since the circumstances left him no choice, he picked himself up stiffly and made his way toward the place at the rail where the big fisherman stood, with as much determination as a twisted wrist and a pair of badly bruised knees permitted.

"Say," he gurgled thickly, coming to a halt in front of the fisherman and leering up at him, "do you know who I am? My name's trouble, an' my father's name was trouble, an' my grandfather's name was trouble. Nice fam'ly. Want to know any of 'em?"

"Sure," the fisherman responded calmly.

Moran hunched his shoulders and drew down his head. "T'row yer fish at me, would yer?" he snarled, making a rush at his opponent and at the same time aiming a blow at the jaw.

The man in the red sweater coolly stepped aside, and, as he did so, one horny hand shot out and seized Moran's collar in the grip of a vise. In the twinkling of an eye Moran was swung from the deck and dangled helplessly in the air, while several lusty kicks from the sea-boots served yet further to inflame his outraged feelings.

"I'll learn yer to come pickin' a fuss with me, yer measly little wharf-rat," his captor panted between kicks. "I'll learn yer good an' plenty. Now think twice before you try it again," he concluded, shaking the limp figure of Moran as a terrier shakes a rat, and then dropping his captive to the deck with force enough to take the wind out of him.

"Get out of here now, an' don't come round here again ki-yoodlin' to your betters about Annabel an' what she done to you. Move, now!"

At this juncture Oily Moran made a fatal mistake. On a nearby hatch-cover lay a row of keen-edged dressing-knives. His eyes fell upon them and at the sight his little yellow soul rejoiced within him.

With the suppleness of a cat he bounded toward them and snatched one up. Before he could use it the big fisherman sprang on him, caught his wrist and twisted it until Moran screamed with pain and the knife fell clattering to the deck. Then, without a word, he dragged Moran to the rail, swung him far over and dropped him into the water.

"Maybe this will teach you to fight fair," he observed, as Oily came to the surface and struck out in the direction of the seiner. "An' say, sonny, if I was you I'd change my name. You seem sorter out of place in the trouble fam'ly."

Moran gained the seiner, scrambled up her side to the deck and thence to the wharf. Here he paused for a moment, shook the water out of his eyes, and then turned to swing a threatening fist at his late antagonist.

"Say, I ain't done with you yet," he yelled. "I'll get square with you yet, an' that ain't no pipe."

The other man made a movement as if he were about to scramble onto the wharf. "Wanter try it now?" he suggested, but Oily Moran was beating an adroit and hasty retreat down the wharf.

Oily made his dripping way down the wharf, crossed the avenue, and turned into a narrow, dirty alley. He paused not in his flight until he reached a certain dingy back door. This he opened and entered a gloomy little room, lighted by a single dim gas-jet and pervaded by the many odors of weird cookery. By the greasy stove a sharp-featured man in a soiled cap and apron was deftly flapping over the cakes on a big griddle.

He glanced up carelessly as Moran entered, noted the water-logged condition of his visitor and grinned sardonically. Oily sank into a rickety chair near the stove and began divesting himself of his outer garments.

"Say, I've been overboard," he explained, "an' I want to get dried out."

"Sure. Hang 'em on that rack behind the stove, an' then come round here in front of the stove," the other directed.

Oily stripped off his coat, his vest, and his trousers and hung them on the rack. Then he moved his chair close before the glowing fire and sat there with steaming undergarments and chattering teeth.

"An' say, Pete," he went on, "I got it in for a fresh guy that give me the souse. I guess I got to do a little borrowin', if you're willin'."

The man in the apron nodded his comprehension. Without a word he unlocked a little closet on the other side of the room and laid before his visitor the entire contents of a rather formidable arsenal. There were three revolvers, a half score of ugly looking knives, a sand-bag, billies, and a fine array of other weapons, offensive and defensive.

Moran made his selection with care—a pair of heavy brass knuckles and a short, thick billy of lignum vitæ. The man by the stove again nodded his complete understanding.

"Goin' to do him?" he inquired casually.

"Some," Moran returned with feeling.

He moved closer to the fire and fell into a period of silent brooding while the man by the stove busied himself with the griddle cakes and his unsavory dishes. Now and then a slide was thrust back, and through it the hoarse voice of a waiter in the room beyond bellowed an order, but Moran and his host, understanding each other perfectly, ventured no further conversation.

It was nearing noon when the clothes were dried sufficiently to don again. Moran put them on, thrust the knuckles and the billy into the inside pocket of his coat and, with a grunt of thanks, took his departure.

It was just after nightfall when he again appeared on the wharf where the trawler was docked. She was quite alone in her glory now, for with the afternoon tide the seiner had dropped down stream and departed seaward. A wraith of fog hung over the harbor and through it the lights along the water-front shone but dimly in the ghostly haloes.

The tide was nearing its full, and the trawler's rail was level with the stringer of the wharf. Oily crept along in the shadow of the sheds. When he had reached a point opposite the schooner, he crouched low and, peering through the mist, scanned eagerly the deck before him.

No one was in sight; the only sound to break the stillness was the grinding of the schooner's bumpers against the stringer of the pier. For something like half an hour he waited there impatiently; then the tread of heavy footsteps sounded along the deck. Oily crouched lower. He saw the big fisherman, pipe in mouth, stride to the starboard rail and perch there, sniffing the fog.

When he was sure the man's back was turned to him, Oily kicked off his shoes, crossed the wharf to the schooner, and, climbing over the rail, stole noiselessly forward toward the bulky figure on the other side. Near the open hatch he paused to slip on the brass knuckles and draw the lignum vitæ billy from his pocket.

Then he started cautiously forward again, but at this juncture there came an unwelcome interruption. Another man came stamping up the after companionway and made his way along the deck straight toward Moran.

It was a case of quick thinking for the redoubtable Oily. Only too well he knew what discovery here would mean; moreover, it was now impossible to retreat to the wharf. Without a moment's hesitation he swung himself into the open hatch and dropped. His stockinged feet landed with a shock on a cake of ice; shiveringly he crept forward into the darkness of the hold and ensconced himself finally on several tubs of spare trawl.

From above a hoarse voice, redolent of the sea, floated down to his hiding-place.

"Better get the hatch on," he heard with sinking heart. "There ain't nothin' like fog for shrinking ice."

There was a scraping sound; the hatch-cover was lifted on and fastened down, while Mr. Moran, somewhat disgruntled, it is true, yet by no means alarmed at his predicament, stretched himself on the trawl tubs. Being thoroughly inured to the vicissitudes of life, and, moreover, possessed of no disquieting imagination, he prepared to spend as comfortable a night as circumstances allowed, trusting on the morrow, by hook or crook, to make good his escape.

Some hours later he awakened with a start. He sat up and rubbed his head in dazed fashion. The swash and hiss of water was plainly audible. His head swam; in the pit of his stomach was a strange, deathly feeling.

All at once he was aware of motion—rolling, wrenching, most unpleasant motion. The combined odors of tar and stale fish yet further added to his misery. Shaking, he got to his feet, only to be thrown violently face downward as the schooner rose on a heavy sea.

Oily Moran could bear suffering and bear it stolidly. Cold he would have laughed at; hunger he would have scouted; thirst and bruises and stiffness of limbs he would have taken with Spartan fortitude as all part of the day's game. But this—this was different. It was something that took the stiffness from his spine, that ate the marrow from his bones, that seemed to tear his very soul from his body, that left him shaken, broken, cringing.

Therefore he sent up a wild wail for help, and after seemingly interminable hours, the hatch-cover was thrown back and two men pulled him roughly to the deck.

Above was a gray, leaden sky; all about, angry, swirling, white-capped seas. He clutched the rail with both hands and clung there, spent and trembling. He was aware that a gray-bearded, heavy-browed man stood before him, lowering savagely and asking him profanely what in many different kinds of things he was doing there; but in his tortured soul he could find no answer.

At last his eyes roved aft and fell on the man at the wheel—a big man in a dingy red sweater and heavy sea-boots. The face was clothed in a leering grin.

"Hey, Charley, take the wheel a minute, will you?" he called, and, as the man addressed came aft and relieved the helmsman, the man in the red sweater and the heavy sea-boots came swinging along the deck to the place where Oily Moran clung tenaciously to the rail.

"It's all right, cap'n," said he of the sea-boots, addressing the white-bearded man. "This feller wants to try bankin' for a while. He wants to go dory mate this trip with me. Ain't that so?" he demanded of Oily. "Ain't that right? Didn't you say you wanted to go dory mate with me? An' didn't you say you didn't want no share, only jest the experience?"

There was only one thing for Moran to say. He said it; from the depths of his unutterable misery he said it. "Sure!" he gurgled faintly.

The captain turned on his heel with a disgusted grunt; the big man bent closer to Oily's ear.

"Let's see, your name's trouble, ain't it?" he purred.

Moran said nothing. Weakly he fumbled in his pocket. A set of brass knuckles struck the water with a dull chug, and a short, thick, lignum vitæ billy went down in the wake of the flying schooner.

"Don't Give Up the Ship"
W. Hanson Durham

Wherein the Lonely Skipper of a Battered
Coaster Derives Unexpected Strength
from an Old Motto

THE LAUGHING MARY SHIFTED HER HELM and stood well out to sea. Probably the Mary was the best-known, and certainly she was the most disreputable-looking, coaster out of Port Haven. She was a little fore-and-aft schooner, with rough, weather-beaten sides and dirty patched sails, which gave her a most unattractive appearance.

On this particular voyage the crew of the Mary, all told, consisted of one man, old "Lige" Bingham, who was captain, and sole owner as well. Her cargo, untold, consisted of a miscellaneous assortment of casks and kegs, which had been loaded on under cover of darkness just over the line on the Canadian side, consigned, duty-free, to certain temperance towns along the Maine coast, Eastport way. Captain Bingham was too eager to deliver this cargo to wait for his tardy assistant.

A dank, heavy fog came rolling in, mist-like, from the open sea beyond Grand Manan, and straight out into its concealing shelter Captain Lige edged the little Mary, not only in order to clear certain sunken reefs, invisible at high tide, but also to avoid a possible inspection from a suspicious-looking craft creeping along past his starboard quarter, a craft which flew the revenue flag of Uncle Sam at her peak and left a low-hanging smudge of soft-coal smoke in her wake.

Rounding Eastport Point in a head wind, Captain Lige had been watching for that little steamer for many hours with anxious eyes. And at last he saw the sun glisten for a moment on her brasswork, and on the tapering tube of her machine gun, on the forward deck. Then it was that he suddenly shifted his helm and stood still farther out to sea.

Although, to all appearances, above decks the Mary was nothing but a simple fisherman beating out, Captain Lige had no intention of coming into closer contact with the government cutter, nor any desire to run the risk of a possible search by her too inquisitive officers.

A mile or more off to starboard Captain Lige could see the blurred shape of Grand Manan looming up grim and forbidding through the fog, and he could hear the solemn clang of her bell-buoy as it rose and fell on the swell of the sea. He grasped the tiller firmly and stood up and scanned the eastern horizon for a sight of the cutter, but in vain, for the fog-bank had rolled in and settled thick between.

"Slipped 'em ergin, by gosh!" ejaculated Captain Lige exultantly as he swung the pounding Mary around closer into the wind.

For nearly half a century Captain Lige had been diligently taking his toll from the sea, pulling his nets and lines, tending his lobster-pots and eel-traps in all winds and weather, with no accumulation except the battered old hulk of the decrepit Mary and of years which were beginning to weigh heavily upon man and boat.

Captain Lige drew a deep sigh of relief as he thought of his little cargo stored away deep below, covered from curious eyes by many nets and traps and other paraphernalia of his calling.

Still keeping the Mary pointed well out, the old man lashed the tiller, made his way slowly forward, and trimmed his jib-sheet. The maneuver brought forth a sudden and surprising spurt of speed from the agile Mary, causing her to heel well over to port and plunge ahead like a race-horse. Her dirty blunt nose buried deep in a smother of green-and-white hissing foam, which broke and fell in splashing spray from her bows, and the creaking and straining of her ancient shrouds and sails mingled unheeded with the steady rush and wash of the sea alongside.

All day long Captain Lige stood faithfully at his post at the helm and coaxed, urged, and drove the plunging Mary through the low-hanging fog and sweltering seas. At sunset he heard the last clang of the bell-buoy far astern, and then, as night gathered and darkness began to settle down over the sea, Captain Lige swung his sidelights.

With a cold bite in one hand and the creaking tiller in the other, he stood and supped in silence.

A drizzling rain began to fall. At midnight the wind shifted suddenly and the fog grew less thick until, when the day broke over the sea, it found the Mary wallowing sluggishly along with idle flapping sails and Captain Lige smoking his morning pipe as he still stood and dozed wearily at the helm.

Then, as the morning sun rose higher in a clearer sky and dispelled the wind-scattered mist, Captain Lige straightened slowly up and gazed long and hard toward the sea-bound horizon. He shaded his dim old eyes with his toil-hardened palm and looked again.

And then his jaw dropped suddenly and his pipe slipped unheeded from his mouth and fell shattered to the deck. Less than a league off, on his port quarter, between the Mary and the open sea, he saw the revenue cutter he had sought to slip away from.

"Wal, I'll be blowed!" muttered the old man brokenly, for he knew that with neither wind nor fog in his favor there was now no chance of escape.

With the knowledge that sighting him meant signaling him, and that signaling meant search, and that search meant confiscation for the Mary and imprisonment for him, he dropped the tiller and staggered down the narrow companionway into the little cabin.

A moment later he reappeared with his ratline-wrapped telescope, and with trembling hands raised the glass to his eye and surveyed the decks of the distant steamer.

One long look was enough to tell him the worst. They had evidently sighted him long before he was aware of their presence, and had slipped down closer upon him as silently as a shadow through the rising fog. Now they were coming straight on toward him.

The old fisherman realized that he was hopelessly cornered at last, and that the Mary was as good as lost to him. The sudden thought that he would never walk her warped old deck again filled his heart with an ache that almost unmanned him. He turned and tottered back down the little companionway, carefully replaced the telescope in its rack over his bunk, and began resolutely to gather his meager dunnage into his old sea-chest preparatory to leaving the Mary forever. She had been the only real home or shelter he had known for over forty years, and his dim old eyes filled with unshed tears as he stood and looked about the little cabin with its low ceiling and rough timbered sides.

Across from his bunk, on the wall, he saw the faded and almost forgotten daguerreotype of his dead first-born, a sturdy little chap with his mother's face and manners. The old man walked across to it, withdrew the salt-rusted tacks which held it, and thrust the picture carefully into the innermost pocket of his ragged coat.

As he turned slowly away, he paused and looked back. There was that bleached and blurred picture of Lawrence lying on the deck of his frigate, just as little Tom had stuck it up there twenty years ago. Captain Lige stood and gazed at the dying hero of the Chesapeake, and as he stared he saw only his last words printed below the picture:

Don't Give Up the Ship!

Like a man aroused at last from a prolonged sleep, Captain Lige started, and slowly raised his wrinkled hand to his forelock. Then, as if awakened anew into action, he turned and crept, muttering, up the companionway and glanced cautiously seaward.

The revenue cutter was still rapidly bearing down upon him, a mile or more yet astern. With a crafty little smile gathering and tightening the corners of his thin old lips, Captain Lige slipped back down the stairs into the cabin again.

Stepping across to the starboard locker, he flung it wide open and knelt down before it. Hurriedly he rummaged about among the damp and musty garments of a generation ago, until, with a sudden grunt of success, he found what he sought. Fishing it out, he held triumphantly up to the light a small American flag of the days when the stars were less numerous.

Back up the companionway he crept, and reached the topmast halyards. With hasty, fumbling fingers he bent on the faded flag and hauled it, fluttering, to his masthead—union down. Then he sank wearily back beside the swinging tiller.

The United States revenue cutter Seabury had been moving slowly through the fog all night, but when the officer of the deck reported, at daybreak, a little schooner on the port quarter the Seabury suddenly changed her course slightly and bore rapidly down upon the suspicious little craft.

"What do you make of her, sir?" inquired the first officer, stepping up as the captain closed his glass and turned away.

"Nothing," replied his chief slowly. "She's a lobster boat, I guess, and an old timer, too," and he passed the glass to his subordinate as he spoke.

The officer raised the glass and looked. Then he turned suddenly to the captain beside him.

"It's the same old tub we sighted yesterday beating out. She slipped us in the fog off Grand Manan."

"What!" cried the captain, and he whirled quickly about, seized the proffered glass, and raised it again. For a moment neither spoke. All was still save for the rush of the sea and the steady, monotonous throb of the engines as the Seabury tore along through the water toward the bobbing Mary.

"You are right, Blake," muttered the captain slowly, with the glass still at his eye. "She's the same, and now she's working in. I guess we'll just take a look at her. Eh, what's that? She's trying to hail us, Blake. She's raised a distress signal!"

As he spoke he saw the fluttering faded flag, union down, creep slowly to the masthead of the Mary.

"By Jove!" exclaimed the captain seriously, "there is something wrong there. She's drifting! Say, Blake, there's an old man lying across the deck aft at the helm. He sees us, and is waving his hand. Lay her up as close as possible, Blake, and board her and see what the trouble is." At his command the first officer stepped to the speaking-tubes, communicated his orders to the engine-room below, and five minutes later the Seabury's engines ceased their throbbing and the little steamer swung slowly around and lay wallowing in the sea.

Captain Lige heard the Seabury as she bore down upon him through the fog. Turning slowly, he waved his hand feebly as he raised himself to a sitting posture on the deck beside the helm, and watched her movements with doubtful eyes. He saw her as she hove to and lowered one of her port boats, and he continued to watch the boat closely as it drew nearer, driven by steady strokes, until it reached and slid alongside the Mary's roughened sides. As it rose on the crest of a wave the first officer leaped for the bulwarks, swung himself on deck, and approached him.

"What's the trouble here?" he demanded, almost gruffly, as he glanced quickly about. Then, as he saw the huddled figure of the old man beside the helm, his manner softened suddenly.

"Rheumatiz'!" groaned Captain Lige painfully. "Got kinder wet last night, an' can't move to-day. I'm goin' er'drift, I reckon. Thought as how I'd hail yer fer a tow in. I'm 'bout used up," and the old man groaned again and shook his head helplessly as he glanced aloft.

"Where are you bound?" asked the officer quickly, and he noted with pity the knotted and pain-distorted fingers grasping the well-worn tiller.

"She's ther Mary—fisherman—out o' Eastport way," replied Captain Lige between intermittent twitches of assumed agony. "Cap'n Elijah Bingham, sir."

"What's aboard?" asked the inquisitive officer, and he turned and stepped quickly toward the companionway as he spoke.

"Eel-pots and lobster-traps, mostly," grunted Captain Lige promptly. "Ther forrard hatch, sir."

The officer made no reply, but turned quickly aside and walked along the heaving deck, lifted the little hatch, and glanced suspiciously below. A confused jumble of ancient odds and ends was all he saw there, together with a tangle of nets, lines, herring-tubs, and lobster-pots. He replaced the hatch and came aft.

"Feeling pretty stiff in the joints, are you?" the officer asked suddenly, and Captain Lige moaned pathetically.

"Tolerably so," he gasped shortly. "It's all in my hands, sir. They hain't what they uster be."

"No, I suppose not," remarked the officer, with sympathy. "Now, shall I make fast a line and take you aboard? I'll leave a man at the helm, here, until we get you well inside," and he stepped forward to assist the old fisherman to his feet. Captain Lige drew quickly back and shook his head resolutely.

"I'll take er tow-line in, an' obleeged ter yer, sir, but I'll jist stick ter my own helum an' keep her head on. Yer can drop me off Eastport way. I reckon I can work her in from thar."

The officer nodded his head and said no more. Making his way forward, he found and cast off several fathoms of line; then stepping to the rail, he leaped down into the cutter's boat waiting alongside.

"Well, just as you say. So long. We'll cast you off any time," and with a wave of his hand he was gone. Captain Lige chuckled inwardly and drew a deeper breath of relief.

"Fooled 'em, by gum!" he muttered grimly.

Tearing off a generous chew of tobacco, he settled himself comfortably against the tiller-post and listened with satisfaction to the sudden rush of the sea past the Mary's blunt bows as the tow-line tightened.

A Crusoe of the Antarctic
Herbert E. Hamblen

Of a Life-Long Vigil in the Frozen Wastes
and the Final Clearing of a Great Ocean
Mystery

FROM THE SUMMIT OF THE SMALL BERG where I stood with Manuel, the Portuguese seaman, I looked out over a barren frozen wilderness. Behind me, hidden from sight, were my men and the whale-boat, caught in the treacherous ice of the Antarctic. Somewhere in the distance was our ship—the question was where.

We had killed the whale that had towed us into this desolation the day before, but unless we could find the ship soon we were likely to pay a high price for it. And now there was no sign of the vessel—only ice and snow.

We had climbed up the berg readily enough, but on the other side the descent was a tough road, steep and slippery. Manuel suggested that we "let go everyt'in'" and slide down. The prospect was alluring, for we were fagged out from the murderous climb, but I distrusted my snow-blind eyes. There might be treacherous crevices and bone-breaking bumps, and we could not afford to risk them.

So, with a word of caution to Manuel, I started, easing myself away and taking advantage of every slight inequality in the glittering surface to safeguard my descent.

I had negotiated two-thirds of the distance and was congratulating myself that the worst was over, when there came a startled grunt from above. Manuel had lost his grip, and in another moment was on top of me. We clutched each other and whirled around, legs outspread, vainly trying to dig elbows, knees, and toes into the granite-like ice.

We brought up with a breath-expelling whack against a pinnacle of ice, on the very verge of a tiny precipice, of whose existence we had no knowledge until that moment.

Manuel peered over, but drew back instantly, exclaiming: "My Lord, Cappy, w'a's dat?"

"Dat" was a huge ice-bear, seated on his haunches and resting his back comfortably against the face of the cliff directly below us. It was a terrifying sight, for no doubt he could easily climb up to us, while we could not possibly escape in any direction. We had nothing but our bare hands with which to defend ourselves, and tradition credits these monsters with a voracious appetite.

Manuel gave me a nudge, preparatory to whispering something in my ear. The movement was just sufficient to dislodge my mittened hand from a smooth knob of ice. Over I went. He grabbed my heels valiantly, but only succeeded in getting himself pulled over along with me. We shot out far enough to clear the bear, landing directly in front of him and a few feet away—Manuel on top. We scrambled to our feet with all possible haste, breathing heavily, but uninjured.

There sat the "bear," displaying an immense, flat, round human face, nearly hidden in a tangle of snowy hair and flowing white beard, and smoking a long bone pipe.

He calmly rose to his feet, regarding us with cool indifference. As he made no hostile movement, I soon regained enough presence of mind to take account of his personal appearance. He seemed to be all of seven feet high, with a corresponding breadth of beam—a formidable presence, indeed, happily robbed of terror by his exceedingly mild facial expression.

He was as fat as a seal, and was clad in a patchwork of hides, clumsily skewered together with fish-bones. He had made no attempt to construct a garment of them, but held them about his great carcass with one hand, for all the world like a Patagonian chief.

We stood there staring at each other in open-mouthed wonder, the three most astonished men, I dare say, on the globe at that moment. The giant broke the spell. Without removing his pipe, he opened one corner of his mouth and rumbled forth an unintelligible something.

The mildness of his manner was so reassuring that I ventured to demand, in an authoritative voice, who the devil he was. Deliberately removing his pipe with his free hand, he responded with something that sounded like:

"I bin der boy."

This answer, coming from the possessor of such a munificent hirsute display, was grotesque, to say the least, yet it was given with such a simple, natural dignity that, somehow, we never thought to laugh. But the pronunciation decided one point: he was some kind of a Dutchman.

As we gaped our astonishment he naively blew a malodorous cloud of smoke down our throats, causing us to veer hastily to windward. From this vantage-point I demanded again:

"Who are you and where did you come from?"

Again he opened that cavernous mouth and spoke, but his reply was absolutely unintelligible. I then discovered that, in addition to a pronounced foreign accent, he was blessed with a hare-lip and also an infantile lisp, a rare combination which so perfected his lingual disabilities that he might almost as well have been dumb.

He seemed to realize his handicap after a while, for with a grunt that sounded like "coom," he turned and waddled toward the face of the cliff, wherein we now saw for the first time an opening like the entrance to an

Eskimo igloo. When he went down on his hands and knees and started to crawl in, he looked more like a bear than ever.

It was not without some misgivings that I followed suit, Manuel bringing up the rear; there was no knowing what he might do inside his den.

The farther we went, the darker it became. I laid hold of the tail of his robe with one hand, to keep a kind of tab on his movements, at the same time ordering Manuel to keep close to me.

We had crawled in this way twenty-five or thirty feet, through a tunnel of solid ice, when I felt a timber under my hand and perceived at the same time that the giant had risen to his feet. With a word of instruction to Manuel, I rose too. There was plenty of head-room here, though it was as dark as a pocket, with an occasional feeling as of planks in the uneven icy surface underfoot.

Our leader took a step up and stopped so suddenly that I butted into him. There was a sense of oppressive heat and a most unpleasant odor. He seemed to be groping for something. Suddenly he struck a light and lit an old-fashioned battle-lantern.

Imagine, if you can, my surprise on finding that we were in an enormous ship's galley, containing the biggest caboose I had ever seen, in which there roared a blazing wood-fire.

Before I had time to become in the slightest degree familiar with this miracle, the giant, without a word of warning, backed deliberately over me, out of the galley. Again we took up the line of march behind our guide, who strode confidently along in what I was able to make out by the dim light of the lantern to be the 'tween-decks of a large vessel.

It was so coated and hung with ice, however, and so hacked and chopped where the surface was visible, as to be almost unrecognizable. Evidently, he had not hesitated to levy upon this interior for his fuel-supply.

At one place he stopped, and holding up his light, called attention to a huge stalactite of ice, issuing from a jagged hole in the upper deck, and disappearing, in a slanting direction, in a corresponding hole in the deck at our feet. It was all of four feet in diameter, completely filling both holes. He went into a long explanation of this strange appearance, but all I could make out was that here something had "come troo," which was easily self-apparent.

I noticed that all of the interior that was visible hereabout was deeply charred, some of the timbers being completely burned through. I wondered how they had managed to extinguish such a severe fire surrounded by everlasting ice.

Presently the giant turned and continued his way until we came to a hatch in the deck at our feet. From somewhere within his fur robe he produced a length of spunyarn, the end of which he bent onto the lantern and lowered it down the hole. I knelt at his side and peered into the black void.

I could see nothing for some time, as the lantern slowly revolved at the end of its lanyard, merely throwing dim shadows into space. Then, as he slowly lowered it, there came into view an icy bottom, with here and there a stiffly frozen human arm or leg, protruding weirdly—and at last a dead face, bewhiskered like his own, stared up at me horribly from right under the lantern.

I jumped to my feet and seized him by the throat. I had no fear of him now.

"You beast!" I cried. "What does this mean? Give an account of yourself quick, or down there you go among them."

He wasn't ruffled in the least. There was no sign of guilt in his great flat face as I held the lantern close to it—it was as expressionless as the bottom of an empty try-pot. He regarded me with fish-like stolidity as he commenced a long, unintelligible harangue, from which, principally by guess, I untangled the information that these were the bodies of the crew—"a hunnert an' eighty mans"—and that he was "der boy."

The gruesome sight unnerved me. I felt weak and sick. Now that I knew what was down there, I fancied a horrible effluvia arising from that ghastly charnel-house; which, of course, was purely imaginary, as the bodies were preserved to all eternity, unless, indeed, a combination of winds and currents should drift the berg into the temperate zone. But I needed air and daylight.

"Come, Manual," said I. "Let's get out of here. Take the lantern away from him." But that was not necessary. However poor his talking apparatus, he understood all right. He led us back to the galley, where he doused the light.

Then I discovered the source of the vile odor of which I had been conscious ever since we struck that galley in the first place. The floor was littered with all manner of refuse; decaying chunks of blubber, bits of green hide, fish offal, scraps of every sort, were scattered all about, reeking in the warm atmosphere of the fire.

Once more in the sweet daylight, I ordered Manuel to bring up the boat's crew. There was warmth and shelter here, the wherewithal to cook, and doubtless something to eat.

After Manuel left I sat me down patiently to question this strange creature, but I learned very little. He seemed not to comprehend that I had no knowledge of him or of the ship; rather, he appeared to have been expecting us, and so failed to catch the importance of being explicit. He would wander from the point, and at times I judged that he lapsed into his native tongue, though I could not be sure of that, so unintelligible was all that he said.

His unbroken stolidity puzzled me. One might have expected him to go into transports of delight at the sight of human beings in this solitude, to have flooded us with questions as to how we came to find him. But not the slightest interest did he manifest, nor did he take the initiative in any manner.

Despairing of learning anything from his incoherent mumblings, I set myself to hammering away at one question, hoping to learn, from ceaseless repetitions, the answer to that. I asked him over and over again what ship it was. That he understood the question was evident, as he invariably made the same reply.

It sounded to me like a Hollandish name, one of those long jawbreakers, consisting of a medley of double o's and a's interspersed with consonants, in which that language seems to abound. After many tiresome repetitions, I jotted down in my note-book my understanding of it as *Thloopyvaarvaathp*.

A happy thought seemed to strike him, and repeating "coom," we returned to the galley. Relighting his lantern, he led me in the opposite direction from the gruesome refrigerator of dead men, till we came to a regulation old-style crossed man-o'-war hatchway ladder, leading to the upper deck.

Ascending this, we emerged into a beautiful grotto of clear ice of no great extent which gave back the lantern's dim rays in a million sparkling scintillations. It was fairy-like in its cold beauty; one might have thought it the ice-queen's private boudoir.

As I gazed about in surprise and wonder at this strange sight, I noticed a spencer-boom, frozen in above my head, forming, as it were, a ridge-pole to this queer room. Then I knew I stood on the spar-deck of the wreck.

But there was nothing here, apparently, to assist in solving the puzzle of her identity. Advancing to the farthest corner of the place, my guide called my attention to what appeared to be the breech of an old thirty-two-pounder protruding slightly from the solid ice; at the same time he kept repeating that outlandish name, *Thloopyvaarvaathp*.

And then the meaning of what he was trying to say dawned upon me.

"Sloop-o'-war?" I asked. And for the first time I detected a gleam of interest, as he nodded his great head ponderously and repeated:

"*Ja, ja; thloopyvaar.*" So I had unexpectedly mastered a part of that long word. The rest must represent her name.

"What country ship is it?" I asked, determined to go slow so as not to lose the slight advantage.

Imagine, if you can, my surprise when he replied:

"*Mericanska.*"

At least, that was the nearest I could make it out, remembering that it would indicate a civilized nationality.

"American?" My manner must have shown my excitement, and it proved contagious, for he replied with more interest than he had yet shown:

"*Ja, ja; Mericanska.*"

"What is her name?" I now felt myself on the right track, and was elated with the fever of discovery. Alas! My hopes were doomed to instant demolition. Resuming his normal air of impenetrable stolidity, he replied:

"*Dervaathp.*"

I made him repeat it over and over again, for it was inconceivable that a United States war-ship should have such an outlandish name as that, but he never varied in the slightest from his original pronunciation. Discouraged by my failure along this line, I took another tack, asking him what his own name was.

"Hanth Olethen," he replied promptly, and it was the first thing he had said that I understood readily. Hans Olesen! It was a Swedish or Norwegian name, and confirmed my first impression that he was some kind of a "Dutchman," for on board American ships all those who say *ja* for yes are indiscriminately called Dutchmen.

I saw no reason to doubt his assertion that she was an American ship, despite her comic-opera name—which I attributed to failing memory or weak intellect on his part, for he could have no possible interest in deluding me, and, anyway, his overpowering guilelessness forbade the thought.

Yet I had no recollection of the loss of a war-ship that would account for her presence here. But how long had she lain here? Those dead bodies in the forepeak would indicate that her entire crew had died during her incarceration in the ice.

And this aged man who called himself "der boy"? What was I to think of it all? It was beyond me. Regretfully I gave it up, hoping hazily that time might in some mysterious way read me this riddle.

We returned to the galley, and, despite the evil odors of the place, I hung over the caboose until the grateful warmth thawed me out.

I was glad, however, to get into the open air again, where I found Manuel and the boat's crew. They had secured the boat and the carcass of the whale to the berg, but in view of Manuel's story that a land of plenty awaited them, had brought nothing with them but the tobacco. We got a chunk of frozen seal from Hans and regaled ourselves heartily on broiled steak.

After a smoke, I called for volunteers to go in search of the ship. Eaton and Jamieson responded. I gave them explicit instructions, a hearty ration of cooked meat, and with a final injunction to hurry, and to be sure to get back before sundown, whether they found her or not, started them off. We watched than out of sight, giving them a hearty cheer as they disappeared over the last hummock.

With Manuel and the lantern, I made a tour of investigation, hoping to find something that would lead to the identification of the wreck. There was nothing. I found I had already penetrated to all the available parts.

She was the nucleus of the berg up whose side we had climbed on leaving the boat. I carefully inspected the great stalactite and the holes in both decks, where Hans said "it" had "come troo," but could make nothing of it except to verify his statement. Some huge projectile certainly had torn its way through there, rending the stout oak planks and beams like brown paper. What it could have been, like everything else about this mysterious ship, could only be guessed at—and that by every one to suit himself.

I tried my hand on Hans again, but he had relapsed into hopeless vacuity, sitting where we first discovered him, with his back against the ice, puffing away stolidly at that horrible pipe.

An hour and a half before sundown the exploring party returned. They brought the best of news. They had found the ship, the mate having hung about, keeping a bright lookout for us. He gave them eight pounds of boiled salt pork, a bag of biscuit, and a bottle of rum.

I offered Hans a biscuit, but he parted his enormous mustache and pointed to his bare and swollen gums. Poor old fellow! I wondered how he had lost his teeth.

We made a big pot of seal stew, thickened with pounded hard-bread and sweetened with shredded pork. Hans ate nearly as much as all the rest of us together, yaffling it down with porcine delight.

I cleaned out his pipe afterward and filled it with tobacco. He whiffed suspiciously at first, but the long-forgotten flavor won him in the end, and we were relieved forever from the unbearable odor of his pipe.

After dinner, in celebration of our good luck, I made a stiff jorum of hot rum-punch. Hans took to it as naturally as to mother's milk, advancing without a qualm from able seaman's to bo's'n's nips. But it went to his weak old head, and he kept us roaring for an hour at his clumsy attempts to sing and dance, before he crawled into the galley and went to sleep in front of the fire.

Toward evening we hauled him out of there and cleaned out the accumulated filth of years. To sweeten the place was impossible, but we got it comparatively clean and built a rousing fire—the last for which the old sloop-o'-war was to furnish fuel—and, stowing ourselves like herrings in a cask, we slept like seals till broad daylight.

We started right after breakfast, Hans having no packing to do, as all his possessions were on his back. True to his unemotional nature, he left his old home without a backward glance, nor did he show the slightest curiosity as to where we were taking him. He was weak in legs and wind, so I had one of the men accompany him, to pull him out of the holes he persisted in tumbling into and to boost him over every little obstruction.

The ship never looked so good to me as she did that afternoon. It was a perfect day, with a whole-sail breeze and the sweet sunshine dimpling the gently breaking seas. The virgin white ice glittered in the dazzling sunshine as though dusted with diamonds, and where the snow had melted and run off the peaks, the delicate blues and greens furnished a delightful contrast which we were able to appreciate now that it was robbed of its terrors.

Hans was completely worn out with the trip. We had to hoist him aboard with a yard-arm whip, as he was unable even to climb the ladder put over the side for his especial benefit. With a single exception, his absolute lack of interest in his surroundings remained unbroken. He didn't look aloft or about the decks, but he did demand rum—which I declined to furnish.

As I intended to keep him aft, I had a couple of the men take him into the galley for a hair-cut, shave, and bath, while the mate and I herring-boned him a suit of clothes of blanket-lined sail-cloth.

For sanitary reasons I gave his fur robe to the sharks, and there was nothing in the slop-chest that could possibly have been stretched over his huge body. A doleful whining and blubbering accompanying the splashings from the galley indicated his lack of appreciation of our efforts in his behalf, but the Portuguese were sturdy fellows, with whom cleanliness was a passion, and I was able to harden my heart to his pleadings to be let alone.

His brother seals and albatrosses would never have known him when the boys turned him out on deck in his new clothes—Mother Hubbard style. He had lost nearly a bushel of hair and whiskers, and his complexion had been improved out of all recognition—he looked almost handsome. But no amount of improvement could materially change that great, moon-like, vacant countenance.

He seemed to have brought us luck. The next morning the sea was alive with whales to the horizon, and thereafter we were kept busy night and day till the ship was full to her hatches. Nobody paid much attention to Hans during this period, except to give him an occasional scrub-down, which he never failed to resent, weeping piteously at the outrage upon his lifelong habits.

He browsed around the try-pots like a huge infant, feasting to his heart's content on the sweet, crisp scraps and the skipjacks and bonitoes which the men caught and fried in the boiling oil for his especial delectation. He slept on deck, the cabin being too confined after his life in the open—for which mercy the rest of us were truly grateful.

The crew being in splendid health, water-casks full, and provisions abundant, I decided to run straight home without calling anywhere. As we approached the temperate zone and Hans was restricted to ship's provisions, his health began to fail, as I had feared it would. I put him on a limited diet, but the crew was unable to resist his plaintive begging, and the cook found it impossible to keep him away from the swill-pail, for he had developed a rare cunning, like a thievish cat.

So, in spite of me, he kept himself in a state of engorgement, with the result that he fell a victim to acute indigestion, caused by the unfamiliar food. The poor old chap suffered intensely, rolling about the deck, while the big tears fell down his fat cheeks and he howled piteously in his misery. I gave him such opiates as the medicine-chest afforded, in increasing doses until they were all gone, but with little effect.

Later, the pain mercifully left him, but he failed more rapidly than before and I saw that the poor old child-giant was doomed. I had a spare sail stretched for him on the poop, and under that he would lie, the clock around, whimpering like a sick puppy, while the train-oil oozed from every pore—and the rest of us with pea-jackets buttoned to our chins.

As the fat came off and he grew weaker his intellect became perceptibly clearer and, to a certain extent, his memory returned. I spent all the time I could with him in those last days, realizing that now, if ever, I must get his story.

If he could have talked intelligibly, what a tale I should have heard— the recital of unparalleled experience in the polar regions; of the almost incredible survival of a human being; and the details of an ocean tragedy already forgotten in the lapse of time.

Every night I made copious notes of what I had learned during the day, so that when we buried the emaciated form of the poor old fellow, a hundred and fifty miles east of Cape St. Roque, I had a mass of these notes, from which I have been able to compile a story of the life of this wonderful man. But, better and—more important still, I have established beyond a reasonable doubt the identity of the frozen wreck, thereby clearing up one of the saddest mysteries in our naval annals.

It is to be understood that what I write here is not what he told me. Hans Olesen was not able to tell a connected story, even had he been able to enunciate distinctly. His mental mechanism was awry; the half century of solitude on that floating berg had benumbed whatever brains he may have had; and when it is remembered that having gone to sea at a very early age he could not possibly have had many educational advantages to start with, it is not to be wondered at that his mind became almost a blank and his soul died under the strain.

And yet, it is probably due to this low mentality that his reason survived. Being incapable of sustained mental effort, his brain gradually reverted to primal conditions, retaining only sufficient activity to enable him to care for his physical necessities, like the birds and animals with whom he consorted.

This story, then, is merely the impression I was able to gather from my conversations with him, consisting of questions and suggestions on my part, to which he replied with nods or shakes of the head or at best in monosyllables. It would therefore be of no value, except for the corroborative evidence I had the good fortune to acquire later on from official sources.

The first valuable discovery I made was the ship's name, which I have recorded as *Dervaathp*. After much patient study, I decided that *Der*, which did not appear when he gave the ship's name and her naval rating all in one word, *Thloopyvaarvaathp*, could be translated as "the." This gave me the *Vaathp*. Being a Swede, his V would be a W in English—the *Waathp*. Then there was the lisp, the elimination of which gave me the Wasp.

The Wasp! Why, every American schoolboy knows the story of the Wasp and the Frolic. It is one of our naval classics! But if my memory served, both vessels were immediately captured by a larger English ship, so how could the Wasp have ended her days under our flag? I had to give it up.

But here is the story as I dragged it piecemeal from Hans. While cook on board a Swedish bark, Hans, then a boy, stowed away in the Wasp's boat, which had boarded the bark for the purpose of taking off a couple of her passengers. They sailed away to the southward, capturing and burning two British merchantmen.

Continuing into extreme cold weather, she was struck one night, during a furious snow-storm, by an immense blazing meteor, which set her afire and started a leak that threatened to founder her. The captain put her before the wind—his only recourse—while part of the crew fought the flames and the rest pumped for their lives.

The volumes of black smoke mingled with the driving snow and formed an impenetrable curtain that preceded the doomed ship in her headlong flight. Without warning she shot up on shelving ice, ran her entire length out of water, pitched over a slight hummock, heeled over to port, and brought up all standing against the face of the solid mass of ice.

The three masts went short off at the deck, sweeping several men to death in the tangle of spars and rigging. As they could not sink now, all hands got at the fire and put it out.

I was unable to get a distinct idea of what happened immediately after that, but think part of the crew took to the boats, seeking relief for their shipmates; this might account for Hans's lack of surprise on seeing us. While his shipmates grew old and died and he himself became a toothless graybeard in the dead-level of that terrible monotony, he probably lost all conception of the flight of time, and so took us for the returning expedition.

On my arrival home, I opened a correspondence with the Secretary of the Navy, and he kindly sent me the records of two Wasps. As I remembered, the first was captured, with her prize, the Frolic, by the British ship-of-the-line Poictiers. But a new Wasp was launched at Portsmouth, New Hampshire, and sailed under command of Captain Blakeley early in the summer of 1814 on her mission of destruction.

She ravaged the North Atlantic until the British ensign was well-nigh a stranger in that ocean. On October 9 she took two American officers out of the Swedish bark Adonis, to the westward of the Cape de Verdes, and was never heard from thereafter. But it is worthy of note that the British merchant ship George III, homeward bound from China ports, sailed from Table Bay on the 23d of October and was never heard from more. Also, the British brig Orion, from Montevideo for London, at about the same time, met a similar fate. These were doubtless the two ships which Hans said that he had seen captured and burned while he was on board the Wasp.

They were the last to douse England's proud ensign at the behest of the invincible Wasp, which then sailed away to meet her strange doom; to be sealed in the heart of an iceberg with her unfortunate crew, there to remain in the frozen wastes, indestructible, as long as the earth endures.

The Lone Mutineer
Charles Francis Bourke

Wherein an Adverse Fate Frowns Upon
a Resourceful Sea Lawyer and an Able
Seaman Is Heartlessly Marooned

THE SOUTHERN SUN SHONE DOWN ON THE LITTLE SCHOONER FLEETWING as she lay, with backed topsail, lifting gently on the long swells of the East Florida coast. At the schooner's lee rail, glancing from the lowered boat, in the water alongside, to the distant Florida beach, the skipper and his mate were engaged in earnest discussion.

"We've simply got to do it, Mr. Parker," the captain said. "We're practically out of provisions, and if we keep that mischief-making animal aboard the Fleetwing he'll raise the crew before we sight Hatteras. And think of all those casks of Jamaica in the hold!"

"Well, sir, it's a responsibility, marooning a man," the mate said doubtfully. "Still, it's a long run to Sandy Hook."

Both officers shifted their gaze inboard to a group of stolid-faced seamen clustered in the waist around a bound figure prostrate on the schooner's deck. The master squared his jaw.

"By George, I'll take no chances," he said. "This ship isn't safe with Isaac Parsons aboard. Keep your gun handy, Parker."

The mate grinned appreciatively, and dropped his hand upon a bulging object that reposed in the side pocket of his pea-jacket.

"I see Isaac Parsons' finish when the old man clicks his jaw," he said as he lounged up the deck after his captain.

Able Seaman Isaac Parsons, trussed like a partridge in the coils of a flag-halyard, glowered up under a shock head of sandy hair at the captain towering above him.

"You're a trouble-brewing, mischief-making mutineer, Isaac Parsons," the master said. "You've been trying to raise the crew all the way up the coast. You've made this ship too hot to hold you."

"S'pose you think if I had my dues I'd be swingin' from the topsail yard-arm," Parsons growled, "but you try it. You just try that on an able seaman!"

The captain shook his head.

"No, you'll get the benefit of the doubt, Parsons. That's more rope than any other ship's master would give you."

He paused as the man snarled up at him with an assured impudence rarely seen on the high seas, where the captain's will is the supreme law. Able

Seaman Parsons was not an ordinary sailor-man.

"Kind o' thought you would," he sneered. The listening seamen grinned—and the mate watched them out of the corner of his eye.

"I'm not going to hang you—this time," the captain went on grimly. "I'm going to turn you loose on that Florida beach yonder."

"Turn me loose on the beach! I dare you! Me, a signed able seaman!"

"You won't be able to raise the devil in anybody but yourself there," the skipper continued calmly. "When you feel a fancy to throw knives at your superiors again you can try it on the crocodiles and land-turtles. And you can put in your spare time thanking Providence you signed under a merciful master."

At the conclusion of the captain's remarks the able seaman burst into hoarse but defiant expostulation.

"You don't dast maroon me. You don't dast dump a dooty-mindin' regular-signed able seaman on a empty uninhabited beach fer crocodiles to devour. You jest try dumpin' me off in them there Everglade Floridy swamps, Mister Cap'n Thompson, an' I'll good and plenty see wot the Board o' Trade does to your ticket.

"Mark me, I know ship law, an' you're goin' to take me back to Bedford, where you signed me from, an' I'll have the law on you then fer stretchin' me with a handspike. Yuss, an' Mister Mate, too!"

"Good!" The master eyed him coolly. "In that case I shall log a charge of inciting mutiny on the high seas. If you're not hanged, Mr. Sea Lawyer, you'll get twenty years, hard. Well?"

A light of fear took the place of the murderous glare in the sailor's eyes. For a long, silent minute he stared at the two officers. Then his gaze swung to the group of stolid-faced seamen and dropped to the deck.

"Well?" the master repeated.

Parsons looked up sullenly.

"Will ye gimme my dunnage, an' a gun?"

"You shall have what is necessary," the captain said shortly. "Now, Mr. Parker, we're lying here losing the trade-wind. Get one of those muskets out of the cabin and ferry him ashore."

Parsons' supplementary remarks, though sufficiently lurid, need not be quoted. His eloquence was rudely interrupted by two of the schooner's hands, who hoisted him over the brig's rail and dropped him unceremoniously into the waiting boat.

The master of the Fleetwing looked over the side as the boat's crew took their places.

"When you dump Parsons' dunnage on the sand, Mr. Parker," he called to the mate, "be careful how you leave that musket with him before you cast loose his lashings."

The boat pushed off for the distant white line of the Florida shore, the lamenting voice of the seaman trailing behind, and growing fainter and fainter as the little craft danced across the blue waters of the Florida coast.

Twenty minutes later, when the landing party returned to the schooner minus Parsons, the captain met the mate at the gangway.

"I told you to be careful about that musket," the captain said anxiously. "What was that shot ashore?"

The mate grinned.

"Oh, I know Isaac Parsons, A.B., of old," he said. "I pitched him the powder-flask when we got twenty yards clear of the beach. Before he got a charge crammed down the barrel we'd pulled well out of range of the old muzzle-loader. He turned the cannon loose on us just the same, together with a handful of pebbles he dropped in her. He's a bad egg—a born trouble-hunter. Don't worry about marooning him, sir."

"Well, he won't starve, with what we left him," the skipper replied. "Besides, the revenue people have got houses of refuge somewhere on the coast. Get the boat in and swing your yard, Mr. Parker. It's murking up. We've got to make sea-room."

Long after the schooner's boat rowed away from the beach and his impotent musket, Isaac Parsons, A.B., danced in incoherent rage on the soft white sand of the Florida seaboard, a solitary, grotesque figure in shirt and dungaree trousers, absolutely alone in the world.

Scattered around him were his sole possessions—a water-breaker, a bag of ship's biscuit, the old smooth-bore army musket, and part of a cake of tobacco, which some sympathetic seaman had tossed from the boat at the last moment.

The seaman's eyes were glued on the departing Fleetwing, the trim little schooner which his rebellious imagination had vaguely dreamed of turning into some kind of a roving beach-comber after he had managed to rouse his milksop shipmates into action and had disposed of her officers in precisely the same manner in which the Fleetwing's master had now disposed of himself.

He shook a ponderous fist at the shimmer of white sails in the distance and gave vent to inarticulate rage.

"I'll have the law on ye, if I have to swim ev'ry fathom back to Noo England. Oh!" Parsons' face flushed in furious yearning. "Ten years I'd give afore the mast jest to had a man-size Gatling gun on this beach afore Jimmy Legs an' Master Mate Parker got away. Jest-fer-ten-con-sec-utive seconds, full loaded!"

It was not until the schooner had become a hazy dot on the horizon that the marooned man took his eyes from her. Then he stared around, to realize to the full his desperate plight.

For miles the white sandy beach stretched away on either hand. Far back from the shore a dull, shadowy background of somber green marked the outer barricade of the Florida Everglades—trackless swamps, he well knew, untrodden by the foot of man. On the other side stretched the wide Atlantic—nothing more!

"Desarted on a des'lit coast like a Robinson Crooso, an' not even a parrit for comp'ny! An' for wot? Jest 'cause I goes an' tries to show them thankless bullies their rights, an' Old Man Thompson accuses me of stretchin' the mate, an' thumpin' the bo'sun an' damagin' that black cook along of the vittles. Only *wait* ontil I git back!"

The immediate outlook promised ill for Mr. Parsons' ambitions. He noticed that the evening wind was swishing in with a salty tang that smelled of a coming storm. Seaman Parsons did not like it.

With a final glare at the empty ocean, he moved the water-breaker and biscuit-bag farther up the beach, and started along the shore, musket in hand.

Far down the beach a vague speck on the sandy whiteness had caught his eye. It might be a house, it might be a hillock, it might be merely a product of his heated imagination. But it was worth investigating, he told himself.

"Anyways, I ain't got no more important engagements. They used to be pearl-fishers an' Semynoles livin' down here. They had to roost somewheres. Anything beats nothing."

The evasive speck was farther off than he at first thought, but as he plodded closer and closer the heart of Able Seaman Parsons beat high with hope. It was a house—a small square building, with glazed port-holes for windows and a red chimney projecting from the roof. It lay back from a neck of land, a sort of miniature Sandy Hook, that enclosed a little cove and formed a small, sheltered lagoon.

When Parsons reached the front of the house he gave a shout of triumph as his eyes fell upon a printed sign over the door of the house.

MARINER'S HOUSE OF REFUGE
U.S. LIFE-SAVING DEPARTMENT

"Ho! Spoutin' whales! wot kind o' luck is this here?" he cried.

Isaac Parsons had not sailed the Atlantic seaboard twenty years for nothing. He was perfectly acquainted with houses of refuge—those little solitary keeperless stations established by a benevolent government on the barren reaches of the Florida coast for the aid and shelter of shipwrecked mariners. He was only amazed that he had not thought of this godsend before, but his amazement gave place to glee.

"So, they turns me adrift to starve, does they? Right bang up 'longside a privit summer villy, provisioned free an' rigged out with relief sassiety clo'es an' galley-stove an' bunks an' grub! Them Fleetwing bullies kin holystone decks an' work ships till they drop, for all me. This here rent-free Floridy cottage suits I. Parsons to a T."

Suddenly he noticed that the door was ajar. He gasped when he shoved it wide open with the butt of his musket.

"Wot's this here? Hello, here's a find!"

It was evident that some one had but recently occupied the station—some one of untidy habits. Tins and provision-boxes were broken open. The stove in the center of the single room was smeared with cooking operations. Tin platters with scraps of food were scattered upon the pine-topped table, and blankets trailed in slovenly folds over the sides of the bunks ranged against the wall on one side of the room.

But the object which caught and held Parsons' covetous gaze was a pile of long, black, shiny skins spread out on the floor.

"Them's 'gator-skins," he ejaculated. "Them black Floridy crocodile-hunters has been bunking here, sure as guns. No Christian—on'y a swamp hunter or a Floridy cracker—ever lef sech a mess."

He eyed the drying skins hungrily, fingering the lock of his musket. "Fifty dollars apiece them 'ud fetch in York, fer boots. I knows. Wonder when will them mud-muckers come back? If they on'y aren't too many of 'em fer one desarted seaman—"

Whatever thought Parsons had in his mind, he did not give it words. After a survey outside the station of the gathering dusk and the rising sea, and the empty landlocked lagoon that stretched a half-mile or so across to the dark swamp's foliage, he proceeded to carry out the alligator-skins and bury them in the sand, scooping out a hole for the purpose with a piece of board.

Then he reentered the house, locked the door, and placed his musket conveniently at hand.

"No use leaving valyables round to tempt folks," he said. "If they does come back I'll bombard 'em. I'm king o' this castle now, an' I'm a goin' to stay king."

But for that night, at least, the marooned man was not called upon to carry out his threats. Long before the brewing storm was well under way, roaring inshore and slithering spray like volleys of bird-shot against the front of the station, he had finished a hearty supper of salt pork, which he took from the station barrel, and was sleeping in perfect peace the sleep of the surfeited.

Isaac Parsons had lived a strenuous life. He had schemed and fought in many ships and under many masters. He was a stranger to ease and luxury, but his newly acquired sovereignty of the house of refuge seemed less satisfactory than it had the night before as he stumbled from his bunk and peered hungrily over the booming morning surf into the spray-swept sea, apostrophizing his departed enemies.

"There they be, an' here I be. That there Fleetwing's getting good an' mauled—an' I ain't. But they can get away, an' I can't. Jest let me run acrost them murderin' marooners agin. Just once. That's all!"

Seaman Parsons was only dimly conscious that a malignant fate sometimes grants undesired boons; but he was superstitious, and now a vague, half-formed panic seized him as he stared with eyes that grew wider and wilder out upon the lashing ocean.

Like a scant-sheeted ghost, a schooner came driving from the mist, far out from the station. Her topmasts were gone, her bowsprit was snapped short off, and her sails were in tatters. But Parsons knew her, and gasped.

A quarter of a mile from the threatening beach the schooner luffed painfully. Then she fell off, with fluttering rags of canvas, and fled inshore again toward the hook of sand that enclosed the lagoon.

"It's her, by the Lord Harry!" the astounded Parsons ejaculated. "She's the Fleetwing. She's washed in on the blow, she has, an' she'll pile up, she will, sure as guns. Ho! Now who's ahead o' this here game!"

He snatched up his musket and ran along the margin of the lagoon, paralleling the course of the hurrying schooner. An insensate rage possessed him. He determined to witness the end of those who had so basely ill-used him, and besides, another thought urged him onward.

"She'll drownd every man jack of 'em in the breakers. But them Jamaica kags won't drownd. An' won't I fish 'em out arterwards, just! That'll learn 'em to maroon me."

A boom and a crash of falling spars made him drop on his hands and knees and peer over the sands with the instinct of a hunted animal, fearful of being seen.

"She's got it! By gum, she's got it! She's took the bar right off the point, an' she's shuck her fo'mast overboard. Now smash up an' drown 'em, hang ye!"

But the fates seemed determined to play upon the strings of Parsons' emotions. His furious joy was of short duration. It vanished even as he watched. He was a seaman of experience, and now he gnashed his teeth with rage and disappointment.

"They've drove her high, an'll get ashore. They've got a boat out. The mate's in. An' there comes Watkins an' Taylor an' the bo'sun. An' now the old man's climbin' down. Wot are they leavin' the cook for?"

He was snuggled in a hollow of the sand when the schooner's boat plunged into the lagoon and made a landing on the inner beach, so close to him that he heard the conversation of the captain and mate, opening with his own name, in no pleasant accents.

"It was Parsons at the refuge station; I saw him plain," the mate said. "By George, while we're refitting I'd make the animal cook for the men in place of the poor old Doctor."

"I wouldn't mind if we hadn't lost the cook," the captain said. "As a matter of safety, as well as discipline, we shall have to iron Parsons and keep him in the schooner, after that murderous attempt of his. Warn the men about the sharks in this lagoon. It's full of man-eaters."

Cautiously peering over the sand, Parsons watched the men troop after the two officers in the direction of the refuge station.

"Iron me, will ye, Mister Orficer?" he growled. "Ye ain't done enough a'ready, marooning a man, but ye'll shackle 'im an' get 'im twenty years hard! Jest wait an' see!"

With only the stretch of lagoon beach between them, the boat was in plain view of the refuge station. But Parsons was desperate. His own liberty and his burning thirst for the schooner's cargo called him. Waiting until he saw the officers enter the station, leaving the men outside, he gathered himself for a rush.

"I hate to leave them 'gator-hides, but I reckon when them swamp hunters comes back they'll massacre the hull gang for pinchin' 'em."

He sprang down the beach, threw his musket into the unguarded boat, and setting his burly shoulder against the bow, shoved it into the lagoon.

"I'll jest git out o' range, in case Mr. Mate's got his gun," he said, as he tumbled into the boat and seized the oars. "That's wot he done when I opened on 'im."

A sense of the ludicrous in this turning of the tables struck him, and he burst into hoarse laughter. He stopped rowing long enough to shake his big fist at the two officers, who were speeding down the beach toward him.

"Who's marooned now, gents o' the Fleetwing?" he yelled. "Come aboard w'enever you feel sociable, s'posin' you got pussonal friends among the sharkses!"

Engaged in flinging ribald messages to the Fleetwing's crew as he rowed away, Mr. Parsons did not take particular note of other things in the lagoon. Though the wind was abating, he had his hands full breasting the sea-wash to the stranded schooner. The gesticulating men on shore he presumed to be addressing himself.

He saw nothing of a large dugout, paddled by half a dozen black men, which put out from the beach behind him on the lower side of the lagoon entrance and reached the schooner while Mr. Parsons was yet a cable's-length away. The wand of fate was preparing to wave once more.

Parsons boarded the schooner sailor-fashion. That is to say, he made the boat-painter fast to the main-chains and slung one leg over the rail, looking back to see that the boat was secure. Then he turned inboard and landed on the deck—to face a row of blacks, headed by a gigantic negro, who surveyed the newcomer with folded arms and scowling disapproval. For the third or fourth time that day, Parsons gasped.

"The 'gator-hunters!" he said.

"What you want here, sah?" the big black demanded. "You desart ship—we take him in charge. Belong to beachcomber now."

"Desart ship!" the seaman stammered. "I didn't desart. I was throwed out—marooned."

"Good," the negro said calmly. "We maroon you again—or throw you there." The big man pointed an eloquent finger at the shark-infested lagoon.

Parsons realized that fate had dealt him a final buffet. On the very verge of ultimate victory, he found himself in a cul-de-sac. On the beach, the tricked crew of the schooner awaited him hungrily; in the lagoon, the sharks were equally hungry.

On the schooner's deck the scowling blacks were already closing in upon him with drawn knives. He was overwhelmed by the sense of crowding calamity, when an unexpected diversion gave him a breathing-spell. During the brief discussion an adventurous spirit had slipped below. Now the negro reappeared, chattering with glee and rolling a small keg before him.

With a unanimous rush the blacks left their intended victim and fell to beating in the head of the keg, howling joyfully. Seaman Parsons grasped the opportunity. Snatching up his musket, he swarmed up the main-shrouds, rapidly planning the impending campaign as he went aloft hand over hand.

"I'll hold 'em off till the brutes are all helpless with the rum. Then I'll drop them overboard—onless I kin pick 'em off from the top. I'll learn 'em to steal schooners from honest seamen."

Before he was fairly settled a negro climbed up after him, gripping a long knife in his shining teeth. Mr. Parsons ceased to temporize. The musket roared, and the black sprawled to the deck, sprinkled with bird-shot. Parsons coolly fell to reloading.

"If that big swine tries that game I'll let him up an' blow the roof off his kinky head. Wot's that smoke out yon, I'd like to know?"

Rapidly surveying his unpropitious surroundings, a black smudge to the northward caught his eye. He viewed it with mingled feelings of doubt and hope.

"If she's coastwise she'll pass far out. S'posin' she's a prowlin' gov'ment cutter wot looks arter these here mariners' shipwreck stations? That would be nuts for them Fleetwing animiles on the beach—an' for me, too, jest now!"

He noticed with growing interest that the negroes on deck had already begun to play havoc with the cargo. One man held a blazing swabbing-brush that he had dipped in the liquor and set afire, and the sailor's anxiety turned to panic when the man slipped and dropped the swab into the spilled liquor.

"The brutes'll roast me like a partridge. Ain't there no way I kin get out o' this here slaughter-house?"

A sullen boom reached him from the sea, like an answer to his question. In watching the roistering negroes he had forgotten the smudge of smoke in the north. Now he turned and uttered an exclamation of surprise.

A white steamer, flying the barred flag of the revenue service, was in the offing, forging toward the schooner under full steam, with smoke pouring from her yellow funnel. A wisp of white floated away from her bow.

Then Parsons' eyes fell upon the refuge station. A man on the roof was "speaking" the steamer with a signal-flag.

"The las' act is arrove!" he muttered. "She's the revenoo relief. Here's where them ship-stealin' gentlemen mixes in a good healthy scrap."

The blacks on the schooner were still oblivious of the cutter, and of the longboat crowded with armed sailors which shot away from her side. They were still dancing round the blazing kegs when the sailors from the cutter poured over the schooner's side, headed by a lieutenant with drawn sword.

Peering down from the top, the besieged seaman cocked his musket and anxiously singled out the huge negro leader who had first accosted him.

"Mebbe they'll make it on'y ten years if I get him," he said. "Ho! Now they're at it 'ammer an' tongs! Go it, bullies!"

For a moment the negroes on deck hung back, glaring at the unexpected invaders. Then, with frantic yells, they flashed out their knives and fell upon the sailors, the big leader howling defiantly as he fell upon the lieutenant.

Yelling on one side and cheering on the other, the fight surged across the deck, the sailors beating the beach-combers back against the rail with their cutlasses.

In the crosstrees, the seaman squirmed and twisted, yelling encouragement to the cutter's boat-crew. He waited, with cocked musket pointed downward, until the sailors had beaten the negroes over the rail and forced them one after another over the side and into the sea.

The negro leader saw how the fight had gone. With a last savage lunge at the revenue officer, he turned to follow his companions.

Parsons caught him fair in the middle of the deck. He pulled at the trigger, and the big black rolled over, howling and kicking. But before the sailors could reach him he staggered to his feet and plunged over the side.

"I know I ain't killed the beast," Parsons remarked. "On'y, that bunch o' bird-shot won't make you forget to remember me for a while."

The roar of the musket above them caused the whole boarding party to turn their attention aloft, for a moment disregarding the still blazing deck. Two sailors were springing up the shrouds when Parsons threw his leg over the edge of the maintop and calmly began to descend.

His quick eye had detected a second boat from the cutter coming toward the schooner from the refuge station, and he recognized the form of the master of the Fleetwing in the stern-sheets.

"It's out o' the fryin'-pan into the fire, but I've got used to that," Mr. Parsons remarked philosophically. "On'y, I prefer the fire jest now, with brass buttons on his coat-front."

On the deck of the schooner the lieutenant stared in surprise at the shock-headed seaman who appeared before him solemnly holding out an old musket in token of submission.

"Who the dickens are you, man? Where did you spring from?" he cried.

"I'm Isaac Parsons, able seaman," Mr. Parsons answered, with a glance over the lee rail at the approaching boat and the dreaded master of the schooner. "I'm a mutineer, marooned from this same schooner Fleetwing. I plugged the mate an' the bo'sun, an' I stole the boat, an' I marooned the hull crew, an' I was stealin' the schooner, on'y them black animiles stole her fust. I got a right to be took by a gov'ment ship. So I surrenders my weapons.

"There ain't on'y one thing, Mr. Lieutenant," Seaman Parsons added earnestly. "There's some allygator-hides over at the station wot I collected my own self. I'd like to have them fetched on your ship along of me. Them skins'll come handy for the lawyer-sharks w'en I'm tried."

The lieutenant grinned appreciatively, with a side glance at the coming boat.

"All right," he said. "I guess we can fix you up with a nice suit of irons. Anything else?"

Mr. Parsons shook his head with a sigh of relief.

"Never—no, never!" he said with feeling. "Never in my hull maritime career did I dream I would be doin' the dee-lighted w'en brass buttons o' the gov'ment cops showed up! It jest shows wot comes o' maroonin' an able seaman."

And Parsons, with an eye to possible eventualities, slipped across to the windward rail as the master of the schooner Fleetwing came over the side.

The Passing of the Waters
Edwin C. Dickinson

Of a Modern David Who on the Hillside of
Culebra Wrought for Peace with Nature's
Giant Weapons

TEN LONG YEARS IT HAD TAKEN TO BUILD THE GREAT CANAL. Millions upon millions of the nation's dollars had gone into its making. Daily, men had given their lives as the price of service beneath that hot sun, and engineers the best years of their existence in carrying forward the great work.

Through fever-laden morasses, over the redoubtable Culebra and down to the Pacific, the waterway had crawled like some monster snail, until one day the two great oceans lay connected and the ships of all nations forsook the turbulent passage of the Horn for the landlocked lees of the great canal.

Then war had come. The strategic possibilities of this connecting link between the Atlantic and the Pacific would now be proved, said the theorists. With New York and San Francisco less than six thousand miles apart, instead of some fifteen, the Atlantic and Pacific squadrons could concentrate to attack or to resist the enemy, separate, and return to their respective posts before the flying squadron of the enemy could hope to round the Horn and ravage the opposite coast.

If the enemy attempted to force the passage of the canal, so much the better. In a single day either squadron, as the case might be, would be in a position to slip from one ocean to the other, and outside the limit set in the canal treaty the united fleets would resist and destroy the enemy.

So the theorists had reasoned. What they had not taken into account was that conservatism in naval affairs for eight long years which had been the result, partly of the reaction from the strenuous life and partly of the enormous cost of the canal, which had diverted the nation's dollars from other directions and left our navy far behind in the race for the supremacy of the seas.

As the world knows, the enemy's first appearance had been off Colon, but, thanks to the wireless "feelers," its fleet had been discovered some thirty-six hours before, and the Pacific squadron, which had anticipated this move and lay in readiness off Panama, was successfully brought through the canal and formed in line with the Atlantic squadron.

So far, the theorists had been vindicated.

Then had come that awful revelation of the Caribbean, when beneath the fires of the new seventeen-inch guns our ships had been held at arm's length and sent to the bottom, like so many perforated tomato-cans, without seriously scarring the enemy.

Early in the evening of that disastrous day the conquering leviathans had steamed singly and majestically through the long sea-level stretch to the first of those great steps which rose to the level of the lakes. This great victory had laid open to them the Pacific coast. Yet, if they were to enjoy its fruits, they must waste no time.

So, that same night the huge battleships and cruisers, which tested the capacity of the thousand-foot locks, rose upward to the lakes. A few hours more and they would descend as they had ascended, only into the wide waters of the Pacific.

But in that time of their exultation a David was already picking the stones for his sling far up the hillside of the Culebra.

It was by a strange turn of fortune that the greatest stroke of the war—that which paralyzed the arm of one of the most powerful maritime nations in the world and brought peace on its heels—should have been performed neither by sailor nor soldier, but by one who might have been called a non-combatant until that one great opportunity had offered.

Baldwin was chief of the resident engineers. Every foot of the canal was as familiar to him as the three rooms of his bungalow.

Through the rainy season he guarded the swollen waters of the Chagres as a vigilant keeper guards a savage beast; through the dry months he nursed its every drop. Its strength and its weaknesses lay before him an open book. The one he had gloried in, the other deplored, until this day when the news of that defeat had been telephoned him.

Then an idea had come to the engineer which left him strangely lightheaded, and which had for its working basis that very weakness—the dam at Gatun that made the artificial lakes which fed all the stretches above those of the sea-level.

None knew so well as Baldwin the awful pressure against this dam which barred the foot of the valley. None knew so well as he the millions of expense, the years of work, and the incalculable loss to the world's commerce which its destruction would entail.

Yet his was an intense patriotism. This had been the work of his people; their best brains, the very life's blood of some of them, had been given to it; their money had made it possible, and until now their and his flag had floated above it. Now the ships of another nation denied through its locks; his country had sown but for another to reap.

What cared he for an international treaty whose provisions he but hazily knew? Below him the sacred waters of his Canal were polluted by the hulls of the enemy's ships, and in his power it lay to avenge this sacrilege and to save his country's western coast.

And so it was that as the ships of the enemy steamed one by one, all that afternoon and evening, into one end of the great canal, near its other end a gang of grim-faced men were drilling deep into the solid masonry of the greatest dam in the world and concealing therein long, slender sticks of the greatest explosive then known. With his own hands Baldwin led the wires which were to discharge these to the bungalow far back on the hillside.

Fortune had favored the enemy's fleet that night. The moon was nearly at its full, and in its soft light the lakes shimmered under the night-breeze which stirred the palms along their borders.

It was easy work for the pilots. Huge, resistless, destroying monsters of the deep, the war-ships of the enemy steamed slowly along in single file.

The very insolence of their might fanned afresh the hate of him who sat in his bungalow, far up the hillside, with the keyboard on which hung their fate before him. That beautiful valley had been the abode of peace until these had brought war—now they should have their fill of it.

An hour passed, and the moon disappeared in a bank of clouds. Out of the darkness the lights of the ships sparkled like so many diamonds, with here and there, at the bend of the lake, the ruby and emerald of the port and starboard lights.

The first had reached the end of the lakes. The turreted wall of the great dam towered before it, stretching away into dim gray lines on either side.

The enemy's spies were as familiar with the locks beyond as they had been with the basin of the lakes through which they had lately piloted the great ships. There was nothing now to bar the way of the victorious fleet to the waters of the Pacific.

And then, far up on the hillside, a man, quick-drawn of breath and with eyes sparkling with some deep emotion, pressed a switch and the night was bright again—awfully and luridly bright—and then darker than ever, while booming up from the valley there came to the watcher a sound beside which the crash of the enemy's seventeen-inch guns was as the crack of a pistol.

Through that ill-fated ship which led the squadron ran a violent shudder. Men were thrown from their feet and the huge guns unshipped.

The crew saw the massive wall totter and melt before their eyes with a boom that rivaled that of the dynamite. The great battle-ship lurched forward—caught like a chip in a mountain torrent. On the brink of that hillside of rushing, roaring water she hung for a moment, and then she plunged with all the tremendous force of gravity behind her.

Her bow drove through the mighty stream and took the ground. The weight of water behind her raised her stern. Men slid down the steep side of her deck; then the huge after turret, with its big seventeen-inch gun, broke loose and swept the deck clean of everything in its path.

Higher and higher she reared, and then she toppled over with a crash of thunder and the dammed current, welled and swept over her.

The clouds thinned and passed away, leaving the valley once more bathed in the soft light of the moon. But it shone no more on a scene of tropic beauty.

Of that beautiful chain of lakes there remained but a thin stream wandering through a pit of glistening mud. Across the foot of the valley yawned a great ugly gap where once had stood the noble turreted wall of the dam. Here and there in that vast pit wallowed huge unshapely things, like stranded monsters of the deep—the remaining ships of the enemy.

For many minutes the watcher on the hillside stared down upon his handiwork—then his head sank forward on his arms.

The End of the Iron Monarch
Charles Doran

Wherein It Is Demonstrated that When the
Captain Does Not Steer Straight a Crash
Is Likely to Follow

PULLING AND TUGGING AT HER ANCHOR, the Iron Monarch seemed to be trying to get out of the hot and sickly little port of San Miguel, where we had been lying sweltering under a tropical sun for nearly a month.

San Miguel was an out-of-the-way Chilean island port, with no trade except that carried on by a handful of blacks who dived for sponges, caught cuttle-fish, and supported themselves out of what the waters of the port would yield.

What had brought the Monarch to this port was a mystery to the crew. She had plenty of water and provisions, and her bunkers contained coal enough to last her until she could reach Panama.

The steamer was a tramp of eight hundred tons, built in Glasgow for the South American trade, and owned in large part by her skipper. She had seen much service, and was beginning to show it in her boilers and engines, when I signed on board of her at Callao as deckhand. I was out of funds at the time, and wishing to get north at any cost, I took the first job open to me.

I had not been aboard the tramp long when I was convinced that the skipper, one Henry Lloyd, a Scotchman, was not steering just straight. There was something I did not like about the man, something strange in his actions, and I hadn't been at sea over a fortnight when I discovered that his mate and engineer were of the same kind of stuff—shady chaps, all of them, I thought. As I had never shipped under men of their stamp without finding myself in hot water before the voyage ended, I looked for trouble.

Well, we beat about, touching at a dozen ports, but always leaving with an empty hold, until one dark night we crept into San Miguel and dropped anchor. The next morning we were told by the skipper that we'd wait there until further orders.

Now, further orders might mean most anything, so, after a week of sweltering in the deserted port, the whites of the crew, six in number, began grumbling and threatening to make trouble, and the blacks—Lloyd had shipped eight or ten of them—tried to desert. At this, the skipper put them in irons and left them in the forecastle day and night.

Lloyd shipped blacks because he could handle them easier, or, as he used to say, as he pleased. When his wrath was spent on one of them he'd land him on the first strip of shore that came in sight—it did not matter to him whether it was inhabited or not. They had no country, so the skipper argued, as most of them were West Indian negroes, and so long as the Monarch never heard of them again, what were the odds?

I was pretty well tired of the Iron Monarch and her master, and was thinking of getting out of her the first chance I had, when one morning there came into San Miguel the first ship we had seen in the place. The newcomer was an ugly-looking tramp, about the tonnage of the Monarch—a French craft, very heavy and clumsy, with high bows and irregular lines. She had come within a cable's-length of us when she dropped anchor.

I do not know why it was, but I was suspicious of the stranger, and I determined to keep an eye on her. After she had come to anchor not a man could be seen on board. We exchanged no signals, and not a boat was put off from either steamer. This was very strange, I thought.

I noticed, too, that the Portuguese cook, to whom I had been assigned as messman, was watching the newcomer as well as I was, and I thought I saw on his sallow face some uneasiness. He looked like a man who expected a dreaded something to happen.

Night came on; the blacks turned in early, and the white members of the crew at two bells. I went forward, crawled into my bunk, but did not get to sleep. Instead, I lay awake until about four bells. Then I cautiously crept aft from where a light was shining through the doorway to the cabin.

As I reached the deck, just above the cabin, I heard voices, and going to the skylight, so that I could see below, I listened.

Four or five men, judging by the number of different voices I heard, were in general conversation about the Iron Monarch. At last I heard one of the speakers, whom I recognized by his voice to be Lloyd, saying:

"Very well, Captain Legros, it's agreed upon—two thousand pounds. It's no good coming after more when the job's done. You have the bearings. Very well; the night of the twentieth, two bells—have you got it all right?" and Lloyd and three men came out of the cabin, went to the sides, and disappeared.

I heard a splash, then the turn of an oar in the lock, and I knew that a boat was pushing off. It was too dark to see anything beyond a couple of yards, so I did not go to the rail.

The captain returned to the cabin, and soon he, the mate, the engineer, and the cook were talking together, and very excited they were, I thought.

"Two thousand! It's a nice slice," one of the men was saying, "but it leaves a cool four thousand to be divided among us. This craft would not fetch a thousand at auction. With her bottom-plates nearly worn through, boilers leaking, and her engines shaky, she isn't worth the price of scrap-iron. But, blow me, it's a mighty skiddish piece of work. What if it gets to the underwriters?"

"Well, it won't if none of us squeals, but if it does, it's at least ten years in Newgate."

"Underwriters! Newgate! Ah!" thought I, as a little light began to dawn on me. "I see. The Monarch is to be sunk. Collision, eh! Insurance," and in my delight at having, as I believed, discovered something to reward me for my pains I overlooked the danger and leaned over the skylight, where I could command an unobstructed view of the entire cabin.

The four of them, captain, mate, engineer, and cook, were seated around the table, upon which were spread out several charts. The mate was figuring, and the others were waiting for the result.

At last the man said: "One hundred and forty, due east, I make it, sir."

And to this the engineer replied:

"Say about twenty hours' steaming, seven knots an hour—those boilers won't stand any great pressure."

"Very good; that will bring us in sight of the Juan Fernandez by two bells, just as I said to Legros, the night of the twentieth; but we must haul out of here to-morrow night at eight bells—the Juan Fernandez is to sail at daylight. Good thing Legros is going to leave us his black pilot, or we'd never get out of this infernal port after night with our bottoms so thick with barnacles."

"But how about getting rid of the men in the crew we won't need. You know, captain, we can't let others into this, and we don't want to take any chances."

"Oh, that's easily fixed, chief. What can you get along with? Will two stokers run you these twenty hours?"

"Yes, sir, if we can keep them at the fires, but likely as not—"

"Put the blacks to stoking; you can keep them at work, I reckon, can't you?"

"Oh, I suppose so."

"Well, then, we can fix up the other trouble—getting rid of the whites; we'll leave them behind. It's easy; give them all the rum they want, then put them ashore. When they get sober we'll be at sea. How about it, Saucher, will the rum hold out?"

At this the cook made some reply and began giggling to himself. The sallow-faced chap was, then, quite a party to the affair, I thought, and I wondered how he could be worth so much to the officers of the Monarch. I suppose he had got wind of the proposed wrecking of the vessel and the rest had to take him into the job to keep him from telling the crew, at least until they could knock him in the head in his bunk at night and throw his body overboard. I think the Portuguese feared some such thing, for he slept with the galley-door locked, hot as it was at San Miguel.

In the morning the harbor presented its usual quiet appearance. The

Frenchman had sailed. Her pilot was on board the Monarch, having doubtless come on during the night.

That day the skipper issued grog at noon, the men drank freely, and in the afternoon the long-boat pulled off to shore loaded with them. I pretended I was as much under the influence of the liquor as any one of the rest.

The mate, cook, and engineer went along with us. After we had landed the men started inland. I went a short distance from the beach, but when I came to a clump of banana-trees I dropped down and waited. From where I was lying I could see the boat, and when the mate had made certain that the drunken men were a safe distance away he, the engineer, and the cook shoved the boat off, jumped in, and bent to the oars. They had deserted us, just as I had expected they would.

The boat reached the steamer, and soon after a little curl of smoke from the funnel told me she was getting up steam. I looked around for something large enough to serve me as a float, but there wasn't anything. If I wanted to reach the steamer—and I didn't want that pack of scoundrels to have everything their own way—I must do so by swimming. I knew that if I got to her I could climb on board by her anchor-chains, but it was a dangerous undertaking, and it would, of course, have to be done after dark.

Now I saw one reason why the captain wished to wait until night before leaving the port. The men on shore, if any of them got over the grog, would not see the steamer leave. In the morning she would be well on her voyage, and with no means of reaching the steamer the poor fellows would be helpless to do anything, even should they discover that they had been marooned.

Still, Lloyd and his followers evidently had some other motive for getting under way after dark. If the men ashore ever got where they could come back at them the skipper could swear that the steamer had waited for them, even sent its boats ashore with a searching party for them. A pretty shrewd man was Lloyd, I thought, as I went to the beach when darkness closed in and prepared to swim out to the Monarch.

The tide was ebbing, the waters of the harbor very calm. I knew that at flood-tide the steamer would heave up her anchor, so as to reach the shallow channel when the water was high. I still had two hours before me, and I sat down to think it all over.

If I were discovered, I thought, I would be knocked on the head, and if not discovered, there was the probability of my going down with the steamer. I knew Lloyd and his mates would not allow any one else to come into their game. It would be rather dangerous, and certainly too costly. They had already one more than they perhaps wanted in the person of the cook. Still, the adventure was worth something, and one never knows what will turn up.

The distance from the shore to the steamer was about half a mile. I was a good swimmer, and knew I could easily reach her in a quarter of an hour. At last it was dark enough, and I waded past the small breakers and struck out in the direction of the steamer.

I had not mistaken my course. Soon the dark sides of the Monarch loomed up before me, and a dozen strokes more brought me within reach of her anchor-chains. I lay motionless on my back for some time, listening. All was quiet on board, and reaching up, I caught the chain. The links were large, and served as rungs in a ladder, my feet passing easily into the openings.

I reached the rail and peered over. The forecastle was deserted as I started to climb down on to it. When I did so I heard a sound behind me, and turning, saw a figure coming up the ladder. Nearer and nearer it came. I crept back and hung motionless to the chain. No head, however, appeared over the side. Perhaps the man had gone down the forward hatch into the forecastle. I climbed up again until I saw the deck.

The forecastle was now deserted. I got over the rail and crept to the forward hatch and looked down. All was still except for the snoring of the two or three blacks who lay stretched out upon the deck below. Poor devils, little did they know how soon the end was to be, I thought, as I descended the ladder and went by them on my way to the door leading onto the steamer's main-deck.

I wanted to get aft to the cabin, where I knew the captain kept his pistols, and hugging the sides so that I could leap overboard if discovered, I crept along until I was within a few yards of the poop-ladder. The darkness of the night had thus far favored me, and I was safe where I stood if the rays of a lantern carried by one of the men going to and from the cabin did not fall upon me.

I felt chilly, my legs were numb from the wet trousers which clung to them, and I was beginning to feel very uncomfortable, when the cabin-door was opened, a ray of light from within shot down the deck a few feet to my side—too far away, fortunately, to reveal my whereabouts—and the captain, mate, and engineer came out.

They stopped and began talking, and I heard the engineer say:

"Yes, sir, the two blacks are below, the fires are going, but how about those devils forward. What are you going to do with them after we get up anchor? We won't need them any longer."

"Oh, the deuce with them! Dope them like you did Sancho; that damned Portuguese's vigilance didn't save him. Reckon when he wakes up down in the forward hold it will be to serve grub to Father Neptune," and the mate laughed.

Just then the black pilot of the Juan Fernandez appeared and the skipper went forward with him. The cabin was deserted. My chance had come. Hurriedly I slipped into the room, and soon had possession of the two revolvers that hung on the skipper's bunk.

Now at least I was not helpless, I thought, as I left the cabin and returned to my hiding-place near the rail.

The steamer was getting under way, the blacks were heaving anchor, a little curl of smoke was slowly ascending heavenward from the funnel. I felt the jarring of the machinery, and could hear the propeller's blades lashing at the muddy waters of the harbor.

The play had begun. I can't say I liked my chances, but there was nothing for me to do but see it through. The mate again appeared on deck. With him were three or four blacks—I could see their forms as they hurried forward and hear the skipper swearing as he now and then shoved or hit one of the wretches with the marlinespike he carried.

I was beginning to feel very sleepy, and as I knew nothing was going to happen for a good many hours yet, I waited until all hands were forward and then went below into the aft hold. There, by the aid of some matches I had helped myself to while in the cabin, I found a partly empty case, crawled into it and lay down.

When I awoke the motion of the steamer told me we were at sea. I was safe so far as the chance of being discovered was concerned, but a dry throat and a pretty stiff appetite, with neither water nor food at hand, made it apparent to me that I should soon have to try to get into the galley storeroom.

Until then I had not thought to examine the pistols. What if they were not loaded? I shuddered at the thought of such a possibility, but fortune had again favored me. Every chamber in the cylinders had a cartridge in it—big forty-eight caliber. Much relieved, I returned the weapons to my belt.

A faint light that penetrated an opening in the hatch-covering, near which I lay, told me that it was day and that I must wait. To attempt to reach the galley until after dark would have been madness. One of the men on deck would have seen me coming up the ladder, and before I could have used my weapons a blow on the head would have been the end of me.

The hours seemed interminable to me, but at last the faint light that had come through the crack in the hatch-covering vanished and I knew that the sun had gone, down.

Another hour passed. I went to the ladder, and climbing up until I could see over the hatch-coaming, I looked about the deck. Not a soul was visible. A few more rungs and I had reached the deck.

The galley-door was open, and I crept through it and was soon in front of a tank of water. Kneeling down, I put my mouth to the spigot and turned on the water. Never before had water tasted so good. When I had drunk copiously I felt around in the room until I came to the bread-chest, found several pilot crackers and devoured them ravenously.

Drink and food strengthened me, and from the galley I crept aft to a place from which I could see into the lighted cabin through the open door.

The clock hung on the wall near the barometers and I could distinctly make out the hour. If the Monarch had lost no time, in another hour she was to be met by the Juan Fernandez.

The old engines were pulsating, the screw turning, everything in the engine-room working well.

As I stood peering into the cabin the mate and engineer came out. They came within a couple of yards of me, talking as they walked.

"Yes, we won't need the pilot any longer."

"Very well. We can fix him as we did the Portuguese."

The two men disappeared into the darkness forward. They had not been gone very long when I saw them coming aft again, this time dragging something. As they came closer I saw that it was the negro pilot. The mate had him by the arms, the engineer by the legs. He was either dead or unconscious, for his form hung limp and lifeless. In the light that was shed along the deck through the open cabin-door I saw that the black was bleeding freely from a wound in the head. They had evidently knocked him on the head.

Into the cabin they dragged him, pulled away the cover leading to the cabin storeroom, and dropped him down the opening. There was a thud, a groan, and the hatch had been covered over again.

"Another one out of it," said the mate as he and the engineer came on deck again. "Now for the stokers, and we'll be through. The skipper's going to attend to the signal, the dinghy is already in the water, and her oars in place. Mind you, it's the midship's guards, just aft the bridge."

"I know; she's to strike us just aft of the funnel. I've opened the compartments and we're taking in water already."

The men again disappeared in the darkness. When they returned, each one had a wretched black by the throat. The poor creatures, evidently dazed by a heavy blow, offered no resistance, and they, too, were shoved into the cabin and thrown head first into the after-hold.

The hatch-covering was now securely fastened with a bolt and padlock, and the men were left like rats in a trap to whatever fate was in store for them.

Going forward, I groped around in the dark until I found the ladder to the bridge, and climbed up it. To the port side, fastened to the rail, was a signal-rocket. This was to tell the Frenchman our position when we had reached the waters where we were to meet her. Near the rocket was a signal-light, the fuse ready for the match.

What if I could knock the man down, perhaps stun him, as he came up the ladder to set the signals off and deal out to the others that might follow the same dose. I would have to put three men out of action—the skipper, mate, and engineer. If I could do this I could rescue the four wretches in the after-hold and save the ship.

As I was considering the possibility of such an undertaking I heard some one ascend the ladder, and a dark form came toward me. The Monarch's engines had stopped, and to starboard, less than a cable's-length away, were the bow and side-lights of a ship. The Juan Fernandez had kept her appointment.

The rocket would tell her we had seen her, the signal-lights would show her our midships, where she was to strike.

I could hear the noise of the Frenchman's propeller as it churned up the water. She was coming nearer and nearer to us with every revolution of her engines.

Involuntarily I looked about in the darkness for something loose on the deck that I could cling to when the ship went down. I thought of the fearful eddy the big iron body would make as she went down. I thought, too, of the poor devils locked in the hold aft to be drowned like a lot of rats.

The man had reached the side and had struck a match. Another second and the rocket would be set off and the signal-light burning. In less than ten minutes the Monarch, her sides crushed in, the water pouring through the open compartments, would be going to the bottom.

The man leaned over; then I saw the light of a match, there was a whiz, and the rocket went rushing up into the heavens.

At once the Frenchman ran a red light up to her peak, evidently a signal that all was ready on board of her. She was now waiting only for the signal where to strike us.

By the light of the match the man had struck I saw that it was Lloyd, the captain. I crept nearer and nearer the rail, my hand clutching the pistol by the butt, so that to me the weapon was a club. Stealthily I moved toward the skipper, and soon I was upon him.

As he struck the second match, the light of which showed me plainly his position, I raised my weapon and brought it down heavily upon his head. He staggered back, gave one wild yell, and fell to the deck below.

In an instant the mate and engineer were on the bridge. The mate saw me, the rays of light cast by the lantern revealing me plainly to him.

He cried out something to the engineer, and before I could raise my weapon the two were upon me. Something hit me on the head.

As I fell I saw a flash; something whizzed by my head; there was a terrific shock, the Monarch quivered from stem to stern, and I heard the crashing of metal, the rushing of waters into her compartments. The vessel began to list to starboard. There was a gurgle, followed by a roar, and volumes of steam and smoke came pouring through the engine-room skylights.

The water had reached the boilers.

I thought, though, of the likelihood of their exploding, and staggering to my feet, bleeding and stunned, crawled aft. As I felt my way about I smelled smoke, and a flame shot out of the cabin-door, lighting up the deck. The ship was afire. A lighted lantern, doubtless, thrown from its fastenings by the shock, had been broken, the oil had ignited, and the fire had spread to the deck and woodwork in the skipper's quarters.

Horror-stricken, I seized a marlinespike and madly went to work to try to break off the galley-door from its hinges. There was no time to lose, for the ship was fast settling.

At last the broken door fell in. I seized it, carried it to the side, and with it in my arms jumped overboard and swam away from the sinking ship.

The flames, now enveloping the poop and leaping up into the shrouds, lighted up the ocean around the doomed ship, and I saw the Frenchman heaved to and waiting. The dinghy from the Monarch was making for her, but there were but two men in her. Where was the skipper? Had I killed him when I struck him, and had he fallen from the bridge to the deck? Brute as he was, I did not like the idea of having his blood upon me.

By this time I was out of reach of danger, so far as the sinking ship was concerned, and climbing on the door, I lay down to rest. I had not lain there long, however, before something heavy struck me, and I saw that it was a spar. Clinging to it was the figure of a man. It was Lloyd.

I called to him, but he did not answer. His face was deathly pale, and blood was pouring from his head. I tried to reach the spar but could not, and in a few minutes I saw his form slip off and disappear in the waters.

The Monarch had now settled so deep that only her stack and her masts were above the waves. The fire had been extinguished by the waters, and the flames gave only a faint light as they licked up some of the dry rigging. This lasted for several minutes; then spar after spar fell into the water as the ropes that held them were burned away and it was dark again.

A light in the distance, fast becoming fainter, told me that the Juan Fernandez had doubtless picked up the Monarch's and was steaming away.

When day broke nothing floated within sight of me to tell that a ship had gone to her end beneath the waves a few miles away. I was all that was left of the steamer, and as I thought of her and the wretched blacks burned to death in the after-hold I forgot for a moment my own position—floating helplessly about, without a drop of water to drink, a scorching tropical sun beating down on me.

That day not a sail came in sight, and by night my thirst had become almost unbearable. My head was on fire with fever, my lips parched and swollen, my eyes aching and nearly burned out of their sockets by the fiery glare of the white ocean.

Night came at last, bringing but slight relief; a few hours and the sun would again be beating down upon me. I was afraid to go to sleep, lest I should be washed overboard from the floating door; so I lay half-awake, looking up at the heavens, and every few minutes surveying the long dark line of the horizon, hoping through the long hours to see a light there.

Another day, and the sun rose over the calm ocean with its usual splendor and fiery intensity. Too weak now to raise my head, I lay half-unconscious across the float, waiting for the end, which I knew could not be far off. At last my eyes refused to keep open a second longer, and I fell into a long sleep.

How long it lasted I shall never know. When I opened my eyes again I was lying on a beach and two blacks were bending over me. The door had floated ashore, and I was saved.

A month later I reached a fort where there was a British consul, to whom I told my story, with the exception, of course, of my knocking the skipper off the bridge and perhaps causing his death. The marine insurance underwriters were notified, and a search for the Juan Fernandez, or a steamer answering to her description was instituted. There was no result, however. Nothing was ever heard of her, and the conclusion reached by the underwriters was that she had sustained a serious injury when she rammed the Monarch and had gone down in the first severe gale she encountered.

One thing is certain—Lloyd deserved his fate; but when I think of how I last saw him, and especially of the poor devils in the Monarch's hold, I am sorry, since I could not save them, that I did not remain with the rest of the crew at San Miguel.

At the Spur of Danger
L. Frank Tooker

*Wherein a Cape Horn Gale Proves Again
that It Is an Ill Wind Which Blows Nobody
Any Good*

F ROM THE PORT SIDE OF THE TAFFRAIL, where he was moodily paying out the log-line, the second mate turned for a moment to glower darkly at the man at the wheel.

The squat figure, ill clad for winter weather at sea; the narrow brow, above which a shapeless, fuzzy brown cap sloped upward like a thatched pent-roof; the dark, half-closed eyes, with their pathetic, furtive look; the curly black hair, disclosing only the tips of the thick ears, with their wire-like gold earrings—he knew the type, the second mate told himself with bitter self-pity.

Irrational and stupid, suspicious and quick to take offense, the man would be a thorn in his side to the last day of the voyage. And now it was just beginning!

Reeves turned abruptly and gazed in bitterness off toward the receding coast, low, snow-clad, with the bare fringe of trees looming black against the horizon. The yellow glare of dying day stretched in a narrow wedge of clearing sky above the land, broadening toward the north, where, beyond the Narrows, the smoke of the great city hung in a dun-colored cloud.

In his mind he saw the picture of its streets, with their noisy bustle and hurrying throngs. Its contrast with the watery waste, that for many weeks would heave and roll about him, deepened his home-leaving sense of the inequalities of human existence.

"It's a dog's life," he muttered—"a dog's life, passed with brutes like that"—he jerked his head toward the man at the wheel—"in cold and wet and danger, and never a pleasant thing to think of but getting home again. And like as not you never do. Good Lord! what fools we are!"

Above his head a bit of canvas fluttered, crackling in the freshening breeze, and he turned in a fury on the helmsman.

"Keep her steady, man—steady!" he snapped. "Can't you steer?"

"Steady, sir," said the sailor, and in his nervous eagerness swung the wheel over too far and the bark fell off broad before the wind.

With a muttered curse, the second mate sprang to the wheel, thrust the man aside, and brought the bark back to her course; then, still in a white heat of rage, he jumped to the binnacle.

"There," he roared, pointing, "do you see that—sou'east by east—do you see that mark? Then, keep her there."

He hurried away forward as the captain came on deck, busying himself with setting the decks in order. He was closing the booby-hatch for the night, when the mate came aft from stowing the anchor and stopped for a moment at his side.

The sting of winter was in the wind that swept crackling and keen across the deck, and both men stood with shoulders hunched forward and hands in pockets. Behind them the white glow of the light on the Navesink Highlands alternately deepened and faded against the last faint glow of day.

"It'll be cold turning out at midnight," said the mate.

"Say, Sparrow, you got all the best of the deal in picking the watches," Reeves said complainingly. "Can't the old man tell a lubber when he sees him?

"I don't believe there's a first-rate man in the starboard watch, and that dago back there at the wheel—Pasquale, or whatever he calls himself—he's a little too much for me. Don't know a handspike from a ball of marline."

The mate laughed.

"Oh, Pasquale's all right," he replied easily, "only you don't want to nag at those fellows; it makes them nervous."

"No," sneered the second mate; "you want to treat them like young ladies—wrap them up in cotton batting, and all that sort of thing. I'll cotton batting him."

He went stormily aft.

In the forecastle, Pasquale was sitting on the edge of his bunk, mechanically holding out his hands toward the stove, and turning his face toward each of his mates as they spoke. He rarely spoke himself. They were sizing up officers and ship.

A big Irishman, lying on his back in a bunk, rolled up to a sitting position, and took his pipe from his mouth.

" 'Tis like this," he said oracularly: "ye get a good ship an' a bad afterguard, or a good afterguard an' a bad ship, wan. 'Tis niver anny diff'rent. Now, thim min aft are mild as hens, so the ship's bad. Wet she'll be, says I—wet as a whale's belly. Remimber me worrds come the time."

He rolled back in his bunk again.

"Ay tank da secont madt iss no hen," ventured a Swede. "He hass some spurs, yas; he iss spunky."

"Right you are, Olaf," spoke up a wiry little Liverpooler. " 'E's no lydy; 'e's achin' for a row." He turned to Pasquale. "What was 'e a bullyraggin' you about, Old Earrings?"

"My name it is Pasquale," the Portuguese replied, with simple dignity. "He say I cannot steer. I steer before he is born, yes."

Behind his back, some one twitched an earring sharply, and he sprang to his feet, instantly livid with passion. As he turned on the boyish young fellow who had tormented, him, his hand flew to his sheath-knife.

The lad sprang back, catching up a heavy sea-boot, but with one bound Mike dropped between the two.

"None o' thot, ye murderin' dago!" he growled. "Drop that boot, b'y!"

He pushed Pasquale back upon his bunk, and turned toward the lad, slowly shaking his pipe in his face.

"Ye young divil, if I catch ye playin' anny more monkey tricks aboard I'll make a deck-swab av ye! Mind me worrds!"

"Ah, g'wan, Irish!" jeered the lad. He dropped by Pasquale's side, throwing an arm across his shoulder. "That's all right, old man," he said soothingly; "only a joke. Didn't mean to throw you off your trolley. Forget it."

" 'Tis forget," replied Pasquale, with his pleasant smile.

But it could not be forgotten by his shipmates. His simple-minded trustfulness, which gave unquestioning faith to all that was told him; his willingness to assist in any task, his normal patience under discomfort, all joined with his singular inclination to flame up in uncontrollable passion at trifles that others lightly disregarded, made him a tempting mark for all the horse-play of the forecastle.

Under the constant fire of the crew he grew bewildered and nervous, and his work suffered. At bottom the best seaman aboard, there were times when, in his perturbation, his mistakes were maddening for their childish lack of judgment.

"I haven't struck him yet," Reeves said to the mate one day, with a modest suggestion of pride in his forbearance clearly apparent in his tone, "but some day I'll break loose. I know I shall."

"And get a knife in your back the first dark night for your pains," warned Sparrow.

"Well," retorted Reeves hotly, "if that dago's running this vessel, then—"

"He ain't running her," broke in the mate, "and nothing's further from his thought. Can't you see he's willing and a good sailor? But between you and the crew you've got him up in the air. He ain't himself."

They were standing at the break of the poop in the soft twilight of the Southern seas. It was the second dog-watch, and the crew were skylarking forward. Suddenly there rose a burst of laughter, then a cry of warning, and an iron belaying-pin came skidding along the deck and struck with a crash against the after bulkhead.

With a bound Reeves dropped to the main-deck and ran forward. The mate turned his back and walked to the mizzen-rigging.

He was still standing there when Reeves, breathing heavily, returned and stopped at his side. Sparrow looked up, scanned Reeves from head to foot, and a grim smile flickered about his mouth.

The second mate's right sleeve hung in shreds; a round red mark, dotted with fiery points, showed on his cheek. He was touching it tenderly with the tips of his fingers.

"Have a good time?" asked the mate dryly.

Reeves laughed shortly.

"Look so, don't I?" he answered, and said no more.

"Come, don't keep a good thing to yourself," the mate went on. "What's the matter with your face?"

"Oh, you're interested, after all, are you?" retorted Reeves. "I thought you weren't, by the way you turned your back."

"I wasn't interested in being a witness at a murder trial," replied Sparrow. "I was willing to give the old fellow that chance."

"Oh, that's it, is it? Well, he drove his heel in my face, if you want to know." Without further explanation, Reeves walked away. The mate's eyes followed him.

"He's ashamed of the business," he muttered. "Well, I hope it ain't too late."

He had his doubts the next morning when, from the poop-deck, he saw Pasquale appear. The man limped across the deck in evident pain, and his distorted face, swollen and bruised, made the mate heart-sick.

But later, when he passed Pasquale from time to time, it was the change in his eyes that chiefly roused the mate's foreboding. The furtive, hunted look was gone, and his eyes glowed with a sinister light, reckless, vindictive.

The change showed also in his work. He went stolidly about his tasks, with an apparent indifference to trifling disturbances that left the high quality of his seamanship clear.

In the forecastle he was at last at peace. The common instinct of a community of interest was roused by the second mate's brutal attack, and the crew gave him boisterous sympathy.

Apparently, he was wholly indifferent. His taciturn nature withdrew more and more within itself, and his old quiet but genial yearning for companionship no longer showed in his actions.

Indeed, he had become the avatar of a single idea—the idea of revenge. In his bunk at night, on watch, at the wheel, at work in his hours on deck, he went over and over the plans he had formed, picturing vividly in his mind, with a morbid joy in the image, the last scene when, in one supreme moment, he would wipe out all scores.

And he planned cunningly; there would be no doubt, no chance of discovery. Some dark night, in the storm, the second mate would go aloft, but would not return; he would cross the wave-washed deck, but never reach the point to which his duty called him.

Meanwhile, some subtle hint of his danger was borne in upon the second mate. He grew nervous and furtive, and on dark nights acquired the habit of the rolling, peering eye. One night, as he came aft, side-stepping and halting at intervals, the mate, who had come on deck before the close of his watch below, gazed at him in wonder.

"What's the matter with you?" he demanded, with a grin. "Been drinking, or practicing fandango steps?"

Reeves laughed shamefacedly.

"If I don't turn up some night at the end of my watch don't be surprised," he said.

The mate looked up quickly.

"Anything happened?" he asked gravely.

"No, it's only a feeling; but Pasquale is after me. I know it."

"I'd make some excuse to take him in my watch if I could," said the mate thoughtfully, "but I don't know as it would do any good."

Reeves shook his head impatiently.

"It wouldn't. And he'd know. I think he knows I understand, and he rather enjoys it. It's a private affair"—he laughed, with a touch of nervousness— "and I guess we'll not make a fuss. I'm going to die game if he gets me. Only, so long against the time when it comes." He walked away.

The captain laughed scornfully when the mate told him the next morning.

"Reeves has got an attack of acute conscience, that's all, and it serves him right," he said. "What do you want me to do? Put the old fellow in irons on suspicion of meditating murder? Nonsense! I never heard of such a thing.

"Tell Reeves to let him alone if he hasn't the nerve to pay the piper when he dances. Why, Pasquale's the best sailorman aboard, and that ain't the kind to take a little unpleasantness to heart if it isn't followed up. You ought to know that, Mr. Sparrow."

With a wave of his hand that dismissed the subject, the captain ambled to his room and closed the door.

It really began to appear that the captain was right. They had been steadily rolling south, and had entered the region of alternating calms and thunder-storms, ten degrees north of the equator.

Night after night, under a moonless sky, they had raced for hours through the blackness of the Pit, with the rain pouring down in blinding sheets and the deck continually swept by the choppy seas of that latitude, and nothing had happened at all.

More than once, when the storm had broken, in the stifling hush, as he walked aft, Reeves had suddenly remembered his fear, forgotten for a moment in the rush of strenuous tasks. There had been chances enough for Pasquale, he had to confess to himself as he recalled some moment at the braces, alone at the lee rail with Pasquale, with the dragging weight of the water roaring about their knees.

He began to be ashamed of his suspicions and his fright.

Pasquale, too, had recognized the chances; had gloated over them—and let them pass. It was with him the instinct of the cat with the mouse, the recognition of adequate power, the pleasure in delaying the moment of supreme joy.

One night, indeed, he had almost shot his bolt. The memory of it lingered on in his mind as a morbid pleasure, though not without something of vague regret that he had let the moment pass.

He had been relieved from the wheel, and, half blinded by the sheets of rain that drove across the deck, he stumbled along the lee gangway on his way to shelter behind the center-house. The gale was crying aloud in the rigging aloft, and the swash of the seas tumbling over the rail and hissing across the deck added to the indescribable tumult of the night. The darkness was intense.

As he advanced he became aware of a singular sound—a muffled, jangling blow that at regular intervals beat against the side of the vessel amidships. His trained sense, alert to its unusualness amid all the orderly noises of a ship in a storm, rightly guessed its meaning.

A lee topsail-brace had parted, and a block attached to it was swaying against the side of the vessel whenever she rolled to port. He quickened his step, meaning to haul it aboard and secure it.

Then suddenly he paused. The second mate had already been drawn to the spot, and was at the moment leaning far out over the rail in his endeavor to seize the hanging missile as it swung against the side. To Pasquale it seemed fate's own hour.

In his quick recognition of it, with a sudden bracing of all his muscles for the spring, he crouched low. Then, in a flash, his mind, in which the brooding thought of revenge had become an obsession, looking beyond the imminent consummation of its desire, saw life a blank. Something of power, he dimly felt, would be gone from him.

With a quick shrinking from the thought of the last act, he stepped back into the encircling gloom. He would wait a little longer.

They passed the equator, with its long days of calms and baffling winds, and caught at last the southeast trades. With sheets hauled aft, yards braced up, and sunlight flooding the watery ways, Reeves' forebodings dropped from him like a fever.

"I guess I gave the old fellow credit for too much spunk," he said to Sparrow one day as they stood at the rail. "If he didn't get me when we were having our little fracas he wouldn't at all. It's a sudden flash, these dagoes' anger, and then all over."

"Well, I hope so," Sparrow replied. "I don't pretend to understand what notions he's got in his head, but whatever they are, I don't believe he's given to changing them. He's a queer old duffer."

"Well, anyway, I don't believe murder's one of them," Reeves answered, with ready lightness.

"All the same, I'd keep my eyes open if I were you," Sparrow warned, with the easy dubiety with which one views the serious problems of his friends. "I steer clear of rows with these Southern peoples, myself."

"I wish you'd had him in your watch at first," retorted Reeves. "It's easy talking about holding your temper when you've got a watch like yours."

He walked away, vexed at the veiled reproof in his superior's answer, and Sparrow seated himself on the rail and leaned back against the mizzen-rigging. It was his watch below, but, unable to sleep, he had sought relief on deck from the stuffy air in his stateroom. He turned idly as he heard Reeves returning.

At the main-hatch, where Pasquale sat patching a heavy lower sail, he paused. Pasquale did not look up. His large, sinewy hand moved swiftly and with regular precision as he thrust the sail-needle through the thick canvas and drew the heavy waxed cord out with a snap that marked unusual strength.

The stitches were as even and close as those of a woman's embroidery. Reeves casually noted that the hand was much the same color as the sailmaker's leather palm that it wore—the hue of weathered mahogany.

"No need to take so much pains with that patch," he said, with a good-natured sharpness of tone. "The sail's about gone, anyway; but that stitching of yours will outlast us both. No need of it."

Sparrow, casually watching them, was drawing his tobacco-pouch from his pocket as Reeves turned to walk away, when suddenly his hand, half-way to his pipe, paused, every faculty arrested by the startling scene upon which he gazed.

Pasquale had not stirred from his stoop-shouldered sewing position, but slowly his eyes turned to follow Reeves; his mouth widened in an unmistakable grin—a grin so charged with malignity that Sparrow felt a chill pass down his back.

In the half-closed eyes of the sailor the same look glittered, implacable, triumphant, sinister. The thin lips, drawn back from the long, yellow teeth, stiffened in wide, thin lines.

Suddenly his hands tautened on the strong waxed cord with which he was sewing, and it parted. A drop of blood fell on the white canvas and spread.

Pasquale stared blankly at it as he lifted the sail to his knee. He had not felt the sting of the cutting cord. Suddenly, as he gazed at it, Sparrow saw him cross himself; his shoulders shook with a soundless laugh.

Shaken by the import of the scene, Sparrow waited until the watch had changed, then, for a moment, slipped down to Reeves' room. As he closed the door softly the second mate turned in his berth, startled.

"What's up?" he demanded.

"Reeves," said the mate, "don't take a step on deck at night without thought, and don't let that Portugee out of your sight. He's crazy with murderous hate."

He told what he had seen.

"Oh, I don't suppose he loves me," Reeves replied, trying to speak lightly, "but I'm not worrying now. We hit it off pretty well together. But you were right about one thing—he's a good sailor. I let him see I know it."

His manner seemed to imply that in his magnanimity lay every assurance of security. But Sparrow shook his head.

"They follow things up, those fellows; they never forget," he said.

Reeves laughed.

"Look out, or he'll get on your nerves, too. You're welcome to him. Still, I don't think there's any harm in him. But I'll keep an eye on him, don't you fear."

"Well, I'll get rid of him somehow in Callao," declared the mate, "if I have to put him in the hospital myself. He ain't safe at large."

Two weeks later they were nearing the Horn, and daily the air grew colder with the approach of the southern winter. The far horizon began to lose the sharp outlines of the region of the trade-winds in an indefinable blurring of sea and sky.

Every morning day broke with only a gray suggestion of light. It was as if they sailed through a formless, dripping world in which the sea seemed only sound and the sky a drab-colored void, half mist, half darkness. Later a watery sun would break through the flying wrack, only to close in again as night fell early.

But at last there came a day when, with all hands shortening sail in the furious rush of the gale, the bark went staggering ahead through the toppling roar of the seas. The fog was gone, and through the gray, thin wrack sweeping up in an arch from the southwest here and there a star shone dim and cold.

A grayish whiteness of the long morning twilight of the far south had diffused itself over the waste of tumbling waters when the mate hurried aft.

"Bowsprit's badly sprung, sir," he screamed in the captain's ear. "May go—any moment. Got—do something. Everything for'ard—go with it. Sprung just inside—cap."

The captain was furious with fate.

"Damn fine place—happen," he roared—"right in the Cape drift—howling gale! Bear off—soon's you can—take all strain off for'ard. Got to fish it—Mr. Sparrow—quick, too. Nice business!"

It was nice business. A royal-yard is an easy chair by the fire compared with the end of a bowsprit in a Cape Horn gale, and before the short day closed more than one man of the crew, working doggedly in that dizzy place, was seasick for the first time in years.

They had run before the wind to lessen the strain on the weakened bowsprit, and with two spare spars lashed along its length, bound the three together, "fishing" it. All day they worked furiously, clinging to downhauls and gaskets whenever the bow dropped and a great sea leaped up, burying them in the cold green water.

Numb with cold, white and spent with toil and sickness, they struggled on in a dumb acquiescence to the necessity that knew no weakness, recognized no human limitation.

Dusk fell before the work was done. Man after man had crawled back to the forecastle-deck, and only Reeves, Olaf, and Pasquale were left for the finishing touch.

Reeves, astride the spar, with his back to the bowsprit-cap, was binding the lashing fast with marline, with Olaf helping him. Behind him Pasquale sat with a marlinespike and the ball. Reeves passed the last bit of marline about the lashing, made it fast, and straightened up.

"Done at last," he muttered.

Throwing one leg over, he stepped off upon the bowsprit-shrouds, and rose stiffly to his feet. Numb with cold, and cramped by long sitting, his left leg had gone to sleep. As his weight dropped upon it, the bow rose high in air, his leg doubled under him, and he fell, striking his head against the spar, and dropping like a log in the hollowed wave below.

A cry of horror rose from the forecastle-deck, but before a man could turn, something dark shot down from the end of the bowsprit, sank, and rose in a welter of spray. Then, as a great gray roller lifted its crest to meet the dropping bow, two dark spots appeared in the whirling foam, an arm shot out, clutched at the rail, and strong hands drew Pasquale and Reeves in safety to the deck.

Pasquale stumbled stiffly to his feet. He shook himself like a dog, and looked about him with a grin.

"Pret' damn' good luck, heh?" he said.

Then suddenly his face changed; he looked almost sheepish. It had suddenly come to him that he had saved the life he had meant to take.

He turned slowly and gazed down at the form of Reeves, just stirring to consciousness. A wave of tenderness swept over him, and he stooped shyly and patted Reeves' shoulder.

"Pret' damn' good luck, heh?" he repeated softly, and turning, walked away.

An hour later Reeves came slowly forward and stopped at the fore-rigging, where Pasquale stood looking out into the darkness to windward.

Reeves touched him on the arm, and he turned quickly, with the red port light in his face.

"You did me a good turn, Pasquale," he said diffidently, "and I won't forget it." He looked away, gulped, and added: "I guess I wasn't just fair to you that—"

Pasquale waved a protesting hand; his smile was pleasant.

"I guess mens what been toget'er where we been they don't have to say how they feel, sir; they *know*. Is it not so, sir?"

A Treasure in Turtle

E.A. Suverkrop

*Of a Professor Who Discovered a Prehis-
toric Specimen and a Chief Engineer Who
Became Interested in Fossils*

ORDINARILY, I AM NOT VERY STRONG ON NATURAL HISTORY, but I have had a
certain affection for turtles ever since an experience, about a year ago,
with a prehistoric specimen, Trionyx by name. The beast may have been
prehistoric, but he certainly was not extinct, for he bit my little toe nearly
off—but I am getting ahead of my yarn.

I was chief engineer of the Pelorus. The morning of sailing day from
Liverpool I had just stepped from my room to run up to the superintendent's
office, when I met a very dignified old gentleman, with an air of refinement
and a pair of blue glasses, who politely asked me if I could direct him to the
chief officer.

As the mate was just at the head of the gangway, I took the old chap
in tow, and heard him introduce himself as Erasmus Masson, Professor of
Paleontology at the Jonessonian Institute.

When I got back from the super's office the mate tackled me.

"Say, Mr. Dudd," he began, "I wish you would keep your snake-charmers
to yourself."

"What's up now?" said I.

"Oh," he replied, "the old duck with the blue port-holes has been talking
the head off me about an extinct Eocene turtle—which isn't extinct, as he
has just dug one out of the ground alive and kicking. I told him if he had
found a kerosene turtle he'd better put Rockefeller next; but the old chump
didn't see the point. For fear I might call it out of its name again, he insisted
on writing it down on a piece of paper.

"Here it is—'Trionyx, Eocene turtle.' He says the beast is probably two
million years old, and— But you tackle the old man yourself. He can tell you
more about that turtle than its own mother could. He has engaged a whole
room for himself and the turtle, which he keeps in a sort of rabbit-hutch."

We cleared that afternoon. The next day I found the old professor on the
promenade deck in a steamer-chair, and alongside him, in another chair, was
a remarkably pretty young woman. She was so remarkably pretty, indeed,
that I spoke to the old man—and incidentally to the girl.

She asked me if one of those gray-painted Belgian oil-tank steamers was
a man-of-war. Rather than disappoint her, I said yes, and even went so far as
to tell her that it was H.M.S. Terrible. After such a sacrifice on my part, it's

not to be wondered at that the girl and I struck up a fast friendship.

She told me a whole lot about the old professor and the work he was doing. It seems he had a theory that many of the prehistoric animals were not extinct, and he had made extended searches in England to try to discover some of the ancient turtles.

The last of these had been crowned with success. In the London clay, at a depth of one hundred and fifty-four feet, he had discovered a living Trionyx, one of the Eocene turtles. This he was bringing home to confound the scientists who had laughed at him and his theories.

Miss Masson and I got along well together after the manner of young people on shipboard, but behind all her friendliness was a sort of reserve that I could not break through. Some fear or apprehension seemed to possess her. The only times that I got her to forget herself were when I told her the experiences I had been through in different parts of the world.

Smuggling yarns pleased her best of all, especially one about running two hundred cases of whisky and fifty thousand cigars ashore at St. Vincent, Cape de Verde, while we had the customs men in irons down in the forepeak and their places on deck taken by four of our own men, with the customs men's uniforms on and their guns over their shoulders.

I chatted a good deal with the old professor, but he used to talk over my head most of the time. He was full up with his turtle, and as a special mark of his favor he took me to his room and showed me the beast. The turtle was not much in comparison with those I have seen in the Dry Tortugas, or even on the turtle islands near Karachi, where I have turned many a one with a handspike.

The most peculiar thing about it was the great thickness of the top shell. I mentioned this to the professor, but he said that local conditions governed the shape and thickness of the shell. Later on I found that this was true.

One evening I had been playing cards in my room with a young fellow who hailed from Kentucky. All of a sudden he dropped his cards, leaned over, and whispered:

"Billy, I like you, and don't want to see you get into trouble. I advise you to cut out the professor and his wife."

"Wife?" said I. "I didn't know he had a wife."

"The girl he calls his daughter is really his wife," said he.

"Well," I retorted, "I do not as a general thing permit any one to dictate to me whom I shall or shall not associate with. Why do you tell me this?"

With that he threw back the lapel of his coat, opened his vest, and there, pinned to his suspenders, was a customs inspector's badge.

"They are a bad lot, but I guess I have them this clip," said he, and then he shut up like a clam.

I was rather hurt to think that Letty was married. Of course, it was none of my business, but I liked the girl, and I had no love for the customs service. Finally it occurred to me that the best thing I could do would be to give the girl a tip that a customs shark was watching her.

The next evening Letty and I were taking a turn on deck. She had discovered that I had a weakness for poetry, and was repeating poem after poem to me—some of Longfellow and some of Kipling. It was a hard thing to think that this innocent-looking girl was a smuggler, but from the tip the secret-service man had given me it was a pretty sure thing she was. However, next day we should be in port, and it would be a shame to see her hustled into a patrol-wagon and unceremoniously carted off to jail.

Well, as I said before, we were pacing up and down, and I was trying to make up my mind to tip her off about the customs man, when he came out of the smoking-room and walked past us. As he passed he gave me a look as much as to say, "I thought I told you to cut that out."

As soon as he was out of ear-shot, Letty turned to me and said:

"Oh, I do hate that man!"

"You hate him? Why?" said I.

"Yes, I hate him, he is so sneaky. I think he's a thief and wants to steal something my father has. I saw him looking through the keyhole in father's door the other night."

That gave me my chance, so I blurted out without further delay:

"He's a secret-service man connected with the customs service. He runs smugglers down."

With that she turned dead white, but never answered. The next moment she excused herself and went below, leaving me alone on deck.

We were due in port the next afternoon, so I went below to make up my report. Although I had an outside room, it was so stuffy that I sent down to the storeroom for a sheet of Muntz metal to make a wind-sail.

I bent the sheet to the circle of the port-hole and pushed it out, the spring of the metal keeping it from falling overboard. The wind, striking the metal scoop, was diverted into the room, making things more bearable, and I worked away till nearly two o'clock in the morning.

I was just about through, and was thinking how very still the night was, the only sound being the faint purring of the engines away below the water-line, when I was suddenly startled by a woman's voice, borne on the night-wind through the port-hole.

"The chief engineer told me so, and I know he would not lie to me."

Then a man's voice whispered back:

"But think what it means—we lose everything!"

"It's better to lose everything and go free than to lose everything and go to jail into the bargain."

This began to get interesting, so I shut off my electric light and stepped out of the room. The alleyway was deserted as I made my way to the companionway and went on deck. Coming from the brightly lighted companionway into the gloom, I went behind the smoking-room and shut my eyes for a moment, in order to get them accustomed to the darkness as soon as possible.

The night was clear, but there was no moon. I looked cautiously around to see who the whisperers might be. Away aft I could just make out two shadowy forms, and—what was that crouching behind the ventilator?

A man! What could he be doing, sneaking out on deck at that hour of the night?

I had a pair of soft slippers on, and I stepped silently over toward him. So intent was he in watching the two shadowy forms—which I now made out to be a man and a woman—that he did not hear me.

I stood and watched him for a minute or two, and as I stood there he slipped his hand into his hip-pocket and pulled a big revolver, half the length of my arm.

"This is about where I begin to make a noise like a chief engineer," I thought. "This looks very much like a case of jealousy, and it may be murder."

I reached down, and grabbed his wrist and sang out:

"You'd better drop that thing, mister. It may be loaded, and go off and hurt some one."

The fellow's nerves were all keyed up, and the shock of my catching hold of him made him pull the trigger. There was a loud report from the gun, a scream from the girl, and in a minute the deck-officers were out. The second mate brought a lamp out of the binnacle to see who it was that had done the shooting.

In the meantime, I had taken the pistol away from the man, and had him pinned down to the deck, nice and comfortable, face down, with my knee in the small of his back and both his arms bent up so that his wrists were lying good and easy against his shoulder-blades—a trick I learned from a Jap wrestler I once knew.

Well, he turned out to be the secret-service agent, and was in a towering rage, fairly frothing at the mouth—wanted me put in irons, or thrown overboard, or anything, so long as I was properly punished.

By this time the captain was on deck and heard my part of the story. The secret-service man babbled to the skipper, but the old man stood pat; said he didn't care a continental if the fellow with the gun was the President of the United States instead of a common dub of a customs man—the Pelorus was his ship, and if he didn't shut his mouth and behave himself he'd be put in irons and clapped down in the lazaretto.

"Mr. Dudd has done perfectly right, and would have been justified in killing you," said the old man.

The customs man blathered and sputtered on about smuggling, and he would not be satisfied till two of the stewardesses went into Letty's room and reported her sleeping soundly. The doctor and the bedroom steward went into the professor's cabin, and found him snoring like a grampus.

The next afternoon we reached quarantine and were boarded by the revenue cutter. The moment she came alongside, the secret-service man buttonholed the inspector, and the Pelorus was anchored in the bay while the cutter returned to the Battery for an extra draft of searchers.

Down they came, and turned the saloon of the old packet upside down and inside out. A female inspector tackled Letty, and a male inspector tackled the professor, but after a three hours' search they seemed to lose hope, and gave it up. Then the secret-service man came in for a lot of hard names.

After the disturbance was all over we steamed to our berth in time to land the saloon and second-cabin passengers and send the steerage down to Ellis Island on a lighter.

That night I was pretty well tired out, from the loss of sleep the night before, so I turned in early. I fell asleep the moment my head touched the pillow.

I had slept I do not know how long, when I was awakened by feeling something moving in the bed. The next moment I felt something grip the little toe of my left foot. With a yell, I sprang out of the bunk, striking my head against a deck-beam, and jumped for the electric switch.

When the light was turned on I found the professor's infernal turtle fast to my toe—and a fine time I had getting him adrift.

I got his jaws apart with a pair of pliers and flung him on the floor good and hard, but not hard enough to hurt him much, for he had a thick shell, and besides, I have the business instinct pretty strong, and it struck me that I could make the professor pay me a better ransom for the beast alive than dead.

Well, he struck the floor, and he bounced to the other end of the cabin. I was the most surprised man you ever saw. I rubbed my eyes and pinched myself to see if I was awake, and then the whole thing dawned on me in an instant. I say the whole thing, but I could not account for the presence of the turtle in my room.

I put the beast in the seat-locker and turned in again, but it was some time before the pain in my toe would let me sleep. Completely worn out, I fell asleep at last, and did not wake till the mess-room boy brought me my coffee.

I had quite a lot to attend to the next day, and it was nearly two o'clock before I had a chance to get ashore with the turtle in my valise. When I reached the customs man at the gate he took a cursory glance at the grip, as

I opened it, and passed it and me through.

I took the Ninth Avenue elevated train down to Cortlandt Street, walked over to the custom-house, on Wall Street, went in, and asked for the collector of the port. He was not in, but his assistant was, telling stories to a couple of his chums, and he did not look a bit cheerful at my interrupting him.

"Well, Mr. Dudd," said he, looking at my card, "what can I do for you?"

"I am just in from a foreign voyage, and I've come here to find out what reward a man gets if he finds people trying to smuggle and informs on them," said I, sort of innocent-like.

"Fifty per cent of what's left after expenses are paid," said he.

So I opened the grip and pulled the turtle out. Then, assuming the professor's best style, I ran my fingers through my hair, puffed out my chest, and began:

"Gentlemen, I have here, as any student of paleontology can see at a glance, the only specimen in existence of a living Eocene turtle. Yes, gentlemen, in the dim twilight of the dawn of time this Trionyx—for such is the generic name—was crawling lazily through the ooze and slime of the then rush-bound shore which later on was to be called the London clay.

"Thousands upon thousands of years this Trionyx has lived, and with ordinary care he ought to last a few years longer. Scientists contend that the Eocene turtles are all extinct, all dead thousands of years ago.

"I ask you, does this specimen look extinct? Put your finger in between his powerful mandibles and see and feel for yourselves whether he be extinct or not. He was found, at a depth of one hundred and fifty-four feet, in the London clay—"

At this moment the assistant collector, not taking the mirror across the room into account, winked at his chums, tapped his forehead, and whispered: "Crazy as a coot." Then raising his voice he said:

"But what has this to do with smuggling?"

"I'm getting down to that," I replied. "This specimen was brought over to this country by a man posing as a professor of paleontology. He lost it, but it had been his intention to smuggle it into the country, and he would have done so if his plans hadn't miscarried."

The young chap was beginning to lose his temper—which was just what I was waiting for—and turned to me again with:

"That may all be true, but what has that to do with actual smuggling?"

"Well," said I, rather lamely, "while no actual attempt was made to smuggle the turtle into the country, for the reasons that I have already given, still, if the turtle had not been lost an attempt would have been made, and I have come to hand the turtle over and collect the reward."

While I was getting this out of my system he reached for a little paper-covered pamphlet, turned over the pages rapidly, winked almost audibly at his chums, and after glancing at a page about the middle of the book, said in melodramatic style:

"Mr. Dudd, on behalf of the customs department of the great United States, which I so unworthily represent, I offer you, not fifty per cent, but one hundred per cent, of the reward. You may take the er—er—what's its name?"

"Trionyx," I interjected.

"Yes, you may take the diamond-back terrapin up-town, sell it, and pocket the proceeds. Thus does a grateful country reward its zealous and patriotic citizens."

His chums sung out "Bravo!" burst into a roar of laughter, and clapped their hands. After the noise had subsided he turned to me.

"Seriously, Mr. Dudd," he said, "according to paragraph 689, turtles are duty-free, so, you see, you have put yourself to a great deal of trouble to come here to tell me of a crime against the United States which could not be committed. If it were not for your evident sincerity in the matter, I should be inclined to think you were trying to joke with me.

"My advice to you is to take the turtle home and get your wife to cook it for you, though I suspect you will find it a trifle tough at its age. I am very busy, as you can see, and I wish you a very good day."

Well, I had done my duty by my country, so I put old Trionyx back in the grip and went up to my hotel, registered, and got the clerk to put the grip in the safe.

Then I strolled down Broadway and east on Maiden Lane to Nassom's jewelry store, where I asked for Mr. Nassom. The clerk said that he was in the private office, and asked me for my card.

I scribbled "important" in the corner, and two minutes later I was ushered into Mr. Nassom's presence. In him I at once recognized old Professor Masson, minus the blue glasses. As soon as he laid eyes on me I could see that he recognized me, too, and if there had been any doubt about it his first words would have settled that.

"There's no use your trying to blackmail me, if that's your game. I'm down and out—I have no money."

"I didn't come here to blackmail you," said I. "I came here on an entirely different errand. Knowing you to be interested in paleontology, and also somewhat of a gourmet, I thought you might be glad to get a chance to buy a prehistoric diamond-back terrapin belonging to the Eocene period, genus Trionyx. It was found at a depth of—"

While I was getting this off, Nassom—or Professor Masson—was a sight to see. He was all crouched up in his chair, his eyes rolling and his talon-like fingers grasping the arms of his chair convulsively. When he found his voice he fairly shrieked:

"Where is it? You can't possibly have it! By now it must be at the bottom of the sea!"

"No," said I, "it's not at the bottom of the sea. It's at the bottom of my valise, in the bottom of the safe, in an hotel at the bottom of a street near here.

"The night before we got in, when you and your daughter were out on deck, about two o'clock in the morning, I was in my room. You and your daughter made such a racket whispering about me above my port that I heard you, and came out on deck to find out what deluded idiot it was that took me for a second Washington, who could not tell a lie.

"It was a good job that I did, for that secret-service man might have filled you full of lead if I hadn't been there to stop him. When he did fire the pistol off you dropped the turtle overboard—as you thought—ran below, turned in, and pretended to be asleep. The turtle struck the wind-sail in my port-hole and bounced into my room.

"As my bed had not been slept in that night, the mess-room boy did not make it up the next day. The turtle happened to get under the bedclothes, and remained there till I turned in last night, when I found him—or, rather, he found me, and nearly took my toe off.

"When he grabbed me by the toe I sprang out of bed, pried his jaws apart, and threw him on the floor. The fossil shell, which you had glued so carefully to the upper shell of a common, everyday, contemporaneous turtle, came off, and I found myself in a veritable Aladdin's cave—the floor strewn with diamonds.

"I put the diamonds back where they came from, glued the extra shell on again, took the turtle—intending to turn it over to the authorities—to the customhouse, and told the collector some one had tried to smuggle it in. He was not in a humor to be disturbed, thought I was crazy, told me—what I knew already—that a diamond-back terrapin—so he facetiously dubbed it—was not dutiable, and told me, also, to take it and clear out, which hurt my feelings. The turtle is no use to me, so I am willing to consider an offer."

The upshot of the matter was that Nassom, or Masson, made me an offer of twice what he would have had to pay as duty. This I accepted, as it would have been impossible for me to dispose of the diamonds myself.

Letty was his daughter, after all, and his accomplice, too; but she was a fine girl, and, in spite of her being a smuggler, I liked her. I don't think she had any hard feelings about what I had done, for the next trip, when I got into port, she gave me a little gold turtle with its back studded with diamonds for a watch-charm.

"How did I know where to find Nassom?"

That was easy. I saw the name Nassom scribbled on the fly-leaf of a book Letty was reading one day, and it struck me as strange that she could make a mistake in writing her own name, so I asked her about it, and she became quite confused.

When I left my hotel I strolled down Maiden Lane with an unformed, vague idea in my mind that I might be able to find a diamond broker who would buy the diamonds. Of course, I would have to be very careful in approaching any one with such fine stones—one at a time would probably be the only way to get rid of them.

Ever judge of character by sizing up a man's name? Well, that's what I was trying to do as I paced along Maiden Lane, reading the signs as I went. When I got opposite 1742, there, staring me in the face, in large gold letters, was, "Jacob Nassom, Diamond Broker."

The fly-leaf of Letty's book flashed into my memory in an instant. It was a queer combination, and I decided to try my luck. The luck was good.

When Famine Drives

George Homer Meyer

*Wherein the Old Question of the Survival
of the Fittest Is Discussed in a New Way
on a Raft at Sea*

BY MIDNIGHT, NOTING THAT THERE WAS NO LONGER ANY SOUND but that of
heavy breathing from the group of sleepers about the broken mast,
Norton thought that his time had come. The waves had gone down, as if in
answer to his unconscious prayer, and the heavy raft scarcely moved upon
the surface of the sea.

The risks in any case were great, but with the slumbers of the five as
sound as they seemed to be, at least there was ground for hope. If only he
could avoid awakening them by his own movements, by the launching of
the little dinghy! If only he could make his way to Evelyn without giving the
alarm! If only!

The Malay lay nearest of the five. He slept with lips apart, and Norton
could see the gleam of his white teeth even in the night. He shuddered with
loathing and hate, remembering that same wolfish whiteness and the cruel
light in the snaky eyes when the dreaded words had been spoken.

And Mariano had spoken them—Mariano the Spaniard, huge and grim,
but upon whose faith and true-heartedness he would, until that fatal instant,
have wagered his own soul!

From the Malay, from Jurgen the Finn, the Cockney Skelly, or Hugo the
Martinique negro, famished and desperate as they were, he was prepared
for any cold-blooded selfishness and cruelty. But, wolfish and wild as the
gleam in their sunken eyes had grown when day followed day with no sign
of rescue, not one had uttered a threatening word.

True, there had been moments when his heart had sickened at the glances
they had turned upon the girl, moments when it had seemed that he must leap
to his feet, scream aloud the suspicion and defiance in his soul, and force at
once the question—but he had invariably controlled himself, lest he should
change into fact what might otherwise prove to be but a needless fear.

In those moments of desperation, when the outbreak trembled on his lips,
he had invariably counted on one man among the five to stand with him to
the end—on Mariano. And Mariano, at the last, had put into spoken words
the horror:

"Better the weak should die and the strong live than that all alike should
perish!"

That was all. Only a whisper in the group of clustered, unkempt heads, of faces haggard with famine—a whisper too low to be heard by the girl who lay awake only a rod away. But the look that came at once upon the faces of the four, the sickening thrill that caused his own frame to shudder, made plain its meaning.

A cry of wrath and loathing had trembled on his lips, checked in the instant of utterance by Mariano's hand upon his arm and the low sternness of his voice:

"Hush! Would you tell her what awaits her? Fool! Let her die but once!"

But not even with that warning had he been able to control his fury absolutely. The Malay, squatting opposite, had turned his snake eyes toward the girl, his lips parted and his white teeth, two of them filed to a point, gleaming like those of a wolf.

Forgetting for an instant his new-born hate for Mariano, Norton leaned suddenly forward and struck the islander on the mouth. There was a quick start, a snarl, and a crooked creese flashed wickedly. The girl screamed, suddenly aroused, and sprang upright, staggering with weakness and fear, just as Mariano's huge hand shot forward and dashed the Malay backward.

Norton was standing erect, his hands clenched, his form quivering. Skelly, the negro, and the Finn did not move, but stared stolidly at the scene.

"Put up your knife," said Mariano coldly, a gesture adding to his meaning. "And you, young sir, be not so hasty with your hands."

The Malay's face twisted into an expression of indescribable viciousness, but he obeyed. Then Mariano added, too low for the frightened girl to hear, but in a whisper that burned into Norton's soul:

"It is settled. We will wait till morning. Perhaps there will come a sail. If not—"

He broke off, and his dark glance swept the circle slowly, meeting last and longest Norton's eyes of fury. And the Malay's teeth gleamed again between his swollen lips.

When they lay down to sleep that night—Norton could have laughed at the thought of sleep—he saw that his own place was so near that of the man he had struck that he could almost have touched the islander. True, he placed himself within reach of that wicked creese, but he chose to risk this. Whoever else moved during the dark watches of the night, Norton vowed it should not be the Malay.

But midnight had come, the islander had never moved, and Norton felt that now or never his work must be done.

With all caution he gained his knees, then waited, listening, a moment in a silence so deep that it was almost appalling. There was no movement about him, no sound save that of breathing.

Catlike, he crept from his place, his feet, covered only by his thick woolen socks, making no sound upon the planks. His low shoes were in the bosom of his shirt. There was nothing else for him to carry.

There had been no food on the raft for three days past, and the last drop of water had been swallowed on the evening before. It was something to remember that the girl—Mariano's black thought had not then been put into words—had been given her share, a share that could not have done more than dampen her parched throat.

Norton remembered even in this moment the unquestioning, confidence with which she had accepted her infinitesimal portion—remembered, too, the surly, savage suspicion with which four of her companions in misery and misfortune, all but Mariano and himself, had viewed the measuring of those last drops, and he caught himself grating his teeth together at the thought of the contrast.

But there was no time now for idle hatred.

In a moment he had crept to where she lay, sleeping soundly enough beneath the sheltering fold of sail-cloth. Gently—ever so gently—he placed his hand upon her cheek, choosing this method of awakening her in order to check the cry of alarm he feared.

"Evelyn—Miss Larston!" he whispered.

She was awake in an instant, but she made no movement and uttered no sound. Dark as it was, he could see the dark eyes staring from the white and wasted face into his own.

Even in that instant of dread and doubt he felt his heart throb at the unbidden thought that in the first instant of her awakening she had known him—had known him and realized that he could only be there to do her service.

But in another second he had crushed aside all but his duty and the task before him.

"Say nothing," he whispered. "Make no sound. Come with me to the boat."

For ten seconds, perhaps, she gazed into his eyes, silently, questioningly. Then she laid her thin hand for an instant upon his with the faintest suggestion of pressure, and more noiselessly than he had believed a human being could move she arose and stood beside him.

Silently he took her hand in his, as one who would lead a child where the way was rough or wearisome, and together they crossed the planking of the raft to where the little dinghy lay. It had been flung from the deck of the sinking steamer at the last moment, possibly with scarcely a thought as to why this was done.

Certainly the tiny craft had little place in the calculations of those shipwrecked far out at sea. It had been no part of the lost steamer's equipment—merely the property of a passenger who had had his own plans for its use. Two persons were all that it could hold on the kindest sea.

But if the boat was small it was also light, and Norton, wasted as were the muscles of his once stalwart arms, had little difficulty in lifting it bodily from the planks, awkward as was its shape. In a moment he had slid it smoothly into the water. Then he knelt upon the edge of the raft, holding the boat so that it should not jar against the planking, and beckoned the girl to step on board.

She did so fearlessly, though trembling with weakness until a touch of his hand steadied her. It was little he could do to aid, fearful as he was of the safety of the frail craft, but in a moment she was safely seated.

He was preparing to follow her, when her lifted hand arrested him.

"The oars," she whispered, so low that he could scarcely hear.

He had all but forgotten them, and it was with almost an audible exclamation of impatience that he turned to reach for them. Then he stopped, staring.

One of the group about the broken mast had raised himself on his elbow and was gazing toward him. There could be but one head, one pair of shoulders, so massive. Dark as it was, Norton knew Mariano.

The blood seemed to leave his heart for an instant, then surged back again with a brave man's fierce determination to yield nothing to this chance of an untoward fate. He stooped forward to lift the oars, resolute to spring with them aboard the dinghy, and trust to good fortune and his own active hands to win free before the wrathful rush which he foresaw could reach him.

And then again he paused, staring once more.

Mariano's huge head had sunk again upon the planking. Norton saw the massive shoulders and neck shift a little in a sleepy man's search for greater comfort. Then the giant lay still.

Norton could scarcely believe what he saw. Moonless as was the night, he had made out clearly the movements of the prostrate man. That his own head and figure, black against the sky, should not be visible was more than he could understand.

But he stooped, still wondering, and lifted the oars—then stumbled over a projection in the rough planking and let them both fall with a crash.

It was but an instant thereafter when, snarling like a pack of starved wolves, the five were upon him.

In an instant, however, he had found time to grasp the oars again and thrust them into the boat. But to get aboard himself, even to push the dinghy from the raft, was impossible in the face of that beastlike rush.

The Malay was first, his white teeth with the two sharpened points gleaming between his parted lips, the crooked blade of his long creese glittering. Norton was still stooping—he saw the thrusting blade, he could almost feel it in his quivering flesh—and then the islander suddenly fell crashing down, his head projecting beyond the edge of the raft and his face splashing in the water.

What he had tripped upon, Norton had no time to think. Mariano's giant figure was looming over him, and just behind the mighty Spaniard was the negro, then the Cockney Skelly, with the slower Finn in the rear.

Norton met the sweeping rush as best he might. For a second or two his hands beat fiercely on breasts and faces as they came within his reach, but it seemed that he had scarcely drawn a breath when he was down. The three crowded above him, snarling and worrying, wolflike in truth now if they had not been before. But no blow reached him at once, though to his dazed eyes it seemed that all were striking at him together.

They were in one another's way, and Mariano's great bulk especially impeded the efforts of his fellows, while his own, for the time, at least, seemed also vain. Even while he looked for death, even while he grew mad with dread for Evelyn, Norton wondered at their awkwardness.

But another was still to be reckoned with. The Malay had writhed backward upon the raft. Now he turned suddenly upon his back, his arm came from beneath him, and Norton saw that the dark hand still held the naked creese.

He had only an instant's glimpse. Mariano, struggling for better footing above him, made a singularly awkward movement with one huge foot and pushed the Malay overboard.

The giant was startled at what he had done.

"He will drown!" he shouted to the two beside him. "Drag him aboard again. Quick! You will be too late."

"Drag 'im your bloomin' self or let the beggar go!" growled Skelly. "Wot's the blasted nigger to me?"

Hugo had been bending forward as if to obey. Now he straightened up in hesitation.

For the instant, Norton's body was free—even Mariano no longer held him. With a swift, writhing slide he dragged himself into the dinghy. In the same second of time he had grasped the oars in his hands.

"Grab 'im—grab 'im! 'E's a goin'!" screamed the Cockney, and rushed to clutch the gunwale of the boat. But Mariano thrust his great bulk in between.

"I will hold him," he said with calm deliberation, as Norton remembered later, and bent forward as if to grasp the boat. Oddly enough, in the effort he struck his huge fist forcibly against it, and the blow sent the light craft gliding swiftly from the raft.

"You bloomin' fool! Now you 'ave done it!" growled the Cockney, and in his wrath he planted his fist hard against Mariano's breast.

Even as Norton sculled madly away he saw the great Spaniard seize his puny assailant in his strong grip and shake him as a dog would a weasel. He saw, too, something flashing in the lifted hand of Skelly, and it seemed, also, that Hugo was rushing into the struggle, while from the sea a black figure was rising over the edge of the planking.

Then the darkness shut in the struggling figures, though for a moment longer there came through the night sounds as of dogs worrying their prey. At the end there was a sudden cry—Norton did not know the voice—and that was all.

The girl lay unconscious in the bottom of the boat, just as she had fallen in the horror of the first rush of her enemies. Even yet Norton did not dare cease his efforts to put the dinghy beyond all chance of reach from the raft, and for a few moments he let the girl lie there, though his heart ached at the sight of her.

Then he threw down the oar and bent above her.

Already the breath was coming back, but the thin, white face, the frailness of the slender figure, the great hollows beneath the closed eyes—all seemed inexpressibly pitiful. With a sudden impulse he bent his head and kissed the wan cheek. And even as he did so she opened her eyes.

She had not moved beneath his caress, but even in the half-darkness she seemed to note the conscious manner in which, for an instant, he turned his face away.

"What is it, Fred?" she said, resting her thin hand upon his own.

"I am ashamed," he muttered, more to himself than to her, in bitter self-reproach.

"Ashamed? For loving me?" she said simply, as a child might have spoken. "I am glad."

"You—oh, Evelyn, you have known? You—"

"Yes, since the wreck. How could I have borne it all else? But you, Fred—you were as blind as you are brave."

"Brave? I have been a coward. If you knew how I have feared during these last few days!"

"For me! I did know."

"You knew? Oh, surely no! Not that Mariano—"

"Mariano? What of him? He was always a friend. Ah, but the others!" and the girl shuddered where she lay.

Norton turned away his head. He was glad that she had not pressed her question as to Mariano. How could he tell her all?

And then his hand fell upon some object in the bottom of the boat. He lifted it toward the starlit sky, and saw that it was a flask. There was liquid within, and somehow both knew in that first instant that it was water. And they knew, too, both of them, that the flask had been Mariano's.

"Norton uttered a half-cry, for something seemed suddenly to break and brighten in his brain.

"He saved it—his own portion—and he placed it here! And his words to the others—they were only a warning to me! Evelyn, you are right. I have been blind—so blind!"

Then he told her something—not all—of the horror that had been his. She listened, breathless.

"If only we could have brought him with us!" she said at last.

Norton turned away. He could not tell her what was in his own soul—the fear born of his last glimpses of the struggle on the raft, faintly seen in the night.

But he put the thought from him. Mariano was a giant in strength; the others, three to one though they might be, were weaklings beside him. Why should he fear that the cry he had heard had been the Spaniard's? There was no reason, he told himself.

And while he thought, the sun rose, the mist melted from the face of the sea, and before them lay an island beautiful with palms.

The Guardian of the Gold
Maitland LeRoy Osborne

A Tale of a Hunt for Buried Treasure on
a Remote Pacific Isle and the Horror That
the Forest Held

F OR THIRTY-SIX HOURS THE PETREL HAD ROLLED AND TOSSED on the unquiet bosom of the South Pacific. In the afternoon of the second day, with the black clouds banked on the far horizon, the sun shining and only the long, slow swells to remind us of the tempest that was past, we gathered on the steaming deck, clad in dry clothes once more, lighted our pipes, and talked lightly of the danger we had escaped.

The Petrel was a seaworthy steamer-yacht of a hundred and fifty tons, built for comfort and stability rather than speed or grace. We were a month out of Yokohama, and had been loafing leisurely southward with no particular port in view, touching casually at the Marquesas and such other of the islands as fancy prompted. By the sailing-master's latest observation, we were in 142 degrees west, 58 degrees south, when the rapidly falling glass gave warning of the approach of one of those fierce tempests that sweep unchecked across that desert waste of waters.

Like a frightened bird the Petrel had staggered before the gale, buffeted mightily by angry waves, often half overwhelmed by towering seas, and shaken from stem to stern by the racing screws when she pitched bow downward into the trough of the seas, only to emerge at last, safe and sound, from the tempest's grasp after being driven a matter of five hundred miles before its fury.

There were on board the Petrel, besides the crew, a party of six congenial souls: Jack Raymond, the owner of the yacht; Professor DuBois, an inexhaustible mine of information and good-fellowship; Hitchcock, who loafed industriously and looked on life as one long holiday; Tommy Raines, gray-haired and sprightly as a boy; Max Nordenfeld, a Swede, low-voiced and gentle and a man of iron nerve, who had hunted and explored in every quarter of the globe; and lastly myself, a free-lance, ready to join any wild-goose chase that promised "copy."

And, indeed, it was a wild-goose chase upon which we were then embarked.

Nordenfeld, stumbling by accident upon a fellow countryman dying in a sailor's dive in Yokohama, had befriended the poor devil, who in token of his gratitude had confided to him the secret of an unknown island in the South Pacific. There, he said, he and another shipwrecked sailor had discovered a cave piled high with chests filled with golden doubloons, ropes of pearls, rare plate and precious stones taken by pirates from the treasure galleons of Spain in ages past.

It was the old, old story that has lured adventurers for untold years—the unquiet wraith of buried treasure for which men have hunted in every land. But in this case the setting was so strange that Nordenfeld had been more than half convinced of its truth by the very novelty of the tale.

The sailors, the only survivors of the crew of a trading vessel which had foundered in a sudden storm, had drifted in an open boat for many days, until at last, half starved and crazed with thirst, they had landed on an island far out of the usual track of ships, where fresh water, fruit, and the eggs of wild fowl soon restored their strength. The island appeared to be of volcanic origin, but the half-active crater in the interior, above which hung a cloud of smoke by day and a pillar of fire by night, had occasioned the sailors little concern.

A copper kettle, half-buried in the sand, and stones heaped together in the form of a rude fireplace showed that some one had visited the island before themselves.

After a time, while wandering farther inland, they had stumbled upon the entrance to a cavern in the volcanic rocks, half concealed by clambering vines.

Prompted by curiosity, they had torn away the vines and entered, and found themselves in a veritable treasure-house, packed with stout brass-bound oaken chests whose massive locks defied their efforts to open them. When, with great labor, they had battered in the lids with rocks they found themselves possessed of wealth to ransom kingdoms.

For a time they had gone crazy with delight and danced and howled like drunken men, dipping their hands elbow deep into the piles of golden coin and tossing handfuls of precious stones into the air to see them sparkle in the sunlight; but when the excitement of their find had somewhat abated and they realized the futility of all the wealth spread out before them, they had wept and cursed alternately, and after a time had fallen into sullen silence.

After that had ensued a period in which, each suspicious of the other, they had lived in terror of their lives, each endeavoring unobserved to watch the other, scarce daring to close their eyes in slumber for fear that they might not wake, and never trusting each other for a moment out of sight.

At last, worn and wearied by constant fear and suspicion, they had made a compact bound by a series of oaths and penalties, and dividing equally the spoils, after infinite labor each carried away his share from the cave and buried it in some spot known only to himself. Then they set about devising means of escape from the island.

Neither of them having any idea how far away or in what direction lay the nearest land, they decided to stock their boat with such food as they could gather, and trust themselves to the chance of reaching some port or falling in with some passing vessel.

"Up to that point," said Nordenfeld, "the man's story was straight and lucid; beyond there it became a jumble of meaningless allusions to some terrible happening upon the island. The most that I can make out of his rambling account of what followed is that, while they were gathering breadfruit with which to provision their boat, some strange animal fell upon them without warning and killed his companion, and that he himself escaped only by running for his life to their boat and rowing out to sea without food or water.

"If the whole thing was not the delusion of a dying man, that sailor had undergone such a terrible experience that the mere memory of it was sufficient to set him gibbering unintelligibly with horror.

"As evidence that the story he told me was not merely a delusion, I have only a couple of Spanish doubloons of early date and a rough chart that he drew for me of the island, on which is indicated the beach on which they landed, the volcano in the interior, the treasure-cave, and the spot where he buried his share of the treasure.

"The only corroborative evidence that I could gather is the undeniable fact that he was picked up unconscious from thirst in an open boat somewhere about latitude 140 degrees west, longitude 50 degrees south, by a trading vessel blown out of her course to Auckland, two months before I stumbled upon him in Yokohama.

"What say you, Jack?" Nordenfeld had asked at the conclusion of the tale. "Are you willing to risk the Petrel in those waters on such a wild-goose chase?"

"I'd like nothing better," responded Raymond heartily. "I've often thought of taking a cruise about that part of the world."

One and all we chimed in with hearty assent—DuBois because he welcomed a chance to enlarge his knowledge of the flora and fauna of the South Pacific, Hitchcock because he could loaf more comfortably and completely afloat than ashore, Raines because he would be lonely without our company, and myself for the reason that the adventure promised "copy."

And so a month later found us embarked on the Petrel. We had touched land first at the Hawaiian Islands; then dropped steadily southward past the Marquesas, crossed Capricorn, and were working westward, when with hardly an hour's warning out of the east the storm had wrapped the Petrel in its mantle.

Now it had left us again, but our wet decks had scarcely dried under the scorching sun when,

"Smoke-ho!" came the lookout's hail, startling us with its suddenness.

"Where away?" called Hitchcock.

"Two points on the port bow, sir," came the answer.

"Might be a tramp steamer blown out of her course," mused Hitchcock. "Are there any volcanic islands in the neighborhood, Mr. Brown?" he asked the grizzled old sailing-master, who was poring over a chart spread out on his knee.

"Shouldn't be at all surprised, sir," he answered, "to run against one any time. They pop up out of the sea overnight in this latitude."

"We'll have a nearer look at that smoke yonder, at any rate," said Hitchcock.

A few hours later the throbbing engine had brought us within sight of a picturesquely beautiful island, covered with a riotous luxuriance of vegetation that from a distance gave it the semblance of an emerald in a silver setting. From a low, irregular mountain in the interior rose straight and unwavering in the still air the pillar of smoke that had betrayed its location to us.

As we drew nearer a long curving stretch of sandy beach became visible, and before the sun had dipped below the horizon the Petrel came to anchor a few hundred yards from shore in a harbor-like cove where the water, as clear as crystal, seemed alive with fish of every hue and shape.

Nordenfeld, poring over a soiled and tattered scrap of paper, nodded slowly.

"This looks like the real thing," he said. "Here's the beach, running halfway round the western side, and the cove a third of the distance from the southern extremity of the beach, and the mountain in the interior two points east by north of the cove, with two low peaks to eastward of the crater.

"According to the chart the treasure-cave should lie a little to the south of a direct line from the upper end of the cove to the crater and about two miles inland, and the private safe-deposit vault that we're to search for is located under the shelving edge of a great rock at the apex of a triangle formed by the treasure-cave and the middle peak of the mountain."

As Nordenfeld pointed out the landmarks one by one and compared them with the rudely drawn chart we verified his statements with eager glances. I think we were all more or less excited. Even Nordenfeld's bronzed cheek showed a spot of higher color and his eyes glowed strangely. For myself, I remember trying to figure mentally what the value of a million Spanish doubloons might be in current coin.

The brief tropic dusk was almost upon us when we landed, so that we could only prowl aimlessly about on the white sand of the beach for a few moments and peer curiously into the dusky shadows of the forest that came down to meet the sea.

With the dawn we were astir and eager for what adventure the day might bring. Nordenfeld it was who took command as soon as we had landed. Our plans had been carefully discussed, and each of us understood exactly the part we were to play.

Raines, with two sailors, was to guard the boat. Brown, the sailing-master, was to keep close watch of the shore from the deck of the Petrel and fire the yacht's cannon as a signal in case of danger. Hitchcock, in consideration of his laziness, was to take his station at the spot where we entered the forest as a sort of rear-guard, and Raymond, DuBois, and myself, with two sailors, were to form the actual exploring force under the lead of Nordenfeld.

We were all well armed, each of us except the sailors having a repeating rifle, revolver, and ship's cutlass, the two seamen carrying axes instead of rifles and cutlasses.

It was hard to believe that danger could lurk in the midst of the riotously beautiful verdure that confronted us. From the narrow strip of beach the forest stretched unbroken to the mountain in the interior. No sign of human occupancy was discernible, and the myriads of gaily plumaged birds that fluttered above our heads, disturbed by our intrusion, were the only living things except ourselves visible upon the island.

But Nordenfeld, impressed by the dying sailor's tale, counseled caution.

First we were to make a preliminary exploration of the beach along the edge of the forest, and shouldering our rifles, we set off for our two-mile tramp over the sand. I could not repress a smile at our ludicrously warlike appearance in that peaceful spot as we straggled along in single file, Nordenfeld in the lead and the sailors, with their axes on their shoulders, bringing up the rear.

We had proceeded perhaps three quarters of a mile in this fashion, scanning the unbroken green line of the forest on our right, when we were startled by a quick exclamation from our leader. He had stopped and was looking intently at some spot further along the beach.

"Do you see that?" he asked, turning to me.

"I see something that looks like a white stone lying on the sand," I replied, shading my eyes from the glare of the sun and gazing at the object toward which he was pointing.

But Nordenfeld's keener eyes were not to be deceived.

"That white stone yonder is a skull," he declared.

A few moments later we were gathered in a wondering group about the skeleton of a man lying in a curiously contorted position upon the sand, with enough tattered remnants of clothing still remaining to show that he had been a sailor. In the skeleton fingers of one hand was clasped a rusted sailor's dirk.

We stood for some moments in silence, busy with our thoughts. I had an instant vision of the man whose skeleton lay before us struck down by sudden death and the other sailor, panic-stricken, fleeing for his life along the sand. I believe I even shivered slightly—not with actual fear, I hope—and glanced back toward the boat.

It looked a long way distant. I caught myself wondering how long it would take a man running for his life to reach it. Then I shook myself together. DuBois was bending over the heap of huddled bones, examining them.

Presently he looked up.

"There is not the faintest evidence of violence," he said. "No bone covering any vital part is even scratched. He did not come to his death by knife or gun or club, yet he died either in the throes of agony or engaged in a desperate struggle for his life. See how his knees were drawn up as though trying to thrust away some heavy body, and his left arm thrown across his face as if to protect himself from danger.

"He could not have been easily overcome, either. Note the size of those shoulder-blades and the length of the leg bones. In life he must have been an unusually large and powerful man."

I let my glance stray for a moment to the green fringe of the dark forest crowding down to meet the sea.

"I don't half like the looks of this," I said to Nordenfeld.

He nodded gravely.

"No more do I," he answered quietly, "but I'm curious to know how this poor chap met his death."

"Shall we bury him?" asked Raymond.

"We'll do that later," answered Nordenfeld. "We'll have to get a shovel from the engine-room."

Retracing our steps to the point which Nordenfeld had chosen for our entrance into the forest, and leaving Hitchcock to his lonely picket duty, we forced our way one by one through the tangle of hanging vines and creepers, which formed a curtain between the forest and the sea, and crept along in single file behind our leader.

The transition from the glaring sunlight on the beach to the semi-twilight of the forest was almost startling in its suddenness. Above us towered the myriad moss-grown trunks of trees, untouched by the hand of man since time began, their canopied tops interlacing like the warp and woof of some ancient weave.

Nordenfeld, with pocket compass in hand and eyes intent upon the guiding needle, strode onward, unmindful of the momentary discomfort of the swaying vines and creepers that threw themselves across our way. From time to time some one of us tripped and sprawled full-length upon the ground, only to kick ourselves free of the serpent-like embrace of the creepers in which we had become entangled, and struggle onward.

As we progressed, the forest grew less dense and walking less difficult, and our way led through open spaces like ancient amphitheaters, where volcanic rocks protruded in grotesque forms whereon huge myriad-colored lizards crawled in the warm sunlight. Again we would plunge into the gloom of the forest, where no living thing save ourselves seemed stirring. We were gradually ascending, the ground sloping gently upward to the mountains that lay beyond.

After nearly three hours of steady tramping we had come to an open space larger than any that we had yet seen, when, with dramatic suddenness, Nordenfeld paused and pointed with outstretched hand.

"Look!" he said in a tone of quiet exultation.

Before us yawned a cavern in the rocks. Speechless for a moment we stood and gazed, then with one impulse dashed forward, heedless of the huge lizards that scuttled from beneath our feet and crowded to the entrance.

"One moment," said Nordenfeld, raising a restraining hand. "The candles."

We drew forth from our pockets the candles with which we were provided and lighted them, and in a moment had plunged into the interior of the cavern. But hardly had we exchanged the bright sunshine for the midnight gloom of the cavern when a sound like the rustling of an unseen host assailed us, a breath of pestilence smote our nostrils, the light of our candles was snuffed as by a mighty breath, and unseen fingers clutched hideously at our unprotected faces or clung fiercely to our garments, while all about us strange forms fluttered fearfully in the dark.

So sudden was the onslaught that we fought in silence, striking out blindly at unseen foes, feeling the impact of soft, furry bodies swarming all about us, smothering us in their warm odious embrace.

Nordenfeld's laughter rang out strangely in the black darkness, echoed and reechoed from side to side, filling the cavern with a flood of sound that rose and fell and died away in faint, mirthful whispers in some far recess of the rocks.

"Bats!" he cried; and "Bats!" a hundred mocking voices echoed in the darkness. A faint light shone, and guarding his relighted candle with his hat he held it upward, revealing a swarm of winged things circling and weaving about our heads.

Still a little shaken by the experience, we relighted our candles. The very suddenness of the onslaught was enough to unbalance nerves already tuned to high tension by our gruesome discovery on the beach; and in truth the whole aspect of the cavern in which we found ourselves was uncanny enough. Each sound we made was flung back at us, multiplied and distorted by curious echoes till a host of hidden elves appeared to mock us from the gloom.

All about lay scattered brass-bound oaken chests with huge fantastic locks and hinges, their covers rent and riven—and all empty.

It was the treasure-cave, despoiled but bearing evidence that the dying sailor's tale was true. We stood presently at the entrance and discussed our plans. Raymond was for extending the search forthwith for the spot where the sailor had buried his share of the treasure, but Nordenfeld's more cautious counsel prevailed.

"It will be nearly dusk when we get back to the shore, even if we start now," he said. "It's a choice of spending the night in these woods or waiting till tomorrow before we look for it. I vote we start fresh in the morning."

So eminently sensible was his advice that we all accepted it as final, and turned our faces once more toward the coast.

Three hours of scrambling over rocks and fallen trees and through clinging vines brought us at length to the forest's edge.

When we appeared Hitchcock was pacing nervously up and down the sand, obviously ill at ease. He greeted us with evident relief.

"If you fellows hadn't shown up within the next half-hour I think I should have thrown away my gun and bolted," he stated solemnly.

He was in a state of high nervous tension, so greatly at variance with his customary poise that I gazed at him in astonishment. He had worn a well-defined path where he had paced back and forth in the sand, and from time to time he cast quick, nervous glances into the shadows of the forest.

"What is the matter?" asked Nordenfeld quietly. "Have you seen anything?"

Hitchcock shook his head slowly in reply.

"No," he said, "I haven't seen anything. It's just nervousness, I guess. I didn't suppose I was such a coward. But for an hour I've felt that something was watching me.

"Were you ever afraid in the dark when you were a boy? It was that sort of feeling. I've been thinking about that poor chap back there on the sand, wondering what it was that came out from those cursed trees and struck him down."

He wiped the moisture from his brow with a hand that shook, gazing at the forest as he did so. Of a sudden I saw his face go ashen gray and a great terror dawn in his eyes.

"There it comes!" he gasped in a choking voice. Casting his gun upon the sand and turning swiftly, he started to run blindly along the shore, with head thrown back and shoulders heaving with the violence of his exertions.

With one accord we turned to discover the cause of Hitchcock's terror. For a moment I think we all doubted the evidence of our own eyes. Stealing across the beach there advanced upon us the most unthinkably grotesque monster to be met with outside the realms of nightmare.

Imagine the most repulsive spider that you ever saw. Imagine it magnified a thousandfold in size, its saucer-like, protruding eyes emitting gleams of rage, its parrot-like mandibles clashing spasmodically as it emits a buzzing sound like the hiss of escaping steam. Imagine its lion-like mane erect with anger and its great hairy legs propelling it yards at every leap. Imagine it rushing forward to crush you in its horrid embrace, to tear your flesh, to smother you under its weight.

Insensibly, on beholding this Thing the mind groped backward through dark ages to prehistoric times when horrors such as this scuttled over the marshes of the Paleozoic age. The remnant of some race of forgotten monsters, it seemed to be more horrible, more grotesque than the mind can conceive.

Its long legs, hairy and deformed and thick, looked powerful enough to crush like iron bands; its horny beak one could fancy tearing vulture-like at its victims, and the huge, brown, misshapen leathern pouch that served it for a body one could fancy slowly distending to sleek, satiated smoothness with the life-blood of its prey.

A moment more and the Thing was upon Hitchcock. One scream of mortal terror, one unavailing struggle to tear himself from its terrible embrace, and Hitchcock was buried under the unclean Thing, that tore hungrily at his flesh as a hideous vulture tears at a piece of carrion.

Nordenfeld's gun rose to his shoulder; there was a flash, a report, a puff of smoke, and the monster of the forest was writhing in its death throes upon the sand.

Then, as with one impulse, we ran to where Hitchcock lay face downward upon the sand, lifted him in our arms, and panting, stumbling in our haste, fled along the beach. When we had reached the boat we tumbled Hitchcock's limp form into it and pulled hurriedly for the yacht.

Once aboard again, our shaking nerves grew steadier and Hitchcock, thanks to the stoutness of his canvas hunting-coat, little the worse for his adventure, came to himself.

"Probably we have killed the last existing specimen of the prehistoric arachnid," said Nordenfeld, "but I, for one, wouldn't set foot in that forest again for all the doubloons ever minted in Spain."

He glanced inquiringly about the circle of faces around the table in the captain's cabin of the Petrel. One by one we shook our heads gravely. Raymond gave an order to the sailing-master, and when the quick dusk of the South Pacific fell, the island was a mere speck on the horizon.

Under the Black Flag
Burke Jenkins

**Wherein Some Agents of the Law Upon
the High Seas Perceive that Honesty Is
the Best Policy**

Tom AND I TOSSED UP A QUARTER; I won, and Tom washed the dishes. Relieved of the necessity of slopping a greasy frying-pan into the salt waters of the little Bay of Corejo, I pulled the dinghy up, jumped in, and rowed ashore in all the languor of a southern sun.

But my stroke quickened when, upon rounding the end of the wharf, I found that the little northern steamer was in and was discharging Yankee cargo. And—joy of all ecstasies—there fell to my lot a New York newspaper, a Sunday edition, Magazine Section, Funny Page, Puzzle-Picture Section, and all complete.

Satisfaction sat on my brown and stubbled cheek as I made my way back with my prize to our little black schooner. I found Tom's pajamaed back braced against the cockpit coaming, while there flowed lazily from his lips the smoke of my corn-cob.

"Get the coffee?" he inquired, without turning to look at me as my boat edged alongside the rail.

"Something better'n that!" I cried enthusiastically.

He probably doubted my judgment; and, besides, Tom's a coffee toper; so, he whirled around in what was for him a display of real feeling. But he spied the variegated hues of my precious purchase and surrendered unconditionally.

For four mortal hours we sat under our little sail-cloth awning and buried our noses in the printer's-ink which had smeared its way over the rollers of a press we had watched on many a Saturday night eating its rolls of wood-pulp paper.

It was homesick work.

"Would be kind of nice to stroll up the line, wouldn't it, Tom—say from Thirty-Third to Forty-Second?"

The next eye-wink I was swimming alongside. From this you can argue that Tom is quick of temper, but bear in mind the provocation. I think he's mild.

Now, when I had dripped my way back to a seat on the cabin-house we planned the campaign.

Here we were in West Indian waters, as the result of an idea of Tom's. It was not a bad idea, either.

Sickened with the strain of a reporter's life, Tom had dreamed of the delights of southern seas, where we could each indulge our muse in loftier flight. He would write "that novel"; I would no longer illustrate "specials," but would catch the wave-edge tints and shame Nature with the mirror of my canvas.

Well, we bought the little schooner, followed down a line of longitude, and for a year and a half had drifted around the coral islets. But somehow or other the muses had gone on strike, and though it cost but a song to live, both Tom and I had become hoarse. And also we had become homesick.

"Cast your eye over this article, Chinkie," said Tom calmly, indicating a column in the Magazine Section with his thumb. But for all his coolness of tone, I could see that he was excited.

The article set forth the fact that a syndicate of thoroughly sober New York business men had become convinced that all previous attempts to recover the sunken treasure of old Spanish galleons, known to have been wrecked in West Indian waters, had been amateurish and half-hearted. Accordingly, this syndicate, as an initial experiment, was fitting up a modest little cutter, equipped with modern diving-gear. This expedition was to start the day after the issue of the paper.

"Don't exactly catch the drift," I said, when I had thoroughly informed myself of these interesting facts.

"You noticed where they say that little cutter's headed?" he asked.

I glanced again at the paper.

"Why, I'll be blowed if they haven't heard of that little islet we use as headquarters!" I exclaimed, becoming interested at once. "They must put more faith in those natives' stories about that sunken ship on the reef than we do."

"Well," replied Tom, "I'm not so doubtful about that treasure, after all."

"It seems too bad," he went on slowly, "that those fellows who are so practical about their businesslike venture should not be awake to the fact that we are not so up-to-date in these waters."

"No daylight yet, Tom," I wheezed, still puzzled.

"They don't mention any armament in the article, do they?"

"Why, no!" I replied.

"Careless of them, too. Ought to have made closer inquiry. Easy enough to ascertain that there are still petty black pirates in these waters, but big enough to tackle their little unarmed cutter."

"What on earth are you driving at?"

"Chinkie," said Tom, pulling down a serious upper lip, "two questions. Just how bad do you want to click your heels on Broadway flagstones? And just how severe a strain can your elastic conscience stand?"

"Well," said I diplomatically, "you know I trot beautifully to the same whiffletree with you on those points. Please hasten the hatching of the idea."

"Well," Tom replied deliberately, "it just struck me that our little schooner's painted black, and that burnt cork can do wonders in the way of disguise."

Once more he yawned.

"Great Scott!" I cried as I slapped my ingenious colleague on the shoulder. "We can get that old Gatling from our sterling friend, the boss of the port here, and lie by in that little bay beyond the bluff, just out of sight of their operations on the reef!"

"Exactly!" acquiesced Tom. "But, mind you, Chinkie," and his tone took on real seriousness, "no bloodshed. Scare it out of 'em, you know."

"Of course. Besides, we're first to come to that island, anyway."

Believe it or not, it wasn't three days before our little rakish craft lay snugly moored in the pocket behind the bluff, and forward, by the bitts, a tattered tarpaulin shut out from prying gaze a rusty machine gun. Tom and I sweated under our burnt cork like two nimble-legged vaudeville artists.

About sundown of the fifth day the cutter hove into view and groped her way about for an anchorage. Either they never spied our little bay or else they were afraid to cross the reef, not knowing the channel. Anyway, they contented themselves with dropping anchor to leeward of the island itself.

"How many do you make 'em to be, Chinkie?" asked Tom from our vantage-point on the edge of the bluff to which we had snaked our way.

"Why, I can't count but four. This first expedition of the syndicate was certainly modest."

"Couldn't be too modest to suit us, Chinkie. All we want them to have is one real energetic diver."

Right here I wish to state in the interests of truth that as we lay by and watched those fellows churn the air-pumps to a companion in the depths not one flicker of conscience ruffled our serene and blackened countenances.

One morning Tom came scuttling down from the bluff with the important information that our victims were about to take their departure.

"That water-line of theirs is some lowered," he grunted. "They've corralled the pieces-of-eight, all right. They're packing away diving-gear and battening down generally, ready for a quick getaway."

Well, we put all her kites on our little craft, for the breeze was very light, and a half-hour saw us rounding that promontory with every little rag drawing.

The channel past the reef led us somewhat off the direct course for our quarry, the treasure-cutter; but we were, nevertheless, near enough for full vision. Tom had the wheel; I was breast-high in the shrouds of the lookout, and ready to cast the tarpaulin from the gun for that "shot across the bows."

I could see one of the fellows aboard the cutter scanning us with a binocular. His head would turn from time to time as he communicated with the other three, who had abandoned their preparations for departure in view of this new interest.

I was nervous. Piratizing didn't set quite as well on my stomach as my appetite for New York had promised. Accordingly, manlike, I attempted the facetious:

"What'll we use as a Jolly Roger, Tom? Think one of those towels will do? Things ought to be done according to Kidd."

There was no response. Sailor that he was, he held the schooner to her course by the "feel," but he was peering intently off to starboard, away from the cutter. I followed his gaze. From a pearl-tinted horizon were rising the twin sails of a rig we both knew well.

"By the ribbons of Blackbeard, *real* pirates!" bellowed Tom. "Two of 'em, at that!"

"What'll we do?" I cried, somewhat to the point.

"Hard-a lee!" he sang out, and the little schooner bore away on a course which would take us past the cutter and dead in line with the black rascals.

"Guess we're white men, aren't we?" offered Tom, by way of explanation. "Clear away forward there and loosen up that infernal machine."

I rustled down the ratlines and obeyed, venturing no remonstrance.

On went our little schooner to meet the unswerving blacks.

"How's the distance?" cried Tom, with a new ring to his throat.

"Good enough!" I answered in like vein. "Bring her up a bit, let her jog, and come forward here and help me."

I backed the jib, and Tom ran up. To have seen our two perspiringly happy faces as we pumped our lead messengers pirateward would more than have repaid Gatling for his invention. I don't know that we did any damage, but in three minutes our arguments had proved incontrovertible, and the Caribbean imitators of Blackbeard were utterly convinced.

"About they went, and, hull down, they disappeared.

We watched them go, and then Tom calmly remarked:

"Now for soap."

Both of us tumbled into the galley and scrubbed away at burnt cork while the schooner jogged.

"Ahoy, aboard the schooner!" This from right alongside.

Up we bobbed on deck to behold the cutter, which had gotten under way during the fusillade.

"That was the slickest piece of work we've ever seen," yelled their spokesman. "Who the deuce are you fellows, anyway?"

"Come aboard and we'll tell you," answered Tom modestly.

"Surest thing you know." Leaving one man to tend the cutter, the three others rowed over to us.

"D'you know you saved us a lot of money by that little trick?"

"Thought so," assented Tom. "You see, we've got to keep in touch with these waters. Coast-guards, you know."

"Well, well," said the skipper. "Didn't know such things existed in these forsaken regions. But we're certainly grateful, and since we'd probably have lost all we've got, we think it's little enough to divide these doubloons, or whatever they are, into six parts. We'll see the right story's told the syndicate."

"Oh, Lord!" grunted Tom in my private ear. "New York, Chinkie!"

The Backslider
Gifford Hall

Of a Hungry Ship and a Shanghaied
Parson and the Fight That He Made with
Himself and Others

WHEN THE SAN FRANCISCO CRIMPS SHANGHAIED the Rev. John Williams, otherwise "Parson Jack" of a certain seamen's mission, they rejoiced. A converted sailor and boarding-house runner himself, Parson Jack had long been a thorn in the side of the crimps. He knew their game thoroughly, and he combated it with all his energies.

He was a hard and dangerous man to shanghai, but they got him aboard the big "lime-juicer" Duncan McLean, with a sand-bag bruise back of his head and some chloroform in his system, and he didn't come to until the McLean was clear of the Farallones.

He talked to the skipper of the McLean earnestly, but to no purpose. The skipper only smiled.

"You were drunk, mon, when ye fetchet aboard an' ye're drunk the noo. Go forrard an' sober up an' get to yer wark."

Parson Jack obeyed the last part of the order, flinging himself into the work as only a fine sailorman could, but he never forgot Captain Murchison's smile. Good, honest Christian though he was, that smile rankled like a barb; the truth in him had been doubted by a hypocrite.

That's just what Captain "Hungry" Murchison was—a hypocrite of the rankest kind. He had clawed his way from foc'sle to cabin by hypocrisy and *Uriah Heap*-like humbleness to his superiors; he had become deacon of a church in his native town by it; he made his ship "Bethel-ship" wherever he touched by it; he lived by it. But Parson Jack read him like a book.

The facts of the Duncan McLean's "hungriness," and that she was what sailors call a "floating workhouse," while her skipper invariably held service on Sunday and continually rebuked his men for trivial slips of the tongue, were not lost upon Parson Jack. As he worked like a mule, took in hole after hole in his belt on "whack" strictly "according to the act," and was preached at for his sins, he presently learned cordially to detest his captain.

No one could have guessed it from his demeanor. The rest of the foc'sle crowd might curse and growl all they liked; Parson Jack worked and starved silently. He even flagellated his silent soul for its antagonism to the hypocrite aft, and prayed that Murchison's nature might be changed even as his own had been.

But the Duncan McLean grew hungrier and hungrier, and harder and harder as she plowed Hornward. Her crew often "shortened down" in bitter weather on nothing but weevily hardtack and so-called tea and coffee for their morning and evening meals, nor was there even the smallest of "bogies" (stoves) in the icy iron hole that housed them when below.

By the time the Horn was reached, the mission parson-sailor was fighting himself hard.

Six feet of brawny manhood, converted to splendid mildness and faith though it may be, can hardly remain angelic under such conditions as existed in the McLean's foc'sle. Parson Jack led a deputation aft one day to ask for a change in the program.

Once again Murchison smiled that crocodile smile of his.

"Ye're gettin' yer whaack accoordin' to the act, ma men," he said, "an' ye'll get na mair. Go forrard every one o' ye an' do yer wark, an' let's hear na mair o' yer growlin', lest I log ye. It's one o' these hard 'Yanks' ye should be in or a 'Bluenose,' an' not a quiet Aberdeener like the McLean.

"Go forrard noo an' let's hear na mair; ye're gettin' nigh as good vittels as I get mysel'."

From the tone of his voice it would have seemed that the grievance was now actually Murchison's instead of the men's. They turned at his bidding and shuffled away—all save Parson Jack.

"You liar!" said he sadly. "You—you damned old fraud!" and he looked Murchison squarely in the eye.

The captain stared down from the break of the poop in petrified silence, till wrath broke it; then he talked.

Twenty minutes later he retired to his cabin, beaten at all turns in originality, quotation, and rebuke by his strange A.B.

"Ma soul, did ye ever hear the like?" he asked his chief officer. "Such a maan ought to be put in irons for blaspheemy."

But he did not put Parson Jack in irons. Narrow, pig-headed, hypocritical though he was, a sort of shame of himself kept him from it. Parson Jack had, after all, but hurled at him the very truths he, Captain Murchison, professed to believe.

But if he failed in direct punishment of his mutinous crew, he scored on them otherwise. He "geehawked" both watches, and often all hands, day and night, and especially called the attention of his officers to that "skulker," John Williams.

Nothing the man could do now was right. His steering was that of a greenhorn, his passing of an earring faulty, and so on, and so on indefinitely. The praying of Parson Jack for patience became incessant.

He went round the decks, gray beneath his tan, his hands clenching and opening again at the slightest word, his eyes like live coals. Once he asked the mate to let up on him lest he grow desperate. The mate told Murchison, and Murchison took to smiling sardonically when ever he and Parson Jack met.

At first Jack did not understand, but shortly the truth came home. Malice of the most diabolical kind was behind it all. Captain Murchison was trying to force him to do something—to become a backslider!

"He shall not, I will not!" declared the parson to his soul, but the day came when he did.

For three days the McLean had been in the teeth of a regular "Cape Stiff" snorter, and the crew was worked almost to the limit of endurance, when the captain had all hands called to wear ship. This seemed to be the proverbial last straw on the camel's back.

It certainly broke the remnant of patience left the McLean's crew. When the port watch, in which was Parson Jack, came below, soaked and cold, to find no opportunity to dry a single rag, and, furthermore, to find the dinner of pea-soup and pork burnt and rotten, hysteria seized it.

It cursed skipper, owners, and ship with many lurid oaths, nor had Parson Jack a word to say against the cursing. He sat on the hatch of the forepeak, with his chin in his hands, and for a long time scared into hell.

At last he rose, stony-faced, and commanding.

"Boys," he said, "we've worked like horses aboard this ship and have been treated like dogs, and now we've reached the limit. Pick up that kit of pork, one of you, and I'll carry the soup. We're going aft to the old man and settle matters once and forever."

A man grabbed the pork kit and Parson Jack the soup, and together they marched aft.

"Captain," said the latter, when they reached the poop, "do you call this fit food for men who have worked as hard as we have this morning? Just smell and taste it. It's not fit for hogs!"

"No-o?" replied the captain suavely. "Let's see, let's see, mon," and he gravely took the spoon handed him.

"An' what's the matter wi' it?" he asked presently, having merely touched his lips with the horrible mess.

"What's the matter—" Parson Jack checked himself on the verge of volcanic explanation, and the captain called the mate.

"They're sayin' the food's bad, Mr. Parbuckle," he said in an aggrieved tone. "Now, would ye say there's anything wrong yersel'?"

"No!" rapped the mate, after pretending to taste. "No, I wouldn't. That food is good enough for any man, let alone a lot of mutinous fellows like these. Get forrard you"—roaring at the men—"get forrard quick or we'll have you in irons, you shenanicking loafers. Only the captain's kindness has kept you out of 'em now."

Parson Jack's eyes literally blazed as he looked at the fellow.

"Good enough for any man, eh?" he snarled. "So be it. I'll try no longer."

He tramped back to the foc'sle and set the kit down by the hatch.

"Eat hardtack," he said to his mates. "I've got a use for this stuff. Now, don't one of you touch it unless you want to get hurt."

But one of the crowd was too hungry to care. He reached out his hand to take his share.

Parson Jack's heavy fist caught him square under the jaw and lifted him back to his bunk, where he lay dazed across his sea-chest.

"I told you," growled the parson. "I'm going to make men of you instead of yellow curs. Next man that reaches, I'll half kill."

The watch ate hardtack. To a man, it was afraid of this strange fire-eyed heavy-weight with the punch of a Fitzsimmons.

"He's gone loony," whispered "Liverpool" to a big Swede. But Parson Jack was not loony in the way "Liverpool" thought.

When the steward's bell rang for the cabin dinner, he dumped the rotten, slushy pork into the yellow soup and picked up the single kit, then watched his chance to get aft without meeting the second mate.

He reached the poop safely and looked down through the skylight at the cabin-table, waiting until captain and mate were comfortably settled. A moment later he smashed the skylight in with a vicious blow from an iron belaying-pin and emptied the contents of his kit on the heads of the officers.

A bigger joke has seldom been perpetrated at sea. It was no joke, however, to Parson Jack and his victims. Filthy with the yellow reeking stuff, they raced on deck to "double-bank" the sailor. He did not run, but faced them with his back against the chart-house.

If Captain Murchison ever really desired the fall from grace of Parson Jack, he got his desire. The leg-of-mutton fist of "Fighting Jack" Williams got him fair on the point of the jaw and sent him senseless over the taffrail to the main deck, and his chief officer got much the same treatment in the end.

The big A.B. forgot everything. He was like a "must" elephant in his rage. It was only when at last he lay ironed in the lazarette, conquered by belaying-pins in the hands of the second and third officers, that he knew he had tried to kill men.

He had fought as one possessed, as a soulless brute seeking to slay, careless of consequences. The very voice of him had been the snarl and roar of some wild beast.

But in the night, one who came near his place of confinement, heard bitter sobbing, and anon the pleading for forgiveness of a faithful but sorely stricken soul.

Nemesis on the High Seas
Herbert Pennell

The Yarn of a Desperate Game That Was
Played with Fate and Who Won the Final
Trick

O N THE 28TH OF JUNE the Black Star Textile Mills of Winterville shut down for good and Stimson went to his comparatively humble home, chased by a myriad of blue devils. Edgar Brown, who had also been thrown out of work and who walked home with Stimson that afternoon, declared that he was going to clear out of the country. The United States was too unsteady and the small men had too little chance.

Stimson could not leave the country. He was tied down. His wife was a hopeless invalid. He dared not tell her that his means of sustenance had been taken from him, so for the ensuing week he kissed her good-by after breakfast and, leaving her to believe that everything was going on as usual, scoured the town for work.

On the 3d of July the Winterville Farmers' Bank closed its doors, ruining in its failure some thousands of modest depositors, among whom was Stimson. He had barely fifty dollars to his name.

There were some who claimed that the Honorable William Perkins, president of the late Farmers' Bank and second vice-president of the defunct textile mills, had allowed the former to fail by sanctioning the acceptance of some very shaky securities, and had by no means lost at the closing down of the latter establishment.

Many people talked against Mr. Perkins. Stimson did not.

Worry and the heat and the racket of an unusually insane Fourth killed Stimson's wife. At least, that's what the physicians said. At any rate, she died in the hot, gunpowdery dusk of the holiday.

Stimson sat in the window of her room all the night through, long after the rockets and Roman candles had ceased to cut into the blackness and the dawn had shown the streets unkempt and strewn with dead pin-wheels and flowerpots.

When the servant knocked at the door at eight o'clock he had come to a grim conclusion. Vengeance was his—so he rose and took his revolver from the chiffonier and went down-stairs.

To the servant, fittingly subdued, he gave a curt good-morning. No, he would not want breakfast until he returned to the house.

He did not return.

On the evening of the fifth the Winterville *Gazette* had a long account on the front page of the murder of the Honorable William Perkins, president of, *et cetera, et cetera.*

The murder, occurring about nine o'clock that morning, had been particularly bold. The murderer, a certain George Stimson, Jr., until recently employed by the Black Star Textile Mills and an alleged loser in the recent bank failure, had made his way into Mr. Perkins' dining-room and in the presence of Mrs. Perkins had shot the worthy banker across the table.

He had then made his escape.

The *Gazette* suggested that Stimson's mind might have been turned. He was out of a job, penniless, and had lost his wife. The *Gazette* even went so far as to hint that had Stimson had money to pay for the best medical attendance, his wife might possibly have lived.

Still, murder had been done.

But Stimson was hard to find. The weeks spread into months and the newspapers forgot the murder. Yet the district attorney, with the aid of the Perkins family, persevered in the hunt for the criminal. Various clues were followed and various detectives, armed with governmental requisitions for extradition papers, were sent to various foreign states.

Late in September there came a cablegram from Buenos Ayres.

> Is here. Start twenty-ninth, Royal Mail.
> GRAYME.

The R.M.S. Meta, for Southampton, was three days out from La Plata when she ran into an equinoctial gale. For a day and a half she was swept eastward, then by a sudden veering of the tornado was carried north and west and out of her course.

To the man who on the unusually scant passenger list was down as Elbert Grayme, and who shared his stateroom with one George Stimson, the storm was fraught with great discomfort. Grayme was an excessively bad sailor. He lay limp in his berth and whimpered at the storm and the sea and his job.

But most of all he whimpered at his captive who, white and disheveled, crouched by the shuttered window and received the remarks of the detective as stoically as he endured the weather.

Stimson knew that all but the final tricks of the game had been played, and he was glad of it.

He had nothing to live for; as a murderer he had lost his citizenship; as a fugitive, his self-respect. The least he could do was to go back and pay his debt more or less decently.

After forty-eight hours of storm a steward, crawling round with untempting food, told them that the wind was falling. That was about half-past seven in the evening. Later, Grayme let Stimson go on deck alone for the first time. Previously the two men had walked together in the evenings, and none had known that it was a pair of steel bracelets that made them so companionable.

But that night the detective had a helpless idea that any one who could move about enough to throw himself overboard, was entitled to the opportunity. Or perhaps he almost wished Stimson would get out of the way. He had sat so quietly by the window.

Stimson climbed and slipped forward along the tilting deck just in time to see a black, unlighted ship slide down the flank of a wave from behind a curtain of rain and crash against the starboard bow of the Meta right under his nose.

There was a shock that sent him skidding at full length across to the port rail; a jerk and a lurch that tumbled him back to starboard. He crawled dizzily to his feet and stared down into the dark.

The two vessels clung and fought together like animals. Above the lashing of the waves that churned in white wrath below came the sound of timbers cracking and the grating of riven iron. From the bridge behind, a ship's officer bellowed through a megaphone, the noise swooping over Stimson's head and off into the rain.

Answering shouts came from the ship below. Then the smaller vessel tore herself loose from the Meta and almost as suddenly she had appeared, swung off again into the dark.

The Meta lifted herself on the edge of a comber and hung for an instant. Then she plunged down, splitting into the next sea that broke high above her rail, the gash in her bow sucking greedily at the body of the wave.

She did not rise again. Stimson, half drowned, felt her careen and settle beneath him.

He shook the water from his eyes and ears and turned about. Five minutes past he had not cared a snap of his fingers for life. Now that it was in immediate peril, he would fight for it. He started on a crazy run for his stateroom.

The whistle was yelping into the night. Somewhere near the stern a gong was being wildly beaten. Lights shone along the deck. Half-clad men and women crowded out into the wet. There were calls and cries and orders.

Stimson found Grayme, pale with illness, pulling on his trousers over his pajamas. The detective glanced up at him in relief and surprise. It came over Stimson then that perhaps it was odd that he should have returned to his captor when such a chance for freedom was offered.

But not a word was spoken. The detective got into his coat, patted his pockets to see if his papers—Stimson's extradition papers—were safe; took the handcuffs—Stimson's handcuffs—and the revolver, and tottered after the murderer and up to the hurricane deck.

Amidships on the port side they found a smaller life-boat, somehow unnoticed. The crowd was greater to starboard.

With dazed tenacity they cleared the boat of the rail, clambered into it, then struggled and tore their hands with the tackle of the paint-clogged falls and lowered themselves in a tipsy, seesaw course that once nearly pitched Grayme out.

In the end they felt the slap of a wave against the keel, and at once they were almost swamped.

Stimson clung with one hand to the slippery tackle that swung taut and free with the fling of the waves; with the other he yanked at the cords that bound the oars to the thwarts and finally unfastened them.

Again they lowered themselves till the tackle hung quite loose, then freed the boat and, paddling and pushing, kept themselves from being crushed against the ship. With infinite labor they made their way to the stern of the Meta, and there the wind caught them and drove them up and down sheer waves, into which they dug their awkward oars.

The lights had gone out on board the ship. Thirty yards away they could see, as they swung up to the ridge of a comber, an occasional lantern, showing where the crowd fought for safety. It did not occur to them to go back to help; they only worked in agony to creep away from the Meta, whose stern rose from the waves like the head of some nosing sea-beast.

Suddenly, as they clung on a glassy slope, the dim hulk lifted itself almost perpendicular, then slipped from sight. The sea sank and flattened itself. The few lights went out.

It was silent destruction, for the wind deafened all other sounds. A new force caught them, dragging them toward the level, unnatural pool over waves each of which was smaller and smoother as the little boat slid back.

Stimson bent in an abandonment of battle. He lunged at the treacherous current, which took his oar and twisted it from his grip.

The handle caught him under the chin and the life went out of him. He collapsed suddenly. His head, resting on a thwart, banged with the motion of the boat.

Hours later he came to.

His lower jaw felt out of all proportion, and when he tried to open his mouth the line of pain that shot upward from the joints below his ears sent him into wide-eyed agony. He caught his breath in terror as he saw the hills of water that flanked the valley in which the lifeboat wallowed.

He pulled himself up until he half lay on a thwart and again forgot everything in his suffering. After a while, however, he remembered the detective and wondered indifferently if Grayme were still alive.

When he again opened his eyes, he saw in the stern the hunched figure of his fellow survivor. The head hung forward, hiding the face in the lapels of the drenched and discolored suit.

Stimson started to call, but with the movement of his jaws came increased pain. After a moment he raised himself, crawled to the detective, and touched him on the knee.

Grayme straightened with a start, open-mouthed, staring. He blinked a moment at Stimson, shivered, and let his head fall again. The other was too ill to move; too ill even to shift his gaze. He lay across the thwarts, his arms stretched out, and looked at the detective.

Time slipped by silently.

Finally Grayme grunted and moved. He forced himself erect and threw his stiff arms wide.

"Lord!" he said, stopping in the middle of the motion. "Lord! I'm thirsty!"

He rose gingerly, and kneeling in the water that filled the boat almost to his middle, brought forth from beneath the stern-thwart a dripping breaker. Greedily he unscrewed the cover.

"Not half full," he muttered as he peered into the breaker, then raised it to his lips.

Stimson watched him dumbly; watched his big Adam's apple rise and fall as he swallowed and swallowed; wondered whether he would ever stop drinking.

At last Grayme lowered the breaker. Stimson reached for it and drank till he was out of breath. They repeated the performance, passing the water back and forth, until at last Grayme dropped the breaker into the water in the boat.

They watched it gurgle, fill and sink, and then lay back in suffering.

The dull morning wore into afternoon. Occasionally Stimson woke from his coma, and while shifting his lame body realized that the wind and sea had fallen.

Late in the day he was roused to action by becoming acutely aware of the water in which he was lying and of the weight of his soaked clothing. For a while he lay listless, then his aimless eye hit upon the inside of his open hand and he noticed that the skin on the ends of his fingers was wrinkled, as though he had stayed too long in a bath. The thought of a simple, civilized bath carried him back to dry land.

Lord! it swept over him, if he ever got back to dry land, how he would run from justice. His nearness to death made him wild to live, fugitive or free.

He rose and with the sunken breaker began to bail out the boat, working tirelessly on and on, without glancing up. Twilight came. Grayme yawned, stretched himself, and turned to sleep again.

By and by Stimson realized that it was almost dark. He stopped in his labors and looked up, and as the boat was poised on a crest he saw across the ridged seas the dotted lights of a ship. Then the boat sank into a trough.

Stimson called inarticulately to Grayme, but could not wake him. In his excitement he threw the breaker toward the detective. It flattered over the thwarts and hit the latter on the shin. He woke with a curse, but his anger changed to jubilation when he saw the distant lights.

The two men yelled and shouted, waving their arms. Stimson took off his long top-coat and flapped it above his head. But darkness was upon them in the middle of their signaling and they knew they had not been seen.

Grayme threw himself down, but Stimson stood erect, swaying with the rocking of the boat, and followed the tiny lights till they faded into the night. Then he clambered over the thoroughly unattractive Grayme (he was whimpering by that time) and curled himself up in the bow and finally went to sleep.

Thirst roused him to another dull dawn. Low clouds covered the sky, except in the east, where beneath their rigid border was a finger-wide line of red.

In the bow, where he had slept, he found another breaker filled with water, and some damp hardtack. He ate and drank moderately, though when he had finished he felt far from comfortable. Then he poured into the empty breaker half the water that was left and divided the food equally, placing a share beside the sleeping Grayme and saving the rest for himself.

When the detective awoke, dry-mouthed, some time later, he grabbed for the breaker beside him and started to drink deep.

"You'd better go easy," said Stimson. "That's all the water you're liable to get for a while."

Grayme paused.

"It's sort o' salty, too," he remarked. "Where'd it come from? Is this all there is?"

Stimson shook his head.

"No; but the rest is mine."

"It's yours if I say so."

Grayme was thoroughly insolent.

"It's mine whether you say so or not."

"Listen," started Grayme, but Stimson broke in.

"You listen!" he cried. "I'm just as good as you in mid-ocean, and don't you forget it."

The conversation languished. Grayme ate and drank immoderately, and then stretched himself out in the bottom of the boat to groan. Stimson stripped himself of his clothes and hung them on thwart and gunwale to dry.

Though there was no wind on the sea, the clouds above were drawn off and the sun blazed forth. Stimson's clothes began to dry and his naked back to burn. From the sleeping huddle that was Grayme floated faint wisps of steam. His drying suit regained its right color; his face flushed, grew red, then purple.

Stimson, who had as it had grown hotter put on piece after piece of protecting clothing, began to fear that the detective would be sunstruck, and at last awoke him and bade him bathe his head. Grayme was about to swear at being roused, but his first movement sent the blood rushing upward and he sank back in black dizziness.

In a moment he crawled to the gunwale and deluged himself with water. He, too, removed his clothes to dry, and emptied the pockets of his coat.

Stimson could have laughed at him. His wet hair lay flat against his bullet head; the water trickled down his purple, unshaven face. He straddled a thwart, his big feet incased in stained and cracking tan bedroom slippers.

Stimson would have laughed had the detective not been laying out the papers which, after all, were the cause of their being thus afloat in mid-ocean. They were splotched with pink from the dye that had run from the detective's pocket-book.

There was Stimson's photograph, his official criminal description, the much-ruled and indorsed extradition document, a pulpy bundle of newspaper clippings that very likely told hysterically of the murder, a pile of cablegrams and of correspondence, doubtless from the United States authorities.

And there were the handcuffs and the revolver, red and rusty.

Again it came over Stimson that he could not go back to black disgrace and the noose or the electric chair.

He peered out from under his top-coat, which he had thrown over his head to protect him from the heat, and prayed for wind to come and blow away all those dreadful documents. He even found himself whistling, cursed himself for a fool, and then laughed.

Grayme looked up in amazement and saw the grin on Stimson's face. He winked cruelly, and Stimson was seized with a desire to spring at the detective and throw him and his authority overboard. Instead, he merely sat silent, dumb with heat and despair.

The day dragged on. Grayme drank most of his water, and slept, and bathed his head, and took occasional glances round the horizon, Stimson remained in a daze, not eating, not drinking, refusing even to answer the detective's questions.

With the night came the wind and it grew almost chilly. Stimson spread his coat as an awning across the thwarts and went to sleep beneath it. Grayme drowsed in the stern till he tumbled forward and went on snoring where he had fallen.

The heat awoke them both next day. Stimson found himself drenched with sweat beneath his shelter. He threw himself up suddenly, tossing the coat back, and sitting erect, gazed at the sky in stiff stupor.

After a time he looked for his coat. It had gone. Evidently he had thrown it overboard when he had wakened.

His anger at his carelessness was so great that he cried. Grayme, who was staring at him, broke into laughter. Whereupon Stimson set to and cursed the detective. For an hour or more they sat at opposite ends of the boat and called each other the worst names they could devise.

They laughed and sang uproariously and bitterly. And each time one would hurl at the other some particularly vicious insult he would rock in his crazy merriment.

All day long the sun zigzagged its white trail across the sky. All day long at intervals the two men muttered and yelled, cried and laughed.

At last a breeze crept up. At the first touch of the air sanity came to Stimson. He lay inert for a while, drinking in the coolness, aware of each definite sensation—the swish of the waves, the tarry smell of the boat, the pain where he had cut himself in his delirium, and suddenly a clinking sound from where he knew Grayme must be sitting.

The first thing he saw as he stood up was the glimmer of the low sun on the hull of a west-bound ship.

He could not even cry out, but a faint sound came from his swollen lips. Grayme looked up. Stimson pointed tremblingly.

"I know," said the detective, and went on fussing with something he held in his lap.

Stimson sat down, dumb with revulsion.

He was saved!

But for what?

Again the clink came from Grayme's end of the boat and Stimson looked up quickly. The detective was scraping the rust from the handcuffs. The unfairness of so cruel a performance made Stimson see red.

"I'm not going to wear those again!" he shouted.

Grayme was so startled that he almost dropped the handcuffs. Then he, too, lost his unsteady temper.

"You most certainly are!" he bellowed. "Come here."

"You go to the devil!" bawled Stimson, and crawled as far forward as he could. The two men were about ready to be swamped in another sea of insanity.

Stimson hung his head and sobbed in impotence. When he looked up again he found Grayme with his revolver leveled upon him.

This made Stimson roar with laughter.

"Why, you fool," he shrieked, "you know as well as I that that gun is no more than a bunch of rust."

Grayme called him a liar, and to prove it held the revolver at arm's length over the boat's side and tried to pull the trigger. He could not budge it. Stimson laughed harder.

Grayme's veins swelled with wrath. He took his knife and with some caution commenced to dig at the chamber of the gun. Stimson watched him a moment, then settled back to stare at the on-coming boat. By and by, he thought, he would get up and wave.

There came a shot, a scream, and a clatter. Stimson turned slowly. All that he could see of the detective were his shins and feet, that stuck ludicrously upward from the other side of a thwart; also the tip of his red chin was just visible.

Stimson's startled heart beat out the minutes, but he did not move, save every little while to wink the sweat from his eyes. Fear cautioned him that Grayme was working some trick, was playing 'possum. For a time he watched the disreputable bedroom slippers as they swayed. Then the silence and inaction became unbearable.

"Grayme!" he called. "Grayme!"

There was no answer. The bedroom slippers still swayed.

Stimson crept forward. The detective was dead. A raw cleft marked his left cheek and terminated in the corner of his eye.

Stimson stood stock-still, strangely lonely and desperate. A silence that seemed final settled down round the boat where rode the dead man and the murderer. Toward them crept the westbound ship.

The live man's ungoverned thoughts gradually ranged themselves round one idea.

After he had waved, which he would in a few minutes, and help came from the ship, they would find him with the dead detective, and at the door of him who was already a murderer they would place another crime.

He didn't reason that the worst couldn't be made worse. He rebelled against having his not particularly good name further damaged. He would not pay the penalty for two deaths. There was no way, of course, in which he could make them believe that—

A new thought came to him and his brain began to spin like a runaway machine. If they would save him from the sea, he could save himself from death. It was strange how much he cared to live now. A week past life had been barren.

With the calm of tense excitement, he kneeled by the body and gingerly fished the papers from the detective's pockets, keeping his eyes on the wagging head to catch the faintest change of expression and ready to duck in a second should Grayme's hand and the revolver be raised against him.

He found all the papers. The clippings he tore into bits and trailed into the ocean; his own splotched photograph he hacked into nothing and sent the scraps flying in the wind. He kept the cablegrams and the correspondence, the extradition papers and all of Grayme's personal letters.

While he was going through the dead man's clothes his finger-nails caught on the tailor's tag on an inside pocket. This might ruin the game, perhaps, so he hacked from the cloth the last mark of identification. He tore from his own suit a like telltale tag, and then placed all his own papers and letters in the detective's pockets.

At last he rose relieved.

Here was a new trick in the game.

Now he was Elbert Grayme, detective. The dead man was George Stimson, Jr., murderer and fugitive from justice.

Stimson was dead. If Grayme disappeared or never returned to the United States, so much the worse for the detective's reputation. The matter was simple.

Stimson laughed craftily, took off his shirt, and waved at the approaching ship.

It would sound plausible enough. He would tell them that the murderer had struggled when he tried to put the handcuffs on him. (His arms began to ache from waving.) Had become unruly, then violent. Finally, in self-defense, he, Grayme, had been forced to shoot him. (He imagined he could see the foam round the bow of the steamship. Would she never answer?)

And imagine the people in Winterville, U.S.A. Still, the criminal had met with his deserts. Yes, a sea-burial would be all that was necessary. (Lord! how tired he was, and would they never come, so that he could tell his story clearly and unhesitatingly?)

The identification was perfect. Yes, he had the papers. They might examine them after he had had food and sleep. And the extradition papers. The Meta—

A flash of steam came from the ship. The whistle boomed distantly. Stimson waved more frantically. Again came the reassuring flash and boom, and then the man's weary arms dropped.

He settled down drowsily. He would sleep. But it came to him that he ought to be sure about those papers, so he tried to read them through eyes that swam with fatigue. He couldn't see much; still, it was perfectly simple.

Then the craftiest of all thoughts roused him. He went again to the body, pried from the stiff fingers the rusty revolver and pocketed it. Under the dead man he found the handcuffs, one of which he unlocked, then fastened about the lifeless wrist; the other he left open and dangling.

Thus the matter was arranged, the play rehearsed, the stage set.

Stimson sank into numbness. Faintly there came to him the sound of voices, the rattle of oars and oarlocks. He smiled and slumbered.

Then with a start he woke. Something had grated along the boat's side.

His weak, half-opened eyes saw above him the trim figure of a blue-suited ship's officer.

Stimson pulled himself to his feet.

"Look!" he said hoarsely. "I'm Elber' Grayme, 'tective, U.S.A. Tha' "—his hand flopped weakly toward the body—" 's George Stims'n, Junior, murd'rer. Had t' kill 'm. Vi'lent. He's murd'rer. I'm 'tective. Got pape's an' ev'thing. Show later. Eat! Sleep! Fo' God's sake, save!"

He swayed forward. The young officer held out his arms invitingly. The steamship in the offing tooted its whistle joyously. Stimson toppled over, senseless.

Dim lights, warm drinks, fresh water, sweet smells, soft beds, and cool air.

Stimson woke occasionally to a drowsy heaven, only to sigh and sleep again.

Finally there came a time when his lassitude left him. He sat weakly on the edge of a berth in a clean, white stateroom.

Half dressed, he slid the shutter from the window and looked out into the late afternoon light, across woven golden waters to a line of brilliant beach, a city of white houses and the shadow of green mountains. The ship lay at anchor.

Instead of the peace which the scene suggested, fear took root in his heart. Here was land; now he must make his escape, and quickly.

He finished dressing in a mad rush and was about to leave the stateroom, when he saw a little pile of papers that lay on the table. Beside them were a revolver and a pair of handcuffs. He gathered up these precious belongings and turned to leave the room.

The door was locked.

His fear knew no bounds. At first he was tempted to crawl out of the window, but the thought that such an act would appear thoroughly suspicious detained him. He must show a good front, so in a moment he rang for a steward.

Interminable minutes passed. At last a knock sounded.

"I'm locked in," cried Stimson boldly. Perhaps, after all, it had been merely a safeguard to keep him, a sick man, from disturbance.

"All right, sir. Just a minute, sir," came politely from outside.

Another long wait. Then, without warning a key clicked in the lock, the door opened, and the room was flooded with light. A bulky figure stood on the threshold and bowed affably. With a cry Stimson sprang toward the door. The man did not move:

"You're feeling better, Mr. ——?" he began, and then paused.

Stimson caught himself in time, and with some semblance of calmness said:

"Grayme—Elbert Grayme."

The man's eyebrows went up.

"Look here," he said rather kindly. "I don't like to seem either disagreeable or curious"—Stimson noted his quick English accent—"but your name and the story you told the second officer, and those papers"—he pointed toward the bare table—"don't fit very well. To be brutal and frank, the description on those papers fits you better than it fits the man we found dead."

Beads of perspiration stood on Stimson's forehead.

"Why," he began. (Lord! why hadn't he destroyed the papers? What need had there been for so involved a story?) "You read the papers when I was—" He stopped in the middle of his question.

The other nodded.

"You see," he said, "I'm employed by a concern of integrity. Our captains and our ships go round the world doing an honest business, and I can't take the responsibility of having a part in any shady work. I'm not thinking so much about how it would affect me, you understand. Now, if you know any one here who can identify you—"

"Where are we?" Stimson could barely talk.

"Rio," said the officer shortly. "Why not see the consul? I can send you up with a man from the ship. I won't be disagreeable enough to call upon the customs officials."

There was nothing else to do. Stimson agreed weakly.

"Of course," the other went on, "I've no doubt that everything is all right. And I'll be waiting to beg your pardon over something cooling. But we have to be careful, you know. Just come with me, please."

Stimson stepped across the threshold.

Life and freedom shone so green and sweet not more than a hundred yards away. He must escape somehow. Perhaps as they went up to the consulate it could be managed. Twilight was falling. He would delay starting till dark.

The officer talked by his side, but his words could not penetrate the fugitive's maze of thoughts and despair.

Vivid as a flame a new sensation flared in Stimson's brain.

A man in a near-by stateroom had laughed. Stimson knew the laugh, but whose it was he could not think. Shortening his stride, he hung back. A fit of trembling seized him and he leaned against the rail.

"What's the matter?" asked the officer. "Not very strong yet, eh?"

A stateroom door slammed open and a man ran out on deck laughing boisterously. He stumbled against the officer, and turned to apologize. Then he caught sight of the pallid Stimson.

"Why, George!" he cried, stretching out his hand.

The officer turned quickly and caught at Stimson's wrist.

All manliness left the murderer. He stood pusillanimous, round-shouldered, drop-jawed.

The man was Edgar Brown, of Winterville.

"Why, George Stimson!" he cried. "Don't you know me?"

Stimson shook his head wearily. He fumbled in his pocket.

"I guess I've lost the game," he whispered.

And the handcuffs clinked as he gave them to the officer.

In the Land of To-Morrow
Epes Winthrop Sargent

THE DISAPPEARANCE AGENT

CARRISFORD HALF ROSE FROM HIS SEAT WITH AN OATH UPON HIS LIPS.

"I am extremely sorry," began the stranger courteously. "It was very awkward of me to knock over the glass. Permit me to order another."

"Do you think that you can undo the harm by replacing the drink?" demanded Carrisford, the angry light still glowing in his eyes. "That was more than ordinary absinthe."

"But the drink I am about to order will be nothing more. Absinthe alone is quite enough of a poison for a brief chat. Perhaps when we have done, you will be glad that the mixture of chloral and absinthe which I destroyed was thrown to the floor."

"This passes the bounds of insolence," stormed Carrisford. "First, you brush my glass from the table, and then add to your offense by declaring that the drink was drugged."

"Mr. Carrisford has my apology—if the drink was not drugged. Let us say that it was not drugged and, by avoiding argument, come the sooner to our conversation."

"How do you know my name?" demanded Carrisford sullenly.

"Surely, the name and personality of Grenville Carrisford are not unknown," was the retort. "As for the rest, observing that you added to your drink from a vial, and knowing that this afternoon you failed to convince the Electric Development Company of the practicability of your current magnifier, the deduction was simple."

"Are you a detective?" demanded Carrisford. "By what right do you dog my footsteps?"

"I am not a detective," replied the other. "You will pardon me if, for the present, I refer to myself with some vagueness as a colonizing agent. You will perhaps recall the disappearance of Taylor Todd?"

Carrisford nodded. Taylor Todd and his disappearance on the heels of his disappointment with his air-ship had been a nine-days wonder.

"Like yourself, Mr. Todd was weary of life because of his inability to convince the public that his idea was right. He sought self-destruction, and found, instead, peace and appreciation."

"In the life beyond?" demanded Carrisford.

"Not in the life beyond the grave, but in the life beyond the confines of time. In the land of a hundred years from now. Would *you* voyage to this unknown country?"

Carrisford looked puzzled. There was no trace of insanity in the other's face. On the contrary, this strange man represented the best type of business man, alert, self-possessed, and well poised. Carrisford passed his hand uncertainly across his forehead.

"Your ideas of humor are somewhat obscure," he said coldly. "Do you wish me to believe that you are possessed of a time-machine?"

"Not a time-machine," was the ready answer. "But I am in earnest when I offer to move you forward a hundred years. You are hurt and disappointed because your invention does not appeal to the Development Company, and they will give you neither funds nor permission to work in their laboratory.

"One hundred years from now the magnification of the electric current will be well understood. Half a dozen cells and a magnifier will suffice to run an automobile or an air-ship. To-day you are a dreamer because you are a hundred years ahead of your time.

"Century Island is also a hundred years in advance of the present day, but to get there you must vanish from the world as absolutely as though you had completed the rash act you were about to undertake when I stayed your hand. If you like, I will tell you more."

"I should be glad to complete my destruction," said Carrisford wearily. "As you say, I am a hundred years ahead of the times. Because my ideas are too great to be comprehended by the men who have capital, my life-work

"This passes the bounds of insolence," stormed Carrisford.

has gone for naught."

"Suppose we seek some place where we may talk more freely," suggested the stranger, "and meanwhile permit me to introduce myself."

He handed Carrisford a slip of cardboard on which was engraved the name:

GIDEON ROUTLEDGE.

There was no address. Carrisford bowed and thrust the card into his pocket.

"I am staying here in the hotel," he said. "We might go to my room."

"On the contrary," demurred Routledge. "Walls—and most particularly hotel walls—have ears. My car is outside. Suppose we take a spin in that? It is a fine night."

Carrisford nodded, and followed his new acquaintance from the café, wondering what the next development would be. He did not fear violence; indeed, he would have welcomed death in any form.

For ten years he had been working on the device for multiplying the energy of the electric current. Every dollar he owned had gone into the experiments, and now that success was almost in sight, he found himself unable to command the small amount which would suffice to demonstrate the correctness of his theory.

He had approached the Electric Development Company last of all, assured that they would steal his ideas if possible, and he had found that they had not even considered his ideas worth the stealing. They had refused even to permit him to use their laboratory, though he had offered in exchange a half right to the completed invention.

He had no more than enough money to pay his bill at the hotel. To return home would be useless, since there was no one to whom he could appeal. He had sought to commit suicide, when Routledge had interfered, and it was without fear that he climbed into the touring-car that stood at the curb.

They soon came to the open country, and Routledge increased his speed until he came to an open space. On one side a cliff fell sheerly to the lake, a hundred feet below. The stunted undergrowth around them did not afford a hiding-place for a cat.

Routledge backed the machine close to the edge of the bluff and shut off the power. Carrisford looked at him inquiringly.

"This seems to be a safe place," explained Routledge, as he lighted a cigar and handed one to his companion. "What I have to say is not for the world in general. I want to be assured that it goes no further. I have your promise that, whatever the outcome may be, you will not divulge anything that passes between us?"

"You have that promise," said Carrisford.

"Unless I were convinced that you would be glad to accept my offer I should not speak at all," went on the other. "To be brief, I would recall to you the numerous instances in the past five years of the sudden disappearance of men who have advanced ideas too ambitious to be grasped by the average mind. The case of Todd is but one of a hundred or more."

"I recall an editorial in one of the papers at that time," said Carrisford. "It was intended to be humorous, and suggested that there must be a freemasonry among inventors of the crank class whereby their fellows expeditiously removed them from the world without the expense of a funeral."

"I remember the thing," said Routledge. "They had a very incomplete list—less than a score of names, all told. I am the agency by means of which they accomplish their effacement from the world."

"You!" Carrisford regarded his companion curiously, but without fear. Routledge puffed complacently upon the big cigar between his lips.

"You can understand now why my business is not engraved upon my card. I am the disappearance agent for Century Island."

"I have never heard of the place," said Carrisford.

"Naturally not. It is the land of a hundred years from now—the refuge of men who are so far ahead of their times that the world is too small for them."

"And it is near by?"

"I can say no more," said Routledge. "If you are fully determined to pass out from life; if you are ready to abandon your place in affairs; if death seems to you more desirable by far than life, I am prepared to offer to you not death, but life—a life in which you live for others as well as yourself, and realize to the full your dreams of conquest over the powers of nature.

"I am employed by the community of Century Island to keep watch over its interests here in America. There is another man, who looks after France and Germany. These three are the inventive nations, and from these we draw the citizens of Century Island. You are encouraged and helped in the development of your ideas, and this forms your contribution to the community.

"Some few of the inventions are given to the world, and these form the revenues of the island. In many ways your magnifier would form an addition to the resources of the island. It would, for instance, complement Todd's airship by providing him with the battery he needs for his motor.

"Are you willing to give up all claim to worldly fame, receiving in return perpetual provision for your comfort and all things needful for further experiments?"

Carrisford drew from his pockets half a dozen coins.

"This is all I possess in the world," he said. "They asked me to settle my bill at the hotel this evening, and it took all that I had except this. It was for this reason that I was about to commit suicide when you interfered.

"I cannot obtain employment, because I am regarded as a crank. Because I cherish a dream that other men cannot comprehend I am a visionary, and my knowledge of electricity is disbelieved since it leads me to so foolish a theory as the amplification of the power of a current. I am penniless, and without hope of obtaining employment from any source."

Routledge drew from his pocket a roll of bills.

"For a few days it will be necessary to remain here in town until I can arrange for transportation," he said. "Meanwhile, enjoy yourself and do not spare expense, for Century Island does not stint its guests.

"You will be taking your last look upon the world as you understand it. Two months from now you will be as much out of the world as though you had never lived. In return, I only require that once you become a member of the colony, you will not try to make your way back to the world."

For a few seconds Carrisford looked down silently upon the lights of the city, shimmering below them.

"Is it likely that I shall want to go back to that?" he asked bitterly. "But for your interference I should be out of it by now."

"I know how it is," Routledge admitted with a smile. "When you feel that way the world seems a veritable hell, and yet there comes a time when the call of your fellow man sounds louder than all else. But from Century Island there is no escape. Once you land there, you are dead to the world. In self-defense, the colony must guard against desertion lest their secrecy be betrayed.

"Until Thursday you will be free of all save the obligation of secrecy. On Thursday I will come for you, and from that time it will be too late to turn back. Should you attempt to escape, I would be forced to kill you, even though my own life should pay the forfeit."

Carrisford buttoned his coat over the money and laughed. "Have no fear," he said as Routledge turned the car in the direction of the city.

Nothing more was said until the hotel was reached. But as they clasped hands at parting, Routledge leaned forward and whispered in his ear:

"Think it all out before Thursday. Afterward will be too late."

II

THE ROAD TO THE LAND OF DEATH

Carrisford's interview with the electric company had taken place on Monday, and until Thursday there was no sign of Routledge. It was late on that afternoon when the disappearance agent sent up his card and followed it to the room.

"Have you changed your mind?" was his greeting. "To-day is the day you take the veil of Science. Just as the novice assumes the veil before the altar of the church, so must you, in your own mind, assume the obligations before the altar of invention."

"I am sick of it all," said Carrisford. "I am sorry that I did not go with you on Monday."

"Think well," urged Routledge. "You are still a young man; not more than two-and-thirty, I should judge."

"I am thirty-three," corrected the inventor.

"Make it thirty-three," continued the other. "You are young, then, good looking and, until disappointment came, full of the joy of living. Your scientific attainments qualify you for membership in the colony, but are you certain that with content there will not come a yearning for the joys of the world you have left behind?"

"Entirely so," declared Carrisford. "I ask nothing better than to leave the world forever."

"You have no friends nor family ties. I have ascertained your debts and paid them in your name. We will leave for San Francisco this evening at five. I have a compartment in the sleeper. Will you meet me at the station or will you come in my car?"

"I will meet you at the station," said Carrisford. "I shall be only too glad to make the start."

"I have ordered some things for you," said the disappearance agent. "It will be best to pay your bill and leave your trunk here. You might take a car in a direction opposite to that in which the station lies. You can transfer to another line, and then turn toward the station. It will serve to confuse the trail slightly. I shall be waiting on the platform, and we will go at once to our compartment."

He shook hands and went out. At the door he turned and faced Carrisford again.

"I will see you to-morrow," he said loudly, as a chambermaid passed. "Come to the office about eleven."

Left to himself, Carrisford went through his trunk. There were a few papers of importance that he wished to carry. For the rest there was little that he regretted leaving.

He went down and paid his bill with a light heart and sauntered out of the hotel, taking a car, as Routledge had suggested. In half an hour he was at the station, and Routledge led him quickly to the compartment.

Before the train pulled out, Carrisford was dressed in a suit very different from the one he had been wearing, the beard had been shaved off, and the thick hair parted in the middle instead of on the side. He looked entirely unlike the man who had entered the compartment, and as soon as they had started he threw from the window the shaving-paper and the suit of clothes he had worn. They dropped into the river below, and Carrisford turned away with a happy laugh.

"Farewell to Grenville Carrisford," he said. "Who am I now?"

"Peter Waldron—until Century Island is reached," answered Routledge, with a smile. After that you become Carrisford again."

"I don't want ever to hear of that failure," he said with a laugh. "I would rather remain Waldron."

"Wait and see," returned Routledge. "You may want to change your mind. Let's go in to dinner. The car is forward."

"Mr. Waldron accepts the invitation with pleasure," was the laughing response as the two left the stateroom.

As they sat in their stateroom after dinner, Carrisford again asked their destination. Routledge flicked the ash from his cigar with a smile.

"I am sorry that I cannot give you the information you ask," he said. "You must take us on trust. I leave you at San Francisco. From there you will sail for Australia. That is all that I can say."

"You mean that I am not to know where I am going until I arrive there?" demanded Carrisford.

"Almost that," admitted the agent. "You see, were some one to blunder by chance upon the island it would spoil everything. No living man knows just where Century Island is until he gets there. Perhaps a dozen of us can make a rough guess. That is all."

"At least, you can tell me what it is like," suggested Carrisford, and again Routledge laughed:

"I have never been there, else I should have stayed. Only the dead in life know just what the island is. We of the world serve the unknown for liberal pay. With that we must be satisfied. I hope that what I say does not dishearten you."

"Quite the contrary," retorted Carrisford. "I am the more anxious to see the place."

Not until San Francisco was reached was the subject even alluded to, and then only in discussing the telegraphic report of Carrisford's alleged death.

"The dead man had no relatives," concluded the report, after explaining that he had committed suicide because of his inability to place his invention with the Electric Development Company. "His remains will be buried by the college fraternity of which he was a member."

"That is odd," said Carrisford, pushing the paper toward Routledge.

The agent laughed.

"The numerous disappearances were beginning to attract attention," he explained. "One of the medical colleges had a cadaver much like you in appearance. Your disappearance was made complete."

"And to-morrow Peter Waldron will disappear from America," said Carrisford, with a smile. "I begin on the last lap of the journey."

Routledge only smiled, but when on the following day Carrisford swung away from the pier, Routledge knew what the inventor did not discover until much later. There were yet three stages of the journey to be taken.

Wellington was his objective point, but here he was met by another agent, who told him that in two days a smaller ship would start from New Zealand.

"I can't tell you where the end of the journey is," said the man. "I do know that the schooner stops at an uncharted island to the east of Antipodes Island. But you will see for yourself in a week."

The two days passed pleasantly enough, and on the third a trim auxiliary yacht bore him out of the harbor. The six men who manned the vessel, in addition to the captain, were all mutes, huge blacks, who went silently about their duties, with never a word or look toward the passenger sitting beside the skipper on the deck.

It seemed almost like a ship of death, and Carrisford wondered that the captain did not go mad. The skipper took his pipe from his mouth when he heard the suggestion.

"It's like a bit o' heaven," he returned. "I take it you're not married, sir?"

Carrisford shook his head. "Never had any inclination that way," he said.

"I was—for ten years," replied the other, as he replaced the short pipe between his teeth.

For three days they headed southeast, passing Antipodes Island, which approximately marks the antipodes of Greenwich, and late on the evening of the third day they ran into a sheltered cove. The captain pointed his pipe at a sheet-iron hut, on the beach.

"That's where you are headed," he said.

Carrisford looked about him in disappointment. In the moonlight the grim face of the cliffs that rose above the beach seemed less forbidding; but outside of the hut there was no sign of human habitation, and he dropped into the launch with many misgivings.

The interior of the hut was divided into two rooms, as Carrisford saw when lamps were lighted. In the outer apartment were utensils for simple cookery, a dinner-table, and a small library. In the other room were two small iron camp-beds, each nicely made up. The captain turned to his companion.

"I suppose you'll want to get to bed?" he suggested.

Carrisford shook his head.

"I think I'll sit up to receive my hosts," he said with a smile.

The captain went over to a cellaret.

The lights seemed suddenly to grow dim, and there was a roaring in his ears.

"Let us drink to your safe journey," he suggested, as he filled two glasses and raised one in a toast.

Carrisford took the other and tossed off the contents. The lights seemed to grow suddenly dim, and there was a roaring in his ears as of the pounding of surf in a storm. He fought desperately to retain consciousness, but at last he sank to the ground.

At a sign from the captain one of the mutes stepped forward, removed Carrisford's outer garments, and laid the inventor on one of the beds. Then they extinguished the lights and softly left the place.

When Carrisford awoke in the morning there was no trace of the schooner, nor could he even discover the footprints of the men in the soft sand. The appearance of the beach suggested a recent storm, though the skies were blue, and the vegetation above the sand-line gave no evidence of having been recently drenched.

Carrisford prepared breakfast from the food he found in the cupboard, and then wandered disconsolately about the beach. He had never felt so strangely lonesome. Before there had always been the feeling that other human beings were near. Now, even the birds were absent, and there was no hum of insect life. Once, far out at sea, a whale spouted, throwing up a great column of water, and Carrisford smiled at the thought that the ocean, at least, contained living animals.

He wandered back to the hut, getting an early lunch merely that he might have something to do. After the scanty meal he sought to occupy himself with a book. For an hour or more he turned the pages, though few of the printed thoughts occupied his mind, and then he suddenly dropped the volume. His quick ear had caught the faint sound of footsteps. He sprang toward the door, but before he reached it a man stepped through the opening.

"This is Mr. Grenville Carrisford?" he asked pleasantly. "Let me introduce myself as Masten Graves."

"Masten Graves!" Carrisford repeated. "The inventor of the turbine-torpedo?"

"The same," he smiled. "Don't look so shocked. You must be prepared to meet dead men on Century Island. Remember that you are dead yourself."

He held forth the clipping from the San Francisco newspaper, and Carrisford started.

"How did you get that down here?" he asked. "Is it magic?"

"Very white magic," explained Graves. "It is a part of your record sent on by our agent, Routledge. But we can talk more conveniently later on. Just now I only want to welcome you and tell you that I am glad to know you. Let us start for the land of the dead."

He led the way out of the hut, carefully closed the door, and started across the sand to the cliff. At the foot of the rock he turned and uncovered a hose, and a heavy spray of water soon obliterated their tracks. The beach was as hard and firm as though it had never been trodden upon.

"To prevent the millionth chance of discovery," said Graves. "Follow me closely, please," and he led the way into a cleft in the rock. "This is the worldly landing of the ferry across the modern Styx to the new land of death."

III

CENTURY ISLAND

Carrisford followed his guide into the cleft in the rock. To all appearances, it was a natural cave, roughly circular in outline, and some forty feet in diameter. At the rear was a second aperture, through which a dazzling white light gleamed, and toward this Graves led the way.

"I suppose you have seen demonstrations of the vibratory light?" he said. "We have it here in its most complete form. It is Breckenridge's contribution to the society of Century Island."

A cry escaped Carrisford as he led the way through the opening. The second cave was clearly the work of man. It was an arched tunnel one hundred feet across, and through the center was a canal in which lay a submarine. A traveling derrick ran down the center of the roof, but now it was at rest at the far end. Two men in white, short-skirted tunics, seated at the mouth of the submarine's hatchway, came forward as Graves approached.

"Our new comrade, Grenville Carrisford," said Graves, indicating the new arrival. "Mr. Carrisford, I wish to present George Hawley and Fergus McPherson."

The two men clasped his hand and led the way down the hatch into the interior of the boat. Graves went back to swing into place the section of rock that closed the entrance, and as the huge mass swung around, Carrisford looked with interest at the lights.

At either end of the tunnel were brass uprights, terminating in two rounded knobs, six inches apart. From these there flamed tongues of electricity so intensely white that it hurt the eye to look upon it. Graves laughed as he returned from the entrance.

"Plenty of time to study that when you arrive in Century," he said. "Suppose we start."

He helped Carrisford over the hatch and followed him down into the cabin, after making all secure. There was a whir from the motor, and then a slight vibration. Hawley took his place at the wheel, and Graves sank into a seat beside Carrisford.

This is the worldly landing of the ferry to the new land of death.

"It speaks well for our planning," he said, "that for fifty years none has dreamed of the existence of Century Island. Now, those men on the schooner are as ignorant as you were of the means by which the material they bring is removed.

"They never see us. A letter in cipher, telling our wants, is placed in a secret cleft in the rocks. They bring what we send for and leave it in the outer cave. They imagine that we come in another schooner and take it away.

"Instead of that, we enter this island from the opposite side. The opening is forty feet below the surface, and the tunnel runs straight to the secret cave. The three of us can easily work the loading machinery, and in no time at all we are ready for the return trip.

"In ten minutes we shall emerge from the tunnel, and in eight hours we shall be at home, one hundred and sixty miles away."

"But do ships never come?" asked Carrisford. "Antarctic exploration is rather a fad now."

"They make for the known lands," was the explanation. "We lie apart from known routes, and a bank of fog is a perpetual screen. There is some warm current flowing toward the South Pole and, striking the colder waters, it creates the fog."

"But I should think that it would make the climate almost unendurable," objected Carrisford. Graves indicated McPherson.

"They say it was until McPherson came. He is the inventor of a plan for the prevention of fog. His suggestion was hooted at in London, but he has turned Century Island into a place of perpetual summer.

"We all contribute here. This boat, for instance, is my invention. Hawley improved it with the gyroscope that steadies it, and permits the use of a more powerful engine without increasing the vibration. With the aid of your invention we hope to make the boat complete by cutting down the size of the storage batteries."

"But where is the crew?" asked Carrisford. "Do you three represent the entire force?"

"Yes," replied Graves. "You see, we have very few servants. We discovered a race of mutes on one of the islands to the north, and when we need slaves we go and get a few of them. In our submarine they look upon us as gods, and it is not difficult to obtain all we need. But, of course, it is not wise to employ more than are necessary, and we have so arranged matters that machinery does most of the work.

"But you will see all that in a short time. Meanwhile, why not assume the costume of the country?"

Graves had thrown off the long black cloak he had worn when he had met Carrisford, and now, like the others, was clothed in the short tunic.

"The toga is our full dress," he explained. "You had better wear this until you take your place with the workers. A week is allowed in which to look over the place."

He brought out the garments and indicated an alcove where the change might be accomplished. In a few minutes Carrisford stepped out again, the transformation complete. His crisp black curls were well in keeping with the costume, which set off the finely cut features to far greater advantage. His fellows regarded him with approval.

"You will find it very easy," declared McPherson, whose brogue had long since disappeared. "The Scots were the wisest. They kept to the kilts long after the rest of the civilized world went over to breeches."

"Perhaps in the new athletic generation bare legs will become fashionable again," laughed Carrisford. "Golf is accomplishing wonders."

"Scots again," murmured McPherson, and they all laughed.

"McPherson is the one resident of Century Island," explained Hawley, "who will not grant that it is the most perfect spot on earth."

"I'm not saying that," protested the Scotchman, "but it has no lochs. We cannot have everything. I'm not asking that."

"I don't blame you for longing for your Scotch scenery," said Carrisford, with quick sympathy. "It is beautiful."

McPherson looked at him gratefully, and Carrisford had made his first friend in Century Island.

Graves moved about the place getting dinner, and presently he placed upon the table a steak cooked upon an electric broiler, while the other dishes and the coffee were also cooked by electricity.

"I rather imagined that you had tabloid meals in such an advanced colony," said Carrisford, as he gave testimony to the excellence of the dinner by eating heartily. Graves smiled.

"There is no necessity for it," he said. "We did try a food tablet in which the necessary elements were administered in a pure state instead of in combination with waste, but it is used now only when it is necessary to give the digestive organs a short rest. As a cure for dyspepsia, it is a huge success, but tabloid meals, or even synthetic food, is unnatural, and therefore unhealthy."

Graves rose from his seat when the dinner was over and an electric apparatus had washed and dried the dishes, and went into the tower. Presently Hawley nodded to him, and he threw over the lever that controlled the air-tight seal. A moment later he had thrown back the hatch and stepped out upon the platform, calling to Carrisford to follow him.

They were moving rapidly through a thick fog. In the interior of the boat an automatic adjuster had maintained an equitable temperature, but in the open, even in spite of the fog, Carrisford was sensible of a marked increase of temperature.

The boat shot out of the enclosing wall of fog, and Century Island stood revealed.

The huge bulk of the submarine slipped through the water so smoothly that Carrisford scarcely realized that they were moving until, without warning, the boat shot out of the enclosing wall of fog and Century Island stood revealed.

The sun had long since sunk below the horizon, for it was winter in the southern hemisphere, and the days were short, but latticed towers crowned by vibratory lights gave an illumination almost equal to daylight.

The city was built upon a gentle slope, rising in terraces. At the foot of the hill ran a broad esplanade, gorgeous with flower-beds. Along the rear was a one-story structure, apparently a mile and a half in length, pierced at intervals with wide gateways. Above this rose tiers of houses identical in design with the lower row save that here they were not more than two hundred feet long, with a fifty-foot space between each. At the top of the hill stood the Palace, or Administration Building—a large structure six stories high.

The esplanade was thronged with people who crowded eagerly about the basin in the center of the plaza, where rose a water-gate. There was the sound of music, and as the submarine shot into view a cheer came faintly across the water.

"It is your welcome to Century Island," said Graves. "Quick; we must prepare for the reception."

Wonderingly, Carrisford followed him down the iron stairway. Now,

McPherson was draped in the same kind of black cloak that Graves had worn at first when he had come to the new arrival. Graves' cloak hung over the back of one of the chairs. He slipped into this, and the two passed to the rear of the boat.

Here a handsome casket stood upon a pair of trestles, and over it hung a long cloth of black stuff. Graves caught this up and began winding it about Carrisford's shoulders.

"It is an ancient custom," he said. "Only the dead come to Century Island. The ceremony does not last very long, and you will find it interesting in the extreme."

As he was speaking he had wrapped Carrisford's legs, and now, catching him up in his arms, he deposited him in the casket.

"You may look," he counseled, "until you hear me call. Then close your eyes until you are commanded to open them again. Now lie quiet, for here come the bearers."

Eight huge blacks entered the hold through the hatch, which they had raised, and caught up the coffin. With this upon their shoulders, they moved over to an elevator in the center of the place. Graves and McPherson took their places behind them, and as the platform began to move upward the sound of a great organ, playing a dead march, pealed through the air.

Slowly the procession crossed the deck, and so across the platform of the water-gate to the entrance, where they set down their burden upon a marble altar. In an instant all of the lights of the city went out save one torch at the head of the casket, and a man in a purple robe advanced toward the gruesome object.

IV

THE LAW OF THE ISLAND

With the extinguishing of the lights the music was hushed until it scarcely seemed sound at all. The man in the purple robe advanced to the side of the casket.

"Who lies here?" he demanded of Graves.

"One who in earth life was called Grenville Carrisford," answered Graves.

"He comes of his own free will?"

Graves bowed.

"He comes because he has no further use for life on earth. Like us all, he has thought far in advance of his time, and he would die in life that he might reach that land where to-morrow is to-day and to-day is yesterday."

"And abandoning the world, as one dead, he comes willingly to our country of to-morrow, seeking the companionship of others who, like himself, have lived in advance of their time?"

"Even as one dead, renouncing the worldly pleasures for the greater joy of life among kindred souls."

"He has accomplished that which is worthy of our land?"

"He brings rare knowledge; thoughts so great that the earth men cannot understand."

The man in purple turned to the casket and looked down upon the man wrapped in his shroud of black.

"Grenville Carrisford," he said impressively. "But for those whom we maintain, already you would have passed the borders of the earth life. Even as your hand was raised against yourself did our agent intervene.

"We hold that we are entitled to the life that we have saved. Upon the body, upon the spirit we claim jurisdiction. Over thy actions in sleep or wakefulness, at work or at diversion, we claim entire control. For as we raised thee from the dead, so shall we take away that life as penalty for disobedience.

"We demand no vows, we ask no promises. Instead, we give assurance that even as we bring thee up out of the coffin, so shall we place thee therein forever if thou are not obedient."

Graves leaned over the casket.

"Close your eyes," he whispered, "and do not open them until the word is given."

Carrisford obediently closed his eyes, and the voice boomed out again. This time, Carrisford knew that he was addressing the people.

"Behold," he cried, "the body of Grenville Carrisford, who is dead on earth, but who shall live in the Land of To-morrow. From the death of the ignorance of the world he rises to the fellowship of his equals, yielding obedience to the laws we have made and accepting the penalty thereof for his disobedience."

The voice ceased, and Carrisford felt them stripping from him his wrappings. Then he was raised up in the coffin, which had been moved in a quarter circle, and he was conscious of a flood of light against his closed eyelids.

"Open your eyes," called the voice. "Look upon those who are to be thy brothers."

At the command Carrisford opened his eyes and looked about him. The lights had been turned on again, and now the music swelled out in a new strain of gladness. Graves helped the man in purple lift him from the coffin, and as Carrisford stood up the entire assemblage raised their right hands high in the air in silent salute. Coached by Graves, Carrisford made reply and turned to be introduced to those on the platform.

The man in purple, he learned, was Paul Beardsley, the president of the

The entire assemblage raised their right hands high in the air in silent salute.

island. Taylor Todd, with a broad band of purple edging his toga, was vice-president, and seven elderly men, who wore two narrow stripes of purple, were the council. The unofficial welcoming was soon over, and Carrisford, accompanied by McPherson, stepped down from the platform and made his way through the crowd.

As those nearest him clasped his hand in welcome, Carrisford marveled at the preponderance of men. Only here and there was a woman to be seen.

McPherson led the way through one of the gates in the long building, and Carrisford found himself ascending by a gentle grade a well-paved street. On either side were square buildings without openings of any sort save for the gateways that opened upon the streets running parallel with the harbor.

"In the morning," explained McPherson, "you will be assigned a permanent place. For to-night you shall be my guest. We turn here."

He led the way down one of the side streets and turned in at a gate. Carrisford could see now that the lights were enclosed in each courtyard. On three sides of the square were suites of rooms, consisting of a bath, a sitting-room, and a sleeping-room. On the fourth side was an open dining-room on one side of the gateway, while on the other was the kitchen.

McPherson led the way into his own suite, and Carrisford noticed that the rooms were large and comfortable. There was no need of artificial light, though a vacuum tube ran around the four walls.

"The lights are turned off at eleven," explained the host. "After that the independent illumination must be used. Except by special permit, all lights must be out by midnight. Now, if you're ready, we'll go to your apartment. It's right next door."

He led the way through the arched passage into the next bedroom. It did not take Carrisford long to throw off his robes, and before the light in the court went out he was already sound asleep and dreaming that, instead of rising from the dead, the coffin had been lowered into the inferno.

He was wakened in the morning by a trumpet call, which seemed to sound in his very room. He jumped into the bathtub, and was getting into his clothes when McPherson came in.

"I'm to devote the day to showing you around," he explained. "I thought I had better start early. Was your bath too cold?"

"Rather chilly," said Carrisford with a smile. McPherson led the way into the bath-room and showed a dial on the wall.

"Set that overnight to the temperature you want," he explained. "It will be just right in time for your bath. The central station throws the current into the bath thermals at five. They wake you at seven by the music transmitter, and the bath is just the right temperature. Let's go to breakfast."

He led the way across the court to the dining-room, where the rest of the company was already seated. Twelve men formed a house-party and ate at the common table.

The food had been put into the electric cookers the night before by the slaves, who also set the tables. Now, the chops were cooked to a turn, the coffee was clear and fragrant, and even the biscuits were light and feathery.

As the meal was finished, a slave came in, cleared the table, and set about tidying the place. The others went about their daily tasks, but McPherson and Carrisford strolled through the city.

McPherson first led the way to the water-front, where the laboratories were located in the long building. Here the scientists worked at their tasks, each in his own domain. Electricity was everywhere; it turned the wheels and provided heat for the furnaces. Apparently, the supply was inexhaustible, and Carrisford made inquiry.

"The radiations of radium," explained McPherson. "The island is volcanic, and President Beardsley devised a scheme for converting the rays directly into electrical impulse.

"There seems to be small need for my invention," laughed Carrisford. "No need to amplify the current when the direct product is so abundant."

"On the contrary, your idea is most welcome. It will relieve the pressure on the feed wires. Then, too, in the submarine we can develop greater power with the same storage capacity. Don't worry. You will find your place."

They went through the vast works, then climbed the hill for the interview with the president. The interview was satisfactory in the extreme, and as they came away Carrisford's face beamed. He had been given *carte blanche* to push his experiments to the utmost. He had been assigned a laboratory to himself, with the necessary helpers, and was to begin work as soon as he was ready.

What pleased him almost as much was his assignment to the quarters he had occupied the night before. He had conceived a genuine liking for McPherson, and was glad of his society.

They were descending the steps of the Administration Building, were congratulating themselves upon their good fortune, when a cry behind them caused them both to turn. Just behind, a girl, descending the steps, had slipped and, in falling, fell directly into Carrisford's arms.

For a moment he held the slender form in his arms, feeling her warm breath upon his cheek and scenting the fragrance of her hair. Then he had set her down, and with a blushing word of thanks she offered him her hand.

"I thank you very much," she said sweetly. "You are Mr. Carrisford, the new arrival, are you not? I am Clio Beardsley. I am glad to welcome you to Century Island."

She passed on down the steps with a pretty nod, and left Carrisford standing dumb with the pressure of his feelings. Carrisford had known many beautiful women in his day, but never before had he seen one so beautiful as Clio Beardsley. She was tall and slender, with great, serious eyes of unfathomable depths. Her face was a regular oval, framed in masses of golden hair, bound in the Grecian style with a purple band, and the robes, flowing in classical simplicity, were also edged with the purple of authority.

McPherson slapped him on the back.

"Come, lad," he admonished. "There is much to see this afternoon. You'll be wanting to have a look at your laboratory, and I want to show you my fog-dispeller."

They passed on down the steps, but Carrisford looked listlessly at the splendid laboratory placed at his disposal, and gave little heed to McPherson's explanation of the machine which had gained him admission to the colony. Even while he listened to the elaborate explanation of how the electrical currents dispelled the moisture of which the fogs were composed, he could see through the banks of mist the sweet girlish face.

In the middle of the explanation he broke in to ask whether it was Miss or Mrs. Beardsley.

"Miss Beardsley, of course," replied McPherson. "Now, you see how we keep the fogs away. Let's take one of the cars and go over to see the gardens."

They took a motor-car and rode out to where the vast fields provided

*For a moment he held the slender
form in his arms.*

the fruits and vegetables needed for the colony. They inspected the droves
of fine cattle and sheep, and visited the vast poultry-yard. It was all very
interesting, but Carrisford was deep in thought of Clio Beardsley.

Late that evening McPherson stole into Carrisford's rooms.

"Are you awake, lad?" he whispered. Carrisford answered. He was too
full of this new wonder of love to compose himself to sleep. McPherson sat
himself down upon the edge of the bed.

"I wanted to tell you, lad," he whispered. "There's only one sort of vital
statistics in Century Island. They are the deaths. It's like heaven in one way,
for there is 'neither marriage nor giving in marriage.' To break the rule means
death."

V

WHAT IS LOVE?

Carrisford half rose from the bed.

"Do you mean to say," he demanded hoarsely, "that marriage is not
permitted here?"

"Just that," assented the Scotchman. "It is a wise provision, lad."

"It is unnatural," insisted Carrisford. "It is an outrage against the very law
of the world."

"You don't understand," said McPherson pityingly. "You see, laddie, this is not a normal colony. Apart from the dumb slaves, we are all brain workers, men and women. The women, you see, have all contributed to the colony ideas of equal value with the men. There was a time when marriage was permitted, but from very horror the thing was stopped."

"I fail to see the horror in such a sacrament," said the younger man. "Why, we should have a race of intellectual giants here on Century Island."

McPherson shook his head.

"I saw some of them," he explained. "Too much intellect for the little bodies. They were all head, laddie—imbeciles. It was a pitiful sight."

"But Clio—Miss Beardsley; she is not abnormal."

"Very true, very true. But she is the only woman who ever came to Century Island who was not a scientist. If we made an exception in her case, all would demand it. No, it is wiser as it is. Most of us are content. The others know that death is the punishment for even speaking of love, and so we look to the earth people to populate our island. In return we give them our inventions when they are ready for them. The income from these goes to maintain our establishments for recruiting."

"And I am to bow meekly to the decree?" demanded Carrisford.

"Either that or death," responded McPherson. "Be careful, laddie. I speak only for your own good."

He patted Carrisford on the shoulder and slipped from the room.

No sleep came to Carrisford that night. In the darkness he could see the sweet face of Clio Beardsley as in a vision, and the more he looked the more determined he was that he should win her for his wife. There were some five thousand inhabitants on Century Island. Surely some of these must be intolerant of the same conditions. He might arrange a revolt.

He came to breakfast haggard and wan. McPherson, watching him anxiously, sighed. Once he had gone through the same experience, but he had come to realize that the existing order was the best.

"I must get over to the south side of the island," he said as they left the dining-pavilion. "Some of the machines are in need of repair, and the fog is coming in on the vegetable garden. Go to your work, lad. You will find forgetfulness there."

The two men walked down the inclined street to the esplanade and as far as Carrisford's laboratory. There McPherson left him with a promise to look in on his way back, and went off to obtain a vehicle to carry him to his battle with the fog.

Carrisford went into the laboratory with far different feelings than he had anticipated the day before when President Beardsley had assured him that everything needed for his experiments would be forthcoming immediately.

The promise had almost overwhelmed him after the days of struggle in America, when a tool meant the sacrifice of a meal or two and the purchase of supplies was frequently delayed several weeks. He had left the reception-chamber aglow with enthusiasm, but the meeting with Clio and the subsequent discovery of the law against marriage had thrown him into the blackest despondency.

And yet, once he became absorbed in his work he went rapidly about his task. Two skilled helpers had been provided, and he soon had his machine started.

The noon meal was served in the shops, and there was little delay. They were hard at work when some one entered the place.

"That you, McPherson?" called Carrisford without looking up. "Come over here; I'm fixing up the magnifier. I think I shall have it done by to-morrow."

"I am glad that Mr. Carrisford makes such excellent progress," said a deep voice behind him, and Carrisford sprang up to salute the president.

"I am very much interested in the invention," went on Beardsley. "It will simplify the wiring when additional power is needed, and in many ways it will work a revolution. My daughter was speaking of it last night. You have met Miss Beardsley," he added as Clio came forward.

Carrisford bent over the little hand with flaming face.

"I persuaded father to bring me down," she said in her low, clear voice. "I am studying electricity myself, you know. I feel so utterly frivolous in the midst of these thousands of clever people."

"I thought you had to be an inventor to obtain citizenship," he said.

Clio smiled proudly.

"They needed father so badly that they waived the rule and let me come, too, though I am sure that I shall never invent anything. Will you show me your machine, please?"

Carrisford went over the details of his device, and was surprised at the intelligent appreciation she displayed. It was evident that she was possessed of a technical knowledge astonishing in a woman of her age, and he became so absorbed in his explanations that he did not realize how late it was until the electric apparatus blew its trumpet call for the cessation of work.

Clio started up with a little exclamation of surprise.

"I had no idea of the time," she said regretfully. "You must dine with us this evening, Mr. Carrisford, and complete the explanation then."

"We shall be most glad to have you," seconded the president, and Carrisford stammered out his acceptance.

Dressing for dinner was no elaborate undertaking on Century Island. After the bath a toga was put on instead of the short tunic. All of the garments were of the same cloth and made in the same fashion.

McPherson found Carrisford splashing about in his tub when he returned from his own work. He shook his head sadly at the announcement that Carrisford was to dine with the president, but he offered no objection.

He walked as far as the steps of the Administration Building with his friend, and as he took his leave, whispered a caution, but it is doubtful if Carrisford even heard it. He realized only that he was to dine with Clio, and he sprang up the steps with a beating heart.

The dinner was precisely the same as that served in every group house, but to the young inventor it seemed a banquet. Taylor Todd was also a guest, and the president carried him off after dinner to discuss some affairs of state.

"Suppose we sit in the court," suggested Clio. "Father will be talking with Mr. Todd for the rest of the evening. Mr. Todd wants to build an air-ship on a new principle."

They passed through the dining-room out on to a covered balcony. The building was arranged around a square and the center was filled with a mass of luxuriant plants. Carrisford had already seen how the buried electrodes forced the growth, and merely marveled at the scientific development that maintained palms and other tropical vegetation a few hundred miles from the South Pole.

But the greater wonder was the glorious beauty of the girl beside him, and as they paced about the court he had eyes only for her. Presently she led the way through an arched passage to a terrace overlooking the town.

Seen from above, the greenery of the courts broke the monotony of the white granite-like composition which was the only material employed in the construction of buildings.

"Sometimes," she said, as they leaned against the balustrade, "I am afraid that I almost grow tired of this absolute regularity. I was such a little girl when I was brought here—not more than five or six, for father knew of radium long before the Curies announced that they had discovered it. I can just remember London, with the crooked streets and the smoke-stained buildings.

"Here everything is so orderly that at times I feel as though I must scream. There are so many houses to a street, each the same as the other, and containing the same number of tenants; we all eat our breakfast at the same hour; we go to work and stop work at the same signal."

"You are unusual in longing for the world," said Carrisford. "Most of us have found the world too formidable a foe."

"I know," assented the girl, with a shudder. "It seems horrible to think that so many of the people here were saved from suicide. The ceremony of reception is a terrible thing."

"It is very impressive," he said, "and a warning against the infraction of the regulations. Yet I should think that Dan Cupid might make trouble at times."

"Dan Cupid?" she asked. "Is he in the electrical, mechanical, or minerals section?"

"He is everywhere—even on Century Island," Carrisford explained. "But he has never gone through the ceremony of reception. He is the god of love."

"Love," she echoed. "We know little of love here, Mr. Carrisford. I suppose you mean love for—for your friends. I have often wondered how it felt to be in love."

"Do you never read romances?"

"Romances are treatises upon love?" she asked.

"Not treatises," he said, with a laugh—"stories of persons who love. Sometimes they move heaven and earth before their tangled affairs are straightened out, and they are married and live happily ever after."

"The libraries here contain only scientific works," she said, with regret. "Only those parts of the magazines are reprinted which concern discoveries and inventions. Father is the editor. Did not Mr. McPherson show you a copy?"

"I have seen the abstract," he admitted, "but I thought that light reading might be permitted."

"It is prohibited," she said. "Mme. Ferrers once wrote a book. She wanted father to print it, but he scolded her and burned the manuscript. I asked her what it was about, but she said she dared not tell. Can you describe love?"

"It's rather hard," said Carrisford, with an uneasy laugh, "and it seems to be prohibited."

"But you will tell me," she urged.

"It is a feeling that there is one person worth more to you than all the world," began Carrisford. "He or she means more to you than even father or mother. For the loved one you are ready to go through any peril or sacrifice."

"It makes you feel strange when you see him?" she asked, placing her hand over her heart.

Carrisford nodded.

"And you want to be with him and help him? You are bashful when you meet him, and you are afraid that he will see that you like him, and then again you are afraid that he will not?"

"Something like that," he assented, the frown deepening on his brow. Clio already loved. There was no hope for him. "Love is a mass of contradictions."

"I know," she said. "You want him to kiss you, and then you know that you will die of shame if he does. I am in love. Is it not odd that I did not know what it was?"

"Not so very," said Carrisford gloomily. "Some people love for years and do not realize it until too late."

"I have only loved since yesterday," she said simply. "Only since you caught me in your arms there on the steps."

VI

REBELLION

For a moment the town seemed to whirl before Carrisford's eyes, and he clutched at the balustrade. Clio regarded him curiously.

"I have alarmed you?" she said. "I am sorry. Let us forget what I said. Perhaps it will pass."

"Forget!" he echoed. "Do you suppose that I want you to forget? Child, ever since that moment down there on the steps I have thought of nothing but you and the hopelessness of my love."

"You love, also?" she asked, as her hand slipped within his own.

"Heaven help us, I do!" he answered. "Don't you understand, dear, that love here, on Century Island, can bring only sorrow and pain?"

"Then, why can't we go away?" she asked. "You are so clever that you will find a way. Perhaps I could coax my father to let us go. He is president, and can do as he pleases."

"He cannot alter the law of the land," declared Carrisford. "If he did but imagine that I have come here to win you, he would kill me in a moment to hide the fact that you had fallen in love. It is perhaps wise in a measure that marriage is prohibited here. Not even for his own daughter may he overrule the law."

"Then, we must keep it secret," she said, "though it seems wrong to be ashamed of what God puts in our hearts. Perhaps in time we shall find a way."

"God grant that we may," he groaned, "else it were better that I had taken my life in that Chicago hotel."

"Do not say that," she pleaded. "It is better to have loved, even though we pay for it with our lives. We at least feel that we are for each other."

Slowly they retraced their steps across the terrace and through the passage leading to the court. The leave-taking was short.

The president regretted that the visit of Todd had caused an interruption, and promised that he would come to the laboratory in the morning to complete his inquiry. Then he escorted his guest to the head of the stairway and watched, with his arm about his daughter, while Carrisford went slowly down the broad flight. Then he turned to Clio.

"What did you and Carrisford find that was so interesting?" he demanded curiously. "You seemed much absorbed in your talk."

"He was asking of the city," she explained demurely, though her cheek still wore a delicate flush. "It was all so new and strange to him. We spoke of other things," she added, "but little that would interest."

The president raised the fair young face and looked down into the untroubled eyes.

"I fear that I acted unwisely in asking him to dinner," he said. "Young men fresh from the worldly life bring foolish notions into this happy country of ours. Be careful, Clio, and see him as little as possible, lest he fill your head with foolish thoughts. Come, child, let us go to our rooms, and think no more of this young man, who will be very useful to us if he possesses discretion to match his other qualities."

"He really is clever, is he not?" she demanded, anxious to hear him praised.

Beardsley shook his head.

"Almost too clever," he said. "I am afraid that even his invention, valuable as it is, will not excuse his introduction here."

Meanwhile, Carrisford was walking down the street toward the esplanade, lifting his feet heavily, as one half dazed. He could not go to his group-house just now. He could not face the shrewd Scotchman in his present mood, and so he kept on until he reached the broad sea-wall.

The smell of the salt water was pleasant, and the light breeze cooled his healed brow. He walked hurriedly along to the east.

Here the esplanade ran into the broad road that led to the plantations, and presently he had left the paving and was hurrying along the macadam. He had gone perhaps a quarter of a mile when he came suddenly around a curve in the road to face two figures locked in an embrace.

For an instant, in the dim light, he thought that he had come upon a fight; but the next moment Taylor Todd came toward him with an upraised knife, and Carrisford saw that the other was a woman.

He was unarmed, but he was younger than Todd, and he had little trouble in gripping the hand that held the knife. Back and forth they struggled upon the smooth surface of the road, but, try as he would, he could not wrest the weapon from the other's grasp.

At last he succeeded in throwing his antagonist, and Todd's elbow striking the hard earth, the knife went flying across the road. Quick as a flash the woman had caught it up, and as the two men rolled over and over she watched her chance to strike.

Gaining new strength in his terror, Todd was besting Carrisford. With one hand he had pinned him to the ground and with the other was reaching for the knife the woman held, when Carrisford wrenched away the hand that was slowly strangling him.

"Hold on, you fool," he whispered. "Why do you want to kill me? I know that the president has given you permission to build a new air-ship. Now I know what you want it for. You need my help. Without my magnifier you can never make land."

Todd relaxed his pressure, but he held the knife threateningly against the other's throat.

"What makes you think I want to leave Century Island?" he demanded.

"It is death to remain here, loving a woman," answered Carrisford. "An air-ship is about the only real means of making an escape. Suppose I were minded to return to the world myself? We could go together."

"Perhaps it would be as well," muttered Todd; but the woman leaned over the pair.

"Perhaps he is a traitor," she whispered. "Perhaps he only seeks to accomplish our undoing. Strike, lest you regret it."

"Strike, and regret it, Mme. Ferrers," retorted Carrisford.

It was a wild guess, but it struck home.

"You see, he knows my name," whispered the woman. "He has been set to watch us."

"It was perfectly natural," explained Carrisford. "I was told this evening by Miss Beardsley that a Mme. Ferrers had written a novel that the president would not permit her to print. There are so few women here who are not completely engrossed in their work that the inference was obvious."

"Hold on, you fool," he whispered.
"Why do you want to kill me?"

"Clio Beardsley told you?" she asked.

Carrisford nodded. She turned away with a short laugh.

"He is safe enough, *mon ami*," she said to Todd. "He and the little Clio have learned to talk of love. It is but natural that they should wish to be fellow passengers."

Carrisford stared at her as he rose from the dust and shook the dirt from his garments. Mme. Ferrers was a rather gaunt Frenchwoman, whose dominant personality had swayed the less determined Todd. She had, he knew, been admitted to the colony because of her skill as a writer of scientific treatises rather than because of her scientific attainments.

She found the colony dull after her beloved Paris, and she was eager to make her escape. One after another, she had sought in vain to win the love of the three men who operated the submarine, and as a last resort she had turned to Todd, urging him to build an air-ship sufficiently strong to permit a passage to Australia or South America. He had fallen a victim to her wiles, and through his important position in the community he had obtained permission to construct a large air-ship.

"You think that you can help me with the ship?" demanded Todd as he turned to Carrisford, after a whispered conversation with the woman.

"I am certain that I can do so," was the confident reply. "How much power do you need?"

"I have not figured yet," he said, "but I am afraid that I cannot use electricity. The storage-batteries would weigh too much, even in the improved form in which we get them."

"I can develop one horse-power with two gravity cells," said Carrisford. "The magnifier weighs as much as a third cell for each pair."

"You are certain of this?" demanded Todd excitedly. "You are sure that the supply of current will be constant?"

Carrisford smiled.

"I would suggest that you come to my laboratory to-morrow," he said. "There I can demonstrate my ideas to your entire satisfaction."

"Then we are indeed fortunate," said Todd. "In a little while we shall be free of all this and back to our own again. Glad indeed am I that the chance has come. Science is but a poor thing to love."

"Science takes all and gives nothing," said Carrisford. "I was not born to be a slave to science alone."

"Look!" Mme. Ferrers pointed to the city, where but a moment before the lights had been glowing. Now all was dark, and the buildings gleamed but faintly in the starlight.

"It is time to part," said Todd reluctantly. "Do you wait for me beyond the bend, Carrisford."

Carrisford walked rapidly toward the turning of the road and then more slowly until Todd caught up. Together they made their way back to the city, and as they walked Todd rapidly sketched a plan of action.

For the first time Carrisford realized that there was an electrified zone about the island, and that to attempt to pass this zone would be to give immediate warning to the watcher in the executive offices.

With the newly found power it might be possible to rise above this zone before heading away from the island, but this could only be accomplished were the authorities kept in ignorance of the power developed by the magnifier through the battery cells.

It was agreed that the magnifier should be developed for the direct current from the central generator, but that the experiments with the cells should appear to be a failure.

With this understanding they parted at Carrisford's street, and he turned up to his group-house. At the entrance one of the mutes saluted, and Carrisford, thinking him one of those who filled the electric kitchens, passed in.

There was still a light in McPherson's quarters, and as Carrisford went past the open door the Scotchman followed him down to his own rooms.

"Where have you been, lad?" he demanded. "The president has called for you three times, and there is a man outside waiting for you—one of the mutes."

"I was only taking a walk," explained Carrisford. McPherson opened his mouth as though to speak, but at that moment the telephone-bell rang, and Carrisford stepped to the instrument.

"Where were you, Mr. Carrisford?" asked President Beardsley.

"I went for a walk," replied Carrisford. "I went along the shore road for a space."

"Midnight walks are not to be recommended," said the voice at the other end of the line. "I trust that I am mistaken, Mr. Carrisford, but for the present it would be as well if you remained in your own apartments after dinner each evening."

Carrisford made reply, and hung up the receiver. He rapidly repeated to McPherson the gist of the message, and the Scotchman's face fell.

"It's but a poor beginning," he said, with a sigh. "Invited to the president's to dinner and then placed under surveillance. Here in Century Island life ends when love begins." McPherson went out, shaking his head.

VII

THE FLIGHT FROM CENTURY

There was little sleep for Carrisford that night. The knowledge that Clio loved him was tempered by the fact that the president suspected at least the affection that existed between them. No doubt they had both displayed their feelings in their faces as they came through the arch into the garden of the court.

That Todd could build an air-ship that would carry them to Australia or South America he did not doubt. Two small ships were in service on the island, though their heavy storage-batteries prohibited extended flights. With his magnifier this obstacle could be overcome. But there was still the question how to get word to Clio when the time should be ripe, for he did not doubt that she would be watched.

He was entirely unprepared for the placing of a guard upon his own movements. As he came from the group-house the following morning a huge mute stood beside the gate and silently fell in behind Carrisford, following him to the laboratory and placing himself unobtrusively within the place.

Paying no attention to him, Carrisford went quietly about his work, with the assistance of the two helpers who had been assigned to him. It was nearly noon when the president came, as he had promised, to complete his inspection of the magnifier.

That he was impressed was easy to be seen. He followed carefully the working of the crude model Carrisford had constructed the previous day, and nodded approvingly.

"I should be sorry to see the work abruptly terminated," he said as he stood beside the door when the visit was over.

"I should share your regret," said Carrisford simply. "I will not pretend to misunderstand your meaning, sir. McPherson explained last night."

"It will soon pass," said Beardsley, with a confidence that he did not seem to feel. "Look," he went on, waving his hand to indicate the vast shops. "All of these are men and women who have at some time been in love. Now they are absorbed in their work and are far happier than they could ever be if married. Do you recall Pschever, Mr. Carrisford? He gave wonderful promise at one time, but he married, and the scientific world knew him no more."

"I met them," returned Carrisford. "He made a fortune from his inventions. He is supremely happy with his wife and children."

Beardsley's brow clouded.

"That is the trouble here," he cried—"the children. Had you seen what I have seen, Mr. Carrisford, you would understand better. The ordinary man leaves his sons and daughters as a heritage to the next generation. The scientist leaves his inventions. Few there are whose children are aught but imbeciles."

"I might suggest yourself as a notable exception," said Carrisford, with a dark smile.

"I married first," explained Beardsley. "Absorption in my work came after my wife died. That does not prove the rule, Mr. Carrisford. Let us not argue the matter further. The laws of Century Island were made by wiser men than you or I, and I am merely here to see that they are enforced—not to upset the structure so carefully reared."

He turned away abruptly and hurried along the esplanade. Carrisford went to the edge of the broad walk and looked down into the water. The mute came silently to the doorway and stood there watching him. Taylor Todd, hurrying along, passed him with a short nod.

"I will run in this afternoon," he said loudly enough for the mute to hear. "I have the president's permission to call upon you for some technical advice."

"I shall be glad to give it," replied Carrisford.

"I have a plan for a new air-ship," Todd went on. "It promises to be a little more difficult than I anticipated, but I am confident of my ultimate success. I will bring in some drawings to show you."

He hurried on, and Carrisford returned to his work much cheered. The words had carried a secret meaning to him. It was evident that Todd was aware of the espionage in which Carrisford was held and sought to give him hope.

This belief became a fact when Todd came in late in the afternoon. He carried under his arm a roll of plans, and immediately launched into a long discussion of the ship he intended to construct.

"The worst of it is," he said briskly, "that I cannot get away from the weight of the storage-batteries. Now, you will see from this table that a ship of these dimensions cannot carry more than sufficient current for twenty-four hours operation."

He laid the plan on the bench and took out a smaller sheet. It contained a table of weights of the various parts of the airship. One set of figures particularly interested Carrisford. They were:

Weight of motor 537
Weight of storage-battery . . . 973
                                  ————
                                 1,510

He laid the table down upon a bench close to an electric furnace, and as Carrisford studied it an additional table was revealed on the paper. It ran:

Weight of motor 537
Weight of batteries 320
Weight of magnifier . . . . . .   ?
                                  ————

"About sixty pounds here," said Carrisford, "giving a leeway of five hundred and sixty-three pounds."

"Then I think we can make it all right," said Todd, with a smile of satisfaction, as he slipped into Carrisford's hand a note folded within a second one. He rolled up his plans, and with the promise of a visit on the morrow, bustled out of the place.

Carrisford could scarcely wait until he returned to his apartment to open and read the letters. The first was a note from Todd, explaining that it was his idea to keep the matter of the batteries a complete secret until such time as they were ready to put them to use. Meanwhile, Beardsley would feel assured that the ship could not sail away from the current base on the island.

The second enclosure was Clio's first love-letter—a faltering little epistle, half shy, half unconsciously frank. Carrisford reread the note until the words seemed engraved upon his brain. Then he tore it into minute particles and carefully burned the fragments with the other note.

Clio wrote that she was being closely watched, but that Mme. Ferrers had asked for a letter, and had told her of their hopes. She warned Carrisford not to attempt to reply, but promised to be ready at the appointed time.

It was with a more quiet mind that Carrisford sought his couch, and he awoke in the morning with his mind refreshed. By nightfall his first large magnifier had been tested and found to work admirably, and he was hailed as a worthy citizen.

The manufacture of the magnifier was commenced upon a large scale, and in the interest aroused by this novelty Todd's new air-ship was entirely forgotten.

But Todd was working with feverish energy. A huge barn had been erected at the end of the esplanade, and in this the machine was rapidly assuming form. It was of the double aeroplane type, without a gas-bag, depending entirely upon air resistance and the power of its motors to keep it at any desired altitude.

He kept in close touch with Carrisford, and together they secretly constructed the cell batteries and a huge magnifier that would yield one horsepower for each pair of cells. This was hidden in the barn under some boxes of tools, and the public test was made with the usual storage-batteries.

Todd also laid in a stock of diamonds artificially produced for use in drills, but as large and perfect as the best stones from the South African mines. The intense heat developed by the furnaces permitted the fusing of several smaller stones into a single large one, and since they were regarded only as material for tools Todd had little trouble in obtaining all he wanted. Platinum was the precious metal of Century Island, and this alone was used for ornaments.

It was four months after Carrisford's arrival that plans were at last completed. Todd met Mme. Ferrers for a final conference, and Carrisford was with him. He had long since been relieved of the espionage of the mute, but he knew that Clio was still watched.

Mme. Ferrers was like a child in her glee at the prospect of delivery from her long imprisonment, and babbled incessantly of what she should do when they were in Paris. She struck up a quaint old-fashioned song that Carrisford remembered having heard years before. It was probably the rage when she left the earth for Century, and he smiled as he thought of the difference she would find in her beloved city.

But as her shrill voice rang out it attracted the attention of a company of mutes on their way into the city with farm products, and the captain of the little band penetrated the grove to investigate the cause of the disturbance.

As he pushed his way into the little glade where the three had met, Carrisford caught sight of him. At his cry Todd also sprang up. The two raced after the intruder, who had already started to run back to the road and his companions.

Laying about them with branches picked up in their rush, Carrisford and Todd soon laid out four of the slaves. The other two did not stop to fight, but started on a run for the city, and were soon beyond reach.

In the emergency, Carrisford took command. Mme. Ferrers had followed them to the road, and now he caught her arm.

"Run to the barn," he cried. "It is our only hope."

Todd caught the idea, and they ran swiftly down the smooth road to the barn, where the air-ship was stored. As they worked over the exchange from storage to cell battery, Mme. Ferrers loaded the lockers with water and the food-tablets that were sometimes used in an emergency.

They had almost completed their task when they heard the soft noise of bare feet on the road outside, and realized that a company of mutes was being rushed to the scene.

At the same time the city lights flared up and people began to rush down to the esplanade. Todd tested the motor, and they all climbed in.

"Too bad we cannot get Miss Beardsley," said Todd. "We had best make a straight dash out to sea."

Carrisford caught his arm.

"We shall do nothing of the sort," he declared sternly. "We shall make for the palace."

For a moment they struggled desperately, but Carrisford was both stronger and more determined. He forced Todd away from the wheel, and with a whir they were out of the barn and circling in the air.

As the ship rose, it headed for the hill. In the bright light, Carrisford could see that the inhabitants of the Administration Building were gathered on the

"Run to the barn," he cried. "It is our only hope."

roof watching the disturbance. His eyes were unusually good, and before he was recognized he had already picked out the purple-fringed tunic that he knew to be Clio's.

She was standing apart from the others. With a skillful touch he steered the machine close to that part of the roof on which she stood, and almost before the others realized that Clio had not come out simply to investigate the cause of the disturbance, Carrisford had swung the girl aboard the ship and turned toward the sea.

Half a dozen mutes came running toward the aeroplane, and one, leaping high in air, caught the lower edge of the platform. Lying down upon the platform, Todd reached over and wrenched loose the man's grip. Relieved of the weight, the car shot forward.

Century did not depend upon firearms for defense. The waters for ten miles about were wired with floats to notify the inhabitants of the approach of a ship, and long before the belt of fog was penetrated, the submarine could destroy the intruder with a torpedo.

Only the smaller air-ships could offer chase, but as they passed the water-gate they could see the crew of the submarine preparing to follow. Carrisford leaned over and shouted a farewell to McPherson, who was just descending the hatchway. In answer to the hail came the reply:

"Good-by, lad, if you do get away; but I'm hoping that we catch you yet."

Then the aeroplane rose higher, and with a wave of the hand toward the glittering city Carrisford turned to the motor, giving the wheel to Todd.

VIII

McPherson to the Rescue

For a few minutes Carrisford busied himself with the buzzing instruments. There had been no time for adjustment before the start, and the magnifier was working badly. But presently the machine ran more smoothly, and the aeroplane shot up in the air as a result of the increased power.

They were above the fog-bank now and were driving rapidly northward. The glittering walls of the town on Century Island were still visible to the south, and Clio stood at the edge of the platform looking backward upon the only home she had known save for the dimly remembered London of her infancy. Her eyes filled with tears as she looked back upon the Administration Building, where she knew that her father must still be watching the flight.

Carrisford slipped his arm about her.

"Do you regret this step?" he asked softly.

For answer she flung her arms about his neck.

"No," she cried. "When I saw that the aeroplane had started without me I felt as though my heart would break. It is not that, but because I shall never see my father again. He is as one dead, even as all are on Century Island. It is horrible that we should be regarded as criminals, deserving of death, because we love each other."

"Many things are horrible, dear," he answered as he wrapped about her the toga which was slipped over the tunic in the evening. "But soon we shall come to a land where marriage is a sacred institution and not a crime."

"And we shall be happy while life lasts?" she demanded.

"So long as life shall last," he declared. "There will be much that is new to grow accustomed to, but it will all come in time."

"I shall have you," she whispered tenderly. "The rest will not matter. Is it not strange, dear, the change that has already come? From that moment when I fell upon the steps I have known that life was larger and more beautiful than I had ever realized."

"We have seen the last of the narrow life of science," he said, drawing her closer to him. Even as he spoke a shaft of light rent the fog, and Carrisford leaned over the rail.

McPherson had started his fog-dispeller, and the powerful machine had bored a tunnel through the fog through which gleamed the ray of a search-light. In the face of the dazzling rays they could barely make out the outline of the submarine, now steaming along the surface of the sea.

"They are trailing us to catch us when we fall," shouted Todd. "They know nothing of the batteries and think that with the storage machines we cannot keep up long enough to make land."

"We shall lead McPherson a merry chase," laughed Carrisford. "He will stick until we land, that's one thing certain."

"He won't get us," declared Todd grimly. "I once saw a man who had sought to escape. They brought him back, and for seven days he lingered, while all were compelled to look upon him and take to heart the lesson. At last—"

He broke off, and, with a white face, pushed over the lever and mounted higher in the air. It was clear that he was not minded to be taken. Clio leaned over to Carrisford.

"You won't let them take me back, will you?" she whispered.

"No danger of that," he said, with a laugh. "This aeroplane will take us clear through to New York if we want to go. Look!" he added as he pointed to the east. "Here comes the sun. At least you will not have to freeze now."

They had passed the fog-belt, and now they could see the submarine slipping through the water directly underneath. McPherson sat on the tiny deck smoking his pipe, and as he caught sight of some one leaning over

Carrisford swung the girl aboard the ship and turned toward the sea.

the rail he waved a good-morning salute. Carrisford replied and turned his attention to the wheel, while Todd got out the food-wafers.

It was a scanty breakfast at best, but Mme. Ferrers enlivened the meal by planning her first dinner in a Paris restaurant. At last Carrisford laughingly begged her to stop.

"I should be content with ham and eggs," he declared as he munched the tasteless compound of elements. "If you talk of truffled capon I shall certainly lose what little appetite I have for this scientific breakfast-food."

"It will only be for a couple of days," said Todd. "We are heading pretty straight for New Zealand. We can do about five hundred and fifty miles a day, and it is about fourteen hundred miles away."

"It will surprise the New Zealanders to see us come fluttering down," said Mme. Ferrers.

"I hope they do not see us," said Carrisford. "I do not want to divulge the secret of Century Island, and it will be enough to explain our costumes without adding to our troubles with an air-ship. I propose to set the machinery in motion and let it fly off. It will be lost in the sea with no one to control it, and of course the metal will sink. It is different from a gas-balloon."

"That is well," declared Mme. Ferrers, "but, *mon ami*, what of the jewels? Suppose that we have to disembark hurriedly?"

"Let's divide them now," proposed Todd. "Then we can each carry our share and dispose of just enough of them to take us to a place where we can sell them to advantage."

Clio packed the breakfast-dishes away, and Todd brought out the bag and divided the jewels into four equal parts. These he tied up in portions of his toga, and each of the quartet fastened one portion about the body. Carrisford lay down to get some rest while Todd took the wheel again, and Mme. Ferrers and Clio curled up in the corner opposite Carrisford.

It seemed to Carrisford that he had been sleeping but a few minutes when Todd's voice wakened him. The sky was black as he opened his eyes.

"Is it night already?" he asked. "I thought that you were to call me in four hours."

"It's only about nine o'clock," explained Todd; "but we are running into a thunder-storm."

Clio had roused herself at the sound of Carrisford's name, and now her terrified cry awoke Mme. Ferrers. The two women, clasped in each other's arms, huddled in their corner, while Carrisford, with ashen face, bent over the motor. The machinery was so delicate that he feared that the natural electrical current might disarrange the magnifier. In such a case the puny batteries could not keep the propeller revolving, and they would inevitably be pitched into the sea.

The driving clouds came rushing toward them, and Todd let the aeroplane sink a little, for there were vivid flashes as the electricity shot from one cloud to another. Lower down it was barely possible that they might escape.

Lower and lower he sank, until they could almost feel the spray from the storm-tossed waters, and the submarine was clearly in view. The hatch was battened down, and the boat was struggling through the buffeting waves at slow speed. McPherson stood on the deck clinging to the railing and anxiously watching the aeroplane, now a little to the rear.

Presently the rain began to fall in torrents, great sheets of water driving into their faces, so that Todd could scarcely see to steer. Only through the compass was he able to keep his head to the storm, and as the wind beat against the inclined planes the aeroplane rose steadily upward, darting into the teeth of the gale like some huge albatross. The submarine would not have been able to keep up with them had it not been for the fact that the great masses of rain hammered down the surface of the sea.

Carrisford gave no heed to the storm. He was bending over the magnifier, adjusting the instrument, as the electrical waves threw it out of order, when a shout of encouragement from Todd caused him to look up. Far in the west the sky was lighter—a promise that the storm had nearly passed.

At that moment there was a blinding flash, a crackling noise, followed by a deafening reverberation, and Carrisford staggered back. A small bolt had struck the knobs of the magnifier, and the instrument was shattered, while the motor itself was burned out.

Half blinded by the flash, Carrisford staggered toward the corner where he knew Clio to be. As the aeroplane trembled and pitched forward he caught the girl in his arms.

"Small danger of going back to Century Island," he whispered. "The sea will end it all in a few moments."

"I am not afraid," said the girl bravely. "I die with you."

For an instant she pressed her lips against his, and, then, with a tremendous splash, the aeroplane struck the water.

Todd had adjusted the planes to break their fall as much as possible, and they were not carried very far under water. As they rose to the surface, Carrisford struck out, and presently he encountered an obstacle. Surprised that the aeroplane should be floating, he looked up. McPherson's huge hand grasped his collar, and in another moment the Scotchman had dragged Carrisford and his sweetheart on board.

They were passed down the hatch while McPherson rescued Mme. Ferrers. Todd had gone down with the aeroplane, and though they cruised about for an hour they could find no trace of him.

"It's no use," sighed McPherson at last. "He must have become tangled in the wires. Let's get under water, where it will be easier going."

He closed the hatch, and presently the pitching ceased as the boat sank beneath the waves. They sank as far as it was safe, but no sign of the aeroplane could they see in the murky depths. At last McPherson gave the command to go ahead.

"It is a pity that you did not let us drown with Todd," said Carrisford bitterly. "Better that than the tortures to which we are doomed."

McPherson turned, with the bottle from which he had been administering stimulant to the rescued ones still in his hand.

"Gren, lad," he said solemnly, "we did not find ye. There's only Graves and me aboard. Hawley did not get down to the dock in time. We decided hours ago that we would let you all drown if you should fall; but we've been good friends, lad, and I couldn't stand and see ye die."

"You mean—" Carrisford sprang from his chair.

"Ye all are dead," said McPherson solemnly. "We followed you until you all dropped into the sea, and then we turned and went home."

"And you won't take us back?" cried Clio. "Oh, it seems too good to be true."

"But it is true," said McPherson kindly. "Carrisford, here, is a fine man. It would be a shame to hold you down to the dry life of the island. You two were not made for science, but for love. I loved once, before I turned to science. I was happy for a little while. I pay that happiness back to you."

"I am not afraid," said the girl. "I die with you."

"If you're thinking of taking a wedding trip," he whispered, "Scotland's a bonny country."

He took Clio's hand and placed it within Carrisford's.

"Take her, boy. Cherish her, and sometimes, in your happiness, think kindly of old Fergus McPherson."

With his left hand Carrisford clasped the other's.

"Won't you come with us, Fergus?" he pleaded. "Come and be happy again in the earth world."

The Scotchman shook his head, though his eyes grew wistful. "I'm too old to go back," he said. "Love is not for us old fellows. It is better that I should stay."

The following night the submarine crept up on the south coast of New Zealand. When the boat beached, McPherson walked with them to the shore.

"Ivercargill lies over there," he said, pointing to the west. "Get some civilized things before you get there. Work your way along the coast to Auckland. Don't go to Wellington, where our agent is. At Auckland you can get a steamer to Australia, and then—home."

His voice lingered over the last word, and for a moment the kindly eyes grew moist.

"You will need some money," he went on. "You cannot sell those diamonds in New Zealand."

He drew a bag from his tunic and handed it to Carrisford.

"That will see you through," he said. "It's the money that was left in the clothes of the new colonists. No one ever thought of the coins, and we just let them lie about the boat."

"You seem to have thought of everything," said Carrisford gratefully.

"Hush," was the embarrassed reply. "Can't you see that it's to my interest to keep you from being discovered. If word was to get back that three people in outlandish dresses were trying to sell diamonds, it would spoil the story I am going to tell in Century. And now, good-by, lad. Think well of an old man who thinks a lot of you, and be good to the lassie."

"That I will," promised Carrisford. "Won't you come with us, Fergus?"

"It's not for me," repeated McPherson. "Out with you for tempting an old man."

He wrung Carrisford's hand, and then turned to Clio and kissed her on the forehead. He shook hands with Mme. Ferrers, and caught Carrisford's hand again.

With a hungry look, he stepped back into the water to wade out to the submarine, but once more he turned back and beckoned Carrisford.

"If you're thinking of taking a wedding trip," he whispered, "Scotland's a bonny country. Take her there and think of old Fergus."

Till Russia Shall Be Free
Charles Stephens

*The Old Order and the New Meet Upon
an Ocean Liner, and the Captain Acts as
Arbiter*

S WINGING ON THE BREAST OF A GREAT WAVE, the liner's bow rose high in the
air and a discordant groan arose from the emigrants sheltered under the
forecastle, as it crashed down again in a caldron of spume.

Along the shell of the ship the emigrants lay in tiers of boarded bunks,
for the harvest was over and the peasants swarmed to America with their
hoardings.

The liner's bells rang the end of the middle watch—musically from the
bridge-deck, like a clarion on the forecastle. Faintly came the cry, "A-all's
we-ell!" and more faintly the assuring, "Lights are burning bright, sir!"

Ivan Egorovitch tossed uneasily in a lower bunk, turned the hot, discolored
thing called a pillow, and lay down again with his hands clasped under his
head. Finally, with an impatient murmur, he slid out of the bunk, threw
himself into a greatcoat and fur cap, and walked to the companionway.

A steward sat by the exit, the occasional movements of his jaws over a
chew of tobacco being the only evidence that he was not asleep. He opened
his eyes at the sound of Ivan's step on the metal stairway.

"Here!" he bellowed. "Get back in there, you crazy Rush'n! Go on!"

"Is it that I am crazy I go to walk in fresh air?" asked Ivan quickly.

"No lip, get back!" said the steward.

A child in a bunk near by wailed. A sick mother's arm drew it closer,
while a weary voice whispered in Bohemian:

"Hush, we will see the father in three days. Sssh!"

"You'll have the whole blamed lot howlin' in a minnit," growled the
steward, but his tone was quieter.

Ivan Egorovitch was looking at him with anger, contempt, and a little
uncertainty. Had this tall, gaunt man, with the great brow and pallid face,
chosen to violate the ship's rule, it was not the steward who could have
prevented him.

Ivan turned and walked back to a pile of trunks and clothing-sacks. He sat
on one, with his hands hanging clasped between his knees and his deep-set,
light-blue eyes fixed on the damp sawdust.

Another Russian, shaggy and past middle age, joined him, and together
they sat in silence. The newcomer put a black pipe between his teeth.

"No smokin', you!" roared the steward.

"But there is not anything in the pipe, and it is comfort," was the reply. But the pipe slunk into a pocket.

Again silence. A heavy sea burst on the liner's bows, and the steel fabric quivered as the ocean roared in the scuppers. A woman's half-suppressed sobbing was heard in a momentary lull.

"Ivan Egor, you do not sleep," said the older Russian.

"How can I sleep, little father?" Ivan replied, without moving. "It is but a month ago, and I have not forgotten."

"Why do you not kill him, Ivan?" whispered the other after a silence. "He is in your hands and cannot escape."

"It may not be, little father. They would imprison me. Where, then, would be my mission—till Russia shall be free? See how the offense of a people's ways crushed the last mission in America."

"Besides," he added after a while, "it was in the shadow, and I may have but fancied it was Vassilievna, for my eyes were fixed on a vision of him in Riga that bloody night. Yet a husband's eyes could not mistake his dear ones' murderer, little father. Aye, it was Vassilievna, but why did God guide him to this ship?"

"Ivan, you are not as we are, and you have strange thoughts," said the older man. "Were he mine enemy I would kill him."

"Little father, you shall be as I am, and Russia shall be of peaceful ways. We must teach the old Russia, for we are the new people. We have slain many, and to what end? Nothing."

"Ivan Egor," said the old man fiercely, "he led the Cossacks that night against your home. Was it not he who sent you to the fortress of Peter and Paul? Is it not enough?"

"Aye, enough," groaned Ivan. "But have I not spoken with Sergius of the police, and did he not say, being one of us and wise, that murder avails nothing to our end? Did he not say our petitions never reached the Czar, because the people have no voice?

"Did he not say, little father, that the voice of other governments must be listened to if they speak? And am not I, Ivan Egorovitch, chosen to speak for our people to the great voices? Shall I, then, come to America in chains?

"No, little father. My heart bursts to feel his presence; my eyes burn to look into his, and my hands reach out—but it may not be, little father. It may not be."

"Quit that talkin'," growled the steward. "This ain't a social hall."

The vessel plunged wildly. A baby cried, and the mother was powerless to assist it. Ivan Egorovitch arose, gathered the strange child in his arms, and passed up and down, humming a Polish lullaby.

"Only a month ago," murmured the older Russian, crawling back into his bunk.

• • •

"Far be it from me to discuss passengers, but of all the hogs that ever sat at my table," said the ship's surgeon, pulling at his pipe in the smoke-room, "that Count Vassiliootsky, or whatever you call him, is the worst. Ever hear him drinking soup?"

"Yes," said M. Nerode, the French automobile-maker, "I hear him. He take a bath in soup; he put hees nose in beef; he turn eet up when he no like pudding. He say 'poof' when Scotchman order pooreedge. He make me seeck, as you would say; he give me pain!"

"Guess that's the way of Russians," put in an American generously. "You must remember that what's not all right here may be O.K. in St. Petersburg."

"Bah!" said the Frenchman. "Eet is the way of old Russia. They speak French and play Pareesian, but they have not the cleverness of Pareesian, but Pareesian veeckedness and Russia bruteness. *Comprenez*?"

"Quite," was the chorus.

"He coom 'board thees ship first day. Spik to all the ladies and tey turn back on heem. Slip hees hand into ladies' arm and look at ladies' fine reengs, and want change reengs wees tems. But tey go red like lobster and pull away teir arm and run to tell the poopa. Ha!"

"Eh?" said an elderly man, suddenly laying down his magazine.

"Twig the bangle he wears?" put in an English youth. "Rotten in a man—a gold bangle with a bit of ribbon on it. Pulled me to one side yesterday and showed me a picture of a ripping girl."

"Ba-a-ah!" howled the Frenchman. "When he show peecture he kees it, an' kees it wees a noise like eating soup. He make me seeck!"

"Thought you French liked Russians?" said the American.

"Poof! We like tem—so!" and the Parisian snapped his fingers. "First day coom 'board, he hear me sing 'Carmen.' He pull me to quiet corner and put hees mouze to my face, an' sing 'Rigoletto' an' 'Rusticana,' an' imitate droom an' 'cello, teel I am crazy.

"He embrace me an' say, 'France—Roosh'a! Roosh'a—France!' and try kees me. I say, 'Bah! Go damn!' And now he is offend wees me."

The laughter that greeted the Frenchman's story was interrupted by high-pitched voices on the promenade.

"Something up!" said the doctor, moving toward the door.

On the promenade an American named Williams was assisting a limping lady to a deck-chair. Count Vassilievna, a man of thirty, of bulldog appearance, but handsome in a brutal way, was sitting in another chair, unconcernedly chewing an orange, throwing pieces of peel and expectorating the pips upon the deck. The accident which had occurred was obvious to all.

Williams, the moment the lady was safely lodged, pounced on the Russian and jerked him out of the chair.

"What d' you mean?" he demanded. "That lady has fallen on your leavings and hurt herself. What do you mean—sitting there without even moving to help her? What do you mean?"

Williams shook the Russian as a dog would a rat. Vassilievna vainly attempted to disengage himself, while his face expressed different shades of wrath.

"You insult!" he cried. "I no understand. Spik French—German—Russian!"

"Plain United States," cried Williams, taking a firmer hold of the count. "Get down and pick up that truck, or I'll—"

"Easy, Mr. Williams, easy," said the doctor, putting forward a restraining hand. "Don't do that. It means irons."

"Well, irons be blowed," said Williams. "He's got to pick it up."

"That's fair enough," interrupted the doctor. Turning to the Russian, he said bluntly:

"Pick that up and chuck it overboard." The Russian looked blankly from face to face. "You don't understand?" The doctor pointed to the relics of the orange, made a gesture of throwing them into the sea, then motioned to the Russian aristocrat to put the suggestion into practise.

Count Vassilievna turned ashy pale, and drew back a step. He lifted a hand to his waxed mustache, and the action caused the ribboned bangle to slip back on his wrist.

"Steward!" he said loftily.

"No—you!" growled Williams. The lady in the chair sniffed hysterically. "You!" he repeated.

The Russian's eyes blazed. He stood still for a moment; then, with a sneer, he began to pick up the pips and bits of orange-peel. When the deck was cleared, he straightened up and deliberately flung the handful in Williams' face.

"God!" gasped the American, raising his hand.

"No!" snapped the doctor, receiving the blow on his shoulder. "Not here. That's right. Hold him, boys! Report to the captain."

Williams, purple with rage, fought and raved, but fellow countrymen restrained him. As for the Russian, he turned with a smile to the weeping lady in the chair and bowed most gallantly.

"Sorry, *madame*. Ver' sorry."

Then he walked forward to the rail overlooking the steerage-waist.

"Let me go! Let me go!" roared Williams.

Then an unexpected thing happened, and even Williams stopped struggling and raving.

Up the steps from the steerage shot a tall, gaunt man, whose great blue eyes blazed and bulged from his head. His long right arm shot out and a claw-hand clutched the count by the throat. Holding him at arm's length, the man threw back his head and glared into the other's face.

"Vassilievna!" he yelled.

The count uttered a gurgling shriek.

"Egorovitch!"

They stood like carved gladiators for five seconds. Then Ivan gave a great sob and covered his eyes with his free hand. With the other he flung the Russian prone on the deck, and dashed down into the steerage, sobbing like a child.

"Very interesting," said the captain. The chief steward was reporting. Behind him stood the ship's surgeon. "Quite entertaining, but it won't go on my ship. Where are these Russians now?"

"One is forrard, sir. The count is locked in his cabin, and'll let no one in, sir. Moosher Nerode can speak French, but he won't come out for him, either, sir. Says there's a conspiracy to kill him, and swears the other fellow's an anarchist."

"Get that French passenger to tell the Russian the captain summons him and that he won't be killed on this ship. If that doesn't bring him out, break the door open."

"Yes, sir."

"Bring the anarchist aft, too. And you, doctor, fetch Mr. Williams and the witnesses."

The count, assured by the Frenchman that he was temporarily safe from violence, was finally induced to open his stateroom door. But the first person to arrive in the captain's cabin on the bridge was Ivan Egorovitch, accompanied by a couple of stewards. The captain merely glanced at him, then said sternly:

"So it's you again. Making more trouble on my ship?"

"Not more trouble," said Ivan quietly. "I make trouble now, but not before."

"You were spokesman the other day in that food complaint from the steerage, were you not?"

"I was, sir. You say yourself the food not good enough and give better. So you make me right."

"Umph!" grunted the captain, somewhat taken aback.

He surveyed the tall figure and the gaunt face. Beyond the rough lines, hollow cheeks, and pained eyes, the commander fancied he saw a strain of nobility.

"Are you one of those fellows who throw bombs and assassinate people?" said he, not unkindly.

"No, sir."

"Oh, one of the socialist breed?"

"Yes—socialist. Not Russian socialist. He is an anarchist, and think progress come with blood. I am world socialist. We war on condition, not individual."

The captain looked bored.

"What are you going to America for?"

"I speak to deeplomat for millions people who choose me, Ivan Egorovitch, because I say revolt must fail while the world press read of one—two—three men assassinate each week. I speak for peace, and so shall the press say we restrain our hands, until the world say to the Czar, 'It is not good.' "

The door opened and Count Vassilievna was ushered in. As his eyes fell upon Ivan he gave a cry of alarm and tried to back out, but a solid body of witnesses blocked the exit. Ivan stood with his face averted, making no sign that he was aware of Vassilievna's presence.

The matter of the orange was quickly disposed of. The captain, who had been informed of the count's undesirable attentions to ladies and of his insolence to other passengers, ordered that he keep to his stateroom for the rest of the voyage.

"Good! Ver' good!" cried the irrepressible Frenchman. "When a lady walk to deck he look at her like a German at a sausage. He—"

"The matter is disposed of, Mr. Nerode," said the captain, raising his hand. He turned to Ivan Egorovitch.

"Now, my man, whatever else you may be, you are a steerage passenger. You violated a rule of the ship by entering that portion of it reserved for first-class passengers. You then assaulted a first-class passenger—Count Vassilievna.

"What you have heard in this cabin regarding that person is none of your business. It has no connection with your affair. What have you to say for yourself?"

"Nothing," said Ivan. "I was wrong. His death would have been the great catastrophe to me and my brothers. But I have suffer much wrong from this Vassilievna, much wrong in Russia. I see him and my hands and my heart do what my brain would not have. I am sorry."

"Ask the count," said the captain to the Frenchman, "if he ever saw this man before."

Nerode put the question. The Russian became strangely excited and apparently confused. Nerode interpreted his answer.

"He says yes, he know him, and ten says no, he not know him. He says Ivan Egorovitch is a liar."

"How does he know his name?" said the captain. "Tell me what this man did to you," he said to Ivan.

Ivan Egorovitch stared at a barometer over the captain's desk for a long time.

"If I do not speak?" he asked at last.

"I will be compelled to put you in irons for menacing other passengers. Your story will probably make no difference, but it may be an extenuation."

Ivan Egorovitch slowly turned his head and looked at Vassilievna. The fierce, joyous light of revenge glared red in his eyes. Vassilievna returned the stare with a mingled look of hatred, fear, and pride.

"This man," said Ivan, and his words came with a snap that was in contrast to their slow utterance, for he spoke in English, "is officer of the army of old Russia. His friends are the friends of the Czar. I was officer of the army of new Russia, and my friends were the friends of Russia. We were loyal to the Czar while the Czar was loyal to Russia.

"I walk in St. Petersburg with a lady which he offend. We meet him. She ask me not to speak, nor stop, but walk as if we do not see.

"That night I am arrest on a charge of conspiracy. I do not know yet what I have supposed to do. I am dishonor and degrade. I am sent to the prison of Peter and Paul. For four years I live like blind mole, half starve, and only cheer by the tapping on the wall of other prisoners.

"In two years I learn what tapping means, and the first message I take from one wall and tap to next wall is: 'Till Russia shall be free.' I think and think, and when I walk free I give my life 'Till Russia shall be free.'

"While I in prison the lady I walk with much persecuted by this man. But she wait for me and work for free Russia. I go with her to Finland, when I am let go, and lead the peaceful fight for freedom. I marry the good woman, and we have one child, a leetle girl.

"I still work for free Russia. I live on small estate near Riga. One day I am to St. Petersburg and Moscow. I see the streets run red. I still speak against blood, but they say I must lead as the cause speaks.

"We have secret plot of war-ships to mutiny and seize St. Petersburg. But one ship rise too soon, and the revolt is crushed. Again bloodshed and failure, because there is not the unity and not the brains and not the knowledge of government."

"Yes," said the captain, "but what of Vassilievna?"

The almost fanatic glory that had burned in Ivan's face died out. He averted his head from Vassilievna. The count's eyes shifted uneasily around the cabin walls and ceiling. Ivan's filled with hot tears and his jaw-muscles worked painfully. When he spoke it was in gulped groups of words.

"When I return—dishearten—to Riga, I find—my house burn—my Nadine, and—baby murder! The Cossacks—he led them—search my papers and find nothing. They break chair and window and drink liquor—and dance and scream. Then—I do not know— but when they have finish—they burn the house!"

"That'll do," said the captain. "Count Vassilievna, if you try to leave your cabin, I'll put you in steel cuffs. Show him below, steward. Ivan Egorovitch, go forward and remain in the forecastle."

As Vassilievna was being escorted out, Ivan raised his hand.

"May I ask him question?" he almost pleaded.

"What about?" asked the captain.

"Remember," said Ivan Egorovitch, "I do not know what she said to make them kill her and baby. I do not know what the Cossacks do. Let me ask. It is the heart of the husband to know."

"Be quick, then," grumbled the captain.

Ivan turned upon Vassilievna. His face became white with agitation, and his eyes glazed like a snake's. He raised an accusing finger, which stretched as if carved out of stone. He spoke in Russian.

"Vassilievna! You know me, Ivan Egorovitch, and that I shall know the truth if I have to tear it from your black teeth.

"Was it not you—yourself—and not one of your men who killed my wife? Was it not you yourself, in your drunken frenzy, who shot my baby? Answer, you coward!"

And the last words were uttered with a thunder that brought a tremor to the knees of the accused man and made the captain doubt the coming situation.

"Ivan Egorovitch," stammered Vassilievna, "I swear to you it is a lie. I swear by—"

"It is no lie, you dog! It was you!" and the accusing finger never moved.

"No—no, I swear it, Ivan Egorovitch. Listen. When we came she barricaded herself in her room with the child. The Cossacks, when drunk, burst open the door. I swear to you, Ivan Egorovitch, none laid a hand on her, for as the door went down she shot her child and then herself."

There was silence. Vassilievna trembled like a wisp of grass. An awe-inspiring change came over Ivan's face. Tears rolled from his eyes. The accusing finger faltered and the arm fell to his side. Then he reeled into the captain's chair, sobbing and laughing.

"Brave Nadine! Thank God!"

The captain coughed.

"We've had enough melodrama," he growled. "Clear out, all of you. Leave him there for a minute."

When he was alone with Ivan, the captain laid a hand on the new Russian's shoulder and said huskily:

"Go forward, lad, and behave yourself."

But Ivan did not move. In his hands was a miniature of a mother and child. The little picture was splashed with tears, and the man was murmuring over and over:

"Nadine! Katherine! Till Russia shall be free."

To the Readers of THE OCEAN
Frank A. Munsey

The name of this publication will be changed with the February issue to THE LIVE WIRE. Mr. Munsey tells briefly why this change is to be made.

THE OCEAN IS DOING FAIRLY WELL, and has done fairly well from the start. That is to say, it is paying a net profit, and has paid a net profit on every issue. But it isn't doing well enough to be tremendously exciting.

I fancy there is too much water in the title, and water isn't especially popular just now. A dash of earth might help it. A good many people are very strong for the earth. They are out for all they can get of it. Some of them would like to corral it all.

I wasn't very keen for "THE OCEAN" as a title in the outset. I should have preferred "The Earth," but I found that that name was already being used. There was, however, the bare chance that tales of the sea might interest a wide circle of readers. The only way to know was to find out—to put the theory to the test. The experiment has been interesting and profitable—profitable both in actual money and in the development of an established magazine.

THE OCEAN, as the title of a magazine, gives no latitude for wanderings on shore, and there are many scenes along the Rialto and in other choice places of earth that furnish themes for good journalism. It is an inelastic, unyielding term, while our new title is as elastic as a man's fancy. Its scope is not bounded by either the depth or the breadth of the world. THE LIVE WIRE suggests the very opposite of everything that is dull and slow.

If our editors measure up to the dimensions of this title, if they grasp the spirit and scope of it and can translate their enthusiasm into an acute actuality, we may reasonably expect to find this revivified magazine "going some." In its new and broader field—broad enough to cover everything of interest in fancy and fact—it should set a red-hot pace.

Fiction will still be a leading feature of the magazine—good dramatic stories that have sweep and go to them, not mere studies of fiberless people and colorless scenes and situations, sometimes called stories. And in addition to the fiction there will be a vast variety of human interest matter of the kind that isn't over our heads—that isn't so scientific or abstruse or technical or hidden in its meaning that we cannot understand it. THE LIVE WIRE will be good easy reading from start to finish—a homely, homy magazine, with plenty of virility and get-up-and-go to it.

With all these changes going into effect, the magazine will naturally require a little time to find itself—to get its gait and hit up the pace. By finding itself I mean the process of crystallizing into a distinct type of its own—a type that is in harmony with the title and is emphatically the outgrowth of the title.

I am saying this so that you will not expect a finished product with the first issue. We shall give you something pretty good, I think, but it takes time for the editors of a new creation in magazine-making to get to know it and to get into the swing of doing things dramatically. They are not sure of their stroke at first, and this is particularly true while the lines of the magazine— its characteristics—are still in the formative period.

I believe we have a conception in THE LIVE WIRE that should develop into a pretty hot magazine, and one that will have its own individuality. It may interest you to know that this title, with the magazine that it stands for, was first scheduled to appear well-nigh two years ago. The reason why it was not launched before THE OCEAN is that we were waiting for some special machinery with which to print it in colors.

As this machinery is not yet ready, and as a change in the title and make-up of THE OCEAN seems advisable, we have thought it best to make the change now and to convert it into THE LIVE WIRE, so that the latter may begin shaping itself up, and so that our editors may get in training before our new machinery comes in.

I have told you frankly the why and wherefore of this change to THE LIVE WIRE. I hope you will like the new magazine, and if you do, will tell your friends about it.

Just a Word or Two by Mr. Munsey About This New Magazine

Frank A. Munsey

THIS MAGAZINE ISN'T EXACTLY NEW. It is THE OCEAN under a new name, but in idea and in its color-printing it is quite as new as if it had had no predecessor.

In the announcement of this change, made in THE OCEAN last month, I said that we should have brought out THE LIVE WIRE more than a year ago but for the fact that we were waiting for machinery with which to print it in colors. And in that statement I said in substance that we had decided to bring THE LIVE WIRE out now and print it in black, pending the incoming of the new machinery.

But since that statement was written we have made a shift which makes it possible to print the first issue of THE LIVE WIRE in colors. While this is better than we had hoped, I wish to make it clear that the color work in this issue is not up to the very high standard we shall reach later on when our new machinery is installed.

This is the first strictly color magazine ever issued by any house. Colored inserts, a few pages in an issue, have appeared and are appearing in the conventional magazines. THE LIVE WIRE is a brand-new creation, and as such cannot be fully developed in art or make-up in the first number.

Now that we have made a beginning, however, we are in line for improvement, and shall make improvement in each succeeding issue. The possibilities for great "stunts" in this color-printed magazine are as wide as the world.

OFF-TRAIL PUBLICATIONS
Specializing in the era of American pulp fiction

THE WEIRD DETECTIVE ADVENTURES OF WADE HAMMOND
By Paul Chadwick
Volume 1: 10 stories, 180 pages, $18
Volume 2: 10 stories, 172 pages, $18
Volume 3: 10 stories, 202 pages, $18
Volume 4: 9 stories, 232 pages, $18

> *The Wade Hammond stories complete in four volumes. In these chilling adventures, all from the classic 1930's pulps,* Detective-Dragnet *and* Ten Detective Aces, *freelance investigator Wade Hammond battles a series of weird enemies. Some of the best of 1930's pulp fiction.*

DOCTOR COFFIN: THE LIVING DEAD MAN
By Perley Poore Sheehan • Introduction by John Wooley
8 novelettes, 178 pages, $16

> *Weird stories from* Thrilling Detective, *1932-33. A former character actor who faked his own death, Doctor Coffin runs a string of mortuaries by night and fights crime at night. One of the strangest detective series.*

SUPER-DETECTIVE FLIP BOOK: TWO COMPLETE NOVELS
From the pulp *Super-Detective*:
"Legion of Robots" (November 1940) by Victor Rousseau • Introduction by John McMahan •• "Murder's Migrants" (March 1943) by Robert Leslie Bellem and W.T. Ballard • Introduction by John Wooley
2 short novels, 174 pages, $18

> Super-Detective *started as a Doc Savage-like adventure pulp, then changed format to hardboiled detective. The* Flip Book *features a novel from each of the two phases with intros exploring the historical background. Exciting!*

PULPWOOD DAYS: VOL 1: EDITORS YOU WANT TO KNOW

Edited by John Locke • 180 pages, $16

> *Numerous articles from the writers' magazines by and about pulp editors, with ample biographical profiles. Editors include: Frank E. Blackwell (Detective Story, Western Story), Ray Palmer (Amazing Stories, Fantastic Adventures), Robert A.W. Lowndes (Columbia Publications), Edwin Baird (Weird Tales, Detective Tales), and many more.*

GANG PULP

Edited by John Locke • 19 stories, 294 pages, $24

> *Hardboiled stories of the criminal underworld from the first year (1929-30) of the gang pulps:* Gangster Stories, Racketeer Stories, *etc. These violent tales came under immediate censorship pressure; the history is explored in an in-depth essay, "Glorifying the American Goon."*

THE GANGLAND SAGAS OF BIG NOSE SERRANO
Volume 1: DAMES, DICE AND THE DEVIL

By Anatole Feldman • Introduction by Will Murray

4 novels, 266 pages, $20

> *The first four Big Nose Serrano novels from* Gangster Stories, *1930-31. Feldman was the best of the gang pulp authors, and Big Nose was his most inspired creation, the berserking king of Chicago gangsters.*

THE CITY OF BAAL
By Charles Beadle • Introduction by John Locke
7 stories, 240 pages, $20

> *Authentic stories of African adventure from an author who had traveled the lands he wrote about. Lost cities, strange tribes, jungle magic. Six stories from* Adventure *(1918-22) and one from* The Frontier *(1925).*

AMAZON STORIES: VOLUME 1: PEDRO & LOURENÇO
By Arthur O. Friel • Introduction by John Locke
10 stories, 222 pages, $18

> *Friel's first ten stories from* Adventure *(1919-20), following the strange experiences of two Amazon Basin rubber workers as they explore the jungle. The best of pulp adventure fiction.*

FROM GHOULS TO GANGSTERS:
THE CAREER OF ARTHUR B. REEVE
Edited by John Locke
Volume 1 (fiction): 21 stories, 264 pages, $20
Volume 2 (nonfiction): 260 pages, $20

> *Reeve was the leading American detective-story writer of the early 20th Century, with his scientific detective, Craig Kennedy. The astonishing breadth of his career is explored for the first time here. Volume 1 includes a cross-sction of fiction from all phases of career, including many never-before-reprinted pulp stories. Volume 2 provides a 40-page biography; an extensive Art Gallery of cover repros, interior illos, ads, etc; a 75-page guide to Reeve's work in all media; and more. An "excellent piece of scholarship"—*Mystery Scene, *Spring 2008.*

Shipping: $3.00 media mail; $6.00 priority
Check or MO to:
Off-Trail Publications
2036 Elkhorn Road, Castroville, CA 95012
Paypal: offtrail@redshift.com

www.ingramcontent.com/pod-product-compliance
Lightning Source LLC
Chambersburg PA
CBHW030329030726
47499CB00003B/700